Praise for Dean Koontz
and His Masterworks of Suspense

"Koontz barely lets the reader come up for air between terrors."
—*The Washington Post*

"Koontz's skill at edge-of-the-seat writing has improved with each book. He can scare your socks off."
—*Boston Herald*

"Koontz's imagination is not only as big as the Ritz; it is also as wild as an unbroken stallion."
—*Los Angeles Times*

"Koontz puts his readers through the emotional wringer."
—*The Associated Press*

"His prose mesmerizes. . . . Koontz consistently hits the bull's-eye."
—*Arkansas Democrat-Gazette*

"First-class entertainment."
—*The Cleveland Plain Dealer*

"An exceptional novelist . . . top-notch."
—*Lincoln Journal-Star* (NE)

"Koontz is an expert at creating believable characters."
—*The Detroit News and Free Press*

"One of our finest and most versatile suspense writers."
—*The Macon Telegraph & News*

"Koontz does it so well!"
—*The Baton Rouge Advocate*

"Koontz's prose is as smooth as a knife through butter and his storytelling ability never wavers."
—*The Calgary Sun*

"Koontz's gift is that he makes his monsters seem 'realer,' and he makes the characters who fight [them] as normal as anyone you'd meet on a street."
—*The Orlando Sentinel*

Also by Dean Koontz

THE EYES OF DARKNESS

THE KEY TO MIDNIGHT

MR. MURDER

THE FUNHOUSE

DRAGON TEARS

SHADOWFIRES

HIDEAWAY

COLD FIRE

THE HOUSE OF THUNDER

THE VOICE OF THE NIGHT

THE BAD PLACE

THE SERVANTS OF TWILIGHT

MIDNIGHT

LIGHTNING

THE MASK

WATCHERS

TWILIGHT EYES

STRANGERS

DEMON SEED

PHANTOMS

WHISPERS

NIGHT CHILLS

DARKFALL

SHATTERED

THE VISION

THE FACE OF FEAR

DEAN KOONTZ

the door to december

 NEW AMERICAN LIBRARY

New American Library
Published by New American Library, a division of
Penguin Group (USA) Inc., 375 Hudson Street,
New York, New York 10014, USA
Penguin Group (Canada), 90 Eglinton Avenue East, Suite 700, Toronto,
Ontario M4P 2Y3, Canada (a division of Pearson Penguin Canada Inc.)
Penguin Books Ltd., 80 Strand, London WC2R 0RL, England
Penguin Ireland, 25 St. Stephen's Green, Dublin 2,
Ireland (a division of Penguin Books Ltd.)
Penguin Group (Australia), 250 Camberwell Road, Camberwell, Victoria 3124,
Australia (a division of Pearson Australia Group Pty. Ltd.)
Penguin Books India Pvt. Ltd., 11 Community Centre, Panchsheel Park,
New Delhi – 110 017, India
Penguin Group (NZ), 67 Apollo Drive, Rosedale, North Shore 0632,
New Zealand (a division of Pearson New Zealand Ltd.)
Penguin Books (South Africa) (Pty.) Ltd., 24 Sturdee Avenue,
Rosebank, Johannesburg 2196, South Africa

Penguin Books Ltd., Registered Offices:
80 Strand, London WC2R 0RL, England

Published by New American Library, a division of Penguin Group (USA) Inc.
Previously published in a Signet edition.

First Trade Paperback Printing, February 2011
1 3 5 7 9 10 8 6 4 2

To Gerda,
with whom I'll always
be opening doors
to the future.

the door to december

part one
THE GRAY ROOM

WEDNESDAY

2:50 A.M.–8:00 A.M.

chapter one

As soon as she finished dressing, Laura went to the front door and was just in time to see the Los Angeles Police Department squad car pull to the curb in front of the house. She stepped outside, slammed the door behind her, and hurried down the walk.

Hard spikes of cold rain nailed the night to the city.

She hadn't bothered with an umbrella. She couldn't remember which closet she'd stuck it in, and she didn't want to waste time searching for it.

Thunder rolled across the dark sky, but she hardly noticed those ominous peals. To her, the pounding of her own heart was the loudest noise in the night.

The driver's door of the black-and-white opened, and a uniformed officer got out. He saw her coming, got back in, reached across the seat, and opened the front door on the passenger side.

She sat next to him, pulled the door shut. With one cold and tremulous hand, she pushed a damp strand of hair away from her face and tucked it behind her ear.

The patrol car smelled strongly of pine-scented disinfectant and vaguely of vomit.

The young patrolman said, "Mrs. McCaffrey?"

"Yes."

"I'm Carl Quade. I'll take you to Lieutenant Haldane."

"And to my husband," she said anxiously.

"I don't know about that."

"I was told they found Dylan, my husband."

"Most likely, Lieutenant Haldane will tell you about that."

She gagged, choked, shook her head in disgust.

Quade said, "Sorry about the stink in here. Arrested a guy for drunken driving earlier tonight, and he had the manners of a pig."

The odor was not what made her stomach twist and roll. She felt sick because, on the phone a few minutes ago, they had told her that her husband had been found, but they hadn't mentioned Melanie. And if Melanie was not with Dylan, where was she? Still missing? Dead? No. Unthinkable. Laura put a hand to her mouth, gritted her teeth, held her breath, waited for the nausea to subside.

She said, "Where . . . where are we going?"

"A house in Studio City. Not far."

"Is that where they found Dylan?"

"If they told you they found him, I guess that's the place."

"How'd they locate him? I didn't even know you people were looking for him. The police told me there was no cause for their involvement . . . it wasn't their jurisdiction. I thought there was no chance I'd ever see him . . . or Melanie again."

"You'll have to talk with Lieutenant Haldane."

"Dylan must've robbed a bank or something." She could not conceal her bitterness. "Stealing a child from her mother isn't enough to interest the police."

"Buckle your seat belt, please."

Laura fumbled nervously with the belt as they drove away from the curb, and Quade hung a U-turn in the middle of the deserted, rain-swept street.

She said, "What about my Melanie?"

"How's that?"

"My daughter. Is she all right?"

"Sorry. I don't know anything about that, either."

"Wasn't she with my husband?"

"Don't think so."

"I haven't seen her in . . . in almost six years."

"Custody dispute?" he asked.

"No. He kidnapped her."

"Really?"

"Well, the law called it a custody dispute, but as far as I'm concerned, it's kidnapping pure and simple."

Anger and resentment took possession of her when she thought of Dylan. She tried to overcome those emotions, tried not to hate him, because she suddenly had the crazy notion that God was watching her, that He was judging her, and that if she became consumed by hatred or dwelt on negative thoughts, He would decide that she wasn't worthy of being reunited with her little girl. Crazy. She couldn't help it. Fear made her crazy. And it made her so weak that for a moment she did not even have sufficient strength to draw a breath.

Dylan. Laura wondered what it would be like to come face-to-face with him again. What could he possibly say to her that would explain his treachery—and what could she say to him that would be adequate to express her outrage and pain?

She had been trembling, but now she began to shake violently.

"You okay?" Quade asked.

"Yes," she lied.

Quade said nothing. With the emergency beacons flashing but without using the siren, they raced across the storm-lashed west side of the city. As they sped through deep puddles, water plumed on both sides, eerily phosphorescent, like frothy white curtains drawing back to let them pass.

"She'd be nine years old now," Laura said. "My daughter, I mean. I can't give you much more of a description. I mean, the last time I saw her, she was only three."

"Sorry. I didn't see any little girl."

"Auburn hair. Green eyes."

The cop said nothing.

"Melanie *must* be with Dylan," Laura said desperately, torn between joy and terror. She was jubilant at the prospect of seeing Melanie again, but afraid that the girl was dead. Laura had dreamed so often about finding Melanie's corpse in one hideous condition or another. Now she suspected the recurring nightmare would prove to have been an omen. "She must be with Dylan. That's where she's been all these years, six long years, so why wouldn't she be with him now?"

"We'll be there in a few minutes," Quade said. "Lieutenant Haldane can answer all your questions."

"They wouldn't wake me at two thirty in the morning, drag me out in the middle of a storm, if they hadn't found Melanie too. Surely they wouldn't."

Quade concentrated on his driving, and his silence was worse than anything he could have told her.

The thumping windshield wipers could not quite clean the glass. A persistent greasy film distorted the world beyond, so Laura felt as though she were riding through a dream.

Her palms were sweating. She blotted them on her jeans. She felt sweat trickle out of her armpits, down her sides. The rope of nausea in her stomach knotted tighter.

"Is she hurt?" Laura asked. "Is that it? Is that why you don't want to tell me anything about her?"

Quade glanced at her. "Really, Mrs. McCaffrey, I didn't see any little girl at the house. I'm not hiding anything from you."

Laura slumped back against the seat.

She was on the verge of tears but was determined not to cry. Tears would be an admission that she had lost all hope of finding Melanie alive, and if she lost hope (another crazy thought), then she might actually be responsible for the child's death because (crazier) maybe Melanie's continued existence was like that of Tinker Bell in *Peter Pan*, sustained only by constant and ardent belief. She was aware that a quiet hysteria had seized her. The idea that Melanie's continued existence depended upon her mother's belief and restraint of tears was solipsistic and irrational. Nevertheless, she clung to the idea, fighting back tears, summoning all the conviction that she could muster.

The windshield wipers thumped monotonously, and the rain drummed hollowly on the roof, and the tires hissed on the wet pavement, and Studio City seemed as far away as Hong Kong.

•

They turned off Ventura Boulevard in Studio City, a community of mismatched architecture: Spanish, Cape Cod, Tudor, colonial, and postmodern homes jammed side by side. It had been named for the old Republic Studios, where many low-budget Westerns had been shot before the advent of television. Most of Studio City's newest residents were screenwriters, painters, artists, artisans, musicians, and craftspeople of all kinds, refugees from gradually but inevitably decaying neighborhoods such as Hollywood, who were now engaged in a battle of lifestyles with the older homeowners.

Officer Quade pulled to a stop in front of a modest ranch house on a quiet cul-de-sac lined with winter-bare coral trees and Indian laurels with heavy foliage. Several vehicles were clustered in the street, including two mustard-green Ford sedans, two other black-and-whites, and a gray van with the city's seal on the door. But it was another van that caught and held Laura's attention, for CORONER was emblazoned across the two rear doors.

Oh, God, please, no. *No.*

Laura closed her eyes, trying to believe that this was still part of the dream from which the telephone had ostensibly awakened her. The call from the police actually might have been part of the nightmare. In which case Quade was part of it too. And this house. She would wake up, and none of this would be real.

But when she opened her eyes, the coroner's van was still there. The windows of the house were heavily curtained, but the entire front was bathed in the harsh glow of portable floodlights. Silvery rain slanted through the bright light, and the shivering shadows of the wind-stirred shrubbery crawled across the walls.

A uniformed policeman in a rain slicker was stationed at the curb. Another officer stood under the roof that overhung the area around the front door. They were prepared to discourage curious neighbors and other onlookers, although the bad weather and late hour seemed to be doing their job for them.

Quade got out of the car, but Laura couldn't move.

He leaned back in and said, "This is the place."

Laura nodded but still didn't move. She didn't want to go inside. She knew what she would find. Melanie. Dead.

Quade waited a moment, then came around the car and opened her door. He held out one hand to her.

The wind sprayed fat droplets of cold rain past Quade, into the car. He frowned. "Mrs. McCaffrey? Are you crying?"

She couldn't shift her gaze from the coroner's van. When it drove off with Melanie's small body, it would carry Laura's hope away, as well, and would leave her with a future as dead as her daughter.

In a voice no less tremulous than the wind-shaken leaves on the Indian laurels, she said, "You lied to me."

"Huh? Hey, no, not at all, really."

She wouldn't look at him.

Blowing air between his lips, making an odd horselike sound that was hardly appropriate to the circumstances, he said, "Well, yeah, this is a homicide case. We've got a couple of bodies."

A scream swelled in her, and when she held it back, the pent-up pressure was a painful burning in her chest.

Quade quickly continued. "But your little girl isn't in there. She's not one of the bodies. Honestly, she isn't."

Laura finally met his eyes. He seemed sincere. There would be no point in lying to her now, because she would soon learn the truth, anyway, when she went inside.

She got out of the car.

Taking her by the arm, Officer Quade led her up the walk to the front door.

The rain pounded as solemnly as drums in a funeral cortege.

chapter two

The guard went inside to get Lieutenant Haldane. Laura and Quade waited under the overhang, sheltered from the worst of the wind and rain.

The night smelled of ozone and roses. Rosebushes twined around support stakes along the front of the house, and in California, most varieties bloomed even in the winter. The flowers drooped, soggy and heavy in the rain.

Haldane arrived without delay. He was tall, broad-shouldered, roughly hewn, with short sandy hair and a square, appealing Irish face. His blue eyes looked flat, like twin ovals of painted glass, and Laura wondered if they always looked that way or whether they were flat and lifeless tonight because of what he had seen in the house.

He was wearing a tweed sport coat, a white shirt, a tie with the knot loosened, gray slacks, and black loafers. Except for his eyes, he looked like a comfortable, easygoing, laid-back sort of guy, and there was genuine warmth in his brief smile.

"Doctor McCaffrey? I'm Dan Haldane."

"My daughter—"

"We haven't found Melanie yet."

"She isn't . . . ?"

"What?"

"Dead?"

"No, no. Good heavens, no. Not your girl. I wouldn't have brought you here if that had been the case."

She felt no relief, because she wasn't sure that she believed him. He was tense, edgy. Something horrible had happened in this house. She was sure of it. And if they hadn't found Melanie, why had they brought her out at this hour? What was wrong?

Haldane dismissed Carl Quade, who headed back through the rain to the patrol car.

"Dylan? My husband?" Laura asked.

Haldane's stare slid away from hers. "Yes, we think we've located him."

"He's . . . dead?"

"Well . . . yeah. Apparently it's him. We've got a body carrying his ID, but we haven't positively tagged him yet. We'll need a dental-records check or a fingerprint match to make it positive."

The news of Dylan's death had surprisingly little effect on her. She felt no loss, because she'd spent six years hating him. But she wasn't happy about it, either: no glee, no triumph or satisfaction, no sense that Dylan had gotten what he deserved. He had been an object of love, then hatred, now indifference. She felt absolutely nothing, and perhaps that was the saddest thing of all.

The wind changed direction. Icy rain blew under the overhang. Haldane drew Laura back into the corner, as far as they could go.

She wondered why he didn't take her inside. There must be something that he didn't want her to see. Something too horrible for her to see? What in the name of God had happened in there?

"How did he die?" she asked.

"Murdered."

"Who did it?"

"We don't know."

"Shot?"

"No. He was . . . beaten to death."

"My God." She felt sick. She leaned against the wall because her legs were suddenly weak.

"Doctor McCaffrey?" Concerned, he took her by the arm, ready to provide support if she needed it.

"I'm okay," she said. "But I expected Dylan and Melanie to be together. Dylan took her away from me."

"I know."

"Six years ago. He closed out our bank accounts, quit his job, and ran off. Because I wanted a divorce. And he wasn't willing to share custody of Melanie."

"When we put his name in the computer, it gave us you, the whole file," Haldane said. "I haven't had time to learn the particulars, but I read the highlights on the mobile VDT in the car, so I'm sort of familiar with the case."

"He ruined his life, threw away his career and everything to be able to keep Melanie. Surely she must still be with him," Laura said exasperatedly.

"She was. She was living here with him—"

"Living here? *Here?* Only ten or fifteen minutes from me?"

"That's right."

"But I hired private detectives, several of them, and nobody could get a lead—"

"Sometimes," Haldane said, "the purloined-letter trick is the best trick of all."

"I thought maybe they'd even left the country, gone to Mexico or somewhere—and all the time they were right here."

The wind subsided, and the rain came straight down, even heavier than before. The lawn would soon be a lake.

"There are some clothes here for a little girl," Haldane said, "several books suitable for a kid her age. There's a box of Count Chocula cereal in the cupboard, and I'm sure none of the adults was eating that."

"None of them? There were more people here than just Dylan and Melanie?"

"We're not sure. We've got . . . other bodies. We think one of them was living here, because there were men's clothes in two sizes, some of which would fit your husband, but some that might fit one of the other men."

"How many bodies?"

"Two others. Three altogether."

"Beaten to death?"

He nodded.

"And you don't know where Melanie is?"

"Not yet."

"So maybe . . . whoever killed Dylan and the others took her away with him."

"It's a possibility," he said.

Even if Melanie wasn't already dead, she was the hostage of a killer. Maybe not just a killer but a rapist.

No. She was only nine years old. What would a rapist want with her? She was hardly more than a baby.

Of course, these days, that didn't make any difference. There were strange animals out there, monsters who preyed on children, who had a special appetite for little girls.

She was far colder than the incessant winter rain.

"We've got to find her," Laura said, and her voice was a thin croak that she didn't even recognize.

"We're trying," Haldane said.

She saw sympathy and compassion in his blue eyes now, but she could take no comfort from him.

"I'd like you to come inside with me," he said, "but I have to warn you it's not a pretty scene."

"I'm a doctor, Lieutenant."

"Yeah, but a psychiatrist."

"And a medical doctor. All psychiatrists are medical doctors."

"Oh, that's right. I didn't think."

"I assume you want me to identify Dylan's body."

"No. I'm not going to ask you to look at it. Wouldn't do any good. The condition . . . no visual identification is really possible. There's something else I want you to see, something I hope you might be able to explain to me."

"What's that?"

"Something weird," he said. "Something damned weird."

chapter three

Every lamp and ceiling light in the house was blazing. Laura blinked against the glare as she looked around. The living room was furnished neatly but without style. The sectional sofa, covered in a bold geometric pattern, clashed with the floral drapes. The carpet was one shade of green, the walls another. Only the bookcases and the few hundred volumes in them appeared to have been collected with genuine interest and to a particular taste. The rest of the room might have been a stage set hastily assembled by a theater company with a small budget.

At the cold fireplace, a cheap black tin container had tipped over, spilling wrought-iron tools across the white-brick hearth. Two lab technicians were dusting powder over exposed surfaces and lifting tape impressions where they found fingerprints.

"Please don't touch anything," Haldane told Laura.

"If you don't need me to identify Dylan—"

"Like I said, it wouldn't do much good."

"Why?"

"Nothing to identify."

"Surely the body can't be that badly . . ."

"Battered," he said. "No face left."

"My God."

They stood in the foyer, by the living-room arch. Haldane seemed as reluctant to take her deeper into the house as he had been to bring her inside in the first place.

"Did he have any identifying marks?" Haldane asked.

"A discolored patch of skin—"

"Birthmark?"

"Yes."

"Where?"

"The middle of his chest."

Haldane shook his head. "Probably won't help."

"Why not?"

He stared at her, then looked away, at the floor.

"I'm a doctor," she reminded him.

"His chest was caved in."

"*Beaten* in?"

"Yeah. Every rib broken and rebroken. Breastbone smashed like a china plate."

"Smashed?"

"Yeah. The word's carefully chosen, Doctor McCaffrey. Not just broken. Not just fractured or splintered. Smashed. Like he was made of glass."

"That's impossible."

"Saw it with my own eyes. Wish I hadn't."

"But the breastbone is solid. That and the skull are the closest things the human body has to armor plating."

"The killer was one big, strong son of a bitch."

She shook her head. "No. You might smash the breastbone in an auto accident, where there are tremendous forces, sudden impacts at fifty and sixty miles an hour, crushing forces and weights. . . . But it couldn't happen in a beating."

"We figure a lead pipe or—"

"Not even that," she said. "Smashed? Surely not."

Melanie, my little Melanie, my God, what's happened to you, where have they taken you, will I ever see you again?

She shuddered. "Listen, if you don't need me to identify Dylan, then I'm not sure what help I can—"

"Like I said, there's something I want you to see."

"Something weird."

"Yeah."

Yet he kept her in the foyer and even seemed to be using his body to prevent her from seeing farther into the house. Clearly, he was torn between his need for the information that she might be able to give him and his dismay at having to drag her through the scene of such bloody murders.

"I don't understand," she said. "Weird? What?"

Haldane didn't answer the question. He said, "You and he were in the same line of work."

"Not exactly."

"He was a psychiatrist too, wasn't he?"

"No. A behavioral psychologist. With a special interest in behavior modification."

"And you're a psychiatrist, a medical doctor."

"I specialize in the treatment of children."

"Yes, I see. Different fields."

"Very."

He frowned. "Well, if you have a look at his lab, you still might be able to tell me what your husband was doing there."

"Lab? He was working here too?"

"He was *primarily* working here. I don't think that he or your daughter led much of a real life in this place."

"Working? Doing what?"

"Experiments of some sort. We can't figure it."

"Let's have a look."

"It's . . . messy," he said, studying her closely.

"I told you—I'm a doctor."

"Yeah, and I'm a cop, and a cop sees more blood than a doctor does, and this was so messy it made me sick."

"Lieutenant, you brought me here, and now you're not getting rid of me until I know what my husband and my little girl were doing in this house."

He nodded. "This way."

She followed him past the living room, away from the kitchen, into a short hallway, where a slender, good-looking Latino in a dark suit was overseeing two men whose uniform jackets were stenciled with the word CORONER. They were stowing a corpse in an opaque plastic body bag. One of the men from the coroner's office pulled up the zipper. Through the milky plastic, Laura saw only a lumpish man-shaped form, no details but a few thick smears of blood.

Dylan?

"Not your husband," Haldane said, as if reading her mind. "This one wasn't carrying any ID at all. We'll have to rely entirely on a fingerprint check."

More blood was spattered and streaked over the walls, pooled on the floor, lots of it, so much that it didn't seem real, like a scene in a cheap horror film.

A plastic runner had been put down along the center of the hall, so the investigating officers and technicians wouldn't have to step in the blood and get their shoes sticky.

Haldane glanced at her, and she tried not to let him see how scared she was.

Had Melanie been here when the murders had taken place? If she had been, and if she was now with the man—or men—who had done this, she was marked for death too, because she had been a witness. Even if she had seen nothing, the murderer would kill her when he was . . . through with her. No doubt about that. He would kill her because he would enjoy killing her. From the look of this place, he was a psychopath; a sane person would not have slaughtered with such savage, blood-spraying glee.

The coroner's two men went outside to get a wheeled stretcher on which the body could be removed.

The slender Latino in the dark suit turned to Haldane. His voice was surprisingly deep: "We've vacuumed the place, Lieutenant, finished with photographs, lifted what prints we could, all the rest of it. We're moving this victim out."

"See anything special in the preliminary exam, Joey?" Haldane asked.

Laura supposed Joey was a police pathologist, although he was badly shaken for someone who should have been accustomed to scenes of violent death.

Joey said, "Looks like nearly every bone in the body was broken at least once. One contusion atop another, hundreds, no way to tell how many. I'm positive an autopsy is going to show ruptured organs, damaged kidneys." He glanced uneasily at Laura, as if not certain he should go on.

She maintained a bland expression of professional interest that she hoped didn't look as phony and sick as it felt.

Joey continued. "Crushed skull. Teeth broken loose. One eye was jarred out of its socket."

Laura saw a fireplace poker on the floor, against the baseboard. "Is that the murder weapon?"

"We don't think so," Haldane said.

And Joey said, "It was in this guy's hand. Had to pry it out of his fingers. He was trying to defend himself."

Staring at the opaque body bag, they fell into a mutual silence. The ceaseless percussion of the rain on the roof was simultaneously a mundane and strange sound—like the rumble of enormous doors sliding open in a dream to reveal a mysterious and unearthly vista.

The other men returned with the wheeled stretcher. One of the wheels wobbled erratically like a malfunctioning supermarket cart: a cold, clattering noise.

Three doors led off the short hall, one on each side and one at the end. All three were ajar. Haldane led Laura around the corpse and into the room at the end of the passageway.

In spite of her warm sweater and lined raincoat, she was cold. Freezing. Her hands were so white they looked dead. She knew the heat was on, because she felt the warm air blowing out of the vents when she passed them, so she knew the chill came from within her.

The room had once been an office-study, but now it was a monument to destruction and chaos. Steel file drawers were ripped from their cabinets, scraped and dented, handles twisted off; the contents were scattered across the floor. A heavy chrome-and-walnut desk was on its side; two of its metal legs were bent, and the wood was cracked and splintered as if it had taken a few blows from an ax. A typewriter had been thrown against one wall with such force that several keys had snapped off and were embedded in the drywall board. Papers were everywhere—typewritten sheets, graphs, pages covered with figures and notations in a small, precise handwriting—many of them shredded or crumpled or wadded into tight balls. And there was blood everywhere: on the floor, the furniture, the rubble, the walls, even on the ceiling. The place had a raw, coppery smell.

"Jesus," she said.

"What I want you to see is in the next room," he said, leading her toward a door at the rear of the demolished study.

She noticed two opaque plastic body bags on the floor.

Looking back at her, Haldane again said, "Next room."

Laura didn't want to stop, but she stopped. She didn't want to look down at the two shrouded bodies, but she looked.

She said, "Is one of these . . . Dylan?"

Haldane had moved ahead of her. Now he returned to her side. "This one had Dylan McCaffrey's ID," he said, pointing. "But you don't want to see him."

"No," she agreed. "I don't." She glanced at the other bag. "Who was this one?"

"According to the driver's license and other cards in his wallet, his name was Wilhelm Hoffritz."

She was astonished.

Her surprise must have been evident, for Haldane said, "Do you know him?"

"He was at the university. One of my husband's . . . colleagues."

"UCLA?"

"Yes. Dylan and Hoffritz conducted a number of joint studies. They shared some of the same . . . obsessions."

"Do I detect disapproval?"

She said nothing.

"You didn't like Hoffritz?" Haldane pressed.

"I despised him."

"Why?"

"He was a smug, self-important, condescending, pompous, arrogant little man."

"What else?"

"Isn't that enough?"

"You're not the kind of woman who would use the word 'despise' lightly," Haldane said.

When she met his stare, she saw a sharp and probing intelligence that she hadn't noticed before. She closed her eyes. Haldane's direct gaze was discomfiting, but she didn't want to look anywhere else because anywhere else was sure to be smeared with blood.

She said, "Hoffritz believed in centralized social planning. He was interested in the use of psychology, drugs, and various forms of subliminal conditioning to reform and direct the masses."

Haldane was silent. Then: "Mind control?"

"That's right." Her eyes were still closed, her head bowed. "He was an elitist. No. That's too kind. He was a totalitarian. He would have made an equally good Nazi or Communist. Either one. He had no politics except the politics of raw power. He wanted to control."

"They do that kind of research at UCLA?"

She opened her eyes and saw that he wasn't kidding. "Of course. It's a great university, a free university. There aren't any overt restrictions on the directions a scientist's research can take—if he can round up the funding for it."

"But the consequence of that kind of research . . ."

Smiling sourly, she said, "Empirical results. Breakthroughs. The advancement of knowledge. *That's* what a researcher is concerned about, Lieutenant. Not consequences."

"You said your husband shared Hoffritz's obsession. You mean he was deep into research with mind-control applications?"

"Yes. But he wasn't a fascist like Willy Hoffritz. He was more interested in modifying the behavior of criminal personalities as a means of reducing the crime rate. At least I think that's what he was interested in. That's what he talked most about. But the more involved Dylan got with any project, the more obsessed with it, the less he talked about it, as if talking used up energy that could be better spent in thought and work."

"He received government grants?"

"Dylan? Yes. Both him and Hoffritz."

"Pentagon?"

"Maybe. But he wasn't primarily defense-oriented. Why? What does that have to do with this?"

He didn't answer. "You told me your husband quit his position at the university when he ran off with your daughter."

"Yes."

"But now we find he was still working with Hoffritz."

"Hoffritz is no longer at UCLA, hasn't been for . . . three or four years, maybe longer."

"What happened?"

"I don't know," she said. "I just heard through the grapevine that he'd gone on to other things. And I had the feeling that he'd been asked to leave."

"Why?"

"The rumor was . . . some violation of professional ethics."

"What?"

"I don't know. Ask someone at UCLA."

"You're not associated with the university?"

"No. I'm not in research. I work at Saint Mark's Children's Hospital, and I have a small private practice besides. Maybe if you talked to someone at UCLA, you'd be able to find out just what it was Hoffritz did to make himself unwelcome."

She no longer felt ill, no longer minded the blood. In fact, she hardly noticed it. There was too much horror to absorb; it numbed the mind. A single corpse and a single drop of blood would have had a more lasting effect on her than this reeking slaughterhouse. She realized why cops could so quickly become inured to scenes of bloody violence; you either adapted or went mad, and the second option was really no option at all.

Haldane said, "I think your husband and Hoffritz were working together again. Here. In this house."

"Doing what?"

"I'm not sure. That's why I wanted you to come here. That's why I want you to see the lab in the next room. Maybe you can tell me what the hell was going on."

"Let's have a look."

He hesitated. "There's just one thing."

"What?"

"Well, I think your daughter was an integral part of their experiments."

Laura stared at him.

He said, "I think they were . . . using her."

"How?" she whispered.

"That's something you'll have to tell me," the detective said. "I'm no scientist. All I know is what I read in the newspapers. But before we go in there, you should know . . . it looks to me as if some parts of these experiments were . . . painful."

Melanie, what did they want from you, what have they done to you, where have they taken you?

She drew a deep breath.

She blotted her sweat-damp hands on her coat.

She followed Haldane into the lab.

chapter four

Dan Haldane was surprised at how well the woman was coping with the situation. Okay, she was a doctor, but most physicians weren't accustomed to wading through blood; at the scene of multiple, violent homicides, doctors could clutch up and lose control as easily as any ordinary citizen. It wasn't just Laura McCaffrey's medical training that was carrying her through this; she also had an unusual inner strength, a toughness and resilience that Dan admired—that he found intriguing and appealing. Her daughter was missing and might be hurt, might even be dead, but until she got the answers to important questions about Melanie, she wasn't, by God, going to break down or be weak in any way. He liked her.

She was lovely too, even though she wasn't wearing any makeup and her auburn hair was damp and frizzy from the rain. She was thirty-six, but she looked younger. Her green eyes were clear, direct, penetrating, and beautiful. And haunted.

The woman would be even more disturbed by what she would see in the makeshift lab, and Dan disliked having to take her in there. But that was the main reason he had called her out in the middle of the night. Although she hadn't seen her husband in six years, no one knew the man better than she knew him. Since she was a psychiatrist as well, perhaps she would recognize the nature of the experiments and research that Dylan McCaffrey had been conducting. And Dan had a hunch that he wasn't going to solve these homicides—or locate Melanie—until he could figure out what Dylan McCaffrey had been doing.

Laura followed him through the doorway.

In the gray room, he watched her face. She registered surprise, puzzlement, and uneasiness.

The two-car garage had been closed off and remodeled into a single large, windowless, relentlessly drab room. Gray ceiling. Gray walls. Gray carpet. Fluorescent ceiling lights glowed softly behind grayish plastic panels. Even the handles on the sliding gray closet doors were painted gray. Though the heating vents must have been bare gray metal in the first place, they also had been painted, apparently because, unpainted, they had been shiny. No spot of color or brightwork had been allowed. The effect was not merely cold and institutional, but funereal.

The most impressive piece of equipment in the room was a metal tank that resembled an old-fashioned iron lung, although it was considerably larger than that. It was painted the same drab gray as the room. Pipes led from it, into the floor, and an electrical cable went straight up to a junction box on the ceiling. Three movable wooden steps provided access to the tank's elevated entrance hatch, which stood open.

Laura went up the steps and peered inside.

Dan knew what she would find: a featureless black interior that was barely illuminated by the meager light that found its way through the hatch; the sound of water stirred by the vibrations transmitted through the steps and into the tank frame; a dampish odor with a hint of salt to it.

"Know what it is?" he asked.

She descended the three steps. "Sure. A sensory-deprivation chamber."

"What was he doing with it?"

"You mean, what are its scientific applications?"

Dan nodded.

"Well, you fill it with a few feet of water. . . . Actually, you use a solution of ten percent magnesium sulfate in water for maximum buoyancy. Heat it to ninety-three degrees Fahrenheit, the temperature at which a floating body is least affected by gravity. Or depending on the nature of the experiment, maybe you heat it to ninety-eight degrees to reduce the differential between body temperature and water temperature. Then the subject—"

"Which is a person—not an animal?"

She looked surprised by the question. Dan Haldane felt woefully undereducated, but Laura didn't disparage him or let any impatience creep into her tone, and he felt at ease again almost immediately.

She said, "Yes. A person. Not an animal. Anyway, when the water's ready, the subject undresses, enters the chamber, closes the door after himself, and floats in total darkness, in total silence."

"Why?"

"To deprive himself of all sensory stimulation. No sight. No sound. Little or no taste. Minimal olfactory stimulation. No sense of weight or place or time."

"But why would anyone want to do that?"

"Well, initially, when the first tanks were used, they did it because they wanted to find out what would happen when someone was deprived of nearly all external stimuli."

"Yeah? And what happened?"

"Not what they expected. No claustrophobia. No paranoia. A brief moment of fear, yes, but then . . . a not unpleasant temporal and spatial disorientation. The sense of confinement disappeared in a minute or so. Some subjects reported being certain they were not in a small chamber but a huge one, with endless space around them. With no external stimuli to occupy it, the mind turns inward to explore a whole new world of internal stimuli."

"Hallucinations?"

For a moment, her anxiety faded. Her professional interest in the functioning of the human mind became evident, and Dan could see that, if she had chosen a career in the classroom, she would have proven a natural-born teacher. She clearly took pleasure in explaining, illuminating.

She said, "Yes, hallucinations, sometimes. But not frightening or threatening hallucinations, nothing like what you'd expect from a drug experience. Intense and extraordinarily vivid sexual fantasies in many cases. And virtually every subject reports a sharpening and clearing of thought processes. Some subjects have solved complex problems in algebra and calculus without even the benefit of paper and pencil, problems that would ordinarily be beyond their abilities. There's even a cult system of psychotherapy that uses deprivation chambers to encourage the patient to concentrate on guided self-exploration."

He said, "From your tone, I think maybe you don't approve of that."

"Well, I don't exactly disapprove," she said. "But if you've got a psychologically disturbed individual who already feels adrift, only half in control of himself . . . the disorientation of a deprivation chamber is almost certain to have negative effects. Some patients need every grip on the physical world, every external stimulus, they can get." She shrugged. "But then again, maybe I'm too cautious, old-fashioned. After all, they've been selling these things for use in private homes, must've sold a few thousand over the past few years, and surely a few of those were used by unstable people, yet I haven't heard of anyone going all the way 'round the bend because of it."

"Must be expensive."

"A tank? Sure is. Most units in private homes are . . . new toys for the rich, I guess."

"Why would anyone buy one for his home?"

"Aside from the hallucinatory period and the eventual clarity of the mental processes, everyone reports being tremendously relaxed and revitalized by a session in a tank. After you spend an hour floating, your brain waves match those of a Zen monk in deep meditation. Call it a lazy man's way to meditate: no studying required, no religious principles to be learned or obeyed, an easy way of packing a week's relaxation into a couple of hours."

"But your husband wasn't using this just to relax."

"I doubt it," she agreed.

"Then what was he after, specifically?"

"I really have no way of knowing." Anguish returned to her face, her eyes.

Dan said, "I think this wasn't just his lab. I think it was your daughter's room too. I think she was a virtual prisoner in here. And I think she slept in this tank every night and maybe spent days at a time in it."

"Days? No. That's not . . . possible."

"Why isn't it?"

"The potential for psychological damage, the risks—"

"Maybe your husband didn't care about the risks."

"But she was his daughter. He loved Melanie. I'll give him that much. He genuinely loved her."

"We've found a journal in which your husband seems to account for every minute of your daughter's time during the past five and a half years."

Her eyes narrowed. "I want to see it."

"In a minute. I haven't studied it closely yet, but I don't think your daughter was ever out of this house in five and a half years. Not to school. Not to a doctor. Not to a movie or the zoo or anywhere. And even if you say it's not possible, I think, from what I've seen, that she sometimes spent as much as three or four days in the tank without coming out."

"But food—"

"I don't think she was fed in that time."

"Water—"

"Maybe she drank a little of what she was floating in."

"She'd have to relieve herself—"

"From what I've seen, there were times when she might have been taken out for only ten or fifteen minutes, long enough to use the bathroom. But in other cases, I think he catheterized her, so she could urinate into a sealed specimen jar without being taken out of the tank and without contaminating the water she was floating in."

The woman looked stricken.

Wanting to get this over with for her sake and also because he was sick of this place, Dan led her away from the tank, to another piece of equipment.

"A biofeedback machine," she told him. "It includes an EEG, an electroencephalograph to monitor brain waves. It supposedly helps you learn to control the patterns of your brain waves and, therefore, your state of mind."

"I know about biofeedback." He pointed past that machine. "And this?"

It was a chair, from which dangled leather straps and wires that ended in electrodes.

Laura McCaffrey examined it, and Dan could sense her growing disgust—and terror.

At last she said, "An aversion-therapy device."

"Looks like an electric chair to me."

"It is. Not one that kills. The current comes from those batteries, not from a wall socket. And this"—she touched a lever on the side of the chair—"regulates the voltage. You can deliver anything from a tingle to a painful shock."

"This is a standard psychological research device?"

"Good heavens, no!"

"You ever see one of these in a lab before?"

"Once. Well . . . twice."

"Where?"

"A rather unscrupulous animal psychologist I once knew. He used electric-shock aversion training with monkeys."

"Tortured them?"

"I'm sure he didn't see it that way."

"All animal psychologists don't do that?"

"I said he was unscrupulous. Listen, I hope you're not one of those new Luddites who think all scientists are fools or monsters."

"Not me. When I was a kid, I never missed Mr. Wizard on TV."

She managed a faint smile. "Didn't mean to snap at you."

"It's understandable. Now, you said you've seen one of these devices twice before. What about the second time?"

The meager glow of her weak smile was suddenly extinguished. "I saw the second one in a photograph."

"Oh?"

"In a book about . . . scientific experimentation in Nazi Germany."

"I see."

"They used it on people."

He hesitated. But it had to be said. "So did your husband."

Laura McCaffrey regarded him not with disbelief as much as with an ardent *desire* to disbelieve. Her face was the color of cold ashes, burnt out.

Dan said, "I think he put your daughter in this chair—"

"No."

"—and I think he and Hoffritz and God knows who else—"

"No."

"—tortured her," Dan finished.

"No."

"It's in the journal I told you about."

"But—"

"I think they were using . . . what you called 'aversion' therapy to teach her to control her brain-wave patterns."

The thought of Melanie strapped in that chair was so disturbing that Laura McCaffrey was profoundly transformed by it. She no longer looked simply burnt out, no longer just ashen; she was now paler than pale, cadaverously pallid. Her eyes appeared to sink deeper into her skull and lose much of their luster. Her face sagged like softening wax. She said, "But . . . but that doesn't make sense. Aversion therapy is the least likely way to learn biofeedback techniques."

Dan had the urge to put his arms around her, hold her close, smooth her hair, comfort her. Kiss her. He had found her appealing from the moment he had seen her, but until now he'd felt no romantic stirrings for her. And that was par for the course, wasn't it? He always fell for the helpless kittens, the broken dolls, the ones who were lost or weak or in trouble. And he always wound up wishing that he had never gotten involved. Laura McCaffrey hadn't initially held any attraction for him because she had been self-confident, self-possessed, totally in control. As soon as she'd begun to flounder, as soon as she could no longer conceal her fear and confusion, he was drawn to her. Nick Hammond, another homicide detective and smart-ass, had accused Dan of having a mother-hen instinct, and there was truth in that.

What is it with me? he wondered. Why do I insist on being a knight-errant, always searching for a damsel in distress? I hardly even know this woman, and I want her to rely entirely on me, put her hopes and fears on my shoulders. Oh, yes, ma'am, you just rely on Big Dan Haldane, nobody else; Big Dan will catch these evil villains and put your broken world back together for you. Big Dan can do it, ma'am, even though he's still an adolescent idiot at heart.

No. Not this time. He had a job to do, and he would do it, but he would be entirely professional about it. Personal feelings would not intrude. Anyway, this woman wouldn't welcome a relationship with him. She was better educated than he was. A lot more stylish. She was a brandy type, while he was strictly beer. Besides, for God's sake, this wasn't a time for romance. She was too vulnerable: she was worried sick about her daughter; her husband had been killed, and that must have its effect on her, even if she had stopped loving the guy a long time ago. What kind of man could think of her as a romantic prospect at a time like this? He was ashamed of himself. But still . . .

He sighed. "Well, once you've studied your husband's journal, maybe you'll be able to prove he never put the girl in that chair. But I don't think so."

She just stood there, looking lost.

He went to the closet and opened the doors, revealing several pairs of jeans, T-shirts, sweaters, and shoes that would fit a nine-year-old girl. All were gray.

"Why?" Dan asked. "What did he hope to prove? What effect was he after with the girl?"

The woman shook her head, too distraught to speak.

"And something else I wonder," Dan said. "All of this, six years of it, took more money than he had when he cleaned out your joint bank accounts and left you. A lot more. Yet he wasn't working anywhere. He never went out. Maybe Wilhelm Hoffritz gave him money. But there must have been others who contributed as well. Who? Who was financing this work?"

"I've no idea."

"And why?" he wondered.

"And where have they taken Melanie?" she asked. "And what are they doing to her now?"

chapter five

The kitchen wasn't exactly filthy, but it wasn't clean, either. Stacks of dirty dishes filled the sink. Crumbs littered the table that stood by the room's only window.

Laura sat at the table and brushed some of the crumbs aside. She was eager to look at the log of Dylan's experiments with Melanie. Haldane wasn't ready to give it to her. He held it—a ledger-size book bound in imitation brown leather—and paced around the kitchen as he talked.

Rain struck the window and streamed down the glass. When an occasional flicker of lightning brightened the night and passed through the window, it briefly projected the random rippling patterns of water from the glass onto the walls, which made the room seem as amorphous and semitransparent as a mirage.

"I want to know a lot more about your husband," Haldane said, pacing.

"Like what?"

"Like why you decided to divorce him."

"Is that relevant?"

"Could be."

"How?"

"For one thing, if there was another woman involved, then maybe she can tell us more about what he was doing here. Maybe she can even tell us who killed him."

"There was no other woman."

"Then why did you decide to divorce him?"

"It was just that . . . I no longer loved him."

"But you had loved him once."

"Yes. But he wasn't the man I married."

"How had he changed?"

She sighed. "He didn't. He was *never* the man I married. I only thought he was. Later, as time went by, I realized how thoroughly I'd misunderstood him, right from the start."

Haldane stopped pacing, leaned against a counter, crossing his arms on his chest, still holding the log book. "Just how had you misunderstood him?"

"Well . . . first, you have to understand something about me. In high school and college, I was never a particularly popular girl. Never had many dates."

"I find that difficult to believe."

She blushed. She wished she could control it, but couldn't. "It's true. I was crushingly shy. Avoided boys. Avoided everyone. Never had any close girlfriends, either."

"Didn't anyone tell you about the right mouthwash and dandruff shampoo?"

She smiled at his attempt to put her at ease, but she was never comfortable talking about herself. "I didn't want anyone to get to know me because I figured they'd dislike me, and I couldn't stand rejection."

"Why should they dislike you?"

"Oh . . . because I wouldn't be witty enough or bright enough or pretty enough to suit them."

"Well, I can't say whether or not you're witty, but then, David Letterman would have trouble coming up with one-liners in this place. But you're clearly intelligent. After all, you earned a doctorate. And I don't see how you could look in a mirror and think you were anything less than beautiful."

She glanced up from the crumb-carpeted table. The lieutenant's gaze was direct, engaging, warm, though neither bold nor suggestive. His attitude was merely that of a policeman, making an observation, stating a fact. Yet, under that surface professionalism, deep down, she sensed that he was attracted to her. His interest made her uneasy.

Self-conscious, studying the vague silvery tracks of rain on the black window, she said, "I had a terrible inferiority complex back then."

"Why?"

"My parents."

"Isn't it always?"

"No. Not always. But in my case . . . mainly my mother."

"What were your folks like?"

"They have nothing to do with this case," she said. "They're both gone now, anyway."

"Passed away?"

"Yes."

"I'm sorry."

"No need to be. I'm not."

"I see."

That was a harsh thing for her to have said. She was surprised to realize that she didn't want him to think badly of her. On the other hand, she was not prepared to tell him about her parents and the loveless childhood she had endured.

"But about Dylan . . . ," she began, and then wasn't sure where she had left off.

Haldane said, "You were telling me why you misjudged him right from the start."

"See, I was so good at fending people off, so good at alienating everyone and keeping myself snug in my shell, that no one ever got close to me. Especially not boys . . . or men. I knew how to turn them off fast. Until Dylan. He wouldn't give up. He kept asking me for dates. No matter how often I rejected him, he came back. My shyness didn't deter him. Rudeness, indifference, cold rejection—nothing would stop him. He pursued me. No one had ever pursued me before. Not like Dylan. He was relentless. Obsessed. But not frightening in any way, not that kind of obsession. It was corny, the way he tried to impress me, the things he did. I knew it was corny at the time, but it was effective just the same. He sent flowers, more flowers, candy, more flowers, even a huge teddy bear."

"A teddy bear for a young woman working on her doctorate?" Haldane said.

"I told you it was corny. He wrote poetry and signed it 'A Secret Admirer.' Trite, maybe, but for a woman who was twenty-six, hardly been kissed, and expected to be an old maid, it was heady stuff. He was the first person who ever made me feel . . . special."

"He broke down your defenses."

"Hell, I was swept away."

As she spoke of it, that special time and feeling came back to her with unnerving vividness and power. With the memories came a sadness at what might have been, a sense of lost innocence that was almost overwhelming.

"Later, after we were married, I learned that Dylan's passion and fervor weren't reserved solely for me. Oh, not that there were other women. There weren't. But he pursued every interest as ardently as he'd pursued me. His research into behavior modification, his fascination with the occult, his love of fast cars—he put as much passion and energy into all those pursuits as he had put into our courtship."

She remembered how she had worried about Dylan—and about the effect that his demanding personality might have on Melanie. In part, she had asked for a divorce because she had been concerned that Dylan would infect Melanie with his obsessive-compulsive behavior.

"For instance, he built an elaborate Japanese garden behind our house, and it consumed his every spare moment for months and months. He was fanatically determined to make it perfect. Every plant and flower, every stone in every walkway had to be an ideal specimen. Every bonsai tree had to be as exquisitely proportioned and as imaginatively and harmoniously shaped as those in the books about classic Oriental landscaping. He expected me to be as caught up in that project—in every project—as he was. But I couldn't be. Didn't want to be. Besides, he was so fanatical about perfection in all things that just about anything you did with him sooner or later became sheer hard labor instead of fun. He was an obsessive-compulsive unlike any other I've ever encountered, a driven man, and though he was wildly enthusiastic about everything, he actually took no pleasure in any of it, no joy, because there simply wasn't *time* for joy."

"Sounds like it would've been exhausting to be married to him," Haldane said.

"God, yes! Within a couple of years his excitement about things was no longer contagious because it was continuous and universal, and no sane person can live at a fever pitch all the time. He ceased to be intriguing and invigorating. He was . . . tiring. Maddening. Never a moment's relaxation or peace. By then, I was getting my degree in psychiatry, going through analysis, which is a requirement for anyone considering psychiatric practice, and finally I realized Dylan was a disturbed man, not just enthusiastic, not just an overachiever, but a severe obsessive-compulsive. I tried to convince him to undergo analysis, but for *that* he had no enthusiasm at all. At last, I told him I wanted a divorce. He never gave me time to file the papers. The next day he cleaned out our joint bank accounts and left with Melanie. I should have seen it coming."

"Why?"

"He was as obsessive about Melanie as he was about everything else. In his eyes, she was the most beautiful, wonderful, intelligent child who ever walked the earth, and he was always concerned that she be perfectly dressed, perfectly groomed, perfectly behaved. She was only three years old, but he was already teaching her to read, trying to teach her French. Only three. He said all learning comes easiest to the youngest. Which is true. But he wasn't doing it for Melanie. Oh, no. Not in the least for her. He was concerned about himself, about having a perfect child, because he couldn't bear the thought that his little girl would be anything but the very prettiest and brightest and most dazzling child anyone had ever seen."

They were silent.

Rain tapped the window, drummed on the roof, gurgled through the gutters and downspouts.

At last, softly, Haldane said, "A man like that might . . ."

"Might experiment on his own daughter, might put her through tortures of one kind and another, if he thought he was improving her. Or if he became obsessed with a series of experiments that required a child as the subject."

"Jesus," Haldane said in a tone that was part disgust, part shock, part pity.

To her surprise, Laura began to cry.

The detective came to the table. He pulled out a chair and sat beside her.

She blotted her eyes with a Kleenex.

He put a hand on her shoulder. "It'll be all right."

She nodded, blew her nose.

"We'll find her," he said.

"I'm afraid we won't."

"We will."

"I'm afraid she's dead."

"She's not."

"I'm afraid."

"Don't be."

"Can't help it."

"I know."

•

For half an hour, while Lieutenant Haldane attended to business elsewhere in the house, Laura studied Dylan's handwritten journal, which was actually just a log detailing how Melanie's days had been spent. By the time the detective returned to the kitchen, Laura was numb with horror.

"It's true," she said. "They've been here at least five and a half years, as long as he's been keeping this journal, and Melanie hasn't been out of the house once that I can see."

"And she slept every night in the sensory-deprivation chamber, like I thought?"

"Yes. In the beginning, eight hours a night. Then eight and a half. Then nine. By the end of the first year, she was spending ten hours a night in the chamber and two hours every afternoon."

She closed the book. The sight of Dylan's neat handwriting suddenly made her furious.

"What else?" Haldane asked.

"First thing in the morning, she spent an hour meditating."

"Meditating? A little girl like that? She wouldn't even know the meaning of the word."

"Essentially, meditation is nothing but redirecting the mind inward, blocking out the material world, seeking peace through inner solitude. I doubt if he was teaching Melanie Zen meditation or any other brand with solid philosophical or religious overtones. He was probably just teaching her how to sit still and turn inward and think of nothing."

"Self-hypnosis."

"That's another name for it."

"Why did he want her to do that?"

"I don't know."

She got up from the chair, nervous and agitated. She wanted to move, walk, work off the frantic energy that crackled through her. But the kitchen was too small. She was at the end of it in five steps. She started toward the hall door but stopped when she realized that she couldn't walk through the rest of the house, past the bodies, through the blood, getting in the way of the coroner's people and the police. She leaned against a counter, flattening her palms on the edge of it, pressing fiercely hard, as if somehow she could get rid of her nervous energy by radiating it into that ceramic surface.

"Each day," she said, "after meditation, Melanie spent several hours learning biofeedback techniques."

"While sitting in the electrified chair?"

"I think so. But . . ."

"But?" he persisted.

"But I think the chair was used for more than that. I think it was also used to condition her against pain."

"Say that again?"

"I think Dylan was using electric shock to teach Melanie how to blank out pain, how to endure it, ignore it the way that Eastern mystics do, the way Yogin do."

"Why?"

"Maybe because, later, being able to tune out pain would help her get through the longer session in the sensory-deprivation tank."

"So I was right about that?"

"Yes. He gradually increased her time in the tank until, by the third year, she would sometimes remain afloat for three days. By the fourth year, four and five days at a time. Most recently . . . just last week, he put her in the tank for a seven-day session."

"Catheterized?"

"Yes. And on an IV. Intravenous needle. He was feeding her by glucose drip, so she wouldn't lose too much weight and wouldn't dehydrate."

"God in Heaven."

Laura said nothing. She felt as though she might cry again. She was nauseated. Her eyes were grainy, and her face felt greasy. She went to the sink and turned on the cold water, which spilled over the stacks of dirty dishes. She filled her cupped hands, splashed her face. She pulled several paper towels from the wall-mounted dispenser and dried off.

She felt no better.

Haldane said ruminatively, "He wanted to condition her against pain so she could more easily get through the long sessions in the tank."

"Maybe. Can't be sure."

"But what's painful about being in the tank? I thought there was no sensation at all. That's what you told me."

"There's nothing painful about a session of normal length. But if you're going to be kept in a tank several days, your skin's going to wrinkle, crack. Sores are going to form."

"Ah."

"Then there's the damn catheter. At your age, you've probably never been so seriously ill that you've been incontinent, needed a catheter."

"No. Never."

"Well, see, after a couple of days, the urethra usually becomes irritated. It hurts."

"I would guess it does."

She wanted a drink very badly. She was not much of a drinker, ordinarily. A glass of wine now and then. A rare martini. But now, she wanted to get drunk.

He said, "So what was he up to? What was he trying to prove? Why did he put her through all this?"

Laura shrugged.

"You must have some idea."

"None at all. The journal doesn't describe the experiments or mention a single word about his intentions. It's just a record of her sessions with each piece of equipment, an hour-by-hour summary of each of her days here."

"You saw the papers in his office, scattered all over the floor. They must be more detailed than the journal. There'll be more to be learned from them."

"Maybe."

"I've glanced at a few, but I couldn't make much sense of them. Lots of technical language, psychological jargon. Greek to me. If I have them photocopied, have the copies boxed up and sent to you in a couple of days, would you mind going through them, seeing if you can put them in order and if you can learn anything from them?"

She hesitated. "I . . . I don't know. I got more than half sick just going through the journal."

"Don't you want to know what he did to Melanie? If we find her, you'll have to know. Otherwise you won't have much chance of dealing with whatever psychological trauma she's suffering from."

It was true. To provide the proper treatment, she would have to descend into her daughter's nightmare and make it her own.

"Besides," Haldane said, "there might be clues in those papers, things that'll help us determine who he was working with, who might have killed him. If we can figure that out, we might also figure out who has Melanie now. If you go through your husband's papers, you might discover the one bit of information that'll help us find your little girl."

"All right," she said wearily. "When you've got it boxed, have the stuff sent to my house."

"I know it won't be easy."

"Damned right."

"I want to know who financed the torture of a little girl in the name of research," he said in a tone of voice that seemed, to Laura, to be exceptionally hard and vengeful for an impartial officer of the law. "I want to know real bad."

He was about to say something else, but he was interrupted by a uniformed officer who entered from the hall. "Lieutenant?"

"What is it, Phil?"

"You're looking for a little girl in all this, aren't you?"

"Yeah."

Phil said, "Well, they found one."

Laura's heart seemed to clench as tightly as a fist: a knot of pain in her breast. An urgent question formed in her mind, but she was unable to give voice to it because her throat seemed to have swollen shut.

"How old?" Haldane asked.

That wasn't the question Laura wanted him to ask.

"Eight or nine, they figure," Phil said.

"Get a description?" Haldane asked.

That wasn't the right question, either.

"Auburn hair. Green eyes," the patrolman said.

Both men turned to Laura. She knew they were staring at her own auburn hair and green eyes.

She tried to speak. Still mute.

"Alive?" Haldane asked.

That was the question that Laura could not bring herself to ask.

"Yeah," the uniformed man said. "A black-and-white team found her seven blocks from here."

Laura's throat opened, and her tongue stopped cleaving to the roof of her mouth. "Alive?" she said, afraid to believe it.

The uniformed officer nodded. "Yeah. I already said. Alive."

"When?" Haldane asked.

"About ninety minutes ago."

His face coloring with anger, Haldane said, "Nobody told me, damn it."

"They were just on a routine patrol when they spotted her," Phil said. "They didn't know she might have a connection to this case. Not till just a few minutes ago."

"Where is she?" Laura demanded.

"Valley Medical."

"The hospital?" Her clenched heart began to pound like a fist against her rib cage. "What's wrong with her? Is she hurt? How badly?"

"Not hurt," the officer said. "Way I get it, they found her wandering in the street, uh, naked, in a daze."

"Naked," Laura said weakly. The fear of child molesters came back to hit her as hard as a hammer blow. She leaned against the counter and gripped the edge of it with both hands, striving not to crumple to the floor. Holding herself up, trying to draw a deep breath, able to get nothing but shallow draughts of air, she said, "Naked?"

"And all confused, unable to talk," Phil said. "They thought she was in shock or maybe drugged, so they rushed her to Valley Medical."

Haldane took Laura's arm. "Come on. Let's go."

"But . . ."

"What's wrong?"

She licked her lips. "What if it's not Melanie? I don't want to get my hopes up and then—"

"It's her," he said. "We lost a nine-year-old girl here, and they found a nine-year-old girl seven blocks away. It's not likely to be a coincidence."

"But what if . . ."

"Doctor McCaffrey, what's wrong?"

"What if this isn't the end of the nightmare?"

"Huh?"

"What if it's only the beginning?"

"Are you asking me if I think that . . . after six years of this torture . . ."

"Do you think she could possibly be a normal little girl anymore," Laura said thickly.

"Don't expect the worst. There's always reason to hope. You won't know for sure until you see her, talk to her."

She shook her head adamantly. "No. Can't be normal. Not after what her father did to her. Not after years of forced isolation. She's got to be a very sick little girl, deeply disturbed. There's not a chance in a million she'll be normal."

"No," he said gently, apparently sensing that empty reassurances would only anger her. "No, she won't be a well-balanced, healthy little girl. She'll be lost, sick, frightened, maybe withdrawn into her own world, maybe beyond reach, maybe forever. But there's one thing you mustn't forget."

Laura met his eyes. "What's that?"

"She needs you."

Laura nodded.

They left the blood-spattered house.

Rain lashed the night, and like the crack of a whip, thunder broke across the sky.

Haldane put her in an unmarked sedan. He clipped a detachable emergency beacon to the edge of the car roof. They drove to Valley Medical with the light flashing and the siren wailing and the tires kicking up water with a hissing sound that made it seem as if the world itself were deflating.

chapter six

The emergency room doctor was Richard Pantangello. He was young, with thick brown hair and a neatly trimmed red-brown beard. He met Laura and Haldane at the admitting desk and led them to the girl's room.

The corridors were deserted, except for a few nurses gliding about like ghosts. The hospital was preternaturally silent at 4:10 in the morning.

As they walked, Dr. Pantangello spoke in a soft voice, almost a whisper. "She had no fractures, no lacerations or abrasions. One contusion, a bruise on the right arm, directly over the vein. From the look of it, I'd say it was an IV-drip needle that wasn't inserted skillfully enough."

"She was in a daze?" Haldane asked.

"Not exactly a daze," Pantangello said. "No confusion, really. She was more like someone in a trance. No sign of any head injury, though she was either unable or unwilling to speak from the moment they brought her in."

Matching the physician's quiet tone but unable to keep the anxiety out of her voice, Laura said, "What about . . . rape?"

"I couldn't find any indication that she'd been abused."

They rounded a corner and stopped in front of Room 256. The door was closed.

"She's in there," Dr. Pantangello said, jamming his hands in the pockets of his white lab coat.

Laura was still considering the way in which Pantangello had phrased his answer to her question about rape. "You found no indications of abuse, but that isn't the same as saying she wasn't raped."

"No traces of semen in the vaginal tract," Pantangello said. "No bruising or bleeding of the labia or the vaginal walls."

"Which there would've had to've been in a child this young, if she were molested," Haldane said.

"Yes. And her hymen's intact," Pantangello said.

"Then she wasn't raped," Haldane said.

A bleakness settled over Laura as she saw the sorrow and pity in the physician's gentle brown eyes.

With a voice as sad as it was quiet, Pantangello said, "She wasn't subjected to ordinary intercourse, no. We can rule that out. But . . . well, I can't say for certain." He cleared his throat.

Laura could see that this conversation was almost as much of an ordeal for the young doctor as it was for her. She wanted to tell him to stop, but she had to hear it all, had to know, and it was his job to tell her.

He finished clearing his throat and picked up where he had left off: "I can't say for certain there wasn't oral copulation."

A wordless sound of grief escaped Laura's lips.

Haldane took her arm, and she leaned against him slightly. He said, "Easy. Easy now. We don't even know if this is Melanie."

"It is," she said grimly. "I'm sure it is."

She wanted to see her daughter, ached to see her. But she was afraid to open the door and step into the room. Her future waited beyond that threshold, and she was afraid that it was a future filled with only emotional pain, despair.

A nurse went by without glancing at them, pointedly avoiding their eyes, tuning out the tragedy.

"I'm sorry," Pantangello said. He took his hands out of the pockets of his lab coat. He wanted to comfort her, but he seemed afraid to touch her. Instead, he raised one hand to the stethoscope that hung around his neck and toyed with it absentmindedly. "Look, if it's any help . . . well, in my opinion, she wasn't molested. I can't prove it. I just feel it. Besides, it's highly unusual for a child to be molested without being bruised, cut, or visibly hurt in some way. The fact that she's unmarked would tend to indicate she wasn't touched. Really, I'd bet on it." He smiled at her. At least she thought it was a smile, although it looked more like a wince. "I'd bet a year of my life on it."

Fighting back tears, Laura said, "But if she wasn't molested, why was she wandering around naked in the street?"

The answer to that question occurred to her even as she spoke.

It occurred to Dan Haldane too. He said, "She must've been in the sensory-deprivation chamber when the killer—or killers—walked into that house. She would have been naked in the tank."

"Sensory deprivation?" Pantangello asked, raising his eyebrows.

To Haldane, Laura said, "Maybe that's why she wasn't killed along with everyone else. Maybe the killer didn't know she was there, in the tank."

"Maybe," Haldane said.

With swiftly growing hope, Laura said, "And she must've gotten out of the tank after the killer left. If she saw the bodies . . . all the blood . . . that would have been so traumatic. It would sure explain her dazed condition."

Pantangello looked curiously at Lieutenant Haldane. "This must be a strange case."

"Very," the detective said.

Suddenly, Laura was no longer afraid of opening the door to Melanie's room. She started to push it inward.

Halting her with a hand on her shoulder, Dr. Pantangello said, "One more thing."

Laura waited apprehensively while the young doctor searched for the least painful words with which to convey some last bit of bad news. She knew it would be bad. She could see it in his face, for he was too inexperienced to maintain a suitably bland expression of professional detachment.

He said, "This state she's in . . . I called it a 'trance' before. But that's not exactly right. It's almost catatonic. It's a state very similar to what you sometimes see in autistic children when they're going through their most passive moods."

Laura's mouth was exceedingly dry, as if she'd spent the last half hour eating sand. There was a metallic taste of fear as well. "Say it, Doctor Pantangello. Don't mince words. I'm a doctor myself. A psychiatrist. Whatever you've got to tell me, I can handle it."

Speaking rapidly now, words running together, anxious to deliver the bad news and be done with it, he said, "Autism, mental disorders in general, they really aren't my field. Evidently, they're more yours. So I probably shouldn't say anything at all about this. But I want you to be prepared when you go in there. Her withdrawal, her silence, her detachment—well, I don't think this condition is going to go away quickly or easily. I think she's been through something damned traumatic, and she's turned inward to escape from the memory. Bringing her back is going to take . . . tremendous patience."

"And maybe she'll never come back?" Laura asked.

Pantangello shook his head, fingered his red-brown beard, tugged on his stethoscope. "No, no. I didn't say that."

"But it's what you were thinking."

His silence was a wounding confirmation.

Laura finally pushed open the door and went into the room, with the doctor and the detective close behind her.

Rain beat on the only window. The sound seemed like the wings of nocturnal birds beating in a frenzy against the glass. Far off in the night, out toward the unseen ocean, lightning pulsed twice, three times, then died in the darkness.

Of the two beds, the one nearer the window was empty, and that half of the room was dark. A light was on above the first bed, and a child lay under the sheets, in a standard-issue hospital gown, her head resting on a single pillow. The upper end of the bed was tilted, raising and angling the girl's body, so her face was entirely visible when Laura entered the room.

It was Melanie. Laura had no doubt about that. The girl had inherited her mother's hair, nose, delicate jawline. She had her father's brow and cheekbones. Her eyes were the same shade of green as Laura's but deeply set like Dylan's. During the past six years, she had become a different child from the one Laura remembered, but her identity was confirmed by more than her appearance, by something undefinable, a familiar aura perhaps, an emotional or even psychic link that snapped into place between mother and daughter the instant that Laura walked into the room. She knew this was her little girl, though she would have had some difficulty explaining exactly *how* she knew.

Melanie resembled one of those children in advertisements for international hunger-relief organizations or a poster child for some rare and debilitating disease. Her face was gaunt. Her skin was pale, with an unhealthy, grainy texture. More gray than pink, her lips were cracked and peeling. The flesh around her sunken eyes was dark, as if it had been smudged when she had wiped away tears with an inky thumb.

The eyes themselves were the most unnerving evidence of her ordeal. She stared at the empty air above her, blinking but seeing nothing— nothing in *this* world. Neither fear nor pain were evident in those eyes. Just desolation.

Laura said, "Honey?"

The girl didn't move. Her eyes didn't flicker.

"Melanie?"

No response.

Hesitantly, Laura moved toward the bed.

The girl seemed oblivious of her.

Laura put down the safety rail, leaned close to the child, spoke her name again, but again elicited no reaction. With one trembling hand, she touched Melanie's face, which felt slightly fevered, and that contact shattered all her reservations. A dam of emotion broke within her, and she seized the girl, lifted her away from the bed, held her close, and hugged her. "Melanie, baby, my Melanie, it's all right now, it'll be okay, really it will, you're safe now, safe with me now, safe with Mommy, thank God, safe, thank God." As she spoke, tears burst from her, and she wept with a lack of self-consciousness and control that she had not experienced since she had been a child herself.

If only Melanie had wept too. But the girl was beyond tears. She didn't return Laura's embrace, either. She hung limply in her mother's arms: a pliant body, an empty shell, unaware of the love that was hers to receive, unable to accept the succor and shelter that her mother offered, distant, in her own reality, lost.

·

Ten minutes later, in the corridor, Laura dried her eyes with a couple of Kleenexes and blew her nose.

Dan Haldane paced back and forth. His shoes squeaked on the highly polished tiles. From the expression on the detective's face, Laura guessed that he was trying to work off some of his anger over what had happened to Melanie.

Maybe some cops cared more than she thought. This one, anyway.

Dr. Pantangello said, "I want to keep Melanie here at least until tomorrow afternoon. For observation."

"Of course," Laura said.

"When she's released from the hospital, she'll need psychiatric care."

Laura nodded.

"What I was wondering . . . well, you don't intend to treat her yourself, do you?"

Laura tucked the sodden tissues in one coat pocket. "You think it would be better for a third party, an uninvolved therapist, to work with her."

"Yes."

"Well, Doctor, I can understand why you feel that way, and in most cases I would agree with you. But not this time."

"Usually, it's a bad idea for a therapist to treat one of his own children. As her mother, you're almost certainly going to be more demanding of your own daughter than you would be of an ordinary patient. And, excuse me, but it may even be possible that the parent is part of the problem in the first place."

"Yes. You're right. Usually. But not this time. I didn't do this to my little girl. I had no part in it. I am virtually as much a stranger to her as any other therapist would be, but I can give her more time, more care, more attention than anyone else. With another doctor, she'd be just another patient. But with me, she'll be my only patient. I'll take a leave of absence from Saint Mark's. I'll shift my private patients to some colleagues for a few weeks or even months. I won't expect fast progress from her because I'll have all the time in the world. Melanie is going to get all of me, everything I have to offer as a doctor, as a psychiatrist, and all the love I have to offer as a mother."

Pantangello seemed on the verge of issuing another warning or offering more advice, but he decided against it. "Well . . . good luck."

"Thank you."

When the physician had gone, leaving Laura and Haldane alone in the silent, antiseptic-scented corridor, the detective said, "It's a big job."

"I can handle it."

"I'm sure you can."

"She'll get well."

"I hope she does."

At the nurses' station, at the end of the hall, a muffled phone rang twice.

Haldane said, "I've sent for a uniformed officer. Just in case Melanie witnessed the murders, in case someone might be looking for her, I thought it was a good idea to post a guard. Until tomorrow afternoon, anyway."

"Thank you, Lieutenant."

"You aren't staying here, are you?"

"Yes. Of course. Where else?"

"Not long, I hope."

"A few hours."

"You need your rest, Doctor McCaffrey."

"Melanie needs me more. I couldn't sleep anyway."

He said, "But if she's coming home tomorrow, won't you have to get things ready for her?"

Laura blinked. "Oh. I hadn't thought about that. I'll have to prepare a bedroom. She can't sleep in a crib any longer."

"Better go home," he said gently.

"In a little while," she agreed. "But not to sleep. I can't sleep. I'll leave her alone here just long enough to get the house ready for her homecoming."

"I hate to bring it up, but I'd like to get blood samples from you and Melanie."

The request puzzled her. "Why?"

He hesitated. "Well, with samples of your blood, your husband's, and the girl's, we can pretty much pin down for sure whether she's your daughter."

"No need for that."

"It's the easiest way—"

"I said, there's no need for that," she told him irritably. "She's Melanie. She's my little girl. I know it."

"I know how you feel," he said sympathetically. "I understand. I'm sure she is your daughter. But since you haven't seen her in six years, six years in which she's changed a great deal, and since she can't speak for herself, we're going to need some proof, not just your instincts, or the juvenile court is going to put her in the state's custody. You don't want that, do you?"

"My God, no."

"Doctor Pantangello tells me they've already got a sample of the girl's blood. It'll take only a minute to draw a few cc's of yours."

"All right. But . . . where?"

"There's an examination room next to the nurses' station."

Laura looked apprehensively at the closed door to Melanie's room. "Can we wait until the guard comes?"

"Of course." He leaned against the wall.

Laura just stood there, staring at the door.

The glass-smooth silence became unbearable.

To break it, she said, "I was right, wasn't I?"

"About what?"

"Earlier, I said maybe the nightmare wouldn't be over when we found Melanie, that maybe it would be just beginning."

"Yeah. You were right. But at least it *is* a beginning."

She knew what he meant: They might have found Melanie's body with the other three—battered, dead. This was better. Frightening, perplexing, depressing, but definitely better.

chapter seven

Dan Haldane sat at the desk that he was using while on temporary assignment to the East Valley Division. The ancient wooden surface was scalloped by cigarette burns around the edge, scarred and gouged and marked by scores of overlapping dark rings from dripping mugs of coffee. The accommodations didn't bother him. He liked his job, and he could do it in a tent if he had to.

In the hour before dawn, the East Valley Division was as quiet as a police station ever got. Most potential victims were not yet awake, and even the criminals had to sleep sometime. A skeleton crew manned the station until the day crew arrived. In these last musty minutes of the graveyard shift, the place still possessed the haunted feeling common to all offices at night. The only sounds were the lonely clatter of a typewriter in a room down the hall from the bull pen, and the knock of the janitor's broom as it banged against the legs of the empty desks. Somewhere a telephone rang; even in the hour before dawn, someone was in trouble.

Dan zipped open his worn briefcase and spread the contents on the desk. Polaroid photographs of the three bodies that had been found in the Studio City house. A random sampling of the papers that had littered the floor in Dylan McCaffrey's office. Statements from the neighbors. Preliminary handwritten reports from the coroner's men and the Scientific Investigation Division (SID). And lists.

Dan believed in lists. He had lists of the contents of drawers, cupboards, and closets in the murder house, a list of the titles of the books on the living-room shelves, and a list of telephone numbers taken from a notepad by the phone in McCaffrey's office. He also had names—every name that appeared on any scrap of paper anywhere in that Studio City residence. Until the case was wrapped up, he would carry the lists with him, take them out and reread them whenever he had a spare moment—over lunch, when he was on the john, in bed just before switching off the light—prodding his subconscious, with the hope of attaining an important insight or turning up a vital cross-reference.

Stanley Holbein, an old friend and former partner from Robbery-Homicide, had once embarrassed Dan at an R&H Christmas party by telling a long and highly amusing (and apocryphal) story about having seen some of Dan's most private lists, including the ones on which he had kept track of every meal eaten and every bowel movement since the age of nine. Dan, who stood listening, amused but red-faced, with his hands deep in his jacket pockets, had finally pretended to want to strangle Stanley. But when he had withdrawn his hands from his pockets to lunge at his friend, he'd accidentally pulled out half a dozen lists that fluttered to the floor, eliciting gales of laughter from everyone present and necessitating a hasty retreat into another room.

Now he gave his latest set of lists a quick scan, with the vague hope that something would jump out at him, like a pop-up figure in a children's book. Nothing popped. He began again, reading through the lists more slowly.

The book titles were unfamiliar. The collection was a peculiar mix of psychology, medicine, physical science, and the occult. Why would a doctor, a man of science, be interested in clairvoyance, psychic powers, and other paranormal phenomena?

He looked over the list of names. He didn't recognize any.

As his stomach grew increasingly acidic, he kept returning to the photos of the bodies. In fourteen years with the LAPD and four years in the army before that, he had seen more than a few dead men. But these were unlike any in his experience. He had seen men who had stepped on land mines yet had been in better shape than these.

The killers—surely there had been more than one—had possessed incredible strength or inhuman rage, or both. The victims had been struck repeatedly after they were already dead, hammered into jelly. What sort of men could kill with such unrestrained viciousness and cruelty? What maniacal hatred could have driven them to this?

Before he could really concentrate on those questions, he was interrupted by the sound of approaching footsteps.

Ross Mondale stopped at Dan's desk. The division captain was a stocky man, five-eight, with a powerful upper body. As usual, everything about him was brown: brown hair, thick brown eyebrows; brown, watchful, narrow eyes; a chocolate-brown suit, beige shirt, dark brown tie, brown shoes. He was wearing a heavy ring with a bright ruby, which was the only spark of color that he allowed.

The janitor had gone. They were the only two in the big room.

"You still here?" Mondale asked.

"No. This is a clever cardboard facade. The real me is in the john, shooting heroin."

Mondale didn't smile. "I thought you'd be gone back to Central by now."

"I've become attached to the East Valley. The smog's got a special savory scent to it out here."

Mondale glowered. "This cutback in funds is a pain in the ass. Used to be, I had a man out sick or on vacation, there were plenty of others to cover for him. Now we got to bring subs in from other divisions, loan out our own men when we can spare them, which we never really can. It's a crock."

Dan knew that Mondale would not have been so displeased about loaned manpower if the loanee had been anyone else. He didn't like Dan. The animosity was mutual.

They had been at the police academy together and later had been assigned to the same patrol car. Dan had requested a new partner, to no avail. Eventually, an encounter with a lunatic, a bullet in the chest, and a stay in the hospital had done for Dan what formal requests had not been able to achieve: By the time he got back to work, he had a new and more reliable partner. Dan was a field cop by nature; he enjoyed being on the streets, where the action was. Mondale, on the other hand, stayed close to the office; he was a born public-relations man as surely as Itzhak Perlman was born to play the violin. A master of deception, ass-kissing, and flattery, he had an uncanny ability to sense pending changes in the currents of power in the department's hierarchy, aligning himself with those superiors who could do the most for him, abandoning former allies who were about to lose power. He knew how to smooth-talk politicians and reporters. Those talents had helped him obtain more promotions than Dan. Rumor ranked Ross Mondale high on the mayor's list of candidates for police chief.

However, as ingratiating as he was with everyone else, Mondale could find no words of praise or flattery for Dan. "You got a food stain on your shirt, Haldane."

Dan looked down and saw a rust-colored spot the size of a dime.

"Chili dog," he said.

"You know, Haldane, each of us represents the entire department. We have an obligation—a *duty*—to present a respectable image to the public."

"Right. I'll never eat another chili dog until I die and go to Heaven. Only croissants and caviar from now on. A higher quality of shirt stains henceforth. I swear."

"You make a habit of wisecracking at every superior officer?"

"Nope. Only you."

"I don't much care for it."

"Didn't think you would," Dan said.

"You know, I'm not going to put up with your shit forever, just because we went to the academy together."

Nostalgia wasn't the reason that Mondale tolerated Dan's abuse, and neither of them had any illusions otherwise. The truth was, Dan knew something about Mondale that, if revealed, would destroy the captain's career, something that had happened when they had been second-year patrolmen, a vital bit of information that would have made any blackmailer swoon with joy. He would never use it against Mondale, of course; as much as he despised the man, he couldn't bring himself to engage in blackmail.

If their roles had been reversed, however, Mondale would have had no compunctions about blackmail or vindictive revelation. Dan's continued silence baffled the captain, made him uneasy, encouraged him to tread carefully each time they met.

"Let's get specific," Dan said. "Exactly how much longer *will* you put up with my shit?"

"I don't have to. Not for long, thank God. You'll be back in Central after this shift," Mondale said. He smiled.

Dan leaned his weight against the unoiled spring-action back of the office chair, which squealed in protest, and put his hands behind his head. "Sorry to disappoint. I'll be sticking around for a while. I caught a murder last night. It's my case now. I figure I'll stay with it for the duration."

The captain's smile melted like ice cream on a hot plate. "You mean the triple one-eighty-seven in Studio City?"

"Ah, now I see why you're in the office so early. You heard about that. Two relatively well-known psychologists get wasted under mysterious circumstances, so you figure there's going to be a lot of media attention. How do you tumble to these things so quickly, Ross? You sleep with a police-band radio beside your bed?"

Ignoring the question, sitting on the edge of the desk, Mondale said, "Any leads?"

"Nope. Got pictures of the victims, though."

He noted, with satisfaction, that all the blood drained out of Mondale's face when he saw the ravaged bodies in the photographs. The captain didn't even finish shuffling through the whole series. "Looks like a burglary got out of hand," Mondale said.

"Looks like no such a thing. All three victims had money on them. Other loose cash around the house. Nothing stolen."

"Well," Mondale said defensively, "I didn't know that."

"You still should've known burglars usually kill only when they're cornered, and then they're quick and clean about it. Not like this."

"There are always exceptions," Mondale said pompously. "Even grandmothers rob banks now and then."

Dan laughed.

"Well, it's true," Mondale said.

"That's just marvelous, Ross."

"Well, it *is* true."

"Not *my* grandmother."

"I didn't say *your* grandmother."

"You mean *your* grandmother robs banks, Ross?"

"Somebody's goddamned grandmother does, and you can bet your ass on it."

"You know a bookie who takes bets on whether or not somebody's grandmother will rob a bank? If the odds are right, I'll take a hundred bucks of his action."

Mondale stood up. He put one hand to his tie, straightening the knot. "I don't want you working here any longer, you son of a bitch."

"Well, remember that old Rolling Stones song, Ross. 'You can't always get what you want.'"

"I can have your ass shipped back to Central."

"Not unless the rest of me gets shipped with it, and the rest of me intends to stay right here for a while."

Mondale's face darkened. His lips pulled tight and went pale. He looked as if he had been pushed as far as he could be pushed for the present.

Before the captain could do anything rash, Dan said, "Listen, you can't take me off a case that's mine from the start, not without some screwup on my part. You know the rules. But I don't want to fight you on this. That'll just distract me. So let's just call a truce, huh? I'll stay out of your hair, I'll be a good boy, and you stay out of my way."

Mondale said nothing. He was breathing hard, and apparently he still didn't trust himself to speak.

"We don't like each other much, but there's no reason we can't still work together," Dan said, getting as conciliatory as he would ever get with Mondale.

"Why don't you want to let go of this one?"

"Looks interesting. Most homicides are boring. Husband kills his wife's boyfriend. Some psycho kills a bunch of women because they all remind him of his mother. One crack dealer offs another crack dealer. I've seen it all a hundred times. It gets tedious. This is different, I think. That's why I don't want to let it go. We all need variety in our lives, Ross. That's why it's a mistake for you to wear brown suits all the time."

Mondale ignored the gibe. "You think we got an important case on our hands this time?"

"Three murders . . . that doesn't strike you as important?"

"I mean something really big," Mondale said impatiently. "Like the Manson Family or the Hillside Strangler or something?"

"Could be. Depends on how it develops. But, yeah, I suspect this is going to be the kind of story that sells newspapers and pumps up the ratings on TV news."

Mondale thought about that, and his eyes swam out of focus.

"One thing I insist on," Dan said, leaning forward on his chair, folding his hands on the desk, and assuming an earnest expression. "If I'm going to be in charge of this case, I don't want to have to waste time talking to reporters, giving interviews. You've got to keep those bastards off my back. Let them film all the bloodstains they want, so they'll have lots of great footage for the dinner-hour broadcast, but keep them away. I'm no good at dealing with them."

Mondale's eyes swam back into focus. "Uh . . . yeah, of course, no problem. The press can be a royal pain in the ass." To Mondale, the cameras and publicity were as nourishing as the food of the gods, and he was delighted by the prospect of being the center of media attention. "You leave them to me."

"Fine," Dan said.

"And you report to me, nobody but me."

"Sure."

"Daily, up-to-the-minute reports."

"Whatever you say."

Mondale stared at him, disbelieving but unwilling to challenge him. Every man liked to dream. Even Ross Mondale.

"With this manpower shortage and everything," Dan said, "don't you have work to do?"

The captain walked off toward his own office, stopped after a few

steps, glanced back, and said, "So far we've got two moderately prominent psychologists dead, and prominent people tend to know other
prominent people. So you might be moving in different circles from
those you muck around in when a dope dealer gets wasted. Besides, if
this does get to be a hot case with lots of press attention, you and I will
probably have meetings with the chief, with members of the commission, maybe even with the mayor."

"So?"

"So don't step on any toes."

"Oh, don't worry, Ross. I wouldn't *ever* dance with any of those
guys."

Mondale shook his head. "Christ."

Dan watched the captain walk away. When he was alone again, he
returned to his lists.

chapter eight

The sky was brightening from black to gray-black. Dawn hadn't crawled out of its hole yet, but it was creeping close, and it would crest the hilly horizon in ten or fifteen minutes.

The public parking lot of Valley Medical was nearly deserted, a patchwork of shadows and evenly spaced pools of jaundiced light from the sodium-vapor lamps.

Sitting behind the wheel of his Volvo, Ned Rink hated to see the night end. He was a night person, an owl rather than a lark. He was not able to function well or think clearly until midafternoon, and he didn't begin to hit his stride until after midnight. That preference was no doubt programmed into his genes, for his mother had been the same way; his personal biological clock was out of sync with those of most people.

Nevertheless, living at night was also a matter of choice: He felt more at home in the darkness. He was an ugly man, and he knew it. He felt conspicuous in broad daylight, but he believed that the night softened his ugliness and made it less noticeable. His forehead was too narrow and sloped, suggesting limited intelligence, although he was actually far from stupid. His small eyes were set too close, and his nose was a beak, and his other features were crudely formed. He was five-seven, with big shoulders and long arms and a barrel chest that were disproportionate to his height. As a child, he'd had to endure the cruel taunting of other kids who had nicknamed him Ape. Their ridicule and harassment had made him so tense that he'd developed an ulcer by the time he was thirteen years old. These days, Ned Rink didn't take that sort of crap from anyone. These days, if somebody gave him a hard time, he just killed his tormentor, blew his brains out with no hesitation and no remorse. That was a great way to deal with stress; his ulcers had healed long ago.

He picked up the black attaché case from the seat beside him. It contained a white lab coat, a white hospital towel, a stethoscope, and a silencer-equipped Walther .45 semiautomatic loaded with hollow-point cartridges that were coated with Teflon to ensure penetration of even bulletproof vests. He didn't have to open the attaché case to make sure that everything was there; he had packed it himself less than an hour ago.

He intended to walk into the hospital, go directly to the public restrooms off the lobby, slip out of his raincoat, put on the white lab coat, fold the towel around the pistol, and head straight to Room 256, where they had taken the girl. Rink had been told to expect a police guard on duty. All right. He could handle that. He would pretend that he was a doctor, make up some excuse to get the cop out of the hallway and into the girl's room, where the nurses couldn't see, then shoot the jerk, shoot the girl. Then the coup de grâce: a bullet in the ear for each of them, just to make sure they were stone dead. The job done, Rink would leave immediately, return to the public restroom, pick up his raincoat and attaché case, and get the hell out of the hospital.

The plan was clean and uncomplicated. There was almost nothing about it that could go wrong.

Before opening the door and getting out of the Volvo, he looked carefully around the parking lot to be sure that he wasn't observed. Although the storm had passed and the rain had stopped falling half an hour ago, light fog marked the direction of a gentle breeze and eddied in lazy patterns off from the main current, shrouding some objects, distorting others. Every depression in the macadam was filled with a pool of rainwater, and the many wind-stirred puddles shimmered with yellow reflections of the light from the tall sodium-vapor lamps.

Except for the drifting fog, the night was perfectly still.

Rink decided he was alone, unseen.

To the east, the gray-black sky had a pale, opalescent, pinkish-blue tint. The first faint glow of dawn's radiant face. In another hour, the quiet night routine of the hospital would begin to give way to the business and busyness of day. It was time to go.

He was looking forward to the work ahead. He had never killed a child before. It ought to be interesting.

chapter nine

Alone, the girl woke. She sat straight up in bed, trying to scream. Her mouth was open wide, the muscles in her neck were taut, the blood vessels in her throat and temples throbbed with the effort that she was making, but she couldn't produce a sound.

She sat like that for half a minute, her small fists full of sweat-soaked sheets. Eyes wide. She wasn't looking at or reacting to anything in the room. The terror lay beyond those walls.

Briefly, her eyes cleared. She was no longer oblivious of the hospital room.

She realized for the first time that she was alone. Remembered who she was. She desperately desired company, someone to hold, human contact, comfort.

"Hello?" she whispered. "S-s-somebody? Somebody? Somebody? *Mommy?*"

If people had been with her, perhaps her attention would have been altogether captured by them and drawn permanently away from the things that so frightened her. Alone, however, she could not shake the nightmare that had its talons in her, and her eyes glazed over again. Her gaze fixed once more on a scene elsewhere.

Finally, with a desperate, wordless whimper, she clambered over the safety railing and got out of bed. She tottered a few steps. Went down on her knees. Breathing hard, wheezing with panic, she crawled into the darker half of the room, past the untenanted bed, into the corner where friendly shadows offered consolation. She put her back to the wall and faced into the room, knees drawn up. The hospital gown bunched at her hips. She wrapped her arms around her thin legs and pulled herself into a tight ball.

She remained in the corner only a minute before she began to whimper and mewl like a frightened animal. She raised her hands and covered her face, striving to block out a hideous sight.

"Don't, please, please, please."

Breathing rapidly and shallowly, with ever-increasing panic, she lowered her hands and squeezed them into fists. She pounded her own breast, hard, harder.

"Don't, don't, don't," she said.

She was pounding hard enough to hurt herself, yet she couldn't feel the blows.

"The door," she said softly. "The door . . . the door . . ."

It wasn't the hospital-room door or the door to the adjoining bath that frightened her. She was looking at neither. She was dimly aware of the world around her, but she was focused instead on things no one else could have seen from any vantage point in that room.

She raised both hands, held them out in front of her, as though pressing on the unseen door, frantically attempting to hold it shut.

"Stop."

The meager muscles in her frail arms popped up, and then her elbows bent, as if the invisible door actually had substantial weight and was swinging open against all her protests. As if something big pushed relentlessly against the other side of it. Something inhuman and unimaginably strong.

Abruptly, with a gasp, she scrambled out of the shadow-shrouded corner and across the floor. She went under the unused bed. Safe. Or maybe not. Nowhere was safe. She stopped and curled into the fetal position, murmuring, hopelessly trying to hide from the thing beyond the door.

"The door," she said. "The door . . . the door to December . . ."

With her arms crossed on her breast, her fingertips pressing hard into her own bony shoulders, she began to weep quietly.

"Help me, help me," she said, but she spoke in a whisper that did not carry to the hall, where nurses might have heard it.

If someone had responded to her cry, Melanie might have clung to him in terror, unable to cast off the cloak of autism that protected her from a world too cruel to bear. Nevertheless, even that much contact with another human being, when she wanted it, would have been a small first step toward recovery. But with the best of intentions, they had left her alone, to rest, and her plea for solace and for a reassuring voice went unanswered.

She shuddered. "Help me. It's coming open. It's . . . open." The last word faded into a low moan of pure black despair. Her anguish was terrible, bleak.

Eventually her breathing grew less agitated, less ragged, and finally normal. The weeping subsided.

She lay in silence, perfectly still, as if in a deep sleep. But in the darkness under the bed, her eyes were still open wide, staring in shock and terror.

chapter ten

When she got home, shortly before dawn, Laura made a pot of strong coffee. She carried a mug into the guest bedroom and sipped at the steaming brew while she dusted the furniture, put sheets on the bed, and prepared for Melanie's homecoming.

Her four-year-old calico cat, Pepper, kept getting in the way, rubbing against her legs, insisting upon being petted and scratched behind the ears. The cat seemed to sense that it was soon to be deposed from its favored position in the household.

For four years, Pepper had been something of a surrogate child. In a way, the house also had been a surrogate child, an outlet for the child-rearing energies that Laura could not direct toward her own little girl.

Six years ago, after Dylan had run off, cleaning out their bank accounts and leaving her with no ready cash, Laura had been forced to scramble, scrape, and scheme to keep the house. It wasn't a mansion, but a spacious four-bedroom, Spanish two-story in Sherman Oaks, on the "right" side of Ventura Boulevard, on a curving street where some homes had swimming pools and even more had hot tubs, where children were frequently sent to private schools, and where the family dogs were not mongrels but full-bred German shepherds, spaniels, golden retrievers, Airedales, dalmatians, and poodles registered with the American Kennel Club. It stood on a large lot, half hidden by coral trees, benjaminas, bushy red and purple hibiscus, red azaleas, and a fence shrouded in bougainvillea, with thick borders of impatiens in every hue along the serpentine, mission-tile walk that led to the front door.

Laura was proud of her home. Three years ago, when she had finally stopped paying private investigators to search for Dylan and Melanie, she had begun to put her spare money into small renovation projects: darkly stained oak base molding, crown molding, and doorframes; new, rich dark blue tile in the master bathroom, with white Sherle Wagner shell sinks and gold fixtures. She'd torn out Dylan's Oriental garden in the back lawn because it was a reminder of him, and had replaced it with twenty different species of roses.

In a sense, the house took the place of the daughter who had been stolen from her: she worried and fussed about it, pampered it, guided it toward maturity. Her concern for keeping the house in good repair was akin to a mother's concern for the health of her child.

Now she could stop sublimating all those maternal urges. Her daughter was finally coming home.

Pepper meowed.

Snatching the cat off the floor and holding it with its legs dangling, face-to-face, Laura said, "There'll still be plenty of love for one pitiful cat. Don't worry about that, you old mouse-chaser."

The phone rang.

She put the cat down, crossed the hall to the master bedroom, and plucked the handset off the cradle. "Hello?"

No answer. The caller hesitated a moment, then hung up.

She stared at the phone, uneasy. Maybe it had been a wrong number. But in the dead hour before dawn, on this extraordinary night, a ringing phone and an uncommunicative caller had sinister implications.

She double-checked the locks on the doors. That seemed to be an inadequate response, but she could think of nothing more to do.

Still uneasy, she tried to shrug off the call, and at last she went into the empty room that had once been the nursery.

Two years ago, she had disposed of Melanie's baby furniture when she had finally admitted to herself that her missing daughter would have by that time outgrown everything. Laura had not refurnished, ostensibly because when Melanie returned, the girl would be old enough to have a say in the choice of decor. Actually, Laura had left the room empty because—though she couldn't face her own fears—deep in her heart she'd felt that Melanie would never be coming back, that the child had vanished forever.

She had saved a few of her daughter's toys, however. Now she took the box of old playthings out of the closet and rummaged through it. Three-year-olds and nine-year-olds didn't have much in common, but Laura found two items that might still be appealing to Melanie: a big Raggedy Ann doll, slightly soiled, and a smaller teddy bear with floppy ears.

She took the bear and the doll into the guest bedroom and set them on the pillows, with their backs against the headboard. Melanie would see them the moment she came into the room.

Pepper jumped onto the bed, approached the doll and the bear with curiosity and trepidation. She sniffed the doll, nuzzled the bear, then curled up beside them, apparently having decided that they were friendly.

The first beams of daylight were streaming through the French windows. By the manner in which the early light fluctuated from gray to gold to gray again Laura could tell, without looking at the sky, that the rain had stopped and that the clouds were breaking up.

Although she'd had only three hours of sleep the previous night, and though her daughter wouldn't be leaving the hospital for six or eight hours, Laura didn't feel like returning to bed. She was awake, energetic. From the stoop outside the front door, she retrieved the plastic-wrapped morning newspaper. In the kitchen, she squeezed two large oranges to make a glass of fresh juice, put a pan of water on the stove to boil, took a box of raisin oatmeal from a cupboard, and popped two slices of bread in the toaster. She was actually humming a tune—Elton John's "Daniel"—when she sat at the table.

Her daughter was coming home.

The front-page stories in the paper—the turmoil in the Middle East, the fighting in Central America, the scheming of politicians, the muggings and robberies and senseless killings—did not discourage or concern her as they usually did. The murders of Dylan, Hoffritz, and the unknown man were not reported: That story had broken too late to make the early edition. If she had seen that slaughter recounted in the *Times*, perhaps she wouldn't have felt so lighthearted. But she saw not a word about those murders, and Melanie would be released from the hospital this afternoon, and all things considered, she had known worse mornings.

Her daughter was coming home.

When she finished her breakfast, she pushed aside the newspaper and sat looking out the window at the damp rose garden. The sodden blooms seemed impossibly bright in the slanting sun, as unnaturally colorful as flowers in a vivid dream.

She lost track of time, might have been sitting there two minutes or ten, when she was snapped out of her reverie by a thump and clatter elsewhere in the house. She sat straight up, rigid, tense, scared, her mind filled with images of blood-spattered walls and cold dead forms in opaque plastic bags.

Then Pepper broke the ominous spell by dashing out of the dining room, into the kitchen, claws clicking on the tile. She scampered into a corner, stood there, the hair raised along her back, ears flattened, staring at the doorway through which she had come. Then with a sudden self-consciousness that was comical, the cat pretended nonchalance, curled up in a furry puddle on the floor, yawned, and turned sleepy eyes on Laura, as if to say, "Who me? Lose my feline dignity? Even for a moment? Never! Scared? Ridiculous!"

"What'd you do, puss? Knock something over, spook yourself?"

The calico yawned again.

"It better not have been anything breakable," Laura said, "or I might finally get those cat-skin earmuffs I've been wanting."

She went through the house, looking for the damage that Pepper had done, and she found it in the guest bedroom. The teddy bear and the Raggedy Ann doll were lying on the floor. Fortunately, the cat had not clawed the stuffing out of them. The alarm clock had been knocked off the nightstand. Laura picked it up and saw that it was still ticking; the glass face wasn't cracked, either. She put the clock back where it belonged, returned the doll and the bear to the bed.

Strange. Pepper had gotten over the reckless-kitten stage three years ago. She was now slightly plump, content, and thoroughly self-satisfied. This rambunctiousness was out of character, yet another indication that she knew her place in the McCaffrey household was no longer second to Laura.

In the kitchen, the cat was still in the corner.

Laura put food in the calico's dish. "Lucky for you nothing broke. You wouldn't like being made into earmuffs."

Pepper rose to a crouch, and her ears perked up.

Tapping the dish with the empty can of 9 Lives, Laura said, "Chow-time, you ferocious mouse-mauler."

Pepper didn't move.

"You'll eat it when you want it," Laura said, taking the empty can to the sink to rinse it before tossing it in the garbage.

Abruptly, Pepper exploded from the corner, streaked across the kitchen, through the doorway, into the living room, gone.

"Crazy cat," Laura said, frowning at the untouched 9 Lives. Usually Pepper was pushing in at the yellow dish, trying to eat even as Laura was scraping the food from the can.

Strange.

part two
ENEMIES
WITHOUT FACES

WEDNESDAY

1:00 P.M.–7:45 P.M.

chapter eleven

At one o'clock, when Laura drove her blue Honda to Valley Medical, a uniformed policeman at the entrance to the main parking lot barred the way. He directed her to the staff lot, which had been opened to the public "until we straighten out the mess here." Eighty to a hundred feet behind him was a cluster of LAPD cruisers and other official vehicles, some with emergency beacons rotating and flashing.

As she followed the patrolman's directions and headed toward the staff lot, Laura glanced to the right, through the fence, and saw Lieutenant Haldane. He was the tallest and biggest man among those at the scene. She suddenly realized that the commotion might have a connection with Melanie and with the murders in Studio City the previous night.

By the time she slotted the Honda between two cars with MD plates and ran back down the hospital driveway to the fence that encircled the public parking lot, Laura had half convinced herself that Melanie was hurt or missing or dead. The patrolman at the gate would not let her through, not even when she told him who she was, so she shouted to Dan Haldane.

He hurried across the macadam, favoring his left leg. Not much, only slightly. She might not have noticed if her senses hadn't been sharply honed by fear. He took her by the arm and led her away from the gate, along the fence, to a spot where they could talk privately.

As they walked, she said, "What's happened to Melanie?"

"Nothing."

"Tell me the truth!"

"That *is* the truth. She's in her room. Safe. Just the way you left her."

They stopped, and she stood with her back to the fence, staring past Haldane toward the pulsing emergency beacons. She saw a morgue wagon with the patrol cars.

No. It wasn't fair. To find Melanie after all these years and then to lose her again so soon—it was unthinkable.

A tightness in her chest. A throbbing in her temples.

She said, "Who's dead?"

"I've been calling your house—"

"I want—"

"—trying to get hold of you—"

"—to know—"

"—for the past hour and a half."

—who's *dead!*" she demanded.

"Listen, it's not Melanie. Okay?" His voice was unusually soft and gentle and reassuring for a man his size. She always expected a roar, but he purred. "Melanie's fine. Really."

Laura studied his face, his eyes. She believed that he was telling her the truth. Melanie was all right. But Laura was still scared.

Haldane said, "I didn't get home until seven this morning, fell into bed. Eleven o'clock, my phone rings, and they want me at Valley Medical. They think maybe there's some link between this homicide and Melanie because—"

"Because what?"

"Well, after all, she's a patient here. So I've been trying to get hold of you—"

"I was out shopping, buying new clothes for her," Laura said. "What happened? Who's dead? Are you going to tell me, for God's sake?"

"A guy in his car. That Volvo over there. Dead in the front seat of his Volvo."

"Who?"

"According to his ID, his name's Ned Rink."

She leaned back against the chain-link fence, her pulse rate gradually slowing from the frantic beat it had attained.

"You ever hear of him?" Haldane asked. "Ned Rink?"

"No."

"I wondered if maybe he was an associate of your husband's. Like Hoffritz."

"Not that I'm aware. The name's not familiar. Why would you think he knew Dylan? Because of the way he died? Is that it? Was he beaten to death like the others?"

"No. But it was odd."

"Tell me."

He hesitated, and from the look in his blue eyes she could see that it was another particularly brutal homicide.

"Tell me," she said again.

"His throat was crushed, as if someone gave him one hell of a whack with a lead pipe, caught him right across the Adam's apple. More than one whack. Lots of damage. Literally pulverized the guy's windpipe, crushed the Adam's apple, the vocal cords. Broke his neck. Cracked his spine."

"Okay," she said, dry-mouthed. "I get the picture."

"Sorry. Anyway, it's not like the bodies in Studio City, but it's unusual. You can see why we might figure they're connected. In both cases, the murders involved an unusual degree of violence. This one wasn't as bad as those, not nearly, but nevertheless . . ."

She pushed away from the fence. "I want to see Melanie."

Suddenly she *had* to see Melanie. It was a strong physical *need*. She had to touch the girl, hold her, be reassured that her child was all right.

She headed away from the parking lot, toward the front entrance of the hospital.

Haldane walked beside her, limping slightly but apparently not in pain.

"You have an accident?" she asked.

"Huh?"

"Your leg."

"Oh. No. Just an old football injury from college. Banged the knee up pretty bad my senior year. Sometimes it acts up in humid weather. Listen, there's more about the guy in the Volvo, Rink."

"What?"

"He had an attaché case with him. Inside, there was a white lab coat, a stethoscope, and a pistol fitted with a silencer."

"He shoot his assailant? Are you looking for someone with a bullet wound?"

"Nope. The piece wasn't fired. But do you see what I'm driving at? The lab coat? The stethoscope?"

"He wasn't a doctor, was he?"

"No. What it looks like to us is that maybe he was going to go into the hospital, put on the lab coat, hang the stethoscope around his neck, and pretend to be a doctor."

She glanced at him as they reached the curb and stepped up onto the sidewalk. "Why would he do that?"

"From a preliminary look, the assistant medical examiner thinks Rink was killed between four and six o'clock this morning, though he wasn't found until nine forty-five. Now, if he was figuring to visit someone in the hospital at, say, five o'clock in the morning, he'd almost have to try to pass himself off as a doctor, because visiting hours don't start until one in the afternoon. If he tried to get on one of the medical floors in civilian clothes at that hour, there's a good chance a nurse or maybe a security guard would stop him. But in a lab coat, with a stethoscope, he could probably breeze right through."

They had reached the front entrance of the hospital. Laura stopped on the sidewalk. "When you say 'visit' you don't mean 'visit.'"

"No."

"So you believe he intended to go into the hospital and kill someone."

"A man doesn't carry a pistol with a silencer unless he means to use it. A silencer's illegal. Law comes down on you hard for that. You get caught with one, you're in deep sh . . . in deep soup. Besides, I haven't learned any details yet, but I'm told Rink has a criminal record. He's suspected of being a freelance hitman for the past few years."

"A hired killer?"

"I'd almost bet on it."

"But that doesn't mean he came here to kill Melanie. Could be someone else in the hospital . . ."

"We already considered that. We've been checking the patient list to see if there's anyone here with a criminal record, or maybe someone who's a material witness in a case that's going to trial soon. Or any known dope dealers or members of any organized-crime family. We haven't found anything so far. Nobody who might've been Rink's target . . . except Melanie."

"Are you saying maybe this Rink killed Dylan and Hoffritz and the other man in Studio City—then came here to kill Melanie because she saw him do the others?"

"Could be."

"But then who killed Rink?"

He sighed. "That's where the logic falls apart."

"Whoever killed him didn't want him to kill Melanie," Laura said.

Haldane shrugged.

She said, "If that's the case, I'm glad."

"What's to be glad about?"

"Well, if someone killed Rink to stop him from killing Melanie, it must mean she doesn't only have enemies out there. It means she has friends too."

With unconcealed pity, Haldane said, "No. That isn't necessarily what it means. The people who killed Rink probably want Melanie just as much as he did—except they want her alive."

"Why?"

"Because she knows too much about the experiments conducted in that house."

"Then they'd want her dead too, just like Rink."

"Unless they need her to continue those experiments."

Laura knew it was true as soon as he said it, and her shoulders slumped under the weight of this new fear. Why had Dylan been working with a discredited fanatic like Hoffritz? And who was financing them? No legitimate foundation, university, or research institute would give a grant to Hoffritz, not since he had been forced out of UCLA. Nor would any reputable institution fund Dylan, a man who had stolen his own child and was hiding from his wife's attorneys, a man who was using his daughter as a guinea pig in experiments that had left her on the verge of autism. Whoever provided the money to support Dylan and to conduct that kind of research was insane, every bit as insane as Dylan and Hoffritz.

She wanted it to be over and done with. She wanted to take Melanie out of the hospital, go home, and live happily ever after, because if anyone on earth deserved peace and happiness it was her little girl. But now "they" weren't going to allow it. "They" were going to try to snatch Melanie away again. "They" wanted the child for reasons and purposes that only "they" understood. And who in the hell were they, anyway? Faceless. Nameless. Laura couldn't fight an enemy she couldn't see or, seeing, recognize.

"They're well informed," she said. "And they don't waste time, either."

Haldane blinked. "What do you mean?"

"Melanie was here at the hospital only a couple of hours before Rink came after her. Didn't take him long to find out where she'd gotten to."

"Not long at all," he agreed.

"Makes you think he had his sources."

"Sources? In the police department, you mean?"

"Could be. And it didn't take Rink's enemies long to learn he was after her," Laura said. "They *all* move damn fast, both groups, whoever they are."

She stood at the front doors of the hospital and studied the traffic moving on the street, as well as the shops and the offices on the other side of the avenue. Sun shining in big plate-glass windows. Sun glinting off the windshields and chrome of the passing cars and trucks. In all that revealing sunlight, she hoped to spot someone suspicious, someone Haldane could chase and catch, but there were only ordinary people doing ordinary things. She was angered by their ordinariness, by the enemy's failure to step up and identify himself.

Irrationally, even the sunshine and the warm air angered her. Haldane had just told her that someone out there wanted her daughter dead and that someone else wanted to snatch Melanie and shove her back into a sensory-deprivation chamber or maybe into another jerry-built electric chair where they could continue to torture her for God knew what purpose. For that kind of news, the atmosphere was all wrong. The storm shouldn't have passed already. The sky should still be low, gray, full of churning clouds; rain should be falling, and the wind should be cold and blustery. It just didn't seem right that the world around her was balmy, that other people were whistling and smiling and strolling in sunshine and having fun, while she was plunging deeper into a bleak, dark, living nightmare.

She looked at Dan Haldane. A breeze stirred his sandy hair, and sunlight sharpened his pleasant features, rendering him more handsome than he really was. Even disregarding the flattery of sun and shadow, however, he was good-looking. In other circumstances, she might have been interested in him. The contrast between his brutish size and gentleness lent him a certain mystique. The lost potential of this relationship was one more thing she held against the unknown "them."

"Why were you so eager to reach me?" she asked. "Why were you calling my place for an hour and a half? It wasn't just to tell me about Rink. You knew I'd be showing up here. You could've waited till then to give me the bad news."

He glanced toward the parking lot, where the morgue wagon was pulling away from the crime scene. When he focused on Laura again, his face was lined, his mouth grim, his eyes direct and dark with worry. "I wanted to tell you to call a private security firm and arrange for an around-the-clock guard at your house, for after you take Melanie home."

"A bodyguard?"

"More or less, yeah."

"But if her life's in danger, won't the police department provide protection?"

He shook his head. "Not in this case. There's not been any direct threat against her. No phone calls. No notes."

"Rink—"

"We don't *know* he was here to get Melanie. We only suspect."

"Just the same—"

"If the state and city weren't always going through a budget crisis, if police funding hadn't been cut, if we weren't chronically short of manpower, maybe we could stretch a point and have your house put under surveillance. But given the current situation, I couldn't justify it. And if I arrange the surveillance without my captain's approval, he'll sell my butt to the Alpo people, and I'll wind up in cans of dog food. He and I don't get along so well to begin with. But a security service, professional bodyguards . . . that's as good as any protection we could supply you even if we had the men to do it. Can you afford to hire them, just for a few days?"

"I suppose so. I don't know how much something like that costs, but I'm not poor. If you think it'll be for only a few days—"

"I have a hunch this one's going to unravel fast. All this killing, all the chances someone's been taking—it indicates they're under a lot of pressure, that there's a time limit of some kind. I haven't the faintest goddamned idea what they've been doing to your kid or why they're so desperate to get their hands on her again, but I sense this situation's like a giant snowball, rolling fast down a mountain, fast as an express train, getting bigger and bigger as it goes. Right now, already, it's real big, gigantic, and it's not far from the bottom of the mountain. When it finally hits, it's going to bust into hundreds of pieces."

As a pediatric psychiatrist, Laura was self-confident, never uncertain as to how she should proceed with a new patient. Of course she deliberated before choosing a course of therapy, but once she had decided on her approach, she implemented it without hesitation. She was a successful healer, a mender, a repairman of the psyche, and her success had given her the confidence and authority that generated more success. But now she was lost. She felt small, vulnerable, powerless. That was a feeling that she hadn't known for a few years, not since she had learned to accept Melanie's disappearance.

She said, "I . . . I don't even know how you . . . how a person goes about finding bodyguards."

Haldane pulled out his wallet, fished in it, withdrew a card. "Most of the private investigators you sent after Dylan, years ago, probably also offer bodyguard service. We're not supposed to make recommendations. But I know these guys are good, and their rates are competitive."

She took the card, looked at it:

CALIFORNIA PALADIN, INC.
PRIVATE INVESTIGATION
Personal Security

A phone number was provided at the bottom.

Laura tucked the card in her purse. "Thanks."

"Call them before you leave the hospital."

"I will."

"Have them send a man here. He can follow you home."

She felt numb. "All right." She turned toward the hospital doors.

"Wait." He handed her another card, his own. "The printed number on the front is my line at Central, but you won't be able to get me there. I'm on assignment to the East Valley Division right now, so I've written that number on the back. I want you to call me if anything occurs to you, anything about Dylan's past or old research that might have a bearing on this."

She turned the card over. "There're two numbers here."

"Bottom one's my home number, in case I'm not in the office."

"Won't your office forward messages?"

"Yeah, but they might be slow about it. If you want to get me in a hurry, I want to be sure you *can*."

"You usually give out your home phone like this?"

"No."

"Then, why?"

"The thing I hate most of all . . ."

"What's that?"

"A crime like this. Child abuse of any kind is so infuriating and frustrating. Makes me sick. Makes my blood boil."

"I know what you mean," she said.

"Yeah, I guess you do."

chapter twelve

Dr. Rafael Ybarra, chief of pediatrics at Valley Medical, met with Laura in a small room near the nurses' station, where the staff took their coffee breaks. Two vending machines stood against one wall. An icemaker chugged, clinked, and clattered. Behind Laura, a refrigerator hummed softly. She sat across from Ybarra at a long table on which were dog-eared magazines and two ashtrays full of cold cigarette butts.

The pediatrician—dark, slim, with aquiline features—was prim, even prissy. His perfectly combed hair seemed like a lacquered wig. His shirt collar was crisp and stiff, tie perfectly knotted, lab coat tailored. He walked as though afraid of getting his shoes dirty, and he sat with his shoulders back and his head up, stiff and formal. He surveyed the crumbs and the cigarette ashes on the table, wrinkled his nose, and kept his hands in his lap.

Laura decided she didn't like the man.

Dr. Ybarra spoke with brisk authority, biting the words off: "Physically, your daughter's in good condition, surprisingly good considering the circumstances. She is somewhat underweight, but not seriously so. Her right arm is bruised from repeated insertion of an IV needle by someone who wasn't very skilled at it. Her urethra is mildly inflamed, perhaps from catheterization. I have prescribed medication for that condition. And that's the extent of her physical problems."

Laura nodded. "I know. I've come to take her home."

"No, no. I wouldn't advise that," Ybarra said. "For one thing, she'll be too difficult to care for at home."

"She's not actually ill?"

"No, but—"

"She's not incontinent?"

"No. She uses the bathroom."

"She can feed herself?"

"In a fashion. You have to start feeding her, then she'll take over. And you've got to keep watching her as she eats because after a few bites she seems to forget what she's doing, loses interest. You have to continue urging her to eat. She needs help to dress herself too."

"I can handle all that."

"I'm still reluctant to discharge her," Ybarra said.

"But last night Doctor Pantangello said—"

At the mention of Pantangello, Ybarra wrinkled his nose. His distaste was evident in his voice. "Doctor Pantangello only finished his residency last autumn and was accredited to this hospital last month. I am the head of pediatrics, and it is my opinion that your daughter should stay here."

"How long?"

"Her behavior is symptomatic of severe inhibited catatonia—not unusual in cases of prolonged confinement and mistreatment. She should remain here for a complete psychiatric evaluation. A week . . . ten days."

"No."

"It's the best thing for the child." His voice was so cold and measured that it was hard to believe he ever gave a thought to what was best for anyone other than Rafael Ybarra.

She wondered how kids could possibly relate to a stuffy doctor like this.

"I'm a psychiatrist," Laura said. "I can evaluate her condition and give her the proper care at home."

"Be your own daughter's therapist?" He raised his eyebrows. "I don't think that's wise."

"I disagree." She wasn't going to explain herself to this man.

"Here, once an evaluation is completed and a course of treatment recommended, we have the proper facilities to provide that treatment. You simply don't have the right equipment at home."

Laura frowned. "Equipment? What equipment? Exactly what kind of treatment are you talking about?"

"That would be a decision for Doctor Gehagen in psychiatry. But if Melanie should continue in this severe catatonic state or if she should sink deeper into it, well . . . barbiturates and electroconvulsive therapy—"

"Like hell," Laura said sharply, pushing her chair away from the table and getting to her feet.

Ybarra blinked, surprised by her hostility.

She said, "Drugs and electric shock—that's part of what her god-damned father was doing to her the past six years."

"Well, of course, we wouldn't be using the same drugs or the same kind of electric shock, and our intentions would be different from—"

"Yeah, sure, but how the hell is Melanie supposed to know what your intentions are? I know there are cases where barbiturates and even electroconvulsive therapy achieve desirable results, but they're not right for my daughter. She needs to regain her confidence, her feeling of self-worth. She needs freedom from fear and pain. She needs stability. She needs . . . to be loved."

Ybarra shrugged. "Well, you won't be endangering her health by taking her home today, so there's no way I can prevent you from walking out of here with her."

"Exactly," Laura said.

•

After the morgue wagon had gone, while the SID technicians were sweeping the parking lot around the Volvo, Kerry Burns, a uniformed patrolman, approached Dan Haldane. "A call came through from East Valley, message from Captain Mondale."

"Ah, the esteemed and glorious captain."

"He wants to see you right away."

"Does he miss me?" Dan asked.

"Didn't say why."

"I'll bet he misses me."

"You and Mondale got a thing for each other?"

"Definitely not. Maybe Ross is gay, but I'm straight."

"You know what I mean. You got a grudge or something?"

"It's that obvious, huh?" Dan asked facetiously.

"Is it obvious that dogs don't like cats?"

"Let's just say, if I was burning to death and Ross Mondale had the only bucket of water in ten miles, I'd prefer to extinguish the fire with my own spit."

"That's clear enough. You gonna go over to East Valley?"

"He ordered me to, didn't he?"

"But are you gonna go? I gotta call back and confirm."

"Sure."

"He wants you right away."

"Sure."

"I'll call back and confirm you're on your way."

"Absolutely," Dan said.

Kerry headed back to his patrol car, and Dan got into his unmarked department sedan. He drove out of the hospital parking lot, turned into the busy street, and headed downtown, in the opposite direction from East Valley and Ross Mondale.

•

Before talking with Dr. Ybarra, Laura had called the security service that Dan Haldane had recommended. By the time she had spoken with Ybarra, had dressed Melanie in jeans and a blue-checkered blouse and sneakers, and had signed the necessary release forms, the agent from California Paladin had arrived.

His name was Earl Benton, and he looked like a big old farm boy who had somehow awakened in the wrong house and had been forced to clothe himself in the contents of a banker's closet. His blond-brown hair was combed straight back from his temples, fashionably razor-cut—by a stylist, not a barber—but it didn't look quite right on him; his blocky face and plain features would probably have been better served by a shaggy, windblown, natural look. His seventeen-inch neck

ed about to pop the collar button of his Yves St. Laurent shirt, and
looked awkward and slightly uncomfortable in his three-piece gray
suit. His huge, thick-fingered hands would never be graceful, but the
fingernails were professionally manicured.

Laura could tell at a glance that Earl was one of those tens of thou-
sands who came to Los Angeles every year with the hope of moving up
in life, which he'd probably already done. He would most likely climb
higher too, once he wore off some rough edges and learned to feel at
home in his designer clothes. She liked him. He had a nice, wide smile
and easy manner, yet he was watchful, alert, intelligent. She met him in
the corridor, outside Melanie's room, and after she explained the situation in more detail than she had given his office on the telephone, she
said, "I assume you're armed."

"Oh, yes, ma'am."

"Good."

"I'll be with you till midnight," Earl said, "and then a new man'll
come on duty."

"Fine."

A moment later, Laura brought Melanie into the hall, and Earl hun-
kered down to her level. "What a pretty girl you are."

Melanie said nothing.

"Fact is," he said, "you remind me a lot of my sister, Emma." Melanie stared through him.

Taking the girl's slack hand, engulfing it in his two enormous hands,
Earl continued to speak directly to her, as though she were holding
up her end of the conversation. "Emma, she's nine years younger than
me, in her junior year of high school. She's raised up two prize calves,
Emma has. She's got a collection of prize ribbons, probably twenty of
them, from all sorts of competitions, including livestock shows at three
different county fairs. You know anything about calves? You like animals? Well, calves are just the cutest things. Real gentle faces. I'll bet
you'd be good with them, just like Emma."

Watching him with Melanie, Laura liked Earl Benton even more
than she had on first meeting him.

He said, "Now, Melanie, don't you worry about anything, okay? I'm your friend, and as long as old Earl's your friend, nobody's going to so much as look crosswise at you."

The girl seemed utterly unaware of his presence.

He released her hand, and her thin arm dropped back to her side, limp.

Earl stood and rolled his shoulders to settle his jacket in place, and he looked at Laura. "You say her daddy was responsible for making her like this?"

"He's one of the people responsible," Laura said.

"And he's . . . dead?"

"Yes."

"Some of the others are still alive, though?"

"Yes."

"Sure would like to meet one of them. Like to talk to one of them. Just me and him alone for a while. Sure would like that," Earl said. There was a hard edge in his voice, a chilling light in his eyes that hadn't been there before: an anger that, for the first time, made him look dangerous.

Laura liked that too.

"Now, ma'am—Doctor McCaffrey, I guess I should call you—when we leave here, I'll go out the door first. I know that's not gentlemanly behavior, but from now on, most times, I'll be just a couple feet ahead of you wherever we go, sort of scouting the way ahead, you might say."

"I'm sure no one's going to start shooting at us in broad daylight or anything like that," Laura said.

"Maybe not. But I still go first."

"All right."

"When I tell you to do something, you right away do it, and no questions asked. Understand?"

She nodded.

He said, "I might not yell at you. I might tell you to get down or to run like hell, and I might say it in a soft voice the same way I might say what a nice day it is, so you have to be alert."

"I understand."

"Good. I'm sure everything'll work out just fine. Now, are you two ladies ready to go home?"

They headed toward the elevator that would take them down to the lobby.

At least a thousand times over the past six years, Laura had dreamed about the wonderful day when she would bring Melanie home. She had imagined that it would be the happiest day of her life. She'd never thought that it would be like this.

chapter thirteen

At Central, Dan Haldane took two folders from the clerk in Records and carried them to one of the small writing tables along the wall.

The name on the first file was Ernest Andrew Cooper. By his fingerprints, he had been identified as the John Doe victim found the previous night with Dylan McCaffrey and Wilhelm Hoffritz in the Studio City house.

Cooper was thirty-seven years old, stood five-eleven, and weighed one hundred and sixty pounds. There were mug shots, related to a particularly serious DUI arrest, but they were of no use to Dan, because the victim's face had been battered into featureless, bloody pulp. He would have to rely on the fingerprint match.

Cooper lived in Hancock Park, on a street of million-dollar and multimillion-dollar homes. He was chairman of the board and majority stockholder of Cooper Softech, a successful computer software firm. He'd been arrested three times within the city limits of Los Angeles, always for drunken driving, and on all three occasions, he had also been driving without a license. He had protested the arrests, had gone to trial in each case, had been convicted of each offense, had been fined, but had served no jail time. In every case, the arresting officers noted that Cooper insisted it was immoral—and a violation of his constitutional rights—for the government to require a man to carry any form of identification whatsoever, even a driver's license. The second patrolman had also written: "Mr. Cooper informed this officer that he (Mr. Cooper) was a member of an organization, Freedom Now, that would bring all governments to their knees, and that said organization would use his arrest as a test case to challenge certain laws, and that this officer was an unwitting tool of totalitarian forces. He then threw up and passed out."

Smiling at that last line, Dan closed the folder. He looked at the name on the second file—Edward Philip Rink—and he was anxious to see what they had on this one.

First he carried both files to the nearest of three VDTs and sat down in front of the computer terminal. He switched it on, typed in his access code, and asked for a profile of Freedom Now.

After a brief pause, information began to appear on the screen:

Freedom Now

▶

A political action committee registered with the federal elections commission and the IRS.

▶

Please note:

Freedom Now is a legitimate organization of private citizens exercising their constitutional rights. This organization is not the subject of any police intelligence division investigation, nor should it be the subject of any such investigation while it is engaged upon the activities for which it was formed and for which it has been cleared by the Federal Elections Commission. All information in this file was accumulated from public records. This file was created for the sole purpose of identifying legitimate political organizations and distinguishing them from subversive

groups. The existence of this file in no way suggests special
police interest in Freedom Now.

The LAPD had taken considerable heat from the American Civil Lib-
erties Union and others for its secret surveillance of political groups
that were suspected of involvement in dangerous subversive activities.
The department was still fully empowered to conduct investigations of
terrorist organizations, but it was enjoined from infiltrating properly
registered political groups unless it obtained evidence sufficient to convince a judge that the organization in question had ties to other groups
of individuals that were intent upon terrorist activities.

The disclaimer at the head of the file was familiar, and Dan didn't
bother to read it. He pressed the cursor key to scroll to see more data.

Freedom Now—current officers
President: Ernest Andrew Cooper, Hancock Park
Treasurer: Wilhelm Stephan Hoffritz, Westwood
Secretary: Mary Katherine O'Hara, Burbank

▶

Freedom Now was chartered in 1989 for the purpose of
supporting those libertarian-oriented candidates with a publicly
expressed intention of working for the eventual abolition of all but
minimalist government and for the eventual dissolution of all
political parties.

Cooper and Hoffritz, president and treasurer, were both dead. And
Freedom Now had been chartered the same year that Dylan McCaffrey
had vanished with his young daughter, which might or might not be a
coincidence.

Interesting, anyway.

Dan needed twenty minutes to read the computer file and make
notes. Then he switched off the VDT and picked up the paper file on
Ned Rink.

The documents were numerous, but he didn't find them boring. Rink, the man found dead in the Volvo that same morning, was thirty-nine. He had graduated from Los Angeles Police Academy when he was twenty-one, had served four years with the force while taking criminal-law courses at USC in the evenings. He'd twice been the subject of LAPD internal investigations subsequent to charges of brutality, but for lack of evidence, no action had been taken as a result of the accusations against him. He had applied to the FBI, had been accepted, after being granted a variance on minimum height requirements to comply with antidiscrimination laws, and had worked for the Bureau for five years. Nine years ago, he had been discharged from the FBI for reasons unknown, though there were indications that he had exceeded his authority and, on more than one occasion, had shown too much zeal during the interrogation of a suspect.

Dan thought he knew the type. Some men chose policework because they wanted to perform a socially useful function, some because their childhood heroes had been policemen, some because their fathers had been cops, some because the job was reasonably secure and offered a good pension. There were a hundred reasons. For men like Rink, the attraction was power; they found a special thrill in issuing orders, exercising authority, not because they took pleasure in leading well, but because they enjoyed telling other people what to do and being treated with deference.

According to the file, eight years ago, following his dismissal from the FBI, Rink had been arrested for assault with intent to kill. The charge had been reduced to simple assault to ensure a conviction, which had been obtained, and Rink had served ten months with time off for good behavior. Six years ago he was arrested again, for suspicion of murder. The evidence didn't hold up, and charges were eventually dropped. After that, Rink was a lot more careful. Local, state, and federal authorities believed he was a freelance killer, serving the underworld and anyone else who would pay for his services, and there was circumstantial evidence linking him to nine murders in the past five years—which was probably just the tip of the iceberg—but no police agency had acquired enough evidence to bring Rink to justice.

Justice had been dealt to him anyway.

By something other than a police agency or a court.

Haldane closed the folder, put it on top of the Cooper file, and withdrew his current batch of lists from his pocket. He spent a few minutes looking through them, and something did pop up this time. A name: Mary O'Hara. One of the officers of Freedom Now. Her name and number had been on the notepad beside the phone in Dylan McCaffrey's office.

He put the lists away and sat for a while, thinking. God, what a mess. Two doctors of psychology, both formerly of UCLA—dead. One millionaire businessman and political activist—dead. One ex-cop, ex-FBI agent, and suspected hit man—dead. A weird gray room hidden in an ordinary suburban house where one little girl had been, among other things, tortured with electric shocks. By her own father. The Great God of Sleazy Journalism was generous to his people: The press was going to love this one.

Dan returned the two files to the Records clerk and rode the elevator up to the Scientific Investigation Division.

chapter fourteen

As soon as they got in the house, Earl Benton went through every room to be sure that the windows and doors were locked. He closed the drapes and blinds and advised Laura and Melanie to stay away from the windows.

After choosing a few magazines from the stack of publications in the brass magazine tray in Laura's study, Earl moved a chair close to one of the front windows of the living room, from which he could see the walk and street beyond. "Might look like I'm just lazing away, but don't worry. Nothing in these magazines will distract me."

"I'm not worried."

"Most of this job is just sitting and waiting. A guy would go nuts if he didn't have a magazine or a newspaper."

"I understand," she assured him.

Pepper, the calico, was more interested in Earl than in Melanie. She circled him warily for some time, studying him, sniffing at his feet. Finally she clambered onto him and demanded to be petted.

"Nice kitty," he said, scratching Pepper behind the ears.

She settled on his lap with a blissful look of contentment.

"She doesn't take to many people that fast," Laura told him.

Earl grinned. "Always have had a way with animals."

It was silly, but Pepper's acceptance of Earl Benton reassured Laura and made her feel even better about him. She trusted him completely now.

And what does that mean? she asked herself. Didn't I trust him completely already? Subconsciously, did I have doubts about him?

He had been hired to protect her and Melanie, and that's what he would do. She had no reason to suspect that he was connected with the people who wanted Melanie dead—or the ones who seemed to want her alive and back in another gray room.

Yet that was exactly what Laura had suspected, just a little, deep down, on a purely subconscious level.

She would have to guard against paranoia. She didn't know who her enemies were: They remained faceless. There was a tendency, therefore, to suspect everyone, to spin grandiose conspiracy theories that could wind up encompassing everyone in the world but herself and Melanie.

After brewing coffee for Earl and for herself, she made hot chocolate for Melanie and carried it into the den, where the girl waited. Laura had made arrangements to take an indefinite leave of absence from St. Mark's and to have her private patients covered by an associate for at least the upcoming week. She intended to begin therapy with Melanie right away, this afternoon, but she didn't want to conduct the session in the same room with Earl, for he would be a distraction.

The study was small but comfortable. Two walls were covered with floor-to-ceiling bookshelves that were filled with an eclectic collection of hardcover titles ranging from exotic volumes on highly specialized areas of psychology to popular fiction. The other walls were covered with beige grasscloth. There were two Delacroix prints, a dark pine desk with an upholstered chair, a rocking chair, and an emerald-green sofa with lots of pillows. Soft amber light came from a pair of brass Stiffel lamps on matching end tables; Earl had closed the emerald-green drapes at both windows.

Melanie was sitting on the sofa, her upturned hands in her lap, staring at her palms.

"Melanie."

The girl gave no indication that she was aware of her mother's presence.

"Honey, I brought you some hot chocolate."

When the girl still did not respond, Laura sat beside her. Holding the mug of cocoa in one hand, she put her other hand under Melanie's chin, tilted the girl's head up, and looked into her eyes. They were still disturbingly empty eyes, and Laura could make no connection with them, elicit no awareness.

She said, "I want you to drink this, Melanie. It's good, tasty. You'll like it. I know you'll like it."

She put the rim of the mug to the girl's lips, and with a lot of coaxing, she managed to get her daughter to sip the cocoa. Some of it dribbled down Melanie's chin, and Laura wiped it away with a paper napkin before it could drip onto the sofa. With more encouragement, the girl began to drink less sloppily. At last her small frail hands came up, and she held the mug firmly enough that Laura was able to let go. Once she had hold of the mug, Melanie drank the remainder of the hot chocolate quickly, greedily. When it was all gone, she licked her lips. In her eyes there was for the briefest moment a flicker of life, an indication of consciousness; and for a second, but no longer than a second, her eyes met her mother's eyes, didn't stare through Laura as before, but *at* her. That precious instant of contact was electrifying. Unhappily, Melanie at once sank back into her secret inner world, and her eyes glazed over again. But now Laura knew the child was capable of returning from her self-imposed exile; therefore, there was a chance, however small, that she could be brought back not just for a second but permanently.

She took the empty mug out of Melanie's hands, put it on one of the end tables, then sat sideways on the couch, facing the girl. She took both of Melanie's hands and said, "Honey, it's been so long, and you were so little when we saw each other last . . . maybe you aren't exactly sure who I am. I'm your mother, Melanie."

The girl didn't react.

She spoke softly, reassuringly, taking the child through it step by step, because she was sure that, at least on a subconscious level, the girl could understand her. "I brought you into this world because I wanted you more than anything. You were such a beautiful baby, so sweet, never any trouble. You learned to walk and talk sooner than I expected, and I was so proud of you. So very proud. Then you were stolen from me, and while you were gone, all I wanted was to get you back. To hold you again and love you again. And now, baby, the most important thing is to make you well, to bring you out of that hole you're hiding in. I'm going to do that, honey. I'm going to make you well. *Help* you get well."

The girl said nothing.

Her green eyes indicated that her attention was far away.

Laura pulled the girl onto her lap, put her arms around her, held her. For a while, they just sat like that, being close, giving it time, because they had to establish bonds of affection in order for the therapy to have a chance.

After a few minutes, Laura found herself humming a lullaby, then crooning the lyrics almost in a whisper. She smoothed her daughter's forehead, used fingers to comb the girl's hair back from her face. Melanie's eyes remained distant, glazed, but she raised one hand to her face and put a thumb in her mouth. As if she were a baby. As she had done when she had been three years old.

Tears welled in Laura's eyes. Her voice quivered, but she kept crooning softly and running her hand through her daughter's silken hair. Then she remembered how hard she had tried to break Melanie of the thumb-sucking habit six years ago, and it seemed funny that she should be so pleased and moved by it now. Suddenly she was half crying and half laughing, and she must have looked ridiculous, but she felt wonderful.

In fact, she felt so good and was so encouraged by the girl's thumb-sucking, by the instant of real eye contact that had followed the drinking of the hot chocolate, that she decided to try hypnosis today, rather than waiting until tomorrow, as planned. In Melanie's conscious but semicatatonic state, the child was withdrawn into deep fantasy and was resistant to being brought up from those sheltering depths of her psyche. Hypnotized, she would be more malleable, more open to suggestion, and might be drawn back at least part of the way toward the real world.

Hypnotizing someone in Melanie's condition could be either much easier than hypnotizing an alert person—or nearly impossible. Laura continued softly singing the lullaby and began to massage the girl's temples, moving her fingertips around and around in small circles, pressing lightly. When the child's eyes began to flutter, Laura stopped singing and said, in a whisper, "Let go, baby. Sleep now, baby, sleep, that's it, I want you to sleep, just relax . . . you are settling into a deep natural sleep . . . settling down like a feather floating down and down through very still warm air . . . settling down and down . . . sleep . . . but you will continue to listen to my voice . . . down and down, lazily turning, like a drifting feather . . . down into sleep . . . but my voice will follow you down into sleep . . . down . . . down . . . and you will listen to me and answer all questions I ask . . . sleep but listen and obey. Listen and respond." And she massaged even more lightly than before, moving her fingertips more slowly, until at last the girl's eyes closed and her breathing indicated that she was sound asleep.

Pepper slunk through the doorway and regarded them with evident curiosity. Then she crossed the room, jumped onto the rocker, and curled in a ball.

Still holding her daughter in her lap, Laura said, "You are all the way down now, deep asleep. But you hear me and you will answer me when I ask you questions."

The girl's mouth was slack, lips parted slightly.

"Can you hear me, Melanie?"

The girl said nothing.

"Melanie, can you hear me?"

The girl sighed, a sound as soft as the light from the amber-shaded brass lamps.

"Uh . . ."

It was the first sound that she had made since Laura had seen her in the hospital last night.

"What is your name?"

The child's brow furrowed. "Muh . . ."

The calico cat raised its head.

"Melanie? Is that your name? Melanie?"

"Muh . . . muh."

Pepper's ears pricked up.

Laura decided to move to another question. "Do you know who I am, Melanie?"

Still sleeping, the child licked her lips. "Muh . . . muh . . . it . . . ah . . . it . . ." She twitched and began to raise one hand as if fending something off.

"Easy," Laura said. "Relax. Be calm. Relax and be calm and sleep. You're safe. You're safe with me."

The girl lowered her hand. She sighed.

When the lines in the girl's face smoothed out somewhat, Laura repeated the question. "Do you know who I am?"

Melanie made a wordless murmuring-whimpering sound.

"Do you know who I am, Melanie?"

Lines of worry or fear returned to the child's face, and she said, "Umm . . . uh . . . uh-uh-uh . . . it . . . it . . ."

Taking a different tack, Laura said, "What are you afraid of, Melanie?"

"It . . . it . . . *there* . . ." Fear was in her voice now as well as carved into the pale flesh of her face.

"What do you see?" Laura asked. "What are you afraid of, honey? What do you see?"

"The . . . there . . . the . . ."

Pepper cocked her head and arched her back. The cat had become tense, watching the girl intently.

The air was unnaturally still and heavy.

Although it wasn't possible, the shadows in the corners of the room seemed darker and larger now than they had been a moment ago.

"It . . . there . . . no, no, no, no."

Laura put one hand on her daughter's creased brow, reassuring her, and waited expectantly as the girl strove to speak. A strange, disconcerting feeling came over her, and she felt a chill creeping like a living thing up the length of her spine.

"Where are you, Melanie?"

"No . . ."

"Are you in the gray room?"

The girl was audibly grinding her teeth, squeezing her eyes shut, fisting her hands, as though resisting something very strong. Laura had been planning to regress her, take her back in time to the gray room in that Studio City house, but it seemed as though the girl had drifted back there without encouragement, as soon as she'd been hypnotized. But that didn't make sense: Laura had never heard of spontaneous hypnotic regression. The patient had to be guided, encouraged backward to the scene of the trauma.

"Where are you, Melanie?"

"N-n-no . . . the . . . *no!*"

"Easy. Be still. What are you afraid of?"

"Please . . . no . . ."

"Be calm, honey. What do you see? Tell me, baby. Tell Mommy what you see. The tank, the deprivation chamber? No one's going to make you go back in there, honey."

But that wasn't what frightened the girl. Laura's reassurance didn't calm her. "The . . . the . . ."

"The aversion-therapy chair? The electric chair? You'll never be put in that again, either."

Something else terrified the girl. She shuddered and began to strain against Laura, as if she wanted to get away, run.

"Honey, you're safe with me," Laura said, holding her tighter than before. "It can't hurt you."

"Opening . . . it's opening . . . no . . . it . . . coming *open* . . ."

"Easy," Laura said. As the chill climbed all the way up her back and reached the nape of her neck, she sensed that something of terrible importance was about to happen.

chapter fifteen

Behind his back, Lieutenant Felix Porteau of the Scientific Investigation Division was called "Poirot," after Agatha Christie's pompous Belgian detective. It was clear to Dan that Porteau preferred to think of himself as Sherlock Holmes, in spite of his stocky legs, potbelly, slumped shoulders, Santa Claus face, and high-domed bald head. To bolster his desired image, Porteau was seldom without a curved-stem pipe in which he smoked an aromatic blend of shag tobacco.

The pipe was not lit when Dan entered Porteau's office, but the SID man snatched it up from an ashtray and used it to point toward a chair. "Sit down, Daniel, sit down. I've been expecting you, of course. I imagine you're here to inquire after my findings in the Studio City affair."

"Amazingly perceptive, Felix."

Porteau rocked back in his chair. "A singular case, this one. Naturally, it will be several days before the full results are in from my laboratory." It was always *my* laboratory with Felix, as if he wasn't in charge of a big-city police department's forensics unit but was, instead, conducting experiments in one room of his private quarters above Baker Street. "However, I could, if you wish, share some of the preliminary findings."

"That would be gracious of you."

Porteau bit on the mouthpiece of the pipe, gave Dan a sly look, and smiled. "You mock me, Daniel."

"Never."

"Yes. You mock everyone."

"You make me sound like a wiseass."

"You are."

"Thanks so much."

"But a nice, witty, intelligent, charming wiseass—and that makes all the difference."

"Now you make me sound like Cary Grant."

"Isn't that how you see yourself?"

Dan thought about it. "Well, maybe half Cary Grant and, right now, half Wile E. Coyote."

"Who?"

"The coyote in the roadrunner cartoons."

"Ah. And how so?"

"I get the feeling a giant boulder just rolled off the edge of a cliff above me, and it's falling toward me right now, going to smash me flat at any second."

"The rock is this case?"

"Yeah. Any latent prints that're going to help us?"

Porteau opened a desk drawer and withdrew a pouch of tobacco. He began to prepare his pipe. "Lots of prints belonging to the three victims. All over the house. Others belonging to the little girl—although those were in the converted garage."

"The lab."

"The gray room, as one of my men called it."

"Then she was always kept in that room?"

"That's certainly the most logical deduction, yes. We do have a few partials from the hall bathroom that conceivably could be hers, but none anywhere else in the house."

"And nothing else? No prints at all that might've belonged to the killers?"

"Oh, certainly, we found numerous other prints, mostly partials. We're putting them through the new high-speed computerized comparison program, trying to match them with prints of known criminals on file, but we've had no luck so far. Not likely to have any, either." He paused, having tamped the tobacco into the generous bowl of his pipe, and searched his pockets for a match. "In your experience, Daniel, how many times has a murderer left clear, unsmudged, and easily identifiable fingerprints at the scene of his crime?"

"Twice," Dan said. "In fourteen years. So we'll get no help from prints. What *have* we got?"

Porteau got his pipe fired up, exhaled sweetish smoke, and shook out the match. "No weapon was found—"

"One of the victims had a fireplace poker."

Porteau nodded. "Mr. Cooper intended to defend himself with it, apparently. But it was never used to strike anyone. The only blood on it was Cooper's own, and only a few drops of that, all part of the natural spray pattern that spotted the walls and the floor around the body."

"So Cooper didn't manage to land any blows on his assailant, and he wasn't hit with the poker himself."

"Precisely."

"Did the vacuum crew come up with anything besides dirt?"

"The results are being analyzed. Frankly, I'm not optimistic."

Porteau usually was optimistic, another Holmesian trait, so his pessimism in the current case was especially disturbing.

Dan said, "What about the scrapings from under the victims' fingernails?"

"Nothing of interest. No skin, no hair, no blood but their own under their nails, which probably means they didn't get a chance to claw at their assailants."

"But the killers had to move in close. I mean, Felix, they beat these people to death."

"Yes. But although they had to get close, none of them seems to have been wounded. We took scores of blood samples from every surface in those rooms, only to discover that all of it belonged to the victims."

They sat in silence.

Porteau puffed clouds of fragrant smoke into the air above his head. A distant look came into his eyes as he pondered the evidence in the case, and if he, like Sherlock, had played a violin, he would have reached for it now.

At last Dan said, "I assume that you saw the photographs of the bodies."

"Yes. Horrible. Incredible. Such fury."

"Do you get the feeling that this one is going to be really weird?"

"Daniel, I find all murder to be weird," Porteau said.

"But this one seems weirder than usual."

"Weirder than usual," Porteau agreed, and smiled, as if pleased by the challenge.

"I'm beginning to get the creeps."

"Look out for that falling boulder, Mr. Coyote."

Dan left the SID lieutenant in his aromatic haze and rode the elevator back down, this time to the basement, where Pathology was located.

chapter sixteen

Still in a hypnotic state, the girl said, *"No!"*

"Melanie, honey, take it easy, take it easy now. Nobody's going to hurt you."

The girl tossed her head, drawing the quick shallow inhalations indicative of panic. A half-born wail of fear and dread was trapped in her throat and issued only as a thin, high-pitched *eeeeeee*. She squirmed and tried to push herself off her mother's lap.

Laura held her. "Stop struggling, Melanie. Relax. Be still. Be calm."

Suddenly the girl struck out at an imaginary assailant, flailing with both hands. Unintentionally she struck her mother on the breast, then on the face, two hard and painful blows.

For an instant Laura was stunned. The blow to the face was hard enough to bring involuntary tears of pain to her eyes.

Melanie rolled off her mother's lap, onto the floor, and began to crawl away from the couch.

"Melanie, stop!"

In spite of the posthypnotic suggestion that required the girl to respond to and obey Laura's commands, she ignored her mother. She crawled past the rocking chair, making pitiful animal sounds of pure, blind terror.

The calico cat stood on the rocking chair, ears flattened, hissing fearfully. As Melanie scrambled past the chair, Pepper leaped over the girl, hit the floor running, and streaked out of the study.

"Melanie, listen to me."

The girl disappeared beyond the desk.

Her left cheek still stinging where the child had struck her, Laura also went behind the desk. Melanie had crawled into the kneehole and was hiding there. Laura stooped down and peered in at her. The girl sat with her knees drawn up, arms locked around her legs, hunched, chin against her knees, peering out with wide eyes that, as before, saw neither Laura nor anything else in that room.

"Honey?"

Gasping for breath as if she had run a long way, the girl said, "Don't let it . . . open. Keep it . . . shut . . . tight shut."

Earl Benton stepped into the doorway. "You okay?"

Laura looked at him over the top of the desk. "Yes. Just . . . my daughter, but she'll be okay."

"You're sure? You don't need me?"

"No, no. I need to be alone with her. I can handle it."

Reluctantly, Earl retreated to the living room.

Laura looked under the desk again. Melanie was still breathing hard, and now she was shaking violently too. Tears were streaming down her cheeks.

"Come out of there, honey."

The girl didn't move.

"Melanie, you will listen to me, and you will do what I tell you. Come out of there right now."

Instead, the girl tried to draw father back into the kneehole, though she had nowhere to go.

Laura had never known a patient to rebel so completely during hypnotic therapy. She studied the girl and at last decided to allow her to remain under the desk for the time being, since she seemed to feel at least marginally safer there.

"Honey, what are you hiding from?"

No answer.

"Melanie, you must tell me—what did you see that you wanted to keep shut?"

"Don't let it open," the girl said miserably, as if responding to Laura for the first time, although her eyes still remained focused on some horror in another time and place.

"Don't let *what* open? Tell me, Melanie."

"Keep it closed!" the girl cried, and she squeezed her eyes shut and bit her lip so hard that she drew a small spot of blood.

Laura reached into the kneehole and consolingly put one hand on her daughter's arm. "Honey, what are you talking about? I'll help you keep it closed if you'll only tell me what you're talking about."

"The d-d-door," the girl said.

"What door?"

"The *door!*"

"The door to the tank?"

"It's coming open, it's coming open!"

"No," Laura said sharply. "Listen to me. You have to listen to me and accept what I tell you. The door isn't coming open. It's shut. Tightly shut. Look at it. See? It's not even ajar, not even open a little crack."

"Not even a crack," the girl said, and now there was no doubt that some part of her could hear Laura and respond, even though she continued to gaze through Laura and even though she remained, for the most part, in some other reality of her own making.

"Not even a crack," Laura repeated, greatly relieved to be exerting some control at last.

The girl calmed a little. She was trembling, and her face was still lined with fear, but she was not biting her lip anymore. A crimson thread of blood sewed a curved seam down her chin.

Laura said, "Now, honey, the door is closed, and it's going to stay closed, and nothing on the other side will be able to open it, because I've put a new lock on it, a heavy dead-bolt lock. Do you understand?"

"Yes," the girl said weakly, doubtfully.

"Look at the door. There's a big shiny new lock on it. Do you see the new lock?"

"Yes," Melanie said, more confident this time.

"A big brass lock. Enormous."

"Yes."

"Enormous and strong. Absolutely nothing in the world could break through that lock."

"Nothing," the girl agreed.

"Good. Very good. Now . . . even though the door can't be opened, I'd like to know what's on the other side of it."

The girl said nothing.

"Honey? Remember the strong lock. You're safe now. So tell me what's on the other side of the door."

Melanie's small white hands pulled and patted the empty air under the desk, as though she were attempting to draw a picture of something.

"What's on the other side of the door?" Laura asked again.

The hands moved ceaselessly. The girl made wordless, frustrated sounds.

"Tell me, honey."

"The door . . ."

"Where does the door lead?"

"The door . . ."

"What kind of room is on the other side?"

"The door to . . ."

"To where?"

"The door . . . to . . . December," Melanie said. Her fear broke under the crushing weight of many other emotions—misery, despair, grief, loneliness, frustration—all of which were audible in the wordless sounds that she made and in her uncontrollable sobbing. Then: "Mommy? Mommy?"

"I'm right here, baby," Laura said, startled to hear her daughter calling for her.

"Mommy?"

"Right here. Come to me, baby. Come out from under there."

Weeping, the girl did not come but cried, again, "Mommy?" She seemed to think she was alone, far from Laura's consoling embrace, though in fact they were only inches apart. "Oh, Mommy! *Mommy!*"

Staring into the shadowy recess beneath the desk, watching her little girl weep and gibber, reaching back in there, touching the child, Laura shared some of Melanie's feelings, especially grief and frustration, but she was also filled with a powerful curiosity. The door to December?

"Mama?"

"Here, right here."

They were so close yet they remained separated by an immense and mysterious gulf.

chapter seventeen

Luther Williams was a young black pathologist working for the LAPD. He dressed as though he were the ghost of Sammy Davis, Jr.—leisure suits and too much jewelry—but was as articulate and amusing as Thomas Sowell, the black sociologist. Luther was an admirer of Sowell and of other sociologists and economists in the burgeoning conservative movement within the black intellectual community, and could quote from their books at length. Too great a length. Several times, he had lectured Dan on pragmatic politics and had expounded upon the virtues of free-market economics as a mechanism for lifting the poor out of poverty. He was such a fine pathologist, with such a sensitive eye for the anomalous details that were important in forensic medicine, that it was almost worth tolerating his tedious political dissections in order to obtain the information he collected from his dissections of the flesh. Almost.

Luther was sitting at a microscope, examining a tissue sample, when Dan entered the green-tiled lab. He looked up and grinned when he saw who was visiting him. "Danny boy! Did you use those tickets I gave you?"

For a moment, Dan didn't know what the pathologist was talking about, but then he remembered. Luther had bought two tickets to a debate between G. Gordon Liddy and Timothy Leary, and then something had come up to prevent him from going. He had run into Dan in the hall a week ago and had insisted that Dan take the tickets. "It'll raise your consciousness," he said.

Now Dan fidgeted. "Well, I told you last week that I probably couldn't make it. I asked you to give the tickets to someone else."

"You didn't go?" Luther asked, disappointed.

"No time."

"Danny, Danny, you've got to make time for these things. There's a battle raging that'll shape our lives, a battle between those who love freedom and those who don't, a quiet war between freedom-loving libertarians and freedom-hating fascists and leftists."

Dan hadn't voted—or even registered to vote—in twelve years. He didn't much care which party or ideological faction was in power. It wasn't that he thought Republicans and Democrats, liberals and conservatives, were all screwups; they probably were, but he didn't really care, and that wasn't the reason for his stubborn political indifference. He figured society would muddle through regardless of who was in charge, and he had no time to listen to boring political arguments.

His main interest, his consuming interest, was murder, which was why he had no time for politics. Murder and murderers. Some people were capable of the most unthinkable brutality, and he was fascinated with them. Not those killers who were obviously lunatics. Not those who killed in mindless fits of rage or passion after being subjected to understandable provocation. But the others. Some husbands could kill their wives without remorse, merely because they had grown tired of them. Some mothers could kill their children, just because they no longer wanted the responsibility of raising them, and they were without grief or even a sense of guilt. Hell, some people out there could kill anybody at all for any reason, even for trivial reasons like being cut off in traffic; they were amoral sociopaths, and Dan was never bored with them or with their aberrant psychology. He wanted to understand them. Were they mentally ill—or throwbacks? Were only certain people capable of cold-blooded murder when there was no element of self-defense involved, or were these killers a special breed? If they were special, wolves in a society of sheep, he wanted to know what made them different. What was missing in them? Why were compassion and empathy unknown to them?

He didn't entirely understand his intellectual fascination with murder. He did not have a particularly ruminative or philosophical bent—or at least he didn't think of himself in those terms. Perhaps, working day after day in a world of violence and blood and death, it was impossible not to grow philosophical with the passage of years. Maybe most other homicide cops spent a lot of time contemplating the dark side of human potential; maybe he wasn't the only one; he had no way of knowing; it wasn't the kind of thing most cops talked about.

In his case, of course, perhaps his need to understand murder and the murderer's mind was related to the fact that both his brother and sister had been murdered. Maybe.

Now, smelling strongly of alcohol and vaguely of other chemicals used in the pathology lab, smiling up at Dan, Luther Williams said, "Listen, Danny, next week there's a really terrific debate between—"

Dan interrupted him. "Luther, I'm sorry, but I don't have time to chat. I need some information, and I need it right away."

"What's the big hurry?"

"I gotta pee."

"Look, Danny, I know politics bores you—"

"No, really, it isn't that," Dan said with a straight face. "I actually gotta pee."

Luther sighed. "Someday the totalitarians will take over, and they'll pass laws so you *can't* pee unless you have permission from the Official Federal Urinary Gatekeeper."

"Ouch."

"Then you'll come to me with your bladder bursting, and you'll say, 'Luther, my God, why didn't you warn me about these people?'"

"No, no. I promise to crawl away somewhere, all by myself, and let my bladder burst in silence. I promise—*swear*—not to bother you."

"Yeah, because you'd rather let your bladder burst than have to hear me say I told you so."

Luther was sitting at the lab table on a wheeled stool. Dan pulled up another stool and sat down in front of him. "Okay. Hit me with the dazzling scientific insights, Doctor Williams. You have three special customers from last night. McCaffrey, Hoffritz, and Cooper."

"They're scheduled for autopsy this evening."

"They haven't been done already?"

"We have a backlog here, Danny. They kill 'em faster than we can cut 'em open."

"Sounds like a violation of free-market principles," Dan said.

"Huh?"

"You've got a lot more supply than you have demand."

"Isn't that the truth? Would you like to go into the cooler, see the tables where we have all the stiffs stacked on top of one another?"

"No thanks, but it sounds like a charming excursion."

"Pretty soon, we'll have to start piling them in the closets with bags of ice."

"You at least *seen* the three I'm interested in?"

"Oh, yeah."

"Can you tell me anything about them?"

"They're dead."

"As soon as the totalitarians take over, they're going to do away with all smart-ass black pathologists, first thing."

"Hey, that's what I'm *telling* you," Luther said.

"You've examined the wounds on those three?"

His dark face darkening even further, the pathologist said, "Never seen anything like it. Each corpse is a mass of overlapping contusions, scores of them, maybe hundreds. Such a mess. Jesus. Yet no two of those blows have the same configuration. Dozens of points of fracture too, but there's no pattern to the bone injuries. The autopsy will tell us for sure, but based on just a preliminary examination, I'd say the bones sometimes look snapped, sometimes splintered, sometimes . . . crushed. Now, there's no damn way a blunt instrument, used as a club, can *pulverize* bone. A blow will crack or splinter bone, but that's strictly impact. Impact doesn't crush—unless it's tremendous impact, like you get when a car rams a pedestrian and pins him against a brick wall.

Generally, you can only crush bone by applying pressure, by *squeezing*, and I'm talking a *lot* of pressure."

"So, what were they hit with?"

"You don't get me. See, when somebody's bashed as hard and as many times as these guys were, you'll find a pattern of the striking face—rough, smooth, sharp, rounded, whatever. And you'll be able to say, 'This fella was wasted with a hammer that had a round striking surface, one inch in diameter, with a gently beveled edge.' Or maybe it's a crowbar, the dull end of a hatchet, a bookend, or a salami. But once you've examined the wounds, you'll usually be able to put a name to the instrument. *But not this time.* Every contusion has a different shape. Every injury appears to've been made by a different instrument."

Pulling on his left earlobe, Dan said, "I suppose we can rule out the possibility that the killer walked into that house with a suitcase full of blunt instruments just because he likes variety. I don't see the victims standing still while he traded the hammer for a shovel and the shovel for a lug wrench."

"I'd think that was a safe assumption. The thing is . . . I didn't notice *one* wound that looked exactly like a hammer blow or like the mark from a crowbar or a lug wrench. Each contusion was not only different from other contusions, but each was unique, oddly shaped."

"Any ideas at all?"

"Well, if this were an old Fu Manchu novel, I'd say we have a villain who's invented a fiendish new weapon, a compressed-air machine that has more force than Arnold Schwarzenegger wielding a sledgehammer."

"Colorful theory. But not too damned likely."

"You ever read Sax Rohmer, those old Fu Manchu books? Hell, they were full of exotic weapons, far-out methods of murder."

"This is real life."

"That's what they say."

"Real life isn't a Fu Manchu novel."

Luther shrugged. "I'm not so sure. You been watching the news lately?"

"I need something better than that, Luther. I need a whole lot of help with this one."

They stared at each other.

Then, without a trace of humor this time, Luther said, "But that is what it looks like, Danny. Like they were beaten to death with a hammer of air."

chapter eighteen

After Laura encouraged Melanie to come out from beneath the desk, she brought the girl up from the hypnotic state. Well, not up exactly: The child didn't rise to full consciousness. Rather, she moved out of the hypnotic trance and more or less sideways, returning to the semi-catatonic state in which she'd been since the police had found her.

Laura had nurtured a small hope that termination of the hypnotic trance would snap the girl out of her catatonia as well. Briefly the child's eyes *did* fix on Laura's, and she put one hand against Laura's cheek as if disbelieving her mother's presence.

"Stay with me, baby. Don't slip away. Stay with me."

But the girl slipped away nevertheless. The moment of contact was poignant but brief, achingly brief.

The therapy session had taken its toll on Melanie. Her face was slack with exhaustion, and her eyes were bloodshot. Laura put Melanie to bed for a nap, and the girl was asleep as soon as her head touched the pillow.

When Laura went out to the living room, she discovered that Earl Benton had left his chair and had taken off his suit jacket. He had also drawn the revolver from his shoulder holster and was holding it in his right hand, down at his side, not as if he would use it that very minute, but as if he thought he might have a need for it soon. He was standing at a French window, staring outside, a worried look on his broad face.

"Earl?" she said uncertainly.

He glanced at her. "Where's Melanie?"

"Napping."

He returned his attention to the street in front of the house. "Better go sit with her."

Her breath caught in her throat. She swallowed hard. "What's wrong?"

"Maybe nothing. Half an hour ago, a telephone-company van pulled up across the street, parked there. Nobody got out."

She stepped beside him at the window.

A gray-and-blue van with white-and-blue lettering was across from the house, slightly uphill, parked half in sunlight and half in the shade of a jacaranda. It looked like all the other phone company vans she had ever seen: nothing special about it, nothing sinister.

"Why's it look suspicious to you?" she asked.

"Like I said, so far as I could see, nobody got out."

"Maybe the repairman's just taking a nap on company time."

"Not likely. Phone company's too well managed to let that sort of thing go on a lot. Besides, it just . . . smells. I get a feeling about it. I've seen this sort of thing before, and what it means to me is that we're under surveillance."

"Surveillance? Who?"

"Hard to say. But phone company vans . . . well, the feds often work that way."

"Federal agents?"

"Yeah."

Astonished, she shifted her attention from the van to Earl's profile. He didn't seem to share her surprise. "You mean, like FBI?"

"Maybe. Or the Treasury Department—Bureau of Alcohol, Tobacco, and Firearms. Maybe even a security arm of the Defense Department. There're all different kinds of feds."

"But why would federal agents have us under surveillance? We're the victims—the potential victims, anyway—not criminals."

"I didn't say it was for sure the feds. I just said they often work this way."

Staring at Earl while he stared at the van, Laura realized that he had changed. He was no longer the aw-shucks guy with a veneer of West L.A. polish. He looked harder, older than his twenty-six years, and his manner was more brisk and professional than before.

Confused, Laura said, "Well, if it's government men, we don't have anything to worry about."

"Don't we?"

"They aren't the ones trying to kill Melanie."

"Aren't they?"

Startled, she said, "Well, of course they aren't. It wasn't the government that killed my husband and the other two."

"How do you know that?" he asked, his eyes still riveted on the telephone company van.

"Oh, for heaven's sake—"

"Your husband and one of the men killed with him . . . *they* used to work at UCLA."

"So?"

"They received grants. For research."

"Yes, of course, but—"

"Some of those grants, maybe even most of them, came from the government, didn't they?"

Laura didn't bother to reply, because Earl obviously knew the answer already.

"Defense Department grants," he said.

She nodded. "And others."

He said, "The Defense Department would be interested in behavior modification. Mind control. The best way to deal with an enemy is to control his mind, make him your friend, without him ever realizing that he's been manipulated. A real breakthrough in that field could put an end to war as we know it. But, hell, as far as that goes, pretty much *any* damn government agency would be interested in mind control."

"How do you know all this about Dylan's work? I didn't tell you all this."

Instead of answering her, Earl said, "Maybe your husband and Hoffritz were still working for the government."

"Hoffritz was a discredited—"

"But if his research was important, if it was producing results, they wouldn't care if he was discredited in the academic community. They'd still use him."

He glanced at her again, and there was a cynicism in his eyes, a weary-of-the-world expression on his face that made him appear utterly different from the way he'd looked earlier.

She could no longer see the farm boy at all, and she wondered if that image of a simple man seeking polish and sophistication from a new life in L.A. had been an act. She was suddenly sure that Earl Benton, even as young as he was, had never been simple.

And she was no longer sure that she should trust him.

The situation had abruptly become so complex, the possibilities so multifarious, that she felt a bit dizzy. "A government conspiracy? But then why would they have killed Dylan and Hoffritz if Dylan was working for them?"

Earl didn't even hesitate. "Maybe they didn't do the killing. In fact, it's highly unlikely. But maybe your husband's research was leading toward a major breakthrough with military applications, and maybe because of that, the other side had him wasted."

"Other side?"

He was watching the street once more. "Foreign agents."

"The Soviet Union went kaput. Maybe you heard. It was in all the newspapers."

"The Russians are still there, and we're a long way from being best buddies with them. Then there's China. Iran and Iraq and Libya. There's never a shortage of enemies in the world. Power-mad men are always with us."

"This is crazy," she protested.

"Why?"

"Secret agents, spy stuff, international intrigue . . . Ordinary people don't get mixed up in that stuff except in the movies."

"That's just it. Your husband *wasn't* ordinary people," Earl said. "Neither was Hoffritz."

She couldn't look away from this man who was undergoing such a

profound metamorphosis—aging, hardening—before her eyes. She repeated
the question that he had not answered before. "All this speculation . . .
you couldn't have thought about any of it unless you knew my husband's field, his personality, the kind of work he might be doing. How
do you know all this about Dylan? I didn't tell you any of it."

"Dan Haldane told me."

"The detective? When?"

"When he called me. Just before noon."

"But I didn't even hire your firm until after one o'clock."

"Dan said he'd give you our card, make sure you called us. He wanted
us to understand all the possible ramifications of the case right from the
start."

"But he never told me there might be FBI agents and, for God's sake,
Russians involved."

"He doesn't know they're involved, Doctor McCaffrey. He just realized there was the possibility that these murders had more than local
significance. He didn't go into it much with you, because he didn't want
to worry you unnecessarily."

"Christ."

The mad, seductive murmur of paranoia swelled in her mind again.
She felt trapped in an elaborate web of conspiracies.

"Better go look after Melanie," Earl said.

Outside, a Chevy sedan drove slowly along the street. The car stopped
beside the phone-company van, then pulled forward and parked in
front of it. Two men got out.

"Ours," Earl said.

"Paladin agents?"

"Yeah. I called the office a while ago, after I decided the van was a
surveillance operation, asked them to send some guys to check it out
'cause I didn't want to go over there myself and leave you two alone."

The two men who got out of the Chevy went to opposite sides of
the van.

"Better go see about Melanie," Earl repeated.

"She's okay."

"Then at least step back from the window."

"Why?"

"Because I'm paid to take risks, and you aren't. And I warned you at the start you'd have to do what I told you to do."

She retreated from the window, but she didn't move completely away from it. She wanted to see what was happening at the phone company van.

One of the Paladin agents was still at the driver's door. The other man had gone around to the rear of the van.

"If they're federal agents, there won't be any shooting," she said. "Not even if they want Melanie."

"That's right," Earl agreed. "We'd have to give her up."

"No," she said, alarmed.

"Yes, I'm afraid we wouldn't have a choice. They're the law. But then at least we'd know who had her, and we could fight to get her back through the courts. But like I said, these guys might not be feds."

"And if they're . . . someone else?" she asked, unable to bring herself to say "Russians."

"Then it might get nasty."

His large, strong hand curled tightly around the revolver.

Laura looked past him, out the window, which was streaked and spotted from the previous night's rain.

The late-afternoon sunlight painted the street in shades of brass and copper.

Squinting, she saw one of the rear doors swing open on the phone company van.

chapter nineteen

Dan left the pathology department but took only a few steps along the hall before a thought stopped him. He went back, opened the door, and leaned into the office as Luther looked up from the microscope again.

"Thought you had to pee," the pathologist said. "You've only been gone ten seconds."

"Peed right here in the hall," Dan said.

"Typical homicide detective."

"Listen, Luther, you're a libertarian?"

"Well, yeah, but there's all kinds of libertarians. You've got your libertarian conservatives, your libertarian anarchists, and your basic orthodox libertarians. You've got libertarians who believe that we should—"

"Luther, look at me, and you'll see the definition of 'boredom.'"

"Then why'd you ask—"

"I just wanted to know if you'd ever heard of a libertarian group called Freedom Now."

"Not that I remember."

"It's a political-action committee."

"Means nothing to me."

"You're pretty active in libertarian circles, aren't you? You would have heard of Freedom Now if they were really a bunch of movers and shakers, wouldn't you?"

"Probably."

"Ernest Andrew Cooper."

"One of the three stiffs from Studio City," Luther said.

"Yeah. Ever hear of him before this?"

"No."

"You sure?"

"Yeah."

"He's supposed to be a big wheel in libertarian circles."

"Where?"

"Here in L.A."

"Well, he's not. Never heard of him before this."

"You sure?"

"Of course I'm sure. Why're you acting like a homicide dick with me?"

"I am a homicide dick."

"You're a dick, that's for sure," Luther said, grinning. "All the people you work with say so. Some of 'em use different words, but they all mean 'dick.'"

"Dick, dick, dick . . . are you fixated on that word or something? What's wrong with you, Luther? Are you lonely, maybe need a new boyfriend?"

The pathologist laughed. He had a hearty laugh and a smile that made you want to smile back at him. Dan couldn't figure why such a good-natured, vital, optimistic, energetic man as Luther Williams had chosen to spend his working life with corpses.

•

Dr. Irmatrude Gelkenshettle, chairperson of the Department of Psychology at UCLA, had a corner office with lots of windows and a view of the campus. Now, at 4:45 in the afternoon, the short winter day was already fading, casting a muddy orange light like that of a fire settling into embers. Outside, the shadows were growing longer by the minute, and students were hurrying in deference to the evening chill, which was creeping in ahead of the darkness.

Dan sat in a Danish-modern chair, while Dr. Gelkenshettle went around the desk to a spring-backed chair behind it.

She was a short, stocky woman in her fifties. Her iron-gray hair was chopped without any sense of style, and although she had never been beautiful, her face was appealing and kind. She wore blue slacks and a man's white shirt, with pocket flaps and epaulets; the sleeves were rolled up, and she even wore a man's watch, a plain but dependable Timex on an expansion band. She radiated competence, efficiency, and intelligence.

Though Dan had just met her, he felt that he knew her well, for his own Aunt Kay—his adoptive mother's sister, a career military officer in the WACs—was just like this woman. Dr. Gelkenshettle obviously chose her clothes for comfort, durability, and value. She didn't scorn those who were concerned about being in fashion; it had simply never occurred to her that fashion might be a consideration when it was time to replenish her wardrobe. Just like Aunt Kay. He even knew why she wore a man's watch. Aunt Kay had one too, because the face was larger than that on a woman's watch, and the numerals were easier to read.

At first he had been taken aback by her. She hadn't been his idea of the head of a major university's psychology department. But then he had noticed that on one full shelf of the bookcase behind her desk were more than twenty volumes that bore her name on their spines.

"Doctor Gelkenshettle—"

She held up a hand, interrupting him. "The name's impossible. The only people who call me Doctor Gelkenshettle are students, those colleagues whom I loathe, my auto mechanic—because you've got to keep those guys at a distance or they'll charge you a year's salary for a tune-up—and strangers. We're strangers, or the next thing to it, but we're also professionals, so let's drop the formalities. Call me Marge."

"Is that your middle name?"

"Unfortunately, no. But Irmatrude's as bad as Gelkenshettle, and my middle name's Heidi. Do I look like a Heidi to you?"

He smiled. "I guess not."

"You're damned right I don't. My parents were sweet, and they loved me, but they had a blind spot about names."

"My name's Dan."

"Much better. Simple. Sensible. Anyone can say Dan. Now, you wanted to talk about Dylan McCaffrey and Willy Hoffritz. It's hard to believe they're dead."

"Wouldn't be so hard if you'd seen the bodies. Tell me about Dylan first. What did you think of him?"

"I wasn't head of the department when Dylan McCaffrey was here. I only moved into the top job a little more than four years ago."

"But you were teaching here then, doing your own research. You were on the faculty with him."

"Yes. I didn't know him well, but I knew him well enough to know I didn't want to know him any better."

"I understand he was very dedicated to his work. His wife—she's a psychiatrist—called him a severe obsessive-compulsive."

"He was a nut," Marge said.

•

The two new Paladin agents walked away from the suspicious telephone company van and came directly to Laura's front door. Earl Benton let them in.

One was tall, the other short. The tall one was thin and gray-faced. The short man was slightly pudgy with freckles across the bridge of his nose and on both cheeks. They didn't want to sit down or have coffee. Earl called the short one Flash, and Laura didn't know if that was his surname or a nickname.

Flash did all the talking while the tall one stood beside him, his long face expressionless. "They're steamed that we blew their cover," Flash said.

"If they don't want to be made, they should be more subtle," Earl said.

"That's what I told them," Flash said.

"Who are they?"

"They showed us FBI credentials."

"You wrote their names down?"

"Names and ID numbers."

"Did the ID look real?"

"Yeah," Flash said.

"What about the men? They seem like Bureau types to you."

"Yeah," Flash said. "Sharply dressed. Very cool, soft-spoken, polite even when they were angry, but that underlying arrogance. You know how they are."

"I know," Earl said.

Flash said, "We're heading back to the office, check this out, see if the Bureau employs agents with those names."

"You'll find the names, even if these guys aren't legit," Earl said. "What you've got to do is get photos of the real agents and see if they look like these guys."

"That's what we figure to do," Flash said.

"Get back to me as soon as you can," Earl said, and the other two turned toward the door.

Laura said, "Wait."

Everyone looked at her.

She said, "What did they tell you? What reason did they give for watching my house?"

"Bureau doesn't talk about its operations unless it wants to," Earl told Laura.

"And these guys didn't want to," Flash said. "They'd no sooner tell us their reasons for watching you than they'd kiss us and ask us to dance."

The tall man nodded agreement.

Laura said, "If they were here to protect Melanie and me, they'd tell us, wouldn't they? So that means they must be here to snatch her back."

"Not necessarily," Flash said.

Earl put his revolver back in his shoulder holster. "Laura, see, the situation may be just as unclear and confusing to the Bureau as it is to us. For instance, suppose your husband was working on an important Pentagon project when he disappeared with Melanie. Suppose the FBI's been looking for him ever since. Now he turns up, dead, in peculiar circumstances. Maybe it hasn't been our government funding him these last six years, in which case they're bound to wonder where he's been getting his money."

Again, Laura felt as if the floor were tilting under her, as if the real world that she'd always taken for granted were an illusion. It almost seemed as though true reality might be the paranoid's nightmare world of unseen enemies and complex conspiracies.

She said, "Then you're telling me they're out in that telephone company van, watching my house, because they think someone *else* may come for Melanie, and they want to nab them in the act? But I still don't understand why they didn't come to me and tell me they were going to be watching."

"They don't trust you," Flash said.

"They were angry with us for revealing their presence not just to anyone who might've been watching out there," Earl said, "but to you as well."

Puzzled, she said, "Why?"

Earl looked uncomfortable. "Because, as far as they know, maybe you've always been in this thing with your husband."

"He stole Melanie from me."

Earl cleared his throat and looked unhappy at having to explain this to her. "From the Bureau's point of view, could be that you let your husband take your daughter, so he'd be able to experiment on her with no notice or interference from family or friends."

Shocked, Laura said, "That's *insane!* You see what's been done to Melanie. How could I be party to that?"

"People do strange things."

"I love her. She's my little girl. Dylan was disturbed, maybe crazy. Okay, so he was too unbalanced to see or even care how he was hurting her, destroying her. But I'm not unbalanced *too*! I'm not like Dylan."

"I know," Earl said soothingly. "I know you're not."

She saw belief in Earl Benton's eyes, trust and compassion, but when she looked at the other two men, she saw an element of doubt and suspicion.

They were working for her, but they didn't entirely believe that she had told them the truth.

Madness.

She was caught in a whirlpool that was carrying her down into a nightmare world of suspicion, deception, and violence, into an alien landscape where nothing was what it appeared to be.

•

Surprised, Dan said, "*Nut?* I didn't know psychologists used words like that."

Marge smiled ruefully. "Oh, not in the classroom, and not in published papers, and certainly not in a courtroom if we're ever asked for testimony in a sanity hearing. But this is in the privacy of my office, just between almost-strangers, and I tell you, Dan, he was a nut. Not certifiable, mind you. Not close. But not merely eccentric, either. His primary area of research was supposed to be the development and application of behavior-modification techniques that would reform the criminal personality. But he was always off on a tangent, riding one odd hobbyhorse or another. He regularly announced a deep commitment—'obsessed' *is* the right word—to some new line of research, but after six months or so, he would completely lose interest in it."

"What *were* some of those hobbyhorses?"

She leaned back in her chair and folded her arms across her breasts. "For a while, he was determined to find a drug therapy that would combat nicotine addiction. Does that sound sensible to you? Help smokers get off cigarettes—by getting them onto drugs? Hell's bells. Then for a while, he claimed to be convinced that subliminal suggestion, subconscious programming, could enable us to set aside our prejudices against a belief in the supernatural and help us open our minds to psychic experiences, so we'd be able to see spirits as easily as we see one another."

"Spirits? Are you talking about ghosts?"

"I am. Or, rather, he was."

"I wouldn't think psychologists would believe in ghosts."

"You're looking at one who doesn't. McCaffrey was one who did."

"I'm remembering the books we found in his house. Some of them were about the occult."

"Probably half his hobbyhorses dealt with that," she said. "One occult phenomenon or another."

"Who would pay for this kind of research?"

"I'd have to look at the files. I imagine the occult stuff was done on his own, without funds, or by cleverly misusing funds meant for other work."

"It's possible to misuse funds that blatantly? Isn't there some accounting required?"

"The government's relatively easy to dupe if you're dishonest. Sometimes thieves make the easiest target for another thief, because they never see themselves as being the victims, only perpetrators."

"Who financed his primary research?"

"He got some of his money from trust funds set up by alumni for research purposes. And corporate grants, of course. And as I said, the government."

"Mostly the government?"

"I'd say mostly."

He frowned. "Well, if Dylan McCaffrey was a nut, why would the government want to deal with him?"

"Oh, well, he was a nut, and his interest in the occult was as peculiar as it was exasperating, but he was brilliant. I'll give him that. With a more stable personality, his intellect would've taken him all the way. He'd have been famous in his field and maybe even to the general public."

"Did he get Pentagon funding?"

"Yes."

"What would he have been working on for the Pentagon?"

"Can't say. For one thing, I don't know. I could check the files, but even if I knew, I couldn't say. You don't have security clearance."

"Fair enough. What can you tell me about Wilhelm Hoffritz?"

"He was slime."

Dan laughed. "Doctor . . . *Marge,* you certainly don't mince words."

"It's only the truth. Hoffritz was an elitist son of a bitch. He wanted in the worst way to be chairman of this department. Never had a chance. Everyone knew what he'd be like if he had power over us. Vicious. Abusive. He'd have run the entire department right into the ground."

"He was doing Defense research too?"

"Almost exclusively. Can't tell you about that, either."

"Rumor has it that he was forced out of the university."

"That was a banner day for UCLA."

"Why was he gotten rid of?"

"There was this young girl, a student—"

"Ah."

"Much worse than you think," Marge said. "It wasn't just moral turpitude. He wasn't the first professor to sleep with a student. Half the men on the faculty would be dismissed, and maybe as much as a fifth of the women, if that rule was well enforced. He was having sex with her, yes, but he also beat her up and put her in the hospital. Their relationship was . . . Kinky is a kind word for it. One night, it got out of hand."

"Are you talking about bondage games or something?" Dan asked.

"Yes. Hoffritz was a sadist."

"And the girl cooperated? She was a masochist?"

"Yes. But she got more than she bargained for. One night Hoffritz lost control, broke her nose, three fingers, her left arm. I went to the hospital, saw her. Both eyes blackened, split lip, badly bruised."

•

Laura and Earl stood at the window, watching Flash and the tall man move down the walk in the deepening twilight.

The telephone company van was only a lumpish shape, all details obscured, as the oncoming night knitted together with the shadows under the curbside jacarandas.

She said, "FBI, huh? They won't go away?"

"No."

"Even though I'm aware of them now."

"Well, they're not *convinced* you were conspiring with your husband. In fact, that would be one of the less likely possibilities in their eyes. They still figure someone—whoever was financing Dylan's research—will come after Melanie, and they want to be here when it happens."

"But I still need you," she said. "In case the FBI itself takes my daughter."

"Yes. If that's what comes down, you'll need a witness in order to go after them in the courts."

She went to the couch and sat on the edge, shoulders hunched, head bowed, arms propped on her thighs. "I feel as if I'm losing my mind."

"Everything'll work out if—"

He was interrupted by Melanie's scream.

•

Dan winced at Marge's description of the battered student. "But Hoffritz has no arrest record."

"The girl wouldn't press charges."

"He did that to her, and she let him get away with it? Why?"

Marge got up, went to the window, and stared down at the campus. The orange light of sunset had given way to the grays and blues of twilight. A few clouds had sailed in from the sea.

At last, the psychologist said, "When we put Willy Hoffritz on suspension and started looking into his previous relationships with students, we found this girl wasn't the first. There were at least four others over the years, four that we know of, all undergraduates, sexually involved with Hoffritz, all playing masochist to his sadist, although none of them had been seriously injured. Until this girl, it was always more of a nasty game than anything. Those first four were willing to talk about it when we insisted, and because of our interviews with them, we uncovered some interesting, appalling . . . and frightening information."

Dan didn't press her to continue. He suspected that it was painful and humiliating for her to admit that a colleague—even one she didn't like—was capable of these things and that the academic community was no more noble than the human race at large. But she was a realist who could face up to unpleasant truths, a rare creature both in and out of academia, and she would tell him everything. She just needed to do it at her own pace.

Still facing the twilight, she said, "None of those first four girls was promiscuous, Dan. Good kids from good families, here to obtain an education, not to escape parental authority and get some kicks. In fact, two of the four were virgins before they fell under Hoffritz's spell. And none was ever involved in sadomasochistic relationships before Hoffritz, and certainly not after. They were repulsed by the memories of what they had let him do to them."

She fell silent again.

He decided that she wanted him to ask a question now, and he said, "Well, if they didn't like it, why did they do it?"

"The answer to that is a bit complex."

"I can handle it. I'm a bit complex myself."

She turned from the window and smiled, but only briefly. What she had to tell him obviated amusement. "We discovered that each of those four girls had been voluntarily involved in undisclosed behavior-modification experiments with Hoffritz. Those experiments included posthypnotic suggestion and a variety of ego-suppressing drugs."

"Why would they want to get involved with something like that?"

"To please a professor, to get a good grade. Or maybe because it actually interested them. Students are sometimes interested in the things they study, even these days, even the low-caliber students we've been getting lately. And Hoffritz did have a certain charm, which was more effective with some people than others."

"Not with you."

"When he turned on the charm, I found him even more slimy than usual. Anyway, he was teaching these girls, and he charmed them, and you mustn't forget that he was well published and well known in his field. He had earned a certain respect."

"And it was after these experiments started that each girl found herself sexually involved with him."

"Yes."

"So you think he used hypnosis, drugs, subconscious programming to . . . well, to convert them?"

"To program their psychological matrices to include promiscuity and masochism. Yes. That's exactly what I think."

•

Melanie's shrill scream filled the house.

Shouting her daughter's name, Laura hurried behind Earl Benton, down the hall. Revolver in hand, the bodyguard entered the child's room ahead of Laura and snapped on the light.

Melanie was alone. The menace that had elicited her screams was one that only she could see.

Dressed in white socks and the pair of white cotton underpants that she had been wearing during her nap, the child was crouched in a corner, hands held in front of her to ward off an invisible enemy, shrieking so fiercely that she must have been hurting her throat. She looked so fragile, so pitifully vulnerable.

Laura was briefly overwhelmed with loathing for Dylan. She almost sagged, almost went limp, almost crumpled under the weight of her anger.

Earl holstered his gun. He reached out to Melanie, but she struck his hands and scrambled away from him, along the baseboard.

"Melanie, honey, stop! It's all right," Laura said.

The girl didn't heed her mother. She reached the next corner, sat down, drew her legs up, fisted her small hands, and held them up defensively. She was no longer screaming, but she made a strange, rhythmic, panicky sound. "Uh . . . uh . . . uh . . . uh . . . uh . . ."

Crouching in front of her, Earl said, "It's okay, kid."

"Uh . . . uh . . . uh . . . uh . . ."

"It's okay now. It really is. It's okay, Melanie. I'll take care of you."

"The d-d-door," Melanie said. "The door. Don't let it open!"

"It's shut," Laura said, hurrying to her, kneeling by her. "The door is shut and locked, honey."

"Keep it *shut!*"

"Don't you remember, baby? There's a big, new, heavy lock on the door," Laura said. "Don't you remember?"

Earl glanced at Laura, obviously puzzled.

"The door is shut," Laura continued. "Locked. Sealed. Nailed shut. Nobody can open it, honey. Nobody."

Fat tears welled in the child's eyes, spilled down her cheeks.

"I'll take care of you," Earl said soothingly.

"Baby, you're safe here. No one can hurt you."

Melanie sighed, and the fear ebbed out of her face.

"You're safe. Perfectly safe now."

The girl put one pale hand to her head and began to twist a strand of hair in that absentminded way that any ordinary girl might twist her hair when preoccupied with thoughts of boys or horses or pajama parties or any of the other things that preoccupied kids her age. Indeed, after the bizarre behavior that she had displayed thus far, after alternating between extremes of hysteria and motionless catatonia, it was both moving and encouraging to see her playing with her hair, because that was such a normal act—a small thing, simple, hardly a breakthrough, not a crack in her hard autistic shield, but *normal*.

Seizing the moment, Laura said, "Would you like to go to a beauty shop with me, baby? Hmmmm? You've never been to a real beauty shop. We'll go and get our hair done together. How would you like that?"

Although her eyes remained somewhat glassy, Melanie's brow furrowed, and she seemed to be considering the proposition.

"Lord knows, you need something done with your hair," Laura said, anxiously trying to preserve the moment, expand upon it, deepen and broaden this unexpected contact with the girl inside the autistic shell. "We'll get it cut and styled. Maybe curled. How would you like your hair curled, honey? Oh, you'd look just great with lots of curls."

The girl's face softened, and a smile threatened to take possession of her mouth.

"And after the beauty shop, we could go shopping for clothes. How about that, honey? Lots of new dresses. Dresses and sweaters. Even one of the glitzy new jackets the kids are wearing. You'd like that, I bet."

Melanie's unfinished smile stopped forming. Although Laura kept talking, the mood was gone as suddenly as it had come. The girl's placid expression gave way to a look of disgust, as if she had seen something in her private world that horrified and repulsed her.

Then she did a startling and disturbing thing: She struck herself with her small fists, struck hard at her knees and thighs, with a loud smacking sound, then pounded her chest—

"Melanie!"

—and swung both fists at the same time, pounding her withered biceps and her shoulders, pummeling herself fiercely, with unexpected strength and fury, trying to hurt herself.

"Stop it! Melanie!" Laura was shocked and frightened by her daughter's sudden self-destructive frenzy.

Melanie punched herself in the face.

"I got her!" Earl shouted.

The girl bit him as he tried to restrain her. She freed one hand and clawed her own chest with sufficient ferocity to draw blood.

"Jesus!" Earl said as the girl kicked him with her bare feet and twisted loose again.

•

Frowning at Marge, Dan said, "Programmed them to be promiscuous and masochistic? Is that sort of thing possible?"

She nodded. "If the psychologist has a deep and broad knowledge of modern brainwashing techniques, and if he's unscrupulous, and if he has either a willing subject or one he can physically detain and control for lengthy periods—then it's possible. But it usually takes a long time, a lot of patience and perseverance. The astonishing and frightening thing in this case is that Hoffritz seems to have been able to program these girls in a matter of weeks, after working with them only an hour or two a day, just three or four times a week. Apparently, he developed some new and damned effective methods of psychological conditioning. But with the first four, it wasn't long-lasting, never longer than a few weeks or months. Eventually, each girl's original personality resurfaced. First she felt guilty about her sexual acrobatics with Hoffritz but continued to take perverse pleasure in the humiliation and pain of her masochistic role. Then she gradually grew to fear and despise the whole sadomasochistic aspect of the relationship. Each of these kids said it was like waking from a dream when they finally began to want to be free of Hoffritz. All four girls eventually found the will to break it off."

"Good God," Dan said.

"I believe there is a good one, but sometimes I wonder why He lets men like Hoffritz walk the earth."

"Why didn't these girls report him to the police . . . or at least to university officials?"

"They were deeply ashamed. And until we found and questioned them, they never suspected that their masochistic aberrations were Hoffritz's work. They all thought those twisted desires had been in them all along."

"But that's amazing They knew they were involved in behavior-modification experiments. So when they started behaving in ways they'd never behaved before—"

She held up one hand, stopping him. "Willy Hoffritz probably implanted posthypnotic directives that inhibited each girl from considering the possibility that he was responsible for her new behavior."

It scared Dan to think the brain was just so much Silly Putty that could be so easily manipulated.

•

Melanie scuttled past Earl and sprang to her feet and took two awkward steps into the middle of the bedroom, where she stopped and swayed and almost fell. She began once more to scourge herself, hammering herself as if she felt that she deserved to be punished or as if she were trying to drive some dark spirit from her traitorous flesh.

Stepping close, grunting as the small fists glanced off her, Laura threw her arms around her daughter, hugging her, trying to pin the child's arms at her sides.

When her hands were restrained, Melanie still didn't settle down. She kicked and screamed.

Earl Benton stepped in behind her, sandwiching her between him and Laura, so she couldn't move at all. She could only shout and weep and strain to break free. The three of them remained like that for a minute or two, while Laura spoke continuously and reassuringly to the girl, and finally Melanie stopped struggling. She sagged between them.

"She done?" Earl asked.

"I think so," Laura said.

"Poor kid."

Melanie looked exhausted.

Earl stepped back.

Docile now, Melanie allowed Laura to lead her to the bed.

She sat on the edge of it.

She was still weeping.

Laura said, "Baby? Are you all right?"

Eyes glazed, the girl said, "It came open. It came open again, all the way open." She shuddered in revulsion.

•

"The fifth girl," Dan said. "The one he beat up and put in the hospital. What was her name?"

The stocky psychologist moved away from the twilight-darkened window, returned to her desk, and slumped in her chair as if these unpleasant memories had drained her in a way that a hard day's work never could. "Not sure I should tell you."

"I believe you have to."

"Invasion of privacy and all that."

"Police investigation and all that."

"Doctor-patient privilege and all that," she said.

"Oh? This fifth girl was your patient?"

"I visited her several times in the hospital."

"Not good enough, Marge. Carefully worded, but not quite good enough. I visited my dad every day when he was in the hospital for a triple heart-bypass operation, but I don't figure a daily visit gives me the right to call myself his doctor."

Marge sighed. "It's just that the poor girl suffered so much, and now to dredge it all up again four years after the fact—"

"I'm not going to find her and dredge up the past in front of a new husband or her parents or anything like that," Dan assured her. "I may look big and dumb and crude, but actually I can be sensitive and discreet."

"You don't look dumb or crude."

"Thank you."

"You *do* look dangerous."

"I cultivate that image. It helps in my line of work."

She hesitated a moment longer, then shrugged. "Her name was Regine Savannah."

"You're kidding."

"Would Irmatrude Gelkenshettle kid about anyone's name?"

"Sorry." He wrote "Regine Savannah" in his small notebook. "You know where she lives?"

"Well, at the time it all happened, Regine was a junior in the undergraduate program. She shared a large off-campus apartment in Westwood with three other girls. But I'm sure she's long gone from that address."

"What happened after she got out of the hospital? Did she drop out of school?"

"No. She finished her studies, took her degree, although there were those who wished she would have transferred. Some felt it was a continuing embarrassment to have her here."

That sentiment baffled him. "Embarrassment? I'd think everyone would've been happy that she recovered sufficiently—physically *and* psychologically—to go on with her life."

"Except that she continued seeing Hoffritz."

"*What?*"

"Amazing, huh?"

"She went on seeing him *after* he put her in the hospital?"

"That's right. Worse, Regine wrote a letter to me, in my capacity as department head, defending Hoffritz."

"Good God."

"She wrote letters to the university president and to a few other faculty members on the review board. She did everything in her power to keep Willy Hoffritz from losing his job."

A creepy feeling settled over Dan again. He was not, by nature, given to melodramatic action or thought, but somehow just talking about Hoffritz was beginning to make his blood run cold. If Hoffritz was able to acquire such control of Regine, what breakthroughs might he and Dylan McCaffrey have achieved once they had combined their demonic talents? For what purpose had they turned Melanie into a near vegetable?

Dan could no longer sit still. He got up. But it was a small office, and he was a big man, and there wasn't much of anywhere to pace. He just stood there by his chair, hands in his pockets, and said, "You would think, after he beat Regine, she would have been able to break his hold on her."

Marge shook her head. "After Willy Hoffritz was booted off the faculty, Regine actually brought him to a number of campus functions as her escort."

Dan gaped at her.

Marge said, "And he was her only guest at graduation."

"Good Lord."

"Both of them enjoyed rubbing our faces in it."

"The girl needed psychiatric help."

"Yes."

"Deprogramming."

A sadness had taken possession of the psychologist's kind face. She took off her glasses as if they were suddenly much heavier than they had been heretofore, an unbearable weight. She rubbed her weary eyes.

Dan had a good idea how the woman felt. She was dedicated to her profession, and she was good at what she did, and she maintained high personal standards. She had scruples and ideals. With her well-developed conscience, she must believe that a man like Hoffritz was a discredit not only to the profession but to all of those who were his associates.

She said, "We tried to see that Regine got the help she needed. But she refused it."

Outside, sodium-vapor lights had come on, but they could not hold back the night.

Dan said, "Evidently, then, the reason Regine didn't turn against Hoffritz was because she *liked* the beating he'd given her."

"Evidently."

"He had programmed her to like it."

"Evidently."

"He'd learned from those first four girls."

"Yes."

"He'd lost control of them, but he'd learned from his mistakes. By the time he'd gotten to Regine, he'd learned how to keep an iron grip." Dan had to move, work off some energy. He took five steps to the bookshelves, returned to his chair and put his hands on the back of it. "I'll never be able to hear the words 'behavior modification' without getting sick to my stomach."

Defensively, Marge said, "It's a justifiable area of research, a reputable branch of psychology. Behavior modification can help us find ways to teach children more easily and make them retain what they learn far longer than they do now. It can help us reduce the crime rate, heal the sick, and perhaps even create a more peaceful world."

As Dan grew increasingly eager for action, Marge seemed, by contrast, to seek relief in lethargy. She slumped down even farther in her chair. She was a take-charge kind of person, the sturdy type who was confident of dealing with anything, but she could not deal with inexplicably monstrous men like Hoffritz. And when she was confronted with something that she could not grasp and control, she looked less like a career WAC and more like a grandmother in need of a rocking chair and a cup of tea and honey. Dan liked her even more because of that vulnerability.

Her voice was tired: "Behavior modification and brainwashing aren't the same thing at all. Brainwashing is a bastard offshoot of behavior modification, a twisted perversion of it, just as Hoffritz was not an ordinary man or an ordinary scientist but a perversion of both."

"Is Regine still with him?"

"I don't know. The last I saw of her was more than two years ago, and she was with him then."

"If she wouldn't drop him after the beating, then I suppose nothing he did would cause her to leave. So she's probably still been seeing him."

"Unless he got tired of her," Marge said.

"From what I've heard of him, he'd never get tired of someone he could dominate and terrify."

Marge nodded grimly.

Checking his watch, anxious to get away now, Dan said, "You told me Dylan McCaffrey was brilliant, a genius. Would you say the same of Hoffritz?"

"Probably. In fact, yes. But his genius was a darker variety, twisted, bent."

"So was McCaffrey's."

"Not half as twisted as Hoffritz," she said.

"But if they started working together, with substantial—maybe even unlimited—funding, with a human subject, with absolutely no legal or moral restrictions, they would be a dangerous combination, wouldn't they?"

"Yes," she said. A pause. "Unholy."

The word—"unholy"—seemed like uncharacteristic hyperbole, coming from Marge, but Dan was sure that she had chosen it carefully.

"Unholy," she repeated, leaving him without a doubt as to the depth of her concern.

•

In the hall bathroom, with some iodine and a Big Patch Band-Aid, Laura was able to take care of the small wound on Earl Benton's hand, where Melanie had bitten him during their struggle.

"It's nothing," he assured Laura. "Don't worry about it."

Melanie was sitting on the edge of the bathtub, staring at the green-tiled wall. She couldn't have been more unlike the hellion who had lashed out at them in the bedroom a few minutes ago.

"A human bite is more likely to become infected than that from a dog or cat or virtually any other animal," Laura said.

"You soaked it good with the iodine, and there's hardly any bleeding. Just a shallow bite. Doesn't even hurt," he said, though she knew it must sting at least slightly.

"Had a tetanus shot lately?" Laura asked.

"Yeah. I was doing skip-tracing work last month. One of the guys I tracked down took exception to being found, pulled a knife on me. He didn't do much damage. Took about seven stitches to close it. That's when I had the tetanus booster. Real recent."

"I'm so sorry about this."

"You already said."

"Well, I am."

"Listen, I know the girl didn't mean it. Besides, it's part of the job."

Laura crouched in front of Melanie and examined the redness on the child's left cheek. It marked the spot where she had punched herself in the midst of her frenzy. It would develop into a bruise, given time. At the open neck of her blouse, scratches showed on her throat and chest, where she had clawed herself. Her lip was still puffy and sore-looking, where she'd bitten it this afternoon at the end of their hypnotic-therapy session.

Dry-mouthed with fear and worry, Laura said to Earl, "How can we possibly protect her? It's not just some faceless enemy out there that wants to get at her. It's not just government agents or Russian spies. She wants to hurt herself too. How can we protect her from herself?"

"Somebody's got to stay with her, watch her every minute."

Laura put a hand under her daughter's chin, turned her head so their eyes met. "This is too much, baby. Mommy can try to deal with the bad men out there who want to get their hands on you. And Mommy can try to deal with your condition, help you come out of this. But now . . . this is just too much. Why do you want to hurt yourself, baby? *Why?*"

Melanie stirred, as if she desperately wanted to answer but as if someone were restraining her. Her stricken mouth twisted, worked, but soundlessly. She shuddered, shook her head, groaned softly.

Laura's heart literally ached as she watched her pale and slender daughter struggle unsuccessfully to cast off the shackles of autism.

chapter twenty

Ned Rink, the ex-cop and former agent for the FBI, who had been found dead in his car in the hospital parking lot earlier in the day, owned a small, tidy, desert-style ranch house on the edge of Van Nuys. Dan drove there straight from his meeting with Marge Gelkenshettle. It was a low house with a flat roof that was covered with white stones, set in the middle of a particularly flat part of the San Fernando Valley, on a flat street of other low, flat houses. The shrubbery—with typical southern California, chlorophyllic exuberance—was the only thing that relieved the harsh geometry of the house and the monotonous tract around it, both of which clearly dated from the late 1950s.

The house was dark. The streetlight in front of the place had a dirty globe and didn't illuminate much. Blank black windows and patches of pale yellow stucco walls could be glimpsed between the shadowy forms of neatly shaped plum-thorn bushes, five-foot-high hibiscus, miniature orange trees, full-size date palms, and sections of a lantana hedge.

Cars were parked along one side of the narrow street. Even though the unmarked police sedan was nestled in darkness, midway between two streetlights, under an immense overhanging laurel, Dan spotted it at once. One man sat in the nondescript Ford, behind the wheel, slumped down, watching the Rink house, barely visible.

Dan drove past the house, circled the block, returned, and parked half a block behind the department sedan. He got out of his car and walked to the Ford. The driver's window was half open. Dan peered inside.

The plainclothes cop on the surveillance detail was an East Valley Division detective, and Dan knew him. His name was George Padrakis, and he looked like that singer from the '50s and '60s, Perry Como.

Padrakis rolled the half-open window all the way down and said, "Are you here to relieve me, or what?" He sounded like Perry Como too: His voice was soft, mellow, and sleepy. He consulted his wristwatch. "Nope, I still have a couple hours to go. It's too early to relieve me."

"I'm just here to have a look inside," Dan said.

Head twisted sideways to stare up at Dan, Padrakis said, "This your case, huh?"

"It's my case."

"Wexlersh and Manuello already tossed the place earlier."

Wexlersh and Manuello were Ross Mondale's right-hand men in the East Valley Division, two career-conscious detectives who had hitched their wagons to his train and were willing to do anything for him, including bend the law now and then. They were toadies, and Dan couldn't stand them.

"They on this case too?" Dan asked.

"Didn't think you had it all to yourself, did you? Too big for that. Four dead altogether. One of them a Hancock Park millionaire. Too big for the Lone Ranger approach."

"What've they got you out here for?" Dan asked, squatting so he was face-to-face with Padrakis.

"Beats me. I guess they figure there might be something in Rink's house that'll tell them who he was working for, and maybe whoever hired him will know it's in there and will come here to get rid of the evidence."

"At which time you nab them."

"Ridiculous, ain't it?" Padrakis said sleepily.

"Whose idea was this?"

"Whose do you think?"

"Mondale," Dan said.

"You win your choice of the stuffed animals."

The chilly breeze suddenly became a chillier wind, rustling the leaves of the laurel overhead.

"You must've been working around the clock if you were at that house in Studio City last night," Padrakis said.

"Pretty nearly around the clock."

"So what're you doing here?"

"Heard there was free popcorn."

"You should be home, having a beer, your feet up. That's where I'd be."

"I'm out of beer. Besides, I'm dedicated," Dan said. "They leave you with a key, George?"

"You're a workaholic, from what I hear."

"You going to psychoanalyze me first, or can you tell me if they left you with a key?"

"Yeah. But I don't know I should let you have it."

"It's my case."

"But the place has already been tossed."

"Not by me."

"Wexlersh and Manuello."

"Tweedledee and Tweedledum. Come on, George, why're you being such a pain in the ass?"

Reluctantly, Padrakis fumbled in a coat pocket for the key to Ned Rink's house. "From what I hear, Mondale wants to talk to you real bad."

Dan nodded. "That's because I'm a brilliant conversationalist. You should hear me discuss ballet."

Padrakis found the key but didn't hand it over right away. "He's been trying to track you down all day."

"And he calls himself a detective?" Dan said, holding his hand out for the key.

"He's been looking for you all day, and then you waltz in here instead of going back to the station like you promised him, and I just give you the key . . . he won't be happy about that."

Dan sighed. "You think he'll be any happier if you refuse to give me the key and then I have to go smash a window to get in that house?"

"You wouldn't."

"Pick a window."

"This is stupid."

"Any window."

Finally, Padrakis gave him the key. Dan went down the sidewalk, through the gate, to the front door, favoring his weak knee. They must be in for more rain; the knee knew. He unlocked the door and stepped inside.

He was in a tiny foyer. The living room on his right was dark except for the pale grayish glow that came through the windows from the distant streetlamps. To his left, back through a narrow hall, a lamp was on in a bedroom or study. It hadn't been visible from the street. Wexlersh and Manuello had apparently forgotten to switch it off when they'd finished, which was just like them: They were sloppy.

He snapped on the hall light, stepped into the darkness on his right, found a lamp, and had a look at the living room first. It was startling. This was a modest house in a modest neighborhood, but it was furnished as though it served as a secret retreat for one of the Rockefellers. The centerpiece of the living room was a gorgeous, twelve-foot-by-twelve foot, three-inch-deep Chinese carpet with a pattern of dragons and cherry blossoms. There were midnineteenth-century French chairs with hand-carved legs and feet, a matching sofa upholstered in a lush off-white fabric that exactly matched the color of the unpatterned sections of the carpet. Two bronze lamps with intricately worked bases had shades of crystal beads. The large coffee table was unlike anything Dan had seen before: It seemed to be entirely bronze and pewter, with a superbly etched Oriental scene on the top; the upper surface curved around to form the sides, and the sides curved under to form the legs, so that the entire piece seemed fashioned from a single flowing slab. On the walls, the landscape paintings, each ornately framed, looked like the work of a master. In the farthest corner, a period French étagère held a collection of crystal—figures, vases, bowls—and each piece was more beautiful than the one before it.

The living-room furnishings alone had cost more than the entire modest house. Clearly, Ned Rink had been making a good living as a hired murderer. And he knew just where to put his money. If he had bought a big house in the best neighborhood, the IRS might eventually have noticed and asked how he could afford it, but here he could appear to be in modest circumstances while living in splendor.

Dan tried to picture Rink in this room. The man had been squat and decidedly ugly. Rink's desire to surround himself with beautiful things was understandable, but sitting here, he would have looked like a roach on a birthday cake.

Dan noticed there were no mirrors in the living room, remembered there had been none in the foyer, and suspected there would be none anywhere in the house except, of necessity, in the bathroom. He almost felt sorry for Rink, the lover of beauty who couldn't stand to look at himself.

Fascinated, he went back down the hall to have a look at the rest of the place, heading first for the room where Wexlersh and Manuello had left a light burning. As he stepped through the door, it suddenly occurred to him that maybe the light couldn't be blamed on Wexlersh and Manuello, that maybe someone else was in the house right now, that maybe someone was there illegally in spite of the fact that George Padrakis was watching the front entrance, and at the same time he glimpsed movement out of the corner of his eye as he went through the doorway, but it was too late. He turned and saw the butt of a pistol swinging at him. Because he turned into the blow, he took it square on the forehead instead of alongside his skull.

He went down.

Hard.

The overhead light went out.

He felt as if his skull had been half crushed, but he wasn't unconscious.

Hearing movement, he realized his assailant was stepping past him toward the door. There was light in the hall, but Dan's vision was blurred, and all he could see was a shapeless form silhouetted by the glow. That silhouette seemed to be gliding up and down and going around in circles at the same time, like a figure on a carousel, and Dan knew his grip on consciousness was tenuous.

Nevertheless, he heaved forward on the floor, gasping as the pain in his head lanced all the way down into his shoulders and back, and he grabbed tenaciously at the fleeing phantom. He caught a fistful of material, a leg of the man's trousers, and jerked as hard as he could.

The stranger staggered, collided with the doorframe, and said, "Shit!"

Dan held on.

Cursing, the intruder kicked him in the shoulder.

Then again.

Dan had both hands on the guy's leg now and was trying to pull him down on the floor, where they would be more evenly matched, but the guy was holding on to the doorframe and trying to shake him loose. He felt as though he were a dog attacking a mailman.

The intruder kicked him again, in the right arm this time, and Dan's right hand went numb. He lost half his grip on the perp's leg. His vision blurred further, and the light seemed to dim. His eyes stung. He gritted his teeth as if to bite into consciousness and hold on to it with his jaws.

The stranger, still a black shape against the vague hall light, bent toward him and clubbed him again with the butt of the gun. On the shoulder this time. Then in the middle of his back. Then in the shoulder again.

Blinking, fighting to clear his burning eyes, Dan let go of the guy's leg but whipped his good left hand up and tried to grab the bastard's throat or face. He got hold of an ear and tore at it.

The stranger squealed.

Dan's hand slipped off the blood-slick ear, but he hooked his fingers in the perp's shirt collar.

The intruder hammered Dan's arm, trying to make him let go.

Dan held fast.

Some of the numbness seeped out of his right arm, and he was able to push himself up with that hand while he pulled himself up with the hand that was hooked in his adversary's shirt. Onto his knees. Then one foot on the floor. Thrusting up, shoving the guy backward. Into the hall. They staggered two or three steps, turning as they moved, like a pair of clumsy dancers. They crashed to the floor, both of them this time.

He was right on top of the guy now, but he still couldn't see what his adversary looked like. His vision wouldn't clear, and the hall light was still dimmer than it should have been. His eyes burned as if acid had gotten into them, and he figured it must be sweat and blood pouring down from the gash in his forehead.

He reached inside his coat and pulled his .38 Police Special out of his shoulder holster, but he couldn't see the other guy swinging at his hand and couldn't duck the blow that came. Something hard whacked his knuckles, and the gun flew out of his grasp.

Grappling, they rolled against the wall, and Dan tried to drive his good knee into the stranger's crotch, but the bastard blocked him. Worse, the guy either kicked or struck Dan's other knee, the bum knee, which was his weak spot. A reptile-quick flash of pain slithered up his thigh and chased its tail around and around in his stomach. Being hit on that knee could sometimes be like taking a kick in the balls; it knocked all the wind out of him, and he almost let go.

Almost.

The guy clambered over him and tried to scramble away, toward the kitchen, but Dan held on to the scumbag's jacket. The perp crawled, and Dan half crawled and was half dragged along behind him.

It might have been funny if they hadn't both been hurting and breathing like well-run horses. And if they hadn't been deadly serious.

Vision swimming and dimming, Dan launched himself forward in one last desperate effort, trying to lever himself on top of the intruder and pin him. But the perp apparently decided that the best defense was a good offense, so he stopped trying to get away and turned back on Dan, cursing so hard he sprayed spittle, pounding and flailing with what felt like four or five arms. They rolled back down the hall a few feet before finally coming to a stop with the intruder on top.

Something cold and hard poked against Dan's teeth. He knew what it was. The barrel of a gun.

"Stop this crap now!" the stranger said.

With the muzzle vibrating against his teeth, Dan said, "If you were gonna kill me, you'd have done it already."

"Push your luck," the intruder said, and he sounded just angry enough to pull the trigger whether he wanted to or not.

Blinking furiously, Dan cleared his vision slightly, not much, just enough so he could see the weapon, blurry, huge as a cannon, jammed into his face. He saw the man beyond the piece too, although not distinctly. The ceiling light in the hall was above and behind the son of a bitch, so his face was still pretty much in shadows. His left ear hung in an odd way, dripping blood.

Dan realized that his own eyelashes were gummed with blood. Blood was still seeping into his eyes along with copious streams of salty sweat, which was half the reason he couldn't clear them.

He stopped struggling.

"Let go . . . you . . . bulldog . . . bastard!" the intruder said, kneeling on top of him, heaving each word out with a new breath, as if the words were lead ingots that had to be cast off with great effort.

"Okay," Dan said, letting go of him.

"You crazy, man?"

"All right," Dan said.

"You half tore my fuckin' ear off!"

"All right, okay," Dan said.

"Don't you know when you're supposed to stay down, you stupid son of a bitch?"

"Now?"

"Yeah, now!"

"Okay."

"Stay down!"

"All right."

The intruder eased back, still pointing the gun at him but no longer holding it against his teeth. He studied Dan warily for a moment, then stood up. Shakily.

Now Dan could see him better, but it didn't much matter, because it was no one he remembered seeing before.

The guy backed off, toward the kitchen. He held the gun with one hand and his bleeding ear with the other.

Defenseless, not daring to move lest he be shot, Dan lay on his back on the hall floor, head raised, blood trickling into his eyes, smelling blood, tasting blood, heart hammering, wanting to go for it, wanting to rush the bastard in spite of the gun, having to control himself, able to do nothing but just watch the guy escape. It made him mad as hell.

The perp reached the kitchen. The back of the house was open, and he reversed through it, hesitated, then ran.

Dan scrambled after his own piece, which was on the floor by the doorway of the room where he'd been ambushed. He snatched up the revolver, heaved and stumbled to his feet, cried out as a grenade of pain went off in his bum knee, somehow shoved the pain down into a little box in his mind and clamped a lid on it, and plunged toward the kitchen.

By the time he reached the back door and stepped out into the cool night air, the intruder was gone. He had no way of knowing over which side of the redwood fence the perp had jumped.

•

Dan washed his face in Rink's bathroom. His forehead was bruised and abraded.

His vision had drifted back into focus and had locked there. Although his head felt as though it had been used as a blacksmith's forge, he knew he wasn't suffering from concussion.

His head was not the only thing that ached. His neck, his shoulders, his back, and his left knee throbbed.

In the medicine cabinet above the bathroom sink, he found a package of gauze, made a compress out of it, and set it aside. He discovered some Bactine too, and he sprayed the scraped flesh of his forehead, blotted it gingerly, sprayed it again. He picked up the gauze compress and held it firmly against his forehead with his right hand, hoping to stop the bleeding altogether, while he prowled around the house.

He went to the room where he had been ambushed, and he switched on the light. It was a study, less elegantly but just as expensively furnished as the living room. One entire wall of bookshelves was built around a television and VCR. Half the shelves were used for books; the other half were filled with videotapes.

He looked at the tapes first and saw some familiar motion-picture titles: *Silver Streak, Arthur,* all the Abbott-and-Costello pictures, *Tootsie, The Goodbye Girl, Groundhog Day, Foul Play, Mrs. Doubtfire,* several Charlie Chaplin films, two Marx Brothers pictures. All the legit movies were comedies, and it figured a professional hit man might need to laugh a little when he came home from a hard day of blowing people's brains out. But most of the movies weren't legit. Most of them were pornographic, with titles like *Debbie Does Dallas* and *The Sperminator.* There must have been two to three hundred porno titles.

The books were of more interest because that was what the intruder apparently had been after. A cardboard carton stood on the floor in front of the bookcases; several volumes had been plucked off the shelves and piled in the box. First, Dan examined the collection and saw that every one of the books was a nonfiction study of one branch of the occult or another. Then, still holding the gauze to his forehead with one hand, he pawed through the seven volumes in the carton and saw they were all by the same author, Albert Uhlander.

Uhlander?

He reached into an inner jacket pocket and pulled out the small address book that he had taken from the Studio City house last night, from Dylan McCaffrey's wrecked office. He paged to the U listings and found only one.

Uhlander.

McCaffrey, who was interested in the occult, had known Uhlander. Rink, who was interested in the occult, had at least read Uhlander; maybe he had known Uhlander too. This was a link between McCaffrey and Ned Rink. But were they on the same side, or were they enemies? And what did the occult have to do with this?

His thoughts were spinning, and not merely because he had been clubbed on the forehead.

Anyway, Uhlander was evidently a key to understanding what was going on. Apparently, the intruder had broken in there only to remove those books from the house, to conceal the Uhlander connection.

Pressing the gauze to his forehead, Dan left the study. Like an electric current, the pain seemed to pass through the gauze, into his hand, up his arm, into his right shoulder, down to the middle of his back, up to his left shoulder, into his neck, along the side of his face, completing the circuit by returning to his forehead, starting all over again.

Favoring his left knee, sorting through things with one hand, feeling like a big crippled bug, he searched the place perfunctorily and found nothing more of interest. Rink was a hit man, and hit men didn't assist police investigations by keeping handy little address books and paper records of their affairs.

In the bathroom again, he removed the compress and saw that the superficial bleeding had, indeed, finally stopped.

He looked like hell. But that was fitting, because he felt like hell too.

chapter twenty-one

When Dan limped out to the curb, carrying the small box of books, George Padrakis was still behind the wheel of the unmarked sedan, sitting in darkness, his window half open. He cranked it all the way down when he saw Dan.

"I was just on the squawk box. Mondale wants . . . Hey, what happened to your forehead?"

Dan told him about the intruder.

Padrakis opened the door and got out of the car. He looked and sounded like Perry Como, and he moved like him too: lazily, casually, with unconscious grace. He was even casual as he reached inside his coat and drew his revolver.

"The guy's gone," Dan said as Padrakis took a step toward Rink's house. "Long gone."

"But how'd he get in there?"

"Through the back."

"This street's been quiet, and I had my window down," Padrakis protested. "I'd have heard breaking glass, anything like that."

"I didn't find a broken window," Dan said. "I think he came in by the kitchen door, probably with a key."

"Well, hell, then they can't blame it on me," Padrakis said, holstering his revolver. "I can't be two places at once. They want to watch the back of the house too, they should have put two men on the place. You get a good look at the joker who jumped you?"

"Not real good." Dan returned the key Padrakis had given him. "But if you see a guy with a badly mangled ear, that's him."

"Ear?"

"I nearly tore his ear off."

"Why'd you do that?"

"For one thing, because he was trying to bash my brains in," Dan said impatiently. "Besides, I'm sort of like a matador. I always try to take a trophy home with me, and this guy didn't have a tail."

Padrakis looked baffled.

A gigantic motor home turned the corner, engine roaring, and lumbered down the block, like a dinosaur.

Frowning at the box in Dan's hands, Padrakis raised his voice above the shrieking engine of the nature lovers' vehicle. "What's that you've got there?"

"Books."

"Books?"

"Assembled sheets of paper with words on them, for the purpose of conveying information or providing entertainment. Now what about the squawk box? What's Mondale want?"

"You taking those books with you?"

"That's right."

"Don't know if you can do that."

"Don't worry. I can manage. They aren't that heavy."

"That's not what I mean."

"What's Mondale want?"

Staring unhappily at the box in Dan's arms, Padrakis waited until the motor home had passed like a brontosaurus making its way through a primeval swamp. Its wake of cold air and exhaust fumes washed over them.

"I called in to let Mondale know you were here."

"How thoughtful of you, George."

"He was about to head over to the Sign of the Pentagram on Ventura."

"Good for him."

"He *really* wants you to meet him there."

"What the hell's the Sign of the Pentagram? Sounds like a bar where werewolves hang out."

"I think it's a bookstore or something," Padrakis said, still frowning at the box of books. "Guy's been killed over there."

"What guy?"

"The owner, I think. Name's Scaldone. Mondale says it's like the bodies in Studio City."

"There goes dinner," Dan said. He headed along the sidewalk, through alternating pools of purple-black shadows and wan amber light, toward his own car.

Padrakis followed him. "Hey, about those books—"

"Do you read, George?"

"They're the property of the deceased—"

"Nothing like curling up with a good book, though they're not nearly so entertaining when you're deceased."

"And this isn't like a crime scene where we can just cart away anything that might be evidence."

Dan balanced the box on the bumper of his car, unlocked the trunk, put the box inside, and said, "'The man who does not read good books has no advantage over the man who can't read them.' Mark Twain said that, George."

"Listen, until a member of his family has been located and gives approval, I really don't think you should—"

Slamming the lid of the trunk, Dan said, "'There is more treasure in books than in all the pirates' loot on Treasure Island.' Walt Disney. He was right, George. You should read more."

"But—"

"'Books are not merely lumps of lifeless paper, but minds alive on the shelves.' Gilbert Highet." He clapped George Padrakis on the shoulder. "Expand your narrow existence, George. Bring color to this drab life as a detective. Read, George, *read*!"

"But—"

Dan got in the car, closed the door, and started the engine. Padrakis frowned at him through the window.

Dan waved as he drove away.

After he turned the corner and went a couple of blocks, he pulled the car to the curb. He got out Dylan McCaffrey's address book. Under the S listings, he found a Joseph Scaldone, followed by the word "Pentagram," a phone number, and an address on Ventura.

Almost certainly, the murders in Studio City, the death of Ned Rink, and now the Scaldone killing were linked. It was looking more and more as if someone out there was desperately trying to cover up a bizarre conspiracy by eliminating everybody involved in it. Sooner or later, they would either eliminate Melanie McCaffrey as well—or snatch her away from her mother. And if those faceless enemies got hold of the girl again, she would vanish forever; she would not be fortunate enough to be saved a second time.

•

At 7:05, Laura was in the kitchen, preparing dinner for herself, Melanie, and Earl. A big pot of water was working up to a boil on the stove, and a smaller pot of spaghetti sauce and meatballs was also heating. The room was filled with mouthwatering fragrances: garlic, onions, tomatoes, basil, and cheese. Laura rinsed off some black olives and added them to a big bowl of salad.

Melanie sat at the table, silent, unmoving, staring down at her hands, which were folded in her lap. Her eyes were closed. She might have been asleep. Or perhaps she was just withdrawn further than usual into her secret, private world.

That was the first meal Laura had made for her daughter in six years, and even Melanie's depressing condition could not entirely spoil the moment. Laura felt maternal and domestic. It had been a long time since she had experienced either of those feelings, and she had forgotten that being a mother could be as satisfying as anything that she accomplished in her profession.

Earl Benton had prepared the table with plates, glasses, silverware, and napkins. Now he sat across the table from Melanie, in his shirtsleeves—and shoulder holster—reading the newspaper. When he came across something surprising or shocking or funny in a gossip column, Dear Abby, or Miss Manners, he would read it aloud to Laura.

Pepper, the calico cat, was curled comfortably in the corner by the refrigerator, lulled by the humming and the vibrations of the motor. She knew that she wasn't allowed on kitchen counters or tables, and she usually kept a low profile while in the room, to avoid being chased out altogether. Abruptly, however, the cat shrieked and popped onto her feet. Her back arched. Her fur bristled. She was wild-eyed, and she spat angrily.

Putting down the newspaper, Earl said, "What's wrong, puss?"

Laura turned from the cutting board where she was making the salad.

Pepper was alarmingly agitated. The calico's ears were flat against her skull, and her lips were drawn back in a snarl, fangs revealed.

"Pepper, what's wrong with you?"

The cat's eyes seemed to bulge in terror from its head and fixed for an instant on Laura. There was nothing of the domestic pet in those eyes, nothing but sheer wildness.

"Pepper . . . ?"

The calico bolted out of the corner squealing in fear or rage or both. She dashed toward a row of cabinets but suddenly wheeled away from them as though she'd seen something monstrous. She streaked toward the sink instead, then shrieked and abruptly changed direction again, claws ticking and scraping on the tile. She chased her own tail for half a dozen revolutions, spitting, and snapping her jaws, then leaped straight into the air as if she'd been stung or swatted. Slashing at the air with her claws, she pranced and twisted on her hind paws in a weird Saint Vitus's dance, came down on all fours, and was moving even as her forepaws touched the tile. She flashed under the table as if running for her life, between the chairs, out the kitchen door, into the dining room. Gone.

It had been an incredible display. Laura had never seen anything quite like it.

Melanie had been unaffected by the cat's performance. She still sat with her hands in her lap, head bowed, eyes closed.

Earl had dropped the newspaper and had risen from his chair. In another part of the house, Pepper let out one last miserable cry. Then silence.

•

The Sign of the Pentagram was a little shop in a bustling block that was the very essence of Southern California hopes and dreams. Photographs of this portion of Ventura Boulevard could have been used in a dictionary as the sole definition of "bootstrap capitalism." One small store or restaurant shouldered up against another, block after block of enterprises owned and managed by entrepreneurs of all ages and ethnic backgrounds, and there was something for every interest and taste, both the exotic and the mundane: a Korean restaurant with maybe fifteen tables; a feminist bookshop; a purveyor of handmade knives; something called the Gay Resource Center; a dry cleaner and a party-supply store and a frame shop and a couple of delis and an appliance store; a bookstore that sold only fantasy and science fiction; Ching Brothers Finance, "Loans to the Reliable"; a tiny restaurant offering "Americanized Nigerian cuisine" and another specializing in "chinois, French-Chinese cooking"; a merchant who sold military paraphernalia of all kinds, although not weapons. Some of these entrepreneurs were getting rich, and some never would, but all of them had dreams, and it seemed to Dan that, in the early-evening darkness, Ventura Boulevard was nearly as well lighted by hope as it was by streetlamps.

He parked almost a block from the Sign of the Pentagram and walked past the Eyewitness News van, similar vehicles from the news departments of KNBC and KTLA, marked and unmarked police cars, and a coroner's wagon. A crowd had gathered on the sidewalk, including curious locals, punk and gangsta-rap kids who wanted to look like street people but probably lived with their parents in three-hundred-thousand-dollar Valley homes, and sensation-hungry media people with the quick-eyed look that always made them seem (to Dan) like jackals. He pushed through the crowd, saw the beat man from the *Los Angeles Times*, and tried to stay out of the range of the active minicam in front of which a reporter and his crew were filming a segment for the eleven o'clock news on Channel Four. Dan edged past a teenage girl with blue-and-green-striped hair twisted into punk spikes; she was wearing knee-high black boots, a minuscule red skirt, and a white sweater with a bizarre pattern of dead babies. The entire front of the shop was covered with amateurishly painted but colorful occult and astrological symbols, and a uniformed LAPD officer was standing directly under a faded red pentagram, guarding the entrance. Dan flashed his badge and went inside.

The extent of the wreckage was familiar. The berserk giant who had smashed his way though that house in Studio City last night had come down his beanstalk again and had stomped through this shop as well. The electronic cash register looked as if someone had slammed a sledge-hammer into it; somehow, a current of life remained in its battered circuitry, and one red number flickered in its cracked digital readout window, an inconstant 6, which seemed analogous to a dying victim's last word, as if the cash register were trying to tell the cops something about its killer. Some of the bookshelves were splintered, and all the volumes were on the floor in mangled heaps of rumpled dust jackets and bent covers and torn pages. But books hadn't been the only mer-chandise offered by the Sign of the Pentagram, and the floor was also littered with candles of all shapes and sizes and colors, Tarot decks, broken Ouija boards, a couple of stuffed owls, totems, tikis, and hun-dreds of exotic powders and oils. The place smelled of attar of roses, strawberry incense, and death.

Detectives Wexlersh and Manuello were among the cops and SID technicians in the shop, and they spotted Dan as soon as he entered. They headed toward him, wading through the debris. Their icy smiles were identical, with no humor in either of them. They were a couple of land sharks, as cold-blooded and predatory as any real sharks in any sea.

Wexlersh was short with pale gray eyes and a waxy white face that seemed out of place in California even in winter. He said, "What hap-pened to your head?"

"Walked into a low tree branch," Dan said.

"Looks more like you were beating up some poor innocent suspect, violating his civil rights, and the poor innocent suspect was foolish enough to resist."

"Is that how you handle suspects in the East Valley Division?"

"Or maybe it was a hooker who wouldn't come across with a free sample just 'cause you flashed your badge at her," Wexlersh said, grinning broadly.

"You shouldn't try to be amusing," Dan told him. "You have about as much wit as a toilet seat."

Wexlersh continued to smile, but his gray eyes were mean. "Haldane, what kind of maniac you think we have on our hands here?"

Manuello, in spite of his name, was not Hispanic in appearance, but tall and blond and square-featured, with a Kirk Douglas dimple in the center of his chin. He said, "Yeah, Haldane, share with us the wisdom of your experience."

And Wexlersh said, "Yeah. You're the lieutenant. We've just lowly detectives, first-grade."

"Yes, please, we await your observations and your profound insights into this most heinous crime," Manuello said mockingly. "We are breathless with anticipation."

Although Dan was a superior officer, they could get away with this sort of petty insubordination because they were from the East Valley Division, not Central, where Dan usually worked, and most of all because they were Ross Mondale's pets and knew the captain would protect them.

Dan said, "You know, you two made the wrong career decision. I'm sure you'd be much happier breaking the law than enforcing it."

"But really, now, Lieutenant," said Wexlersh, "you must have some theories by this time. What sort of maniac would go around beating people into piles of strawberry preserves?"

"For that matter," Manuello said, "what sort of maniac was this particular *victim*?"

"Joseph Scaldone?" Dan said. "He ran this place, right? What do you mean, he was a maniac?"

"Well," Wexlersh said, "he sure to God wasn't your ordinary businessman."

"Don't think they'd have wanted him in the Chamber of Commerce," Manuello said.

"Or the Better Business Bureau," Wexlersh said.

"A definite lunatic," Manuello said.

"What are you two babbling about?" Dan asked.

Manuello said, "Don't you think it'd take a lunatic to run a shop"—and reached into a coat pocket, withdrew a small bottle the same size and shape as those that olives often came in—"a shop selling stuff like this."

At first the bottle did, indeed, appear to contain small olives, but then Dan realized they were eyeballs. Not human eyes. Smaller than that. And strange. Some had yellow irises, some green, some orange, some red, but although they differed in color, they all had approximately the same shape: They were not round irises, as in human and most animal eyes, but oblong, elliptical, supremely wicked.

"Snake eyes," Manuello said, showing him the label.

"And how about this?" Wexlersh said, taking a bottle from his jacket pocket.

This one was filled with a grayish powder. The neatly typed label read BAT GUANO.

"Bat shit," Wexlersh said.

"Powdered bat shit," Manuello said, "smake eyes, tongues of sala-manders, necklaces of garlic, vials of bull blood, magic charms, hexes, and all sorts of other weird crap. What kind of people come in here and buy this stuff, Lieutenant?"

"Witches," Wexlersh said before Dan could speak.

"People who *think* they're witches," Manuello said.

"Warlocks," Wexlersh said.

"People who *think* they're warlocks."

"Weird people," Wexlersh said.

"Maniacs," Manuello said.

"But this place, it accepts Visa and MasterCard," said Wexlersh. "With, of course, acceptable ID."

Manuello said, "Yeah, these days, warlocks and maniacs have Master-Card. Isn't that amazing?"

"They pay off their bat-shit and snake-eye bills in twelve easy monthly installments," Wexlersh said.

"Where's the victim?" Dan asked.

Wexlersh jerked a thumb toward the rear of the shop. "He's back

the door to december   161

there, auditioning for a major role in a sequel to *The Texas Chainsaw Massacre*."

"Hope you guys at Central have strong stomachs," Manuello said as Dan headed toward the back of the store.

"Don't barf in here," Wexlersh said.

"Yeah, no judge is going to allow evidence into court if some cop barfed on it," Manuello said.

Dan ignored them. If he felt like barfing, he'd be sure to do it on Wexlersh and Manuello.

He stepped over a heap of mangled books that were saturated with spilled jasmine oil, and he moved toward the assistant medical examiner who was crouched over a shapeless crimson thing that was the last of Joseph Scaldone.

•

Working on the theory that the calico cat might have detected a stealthy sound too soft to be detected by human hearing and might have been frightened by the presence of an intruder in another part of the house, Earl Benton went from room to room, checking windows and doors. He searched in closets and behind the larger pieces of furniture. But the house was secure.

He found Pepper in the living room, no longer frightened but wary. The cat was lying on top of the television. She allowed herself to be petted, and she began to purr.

"What got into you, puss?" he asked.

After being petted awhile, she stretched one leg over the side of the TV and pointed at the controls with one paw. She gave him a look that seemed to inquire if he would be so kind as to switch on the heater-with-pictures-and-voices, so her chosen perch would warm up a bit.

Leaving the TV off, he returned to the kitchen. Melanie was still sitting at the table, as animated as a carrot.

Laura was at the counter where Earl had left her, still holding a knife. She didn't seem to have been working on dinner while he'd been gone. She'd just been waiting, knife in hand, in case someone else returned in Earl's place.

She was obviously relieved when she saw him, and she put the knife down. "Well?"

"Nothing."

The refrigerator door suddenly came open of its own volition. The jars, bottles, and other items on the glass shelves began to wobble and rattle. As though touched by invisible hands, several cupboard doors flew open.

Laura gasped.

Instinctively, Earl reached for the gun in his holster, but he had no one to shoot at. He stopped with his hand on the butt of the weapon, feeling slightly foolish and more than a little perplexed.

Dishes jiggled and clattered on the shelves. A calendar, hanging on the wall by the back door, fell to the floor with a sound like frantic wings.

After ten or fifteen seconds, which seemed like an hour, the dishes stopped rattling, and the cupboard doors stopped swinging on their hinges, and the contents of the refrigerator grew still.

"Earthquake," Earl said.

"Was it?" Laura McCaffrey said doubtfully.

He knew what she meant. It had been similar to the effects of a moderate earthquake yet . . . somehow *different*. An odd pressure change had seemed to condense the air, and the sudden chill had been too harsh to be attributed entirely to the open refrigerator door. In fact, when the trembling stopped, the air warmed up in an instant, even though the refrigerator door was still open.

But if not a quake, what had it been? Not a sonic boom. That wouldn't explain the chill or the pressure in the air. Not a ghost. He didn't believe in ghosts. And where the hell had such a thought come from, anyway? He'd run *Poltergeist* on his VCR a couple nights ago. Maybe that was it. But he was not so impressionable that one good scary movie would make him reach for a supernatural explanation here, now, when a considerably less exotic answer was so evident.

"Just an earthquake," he assured her, although he was far from convinced of that.

•

They figured he was Joseph Scaldone, the owner, because all the paper in his wallet was for Scaldone. But until they got a dental-records confirmation or a fingerprint match, the wallet was the only way they could peg him. No one who knew Scaldone would be able to make a visual identification because the poor bastard didn't have a face left. There wasn't even much hope of getting an ID based on scars or on other identifying marks, because the body was smashed and torn and flayed and gouged so badly that old scars or birthmarks were lost in the bloody ruins. Splintered ribs poked up through holes in his shirt, and a jagged lance of bone had pierced both his leg and trousers.

He looked . . . squashed.

Turning from the body, Dan encountered a man whose biological clock seemed to be suffering from chronological confusion. The guy had the smooth, unlined wide-open face of a thirty-year-old, the graying hair of a fifty-year-old, and the age-rounded shoulders of a retiree. He wore a well-cut dark blue suit, a white shirt, a dark blue tie, and a gold tie chain instead of a clip or tack. He said, "You're Haldane?"

"That's right."

"Michael Seames, FBI."

They shook hands. Seames's hand was cold and clammy. They moved away from the corpse, into a corner that was clear of debris.

"Are you guys on this one now?" Dan asked.

"Don't worry. We aren't pushing you out of it," Seames assured him diplomatically. "We just want to be part of it. Just observers . . . for the time being."

"Good," Dan said bluntly.

"I've talked to everyone else working on the case, so I just wanted to tell you what I've told them. Please keep me informed. Any development at all, no matter how unimportant it seems, I want to be informed."

"But what justification does the FBI have for stepping into this at all?"

"Justification?" Seames's face creased with a pained smile. "Whose side are you on, Lieutenant?"

"I mean, what federal statutes have been broken?"

"Let's just say it's a national-security matter."

In the middle of his young face, Seames's eyes were old, ancient, and watchful. They were like the eyes of a reptilian hunter that had been around since the Mesozoic Era and knew all the tricks.

Dan said, "Hoffritz used to work for the Pentagon. Did research for them."

"That's right."

"Was he doing defense research when he was killed?"

"No."

The agent's voice was flat, without emotion or inflection, and Dan couldn't be sure if he was lying or telling the truth.

"McCaffrey?" Dan asked. "Was *he* doing defense-type research?"

"Not for us," Seames said. "At least not lately."

"For someone else?"

"Maybe."

"Russians?"

"More likely to be Iraq or Libya or Iran these days."

"You're saying it was one of them who financed him?"

"I'm saying no such thing. We don't know," Seames claimed in that same bland voice that might easily conceal deception. "That's why we want in on this. McCaffrey *was* on a Pentagon-funded project when he disappeared six years ago with his daughter. We investigated him back then, at the request of the Defense Department, and decided he hadn't run off with any new, valuable information related to his research. We figured it was nothing more than what it seemed to be—entirely a personal matter having to do with a nasty child-custody dispute."

"Maybe it was."

"Yes, maybe it was," Seames said. "At first, anyway. But after a while McCaffrey apparently got involved in something important . . . maybe something dangerous. At least that's certainly how it seems when you get a look at that gray room in Studio City. As for Willy Hoffritz . . . eighteen months after McCaffrey disappeared, Hoffritz finished a long-running Pentagon project and declined to accept any additional defense-related work. He said that kind of research had begun to bother his conscience. At the time, the military tried to persuade him to change his mind, but eventually they accepted his refusal."

"From what I know of him," Dan said, "I don't believe Hoffritz *had* a conscience."

Seames's penetrating, hawkish eyes never left Dan's. He said, "You're right about that, I think. At the time Hoffritz did his mea culpa routine, the Defense Department didn't ask us to verify his sudden turn toward pacifism. They accepted it at face value. But today I've been looking more closely at Willy Hoffritz. I'm convinced he stopped taking Pentagon grants only because he no longer wanted to be subject to random, periodic security investigations. He didn't want to worry that anyone might be watching him. He needed anonymity for some project of his own."

"Like torturing a nine-year-old girl," Dan said.

"Yes. I was in Studio City a few hours ago, had a look in that house. Nasty."

Neither the expression on his face nor that in his eyes matched the distaste and disapproval in his voice. Judging from his eyes, in fact, one might suspect that Michael Seames found the gray room more interesting than repulsive.

Dan said, "Why do you think they were doing those things to Melanie McCaffrey?"

"I don't know. Bizarre stuff," Seames said, wide-eyed, shaking his head with amazement. But his sudden expression of innocence seemed calculated.

"What effect were they trying to obtain?"

"I don't know."

"They weren't just involved in behavior-modification studies at that house."

Seames shrugged.

Dan said, "They were into brainwashing, total mind control . . . and something else . . . something worse."

Seames appeared to be bored. His gaze drifted away from Dan, and he watched the SID technicians as they sifted through the blood-spattered rubble.

Dan said, "But why?"

"I really don't know," Seames said again, impatiently this time. "I only—"

"But you're desperate to find out who was funding this whole hellish project," Dan said.

"I wouldn't say desperate. I'd say *frantic*. Quietly frantic."

"Then you must have *some* idea of what they were up to. You know something that's *making* you frantic."

"For Christ's sake, Haldane," Seames said angrily, but even his anger seemed calculated, a ruse, calculated misdirection. "You've seen the condition of the bodies. Prominent scientists, formerly funded by the Pentagon, wind up murdered in an inexplicable fashion . . . hell, of course, we're interested!"

"Inexplicable?" Dan said. "It's not inexplicable. They were beaten to death."

"Come on, Haldane. It's more complicated than that. If you've talked to your own coroner's office, you've learned they can't figure out what the hell kind of weapon it was. And you've learned the victims never had a chance to fight back—no blood, skin, or hair under their fingernails. And many of the blows couldn't have been struck by a man wielding a club, because no man would have the strength to crush another man's bones like that. It would take tremendous force, mechanical force . . . inhuman force. They weren't just beaten to death, *they were smashed like bugs*! And what about the doors here?"

Dan frowned. "What doors?"

"Here, this shop, the front and back doors."

"What about them?"

"You don't know?"

"I just got here. I've hardly talked with anyone."

Seames nervously adjusted his tie, and Dan was unsettled by the sight of a nervous FBI agent. He had never seen one before. And Michael Seames's nervousness was one thing that he didn't appear to be faking.

"The doors were locked when your people arrived," the agent said. "Scaldone had closed up for the day just before he was killed. The back door had probably been locked all along, but just before he was killed, he'd closed the front door, locked it as well, and pulled down the shade. He would most likely have left the place by the rear door—his car's out back—once he'd finished totaling the day's receipts. But he didn't finish. He was hit while the doors were still locked. First officer on the scene had to kick out the lock on the front door."

"So?"

"So only the victim was inside," Seames said. "Both doors were locked when the first cops arrived, but the killer wasn't here with Scaldone."

"What's so amazing about that? It just means the killer must have had a key."

"And paused to lock up after himself when he left?"

"It's possible."

Seames shook his head. "Not if you know how the doors were locked. In addition to a pair of dead bolts on each, there was a bolt latch, a manually operated bolt latch that could be engaged only from *inside* the shop."

"Bolt latches on both doors?" Dan asked.

"Yes. And there're only two windows in the shop. The big show window there, which is fixed in place. Nobody could leave that way without first throwing a brick through it. The other window is in the back room, the office. It's a jalousie window for ventilation."

"Big enough for a man?"

"Yes," Seames said. "Except there're bars on the inside of it."

"Bars?"

"Bars."

"Then there must be another way out."

"You find it," Seames said in a tone of voice that meant that it couldn't be found.

Dan surveyed the wreckage again, put a hand to his face as if he might be able to wipe off his weariness, and winced as his fingertips brushed the still-sticky wound on his forehead. "You're telling me Scaldone was beaten to death in a locked room."

"Killed in a locked room, yes. I'm still not sure about the 'beaten' part."

"And there's no way the killer could have gotten out of here before the first squad car arrived?"

"No way."

"Yet he isn't here now."

"Right." Seames's too-young face seemed to be straining toward a more harmonious relationship with his graying hair and his stooped shoulders: It appeared to have aged a few years in just the past ten minutes. "You see why I'm frantic, Lieutenant Haldane? I'm frantic because two top-notch former defense researchers have been killed by persons or forces unknown, by a weapon that can reach through locked doors or solid walls and against which there seems to be absolutely no defense."

•

Something about it had been different from an earthquake, but Laura couldn't precisely define the difference. Well, for one thing, she couldn't remember the windows rattling, although in an earthquake strong enough to fling open the cupboard doors, the windows would have been thrumming, clattering. She'd had no sense of motion either, no rolling; of course, if they had been far enough from the epicenter, ground movement wouldn't have been easy to detect. The air had felt strange, oppressive, not stuffy or humid, but . . . charged. She'd been through a number of quakes before, and she didn't remember the air feeling like that. But something else still argued against the earthquake explanation, something important on which she couldn't quite put her finger.

Earl returned to the table and newspaper, and Melanie continued to stare down at her hands. Laura finished making the salad. She put it in the refrigerator to chill while the spaghetti was cooking.

The water had begun to boil. Steam plumed from it.

Laura was just taking the vermicelli out of the Ronzoni box when Earl glanced up from the newspaper and said, "Hey, that explains the cat!"

Laura didn't understand. "Huh?"

"They say animals usually know when an earthquake is coming. They get nervous and act strange. Maybe that's why Pepper got hysterical and chased ghosts all over the kitchen."

Before Laura even had time to consider what Earl had said, the radio clicked on as if an unseen hand had twisted the knob. Living by herself, as she had for the past six years, Laura sometimes found the silence and emptiness of the house to be more than she could bear, and she kept radios in several rooms. The one in the kitchen, by the bread box, only a few feet away from where Laura was standing, was a Sony AM-FM with a clock, and when it snapped on all by itself, it was tuned to KRLA, where she had set the dial the last time that she'd used it. Bonnie Tyler was singing "Total Eclipse of the Heart."

Earl had put down his paper. He was standing again.

Laura stared at the radio in disbelief.

Of its own accord, the volume knob began to rotate to the right. She could see it moving.

Bonnie Tyler's throaty voice grew louder, louder.

Earl said, "What the hell?"

Melanie drifted unaware in her private darkness.

The voice of Bonnie Tyler and the music enfolding her words now bounced back and forth off the kitchen walls and made the windows rattle in a way that the "earthquake" hadn't done.

Aware that a chill had settled over the room once more, Laura took a step toward the radio.

In another part of the house, Pepper was screeching again.

•

As Dan was turning away from Michael Seames, the FBI agent said, "By the way, what happened to your forehead?"

"I was trying on hats," Dan said.

"Hats?"

"Tried on one that was too small for me. Had a hell of a time getting it off. Pulled skin right along with it."

Before Seames could respond, Ross Mondale stepped through a door at the back of the store, behind the sales counter. He spotted Dan, and he said, "Haldane, come here."

"What is it, Chief?"

"I want to talk to you."

"What about, Chief?"

"Alone," Mondale said fiercely.

"Be right there, Chief."

He left Seames blinking and puzzled. He picked his way through the wreckage, past the corpse, around the counter. Mondale motioned him through the door back there, then followed him.

The rear room was as wide as the store but only ten feet deep, with concrete-block walls. It doubled as an office and storage area. On the left were piles of boxes, apparently filled with merchandise. On the right were a desk, an IBM PC, a few file cabinets, a small refrigerator, and a worktable on which stood a Mr. Coffee machine. No violence had been done there; everything was neat and orderly.

Mondale had been going through the desk drawers. Several items, including a slim little address book, were piled on the blotter.

As the captain closed the door, Dan went around behind the desk and sat down.

"What do you think you're doing?" Mondale asked.

"Taking a load off my feet. It's been a long day."

"You know that's not what I mean."

"Oh?"

As usual, Mondale was wearing a brown suit, light beige shirt, brown tie, brown socks and shoes. His brown eyes seemed to flicker with a murderous light similar to that refracted within his ruby ring. "I wanted to see you in my office by two thirty."

"I never got your message."

"I know damn well you did."

"No. Really. I'd have come running."

"Don't screw with me."

Dan just stared at him.

The captain stood several steps from the desk, his neck stiff, his shoulders tense, arms straight down at his sides, hands flexing and twitching as if he had to struggle to keep from forming them into fists and coming for Haldane. "What have you been doing all day?"

"Contemplating the meaning of life."

"You were at Rink's place."

"You don't need to be in a church. It's possible to contemplate the meaning of life almost anywhere."

"I didn't send you to Rink's place."

"I'm a full-fledged detective-lieutenant. I usually follow my own instincts in an investigation."

"Not in this one. This one's big. In this one, you're just part of the team. You do what I tell you, go where I tell you. You don't even shit unless I tell you it's okay."

"Careful, Ross. You're beginning to sound power crazy."

"What happened to your head?"

"I've been taking karate lessons."

"What?"

"Tried to break a board with my head."

"Like hell."

"Okay, then what happened was George Padrakis told me you wanted to see me here, and at the mention of your name, I dropped right to my knees and bowed down so fast I scraped my head on the sidewalk."

For a moment Ross couldn't speak. His brown face had flushed. He was breathing hard.

Dan more closely examined the items that Mondale had taken from the drawers and piled on the blotter: the address book, a ledger-size checkbook for an account in the name of the Sign of the Pentagram, an appointments calendar, and a thick sheaf of invoices. He picked up the address book.

"Put that down and listen to me," Mondale said sharply, finally recovering his voice.

Dan favored him with a sweet smile of innocence and said, "But it might contain a clue, Captain. I'm investigating this case, and I wouldn't be doing my job well if I didn't pursue every possible clue."

Mondale came toward the desk, furious. His hands had finally tightened into twin hammers of flesh and bone.

Ah, at last, Dan thought, the showdown we've both been wanting for years.

•

Laura stood in front of the Sony, staring at it, afraid to touch it, shivering in the chilly air. The cold seemed to be radiating from the radio, carried on the pale green light that shone forth from the AM-FM dial.

That was a crazy thought.

It was a radio, not an air conditioner. Not a . . . Not anything. Just a radio. An ordinary radio.

An ordinary radio that had turned itself on without help from anyone.

Bonnie Tyler's song had faded into a new tune. It was a golden oldie: Procul Harum singing "A Whiter Shade of Pale." That was at top volume too. The radio vibrated against the tile counter on which it stood. The thunderous song reverberated in the windows, hurting Laura's ears.

Earl had moved up behind her.

If Pepper was still squealing in another part of the house, the cat's voice was lost in the explosively loud music.

Hesitantly, Laura put her fingers on the volume knob. Freezing. Shuddering, she nearly snatched her hand away, not simply because the plastic was impossibly cold but because it was a different kind of coldness from any she'd felt before, a strangeness that chilled not only the flesh but the mind and soul as well. Nevertheless, she held on to it and tried to reduce the volume, but the knob wouldn't budge. She couldn't turn Procul Harum down, and since the volume control was also the on-off switch, she couldn't shut the music off either. She strained hard, felt the muscles bunching in her arm, but still the knob would not respond.

She was shaking.

She let go of the knob.

Although "Whiter Shade of Pale" was a melodic and appealing song, it sounded harsh and even curiously ominous at that volume. Each thump of the drums was like the approaching footsteps of some threatening creature, and the wailing of the horns was the same beast's hostile cries.

She grabbed the cord of the radio, jerked on it. The plug popped out of the wall socket.

The music died instantly.

She had been half afraid that it would go on playing, even without power.

•

When Dan didn't put down Joseph Scaldone's address book—a pocket-size booklet, actually—Mondale reached across the desk, clamped his right hand over Dan's right hand, and squeezed hard, trying to make him drop the thing.

Mondale was not a tall man, but he was thick in the shoulders and chest. He had powerful arms out of proportion to the rest of him, thick wrists, big hands. He was strong.

Dan was stronger. He didn't let go of the address book. His eyes fixed unwaveringly on Mondale's eyes, and he put his left hand on Mondale's hand and tried to pry the bastard's fingers loose.

The situation was ludicrous. They were like a couple of idiot teenagers determined to prove that they were macho: Mondale trying to crush Dan's right hand, and Dan refusing to flinch or in any way reveal his pain while he struggled to free himself.

He got a grip on one of Mondale's fingers and began to bend it backward.

Mondale's jaw clenched. The muscles popped up, quivering.

The finger bent back and back. Mondale resisted that effort even as he attempted to apply a stronger grip to Dan's right hand, but Dan wouldn't relent, and the finger bent back farther, farther.

Sweat had appeared on Mondale's brow.

My dog's better than your dog, my mom's prettier than your mom, Dan thought. Jesus! How old are we, anyway. Fourteen? Twelve?

But he kept his eyes on Mondale's eyes, and he refused to let the captain see that he was hurting. He bent that goddamned finger back farther, until he was sure that it would snap, then farther, and abruptly Mondale gasped and let go.

Dan remained in possession of the address book.

He kept a grip on Mondale's finger for a second or two, long enough so there could be no mistake about who had relented first. The contest had been silly and juvenile, but that was no reason to believe Ross Mondale didn't take it seriously. He was dead serious. And if the captain thought he could teach Dan a lesson with physical force, then perhaps—just perhaps—he could *learn* a lesson himself by the same method of instruction.

•

They stood in the silent kitchen, staring at the radio. Then Earl said, "How could it—"

"I don't know," Laura said.

"Has it ever—"

"Never."

The radio had ceased to be a harmless appliance. Now it was a brooding, menacing presence.

Earl said, "Plug it in again."

Laura was irrationally afraid that if they brought the radio back to life, it would sprout crablike legs of plastic and begin to crawl across the counter. That was an uncharacteristically bizarre thought, and she was surprised at herself, startled by the sudden rush of superstitious dread, for she thought of herself as a woman of science, always logical and reasonable. Yet she couldn't shake the feeling that some malignant force was still within the radio, and that it waited eagerly for the plug to be reinserted in the wall socket.

Nonsense.

Nevertheless, stalling, she said, "Plug it in? Why?"

"Well," Earl said, "I want to see what it does. We can't just leave it like this. It's too damned weird. We've got to figure it out."

Laura knew he was right. Hesitantly, she reached for the cord. She half expected it to wriggle in her hand and feel slimy-cold like an eel. But it was only a power cord: lifeless, nothing unusual about it.

She touched the volume control on the radio, and she found that it could be moved now. She twisted it all the way down, clicked it to the OFF position.

With considerable apprehension, she put the plug in the socket again.

Nothing.

Five seconds. Ten. Fifteen.

Earl said, "Well, whatever it was—"

The radio snapped on.

The dial lit up.

The air was arctic again.

Laura stepped away from the counter, backed toward the table, afraid that the radio would fling itself at her. She stopped beside Melanie and put one hand on the girl's shoulder, to reassure her, but Melanie appeared to be as oblivious of these strange events as she was of everything else.

The volume dial moved. This time, the dial didn't peg out at the top, but stopped halfway. The latest piece of gangsta-rap thumped from the radio. The beat-heavy music was loud, although not unbearable.

Another knob spun as if an invisible hand were adjusting it. This one was the frequency selector. The red indicator dot glided fast across the luminous green dial, leaving the rap song behind, flitting rapidly to the right end of the scale, bringing them only flashes of songs, commercials, news reports, and deejay voices on a score of other stations. It reached the end of the radio band and moved back to the left, all the way, then swept to the right again, faster, so that the snatches of various broadcasts blended together in an eerie electronic ululation.

Earl moved closer to the Sony.

"Careful," Laura said.

She realized it was ridiculous to be warning him about a mere radio. It was an inanimate object, for God's sake, not a living creature. She'd owned it for three or four years. It had brought her music and kept her company. It was only a radio.

•

When Mondale got his hand back, he didn't rub it or even try to flex the pain out of it. Like a simpleminded high school jock with wounded pride, he went right on pretending that he was the toughest. He casually put his hand in his pocket, as if checking for change or keys, and he kept it there.

He poked his other hand toward Dan, pointed a finger at him. "Don't you screw this up for me, Haldane. This is an important case. It's going to mean heat, lots of heat. We're gonna feel like we're working in a damned furnace. I've got the press nipping at my heels and the FBI on my back, and I've already had calls from the mayor and from Chief Kelsey, wanting results. I don't intend to screw this one up. My career might ride on this one. I'm keeping *control*, Haldane, tight control. I'm not letting some hotshot Lone Ranger type put my ass in a sling *for* me. If my ass ends up in a sling, it'll be because *I* put it there. This is a team effort, see, and I'm the captain and coach and quarterback, all rolled into one, and anybody who *can't* play it as a team effort just isn't even going to get on the field. You got me?"

So this wasn't going to be the final showdown, after all. Ross was just going to bluster and fume. He felt tough and important when he could point his finger at a subordinate, glower, and chew ass for a while.

Dan sighed with some disappointment and leaned back in the office chair, folding his hands behind his head. "Furnaces, football fields . . . Ross, you're getting your metaphors mixed up. Face it, old buddy, you'll never be an inspiring speaker . . . or a disciplinarian. General Patton, you ain't."

Glaring at him, Mondale said, "At Chief Kelsey's request, I'm putting together a special task force to handle this case, just like they did for the Hillside Strangler business several years back. All assignments come straight from me, and I'm assigning you to a desk at HQ for the duration. You'll coordinate the files on some aspects of the investigation."

"I'm not a desk man."

"Now you are."

"I'm deskophobic. You force me to work at a desk, I'll have a complete nervous breakdown. It's going to mean a major worker's compensation claim."

"Don't screw with me," Mondale warned again.

"I'm scared of desk blotters too—and those can-type holders for pencils just spook the bejesus out of me. So I thought, first thing tomorrow, I'd start looking into this Freedom Now group and maybe—"

"Wexlersh and Manuello are going to handle that," Mondale said. "They'll also be talking to the head of the psychology department at UCLA. But *you* will be at your desk, Haldane—at your desk, doing what you're told."

Dan didn't reveal that he had already been to UCLA and that he'd spoken with Irmatrude Heidi Gelkenshettle. He wasn't giving Mondale anything right now.

Instead, he said, "Wexlersh is no detective. Hell, he has to paint his pecker bright yellow so he can find it when he has to pee. And Manuello drinks."

"The hell he does," Mondale said sharply.

"He drinks on duty more often than not."

"He's an excellent detective," Mondale insisted.

"Your definition of 'excellent' is the same as your definition of 'obedient.' You like Manuello because he sucks up to you. You're a tremendous self-promoter, Ross, but you're a lousy cop and a worse leader. For your sake as much as anyone's, I'm going to have to ignore the desk assignment you've given me and play the investigation my own way."

"That's it, you insolent bastard. That's *it*! You're through. You're finished here. I'll call your boss. I'll call Templeton, and have him yank your insubordinate ass back to Central, where you belong!"

The captain swung away from Dan and started toward the door. Dan said, "If you make Templeton pull me off this assignment, I'll have to tell him—and everyone else—about Cindy Lakey."

Mondale stopped with his hand on the doorknob, breathing hard, but he didn't face Dan.

To Mondale's back, Dan said, "I'll have to tell them how little Cindy Lakey, that poor little eight-year-old girl, would still be alive today, a young woman now, maybe married with a girl of her own, if it wasn't for you."

•

Laura stayed at Melanie's side, one hand on the girl's shoulder, ready to grab her and run if it came to that.

Earl Benton leaned close to the radio and seemed mesmerized by the magically spinning knob and the floating red station selector that whipped back and forth across the lighted dial.

Abruptly the red dot stopped, but only for a moment, only long enough to let a deejay speak one word—

". . . something's . . ."

—and then spun across the dial and stopped again at another frequency. Again it only dipped into the announcer's patter for a single word—

". . . coming . . ."

—then zipped farther along the glowing green band, paused once more, this time plucking one word out of the middle of a song—

". . . something's . . ."

—then spun away to a new station, popped into the middle of an advertisement—

". . . coming . . ."

—and swept on down the band again.

Laura suddenly realized there was an intelligent purpose to the pauses of the frequency selector.

We're being sent a message, she thought.

Something's coming.

But a message from whom? From where?

Earl looked at her, and the astonishment on his face made it clear that the same questions were in his mind.

She wanted to move, run, get out of here. She could not lift her feet. Her bones had locked at every joint. Her muscles had petrified.

The red dot stopped moving for no more than a second, perhaps only a fraction of a second. This time Laura recognized the tune from which the word was plucked. The Beatles were singing. Before the red dot continued on its way, the single word that came from the radio's speaker was also the title of the song: "Something . . ."

The selector glided farther along the green-lit band, paused for an instant: ". . . is . . ."

It slipped off that station, sped to another: ". . . coming . . ."

The air was frigid, but that wasn't the only reason Laura was shivering.

Something . . . is . . . coming. . . .

Those three words were not merely a message. They were a warning.

•

Without opening it, Mondale had turned away from the door that connected the late Joseph Scaldone's office to the sales room at the Sign of the Pentagram. He faced Dan again, and both his anger and indignation had given way to a more fundamental emotion. Now his face was carved and his eyes were colored by pure hatred.

Dan had mentioned Cindy Lakey for the first time in more than thirteen years. This was the dirty secret that they shared, the ever-spreading malignancy at the core of their relationship. Now, having brought it into the open, Dan was exhilarated by the prospect of forcing Mondale to face up to the consequences of his actions at long last.

In a low, intense voice, the captain said, "I didn't kill Cindy Lakey, damn it!"

"You allowed it to happen when you could have prevented it."

"I'm not God," Mondale said bitterly.

"You're a cop. You have responsibilities."

"You smug bastard."

"You're sworn to protect the public."

"Yeah? Really? Well, the fuckin' public never cries over a dead cop," Mondale said, still speaking softly in spite of his ferocity, guarding this conversation from the ears of those in the nearby shop.

"You've also got a duty to stand up for a buddy, to protect your partner's backside."

"You sound like some half-baked little Boy Scout," Mondale said scornfully. "*Esprit de corps.* One for all and all for one. Crap! When it gets down to the nitty-gritty, it's always every man for himself, and you know it."

Already, Dan wished he had never mentioned Cindy Lakey's name. The exhilaration that had lifted him a moment ago was gone. In fact, his spirits sank lower than they had been. He felt bone weary. He had intended to make Mondale face up to his responsibilities after all these years, but it was too late. It had always been too late, because Mondale had never been the kind of man who could admit weakness or error. He always slipped out from under his mistakes or found a way to make others pay his penance for him. His record was clean, spotless, and probably would always remain spotless, not just in the eyes of most others but in his own eyes as well. He couldn't even admit his weaknesses and errors to himself. Ross Mondale was incapable of guilt or self-reproach. Right now, standing before Dan, he clearly felt no responsibility or remorse for what had happened to Cindy Lakey; the only emotion boiling through him now was irrational hatred directed at his ex-partner.

Mondale said, "If anyone was responsible for the death of that girl, it was her own mother."

Dan didn't want to continue the battle. He was as weary as a centenarian who had danced away his birthday night.

Mondale said, "Crucify her goddamned mother, not me."

Dan said nothing.

Mondale said, "Her mother was the one who dated Felix Dunbar in the first place."

Staring at the captain as if he were a pile of some noxious and not-quite-identifiable substance found on a city sidewalk, Dan said, "Are you actually telling me Fran Lakey should have known Dunbar was unstable?"

"Hell, yes."

"He was a nice guy, by all accounts."

"Blew her fuckin' head off, didn't he?" Mondale said.

"Owned his own business. Well dressed. No criminal record. A steady churchgoer. By all appearances, he was a regular upstanding citizen."

"Upstanding citizens don't blow people's heads off. Fran Lakey was dating a loser, a creep, a real screwball. From what I heard later, she dated a lot of guys, and most of them were losers. She put her daughter's life in danger, not me."

Dan watched Mondale the way he might have watched a particularly ugly bug crawl across a dinner table. "Are you saying she should have been able to see the future? Was she supposed to know that her boyfriend would go off his rocker when she finally broke up with him? Was she supposed to know he would come to her house with a gun and try to kill her and her daughter just because she wouldn't go to a movie with him? If she could see the future that well, Ross, she'd have put every psychic and palm reader and crystal-ball gazer out of business. She'd have been famous."

"She put her daughter's life in danger," Mondale insisted.

Dan leaned forward, hunching over the desk, lowering his voice further. "If she could've seen into the future, she would have known it wouldn't help to call the cops that night. She'd have known you'd be one

the door to december   181

of the officers answering the call, and she'd have known you'd choke up, and—"

"I didn't choke up," Mondale said. He took a step toward the desk, but as a threatening gesture it was ineffective.

•

"Something's . . . coming. . . ."

Fascinated, Earl watched the radio.

Laura looked at the door that opened onto the patio and the rear lawn. It was locked. So were the windows. The blinds were drawn. If something did come, where would it come from? And what would it be, for God's sake, *what would it be?*

The radio said: "Watch . . ." Then: "Out . . ."

Laura fixated on the open door to the dining room. Whatever was coming might already be in the house. Maybe it would come from the living room, through the dining room. . . .

The frequency selector stopped again, and a deejay's voice boomed through the speaker. It was swift patter with no purpose but to fill a few seconds of dead air between tunes, yet for Laura it had an unintended ominous quality: "Better beware out there, my rock-'n'-roll munchkins, better beware, 'cause it's a strange world, a mean and cold world, with things that go bump in the night, and all you got to protect you is your Cousin Frankie, that's me, so if you don't keep that dial where it is, if you change stations now, you better beware, better be on the lookout for the gnarly old goblins who live under the bed, the ones who fear nothing but the voice of Uncle Frankie. Better look out!"

Earl put one hand on top of the radio, and Laura half expected a mouth to open in the plastic and bite off his fingers.

"Cold," he said as the tuning knob moved toward another station.

Laura shook Melanie. "Honey, come on, get up."

The girl didn't stir.

One clear word burst from the radio as the tuning knob stopped again in the middle of a news report: ". . . murder . . ."

•

Dan wished that he could magically transport himself out of the dreary spook-shop office and into Saul's Delicatessen, where he could order a huge Reuben sandwich and drink a few bottles of Beck's Dark. If he couldn't have Saul's, he'd settle for Jack-in-the-Box. If he couldn't have Jack-in-the-Box, then he'd rather be at home, washing the dirty dishes that he had left in the kitchen. Anywhere but in a confrontation with Ross Mondale. Dredging up the past was pointless and depressing.

But it was too late to stop now. They had to go through the whole Lakey killing again, pick at it as if it were a scab, peel and pick and pluck at it to see if the wound was healed underneath. And of course that was a waste of time and emotional resources, for both of them knew already that it wasn't healed and never would be.

Dan said, "After Dunbar shot me there on the front lawn of the Lakey house—"

"I suppose that was my fault too," Mondale said.

"No," Dan said. "I shouldn't have tried to rush him. I didn't think he'd use the gun, and I was wrong. But after he shot me, Ross, he was stunned for a moment, stupefied by what he'd done, and he was vulnerable."

"Bullshit. He was as vulnerable as a runaway Sherman tank. He was a maniac, a flat-out lunatic, and he had the biggest goddamned pistol—"

"A thirty-two," Dan corrected. "There're bigger guns. Every cop comes up against bigger guns than that, all the time. And he was vulnerable for a moment, plenty long enough for you to take the son of a bitch."

"You know one thing I always hated about you, Haldane?"

Ignoring him, Dan said, "But you ran."

"I always hated that wide, wide streak of self-righteousness."

"If he'd wanted to, Dunbar could have put another slug in me. No one to stop him after you ran off behind the house."

"As if you never made a mistake in your goddamned life."

They were both almost whispering now.

"But instead he walked away from me—"

"As if *you* were never afraid."

"—and he shot the lock off the front door—"

"You want to play the hero, go ahead. You and Audie Murphy. You and Jesus Christ."

"—and he went inside and pistol-whipped Fran Lakey—"

"I hate your guts."

"—and then made her watch—"

"You make me sick."

"—while he killed the one person in the world she really loved," Dan said.

He was being relentless now because there was no way to stop until it had all been said. He wished he had never begun, wished he'd left it buried, but now that he had started, he had to finish. Because he was like the Ancient Mariner in that old poem. Because he had to purge himself of an unrelenting nightmare. Because he was *driven* to follow it to the end. Because if he stopped in the middle, the unsaid part would be as bitter as a big wad of vomit in his throat, unheaved, wedged there, and he'd choke on it. Because—and here it was, here was the truth of it, no easy euphemisms this time—after all these years, his own soul was still shackled to a ball of guilt that had been weighing him down since the death of the Lakey child, and maybe if he finally talked about it with Ross Mondale, he might find a key that would release him from that iron ball, those chains.

●

The radio was at full volume again, and each word exploded like one round of a cannonade.

". . . blood . . ."

". . . coming . . ."

". . . run . . ."

More urgently than she had spoken before, afraid of what might be coming, wanting Melanie to be on her feet and ready to flee, Laura said, "Honey, get up, come on."

From the radio: ". . . hide . . ."

And: ". . . it . . ."

And: ". . . coming . . ."

The volume grew louder.

". . . it . . ."

Jarring, earsplitting: ". . . loose . . ."

Earl put his hand on the volume knob.

". . . it . . ."

At once, Earl jerked his hand off the knob as if he had taken an electric shock. He looked at Laura, horrified. He vigorously wiped his hand on his shirt. It hadn't been an electric shock that had sizzled through him; instead, he had felt something weird when he touched the knob, something disgusting, repulsive.

The radio said: ". . . death . . ."

•

Mondale's hatred was a dark and vast swamp into which he could retreat when the uncomfortable truth about Cindy Lakey rose to haunt him. As the truth drew nearer and pressed upon him more insistently, he withdrew further into his all-encompassing black hatred and hid there amid the snakes and bugs and muck of his psyche.

He continued to glare at Dan, to loom threateningly over the desk, but there was no danger that his hatred would propel him to action. He would not throw a single punch. He didn't need or want to relieve his hatred by striking out at Dan. Instead, he needed to nurture that hatred, for it helped him to hide from responsibility. It was a veil between him and the truth, and the heavier that veil, the better for him.

That was how Mondale's mind worked. Dan knew him well, knew how he thought.

But, though Ross might try to hide from it, the truth was that Felix Dunbar had shot Dan—and Mondale had been too scared to return the fire. The truth was that Dunbar then went inside the Lakey house, pistol-whipped Fran Lakey, and shot eight-year-old Cindy Lakey three times while Ross Mondale was God-knew-where, doing God-knew-what. And the truth was that, wounded and bleeding badly, Dan had retrieved his own gun, crawled into the Lakey house, and killed Felix Dunbar before Dunbar could blow off Fran Lakey's head too. All the while, Ross Mondale was maybe puking in the shrubbery or losing control of his bladder or sprawled flat on the rear lawn and striving hard to look like a natural feature of the landscape. He had come back when it was all over, sweat-damp and slug-white, shaky, reeking of the sour smell of cowardice.

Now, still behind Joseph Scaldone's desk, Dan said, "You try forcing me off this case or you try keeping me out of the action, and I'll tell the whole rotten story about the Lakey shootings, the truth, to anyone who'll listen, and that'll be the end of your dazzling career."

With a smugness that would have been infuriating if it hadn't been so boringly predictable, Mondale said, "If you were going to tell anyone, you'd have told them years ago."

"That must be a comforting thought," Dan said, "but it's wrong. I covered for you then because you were my partner, and I figured everyone has a right to screw up once. But I've lived to regret the way I handled it, and if you give me a good excuse, I'd enjoy setting the record straight."

"It all happened a long time ago," Mondale said.

"You think no one cares about dereliction of duty just because it happened thirteen years ago?"

"No one'll believe you. They'll think it's sour grapes. I've moved up, made friends."

"Yeah. And they're the kind of friends who'd sell their mothers for lunch money."

"You've always been a loner. A wiseass. No matter what you think of them, I have people who'll rally around me."

"With a lynching rope."

"Power makes people loyal, Haldane, even if they'd rather not be. Nobody'll believe any crap you care to throw at me. Not a rotten wiseass like you. Not a chance."

"Ted Gearvy will believe me," Dan said, and if he had spoken any more quietly, he would have been inaudible.

Yet, in spite of his quiet delivery, he might as well have swung a hammer at Mondale instead of those five words. The captain looked stricken.

Gearvy, ten years their senior, was a veteran patrolman and had been

Mondale's partner during his probationary rookie year. He had seen Mondale make a few mistakes—although nothing as serious as what happened at the Lakey house later, when Dan had replaced Gearvy as Mondale's partner. Just disquieting errors of judgment. A too-meager sense of responsibility. Gearvy had thought he detected cowardice in Ross too, but had covered up for him, just as Dan would do in times to come. Gearvy was a big, gruff, easygoing guy, three-quarters Irish, with too much sympathy for rookies. He had not given Mondale high ratings in his rookie year; the Irishman was good natured and sympathetic but not irresponsible. But he didn't give Mondale really bad ratings, either, because he was too softhearted for that.

A few months after the Lakey incident, when Dan was back at work with a new partner, Ted Gearvy had come around, quietly feeling Dan out, dropping hints, worried that he had made a serious mistake in covering up for Ross. Eventually, they had swapped information and discovered they had both been misguidedly shielding Mondale. They realized his misconduct was not just a rare or even a sometime thing. But by then it had seemed too late to come forth with the truth. In the eyes of the department brass, Gearvy's and Dan's failure—even temporary failure—to report Mondale's dereliction of duty would be nearly as bad as that dereliction itself. Gearvy and Dan would have found themselves standing in the dock beside Mondale. They weren't prepared to damage or perhaps even destroy their own careers.

Besides, by then Mondale had wheedled as assignment to the Community Relations Division; he was no longer working on the street. Gearvy and Dan figured Ross would do well in community relations and would never return to a regular beat, in which case he would never again be in a position to hold someone else's life in his hands. It seemed best—and safest—to leave well enough alone.

Neither of them imagined that Mondale would one day be a serious contender for the chief's office. Maybe they would have taken action if they could have foreseen the future. Their failure to act was the thing that both of them most regretted in all their years of service.

Clearly, Mondale had not known that Gearvy and Dan had compared notes. Their consultation was a nasty shock to him.

•

The radio boomed:

"IT!"

"COMING!"

"HIDE!"

"COMING!"

The disconnected words exploding from the Sony were impossibly loud, delivered with considerably more volume than the speakers were capable of providing. Thunderous, volcanic. Wall-shaking. The speakers should have disintegrated or burned out as those tremendous bursts of sound smashed through them, but they continued to function. The radio vibrated against the counter.

"LOOSE!"

"COMING!"

Each word crashed through Laura and seemed to pulverize more of her self-control. Panic and fear surged through her.

The kitchen lights pulsed, dimmed. At the same time the green glow that illuminated the radio dial became brighter, unnaturally bright, as if the Sony had acquired both a consciousness and a greedy thirst for electricity, as if it were drawing off all available power for itself. But that didn't make sense, because regardless of how much power the radio received, the dial was still equipped with a low wattage bulb that couldn't produce this brilliant glow. Yet it did. As the ceiling lights grew dimmer still, dazzling emerald beams sprayed out through the Plexiglas panel on the front of the radio, painting Earl Benton's face, glinting off the chrome on the stove and refrigerator, imparting to the air a rippling murkiness: The room seemed to be underwater.

". . . RIPPING . . ."

". . . APART . . ."

The air was freezing.

". . . TEARING . . ."

". . . APART . . ."

Laura didn't understand that portion of the message—unless it was a threat of physical violence.

The Sony was vibrating faster than the stones in a rattlesnake's rattle. Soon it would be bouncing across the counter.

". . . SPLITTING . . . IN . . . TWO . . ."

•

Dan said, "If I go public, Ted Gearvy probably will too. And maybe there's even someone else out there who's seen you at your worst, Ross. Maybe they'll come forward when we do. Maybe they'll have a conscience too."

Judging by the expression on Mondale's face, there evidently *was* someone else who could blow his career out of the water. He was no longer smug when he said, "One cop *never* rats on another, damn it!"

"Nonsense. If one of us is a killer, we don't protect him."

"I'm no killer," Mondale said.

"If one of us is a thief, we don't protect him."

"I've never stolen a goddamned dime."

"And if one of us is a coward who wants to be chief, we have to stop protecting him too, before he gets into the front office and plays fast and loose with other men's lives, the way some cowards do when they get enough power to be above the fight themselves."

"You take the goddamned cake! You're the snottiest, most self-satisfied son of a bitch I've ever seen."

"Coming from you, I'll take that as a compliment."

"You know the code. It's us against them."

"Why, for heaven's sake, Ross. Just a minute ago, you told me it was always every man for himself."

Irrationally trying to separate his own conduct at the Lakey house from the code of honor that he now so strenuously professed to embrace, Mondale could do no more than repeat himself: "It's us against them, damn it!"

Dan nodded. "Yes, but when I say 'us,' I don't include you. You and I can't possibly belong to the same species."

"You'll destroy your own career," Mondale said.

"Maybe."

"Definitely. The Internal Affairs Division is gonna want to know why the hell you covered up this so-called dereliction of duty."

"Misguided allegiance to another man in uniform."

"That won't be good enough."

"We'll see."

"They'll have your ass for breakfast."

Dan said, "You're the one who actively screwed up. My moral irresponsibility was a passive act, passive sin. They might suspend me for that, reprimand me. But they're not going to throw me off the force because of it."

"Maybe not. But you'll never get another promotion."

Dan shrugged. "Doesn't matter. I've gone as far as I really care to. Ambition doesn't rule me, Ross, the way it does you."

"But . . . no one'll trust you after you've done a thing like this."

"Sure they will."

"No, no. Not after you've ratted on another cop."

"If the cop was anyone but you, that might be true."

Mondale bristled. "I have *friends*!"

"You're well liked by the high brass," Dan said, "because you always tell them what they want to hear. You know how to manipulate them. But the average cop on the beat thinks you're a jerk-off."

"Bullshit. I have friends everywhere. You'll be frozen out, isolated, shunned."

"Even if that's true—and it isn't—so what? I'm just a loner anyway. Remember? You said so yourself. You said I'm a loner. What do I care if I'm shunned?"

For the first time, more worry than hatred was evident in Ross Mondale's face.

"You see?" Dan said. He smiled again, more broadly than before. "You don't have any choice. You have to let me work on this case the way I want to work on it, without any interference, just as long as I want. If you mess with me, I'll destroy you, so help me God, even if it means problems for me too."

•

The overhead lights grew even dimmer. But the radio's eerie green radiance was now so bright that it hurt Laura's eyes.

"... STOP ... HELP ... RUN ... HIDE ... HELP ..."

The Plexiglas that shielded the radio dial suddenly cracked down the middle.

The Sony vibrated so violently that it began to move across the counter.

Laura remembered the nightmarish image that had come to her a few minutes ago: crablike legs sprouting from the plastic casing. . . .

The refrigerator door flew open again all by itself.

With a hiss and squeak of hinges, with scattered thumping sounds, every cupboard door in the room abruptly and simultaneously flung itself wide open. One of them banged against Earl's legs, and he almost fell.

The radio had stopped emitting selected words from various stations. Now it was simply spewing out a shrill electronic noise at higher than full volume, as if attempting to shatter their flesh and bones as a perfectly sung and sustained high-C could shatter fine crystal.

•

Ross Mondale sat on a shipping crate and buried his face in his hands, as if weeping.

Dan Haldane was startled and disconcerted. He had been certain that Mondale was incapable of tears.

The captain didn't sob or wheeze or make any other sounds, and when he looked up again, after half a minute or so, his eyes were perfectly dry. He hadn't been weeping after all—merely thinking. Desperately thinking.

He had also been putting on a new expression, a conscious act not unlike exchanging one mask for another. The fear and worry and anger were completely gone. Even the hatred was fairly well hidden, although a dark rime of it was still visible in the captain's eyes, like a film of black ice on a shallow puddle at the edge of winter. Now he was wearing his patented friendly-and-humble face, which was transparently insincere.

"Okay, Dan. Okay. We were friends once, and maybe we can be friends again."

We were never really friends, Dan thought.

But he said nothing. He was curious to see how conciliatory Ross Mondale would pretend to be.

Mondale said, "At least we can start by trying to work together, and I can help by acknowledging that you're a damned good detective. You're methodical, but you're also intuitive. I shouldn't try to rein you in, because that's like refusing to let a natural-born hunting dog follow its own nose. Okay. So you're on your own in this case. Go wherever you want, see who you want, when you want. Just try to fill me in once in a while. I'd appreciate it. Maybe if we both give a little, both of us bend a little, then we'll find that we not only can work together but can even be friends again."

Dan decided that he liked Mondale's anger and unconcealed hatred better than this smarmy appeasement. The captain's hatred was the most honest thing about him. Now, the honey in his voice and manner didn't soothe Dan; in fact, it made his skin crawl.

"But can I ask you one thing?" Mondale said, leaning forward from his perch on the packing crate, looking earnest.

"What's that?"

"Why this case? Why're you so passionately committed to it?"

"I just want to do my job."

"It's more than that."

Dan gave nothing.

"Is it the woman?"

"No."

"She's very good-looking."

"It's not the woman," Dan said, though Laura McCaffrey's beauty had not escaped his attention. It did indeed play at least a small role in his determination to stay with the case, though he would never reveal as much to Mondale.

"Is it the kid?"

"Maybe," Dan said.

"You've always worked hardest on cases where a child was abused or threatened."

"Not always."

"Yes, always," Mondale said. "Is that because of what happened to your brother and sister?"

•

The radio vibrated harder, faster. It rattled against the counter with sufficient force to chip the tiles—and abruptly floated into the air. Levitated. It hung up there, swaying, bobbing at the end of its cord as a helium-filled balloon might bobble at the end of a string.

Laura was beyond surprise. She watched, immobilized by awe, no longer even terribly afraid, simply numb with cold and with incredulity.

The electronic whine became more shrill, thin, spiraled up, like the tape-recorded descent of a bomb played in reverse.

Laura looked down at Melanie and saw that the girl had at last begun to rise out of her stupor. She hadn't opened her eyes yet—in fact, she was now squeezing them shut—but she had raised her small hands to her ears, and her mouth was open too.

Snakes of smoke erupted from the miraculously suspended radio. It exploded.

Laura closed her eyes and ducked her head just as the Sony blew up. Bits of broken plastic rained over her, snapped against her arms, head, hands.

A few large chunks of the radio, still attached to the cord, fell straight to the floor—the invisible hands no longer providing support—and hit the tiles with a clank and clatter. The plug pulled from the wall, and the cord slithered across the counter; it dropped onto the floor with the rest of the shattered Sony, and was still.

When the explosion had come, Melanie had finally responded to the chaos around her. She erupted from her chair, and even before the flying debris had finished falling, she scurried on hands and knees into the corner by the back door. Now she cowered there, head sheltered under her arms, sobbing.

In the silence following the cessation of the radio's banshee wail, the child's sobs were especially penetrating. Each, like a soft blow, landed on Laura's heart, not with physical force but with enormous emotional impact, hammering her alternately toward despair and terror.

•

When Dan didn't respond, Mondale repeated the question in a tone of innocent curiosity, but his undertone was taunting and mean. "Do you work harder on those cases involving child abuse because of what happened to your brother and sister?"

"Maybe," Dan said, wishing he had never told Mondale about those tragedies. But when two young cops share a squad car, they usually spill their guts to each other during the long night patrols. He had spilled too much before he'd realized that he didn't like Mondale and never would. "Maybe that's *part* of why I don't want to let go of this case. But it's not the whole story. It's also because of Cindy Lakey. Don't you see that, Ross? Here's another case where a woman and child are in danger, a mother and her daughter threatened by a maniac, maybe more than one maniac. Just like the Lakeys. So maybe it's a chance for me to redeem myself. A chance to make up for my failure to save Cindy Lakey, to finally get rid of a little of that guilt."

Mondale stared at him, astonished. "*You* feel guilty because the Lakey kid was killed?"

Dan nodded. "I should have shot Dunbar the moment he turned toward me with that gun. I shouldn't have hesitated, shouldn't have given him a chance to drop it. If I'd wasted him right away, he'd never have gotten into that house."

Amazed, Mondale said, "But, Christ, you know what it was like back then. Even worse than now. The grand jury was looking into half a dozen charges of police brutality, whether the accusations had substance or not. Every half-assed political activist had it in for the whole department in those days. Even worse than now. Even when a cop shot someone in a clear-cut act of self-defense, they howled for his head. Everyone was supposed to have rights—except cops. Cops were supposed to just stand there and take bullets in the chest. The reporters, politicians, the ACLU—they all talked about us like we were bloodthirsty fascists. Shit, man, you remember!"

"I remember," Dan said. "And that's why I didn't shoot Dunbar when I should have. I could *see* the guy was unbalanced, dangerous. I knew intuitively that he was going to kill somebody that night, but in the back of my mind I was thinking about all the heat we were under, all the accusations about being trigger-happy cops, and I knew if I shot him, I'd have to answer for it. In the climate we had back then, I figured nobody would listen to me. I'd be sacrificed. I was worried about losing my job, being booted off the force. I was afraid of destroying my career. And so I waited until he brought the gun around, waited until he pointed it right straight at me. But I gave him just a second too long, and he got me, and because I didn't go with my instincts or with my intellect, he had a chance to get Cindy Lakey too."

Mondale shook his head adamantly. "But none of that was your fault. Blame the goddamned social reformers who take sides without any understanding of the goddamned situation we face, without knowing what it's like out there on the streets. They're to blame. Not you. Not me."

Dan glared at him. "Don't you dare put yourself in the same boat with me. Don't you dare. You *ran,* Ross. I screwed up because I was thinking about my own ass—about my pension, for God's sake!—when I should have been thinking about nothing other than doing the job the best way I could. That's why I have guilt to live with. But don't you ever imply the burden lies equally on you and me. It doesn't. That's crap, and you know it."

Mondale was trying to look earnest and concerned, but he was having increasing difficulty suppressing his hatred.

"Or maybe you *don't* know it," Dan said. "That's even scarier. Maybe you aren't just covering your own backside. Maybe you really think that looking out for number one is the only moral position that makes sense."

Without replying, Mondale got up and went to the door.

Dan said, "Is your conscience actually clear, Ross? God help you, I think maybe it is."

Mondale glanced back at him. "You do what you want to do on this case, but stay out of my way."

"You haven't lost a single night's sleep over Cindy Lakey, have you, Ross?"

"I said, stay out of my way."

"Happily."

"I don't want to have to listen to any more of your carping and whining."

"You're incredible."

Without replying, Mondale opened the door.

"What planet are you from, Ross?"

Mondale walked out.

"I'll bet there's only one color on his home planet," Dan said to the empty room. "Brown. Everything must be brown on his world. That's why his clothes are all brown—they remind him of home."

It was a weak joke. Maybe that was why he couldn't make himself smile. Maybe.

•

The kitchen was still.

The silence held.

The air was warm once more.

"It's over," Earl said.

Paralysis relaxed its grip on Laura. A circuit board from the demolished radio crunched under her foot as she stepped across the kitchen and knelt beside Melanie.

With soothing words, with much patting and stroking, she calmed her daughter. She wiped the tears from the child's face.

Earl began picking through the debris, studying the pieces of the Sony, mumbling to himself, baffled and fascinated.

Sitting on the floor with Melanie, pulling the girl onto her lap, holding her, rocking her, immensely relieved that the child was still there to be comforted, Laura would like to have wished away the events of the past few minutes. She would have given anything to be able to deny the reality of what she had seen. But she was too good a psychiatrist to allow herself to indulge in any of the little mind games that would minimize this bizarre development; nor would she permit herself to rationalize it away with the standard jargon of her profession. She hadn't been hallucinating. This paranormal episode—this supernatural phenomenon—couldn't be explained away as just sensory confusion, either; her perceptions had been accurate and reliable in spite of the impossibility of what she had perceived. She had not been overlaying a logical series of events with an illogical and subjective fantasy, in the manner of many schizophrenics. Earl had seen it too. And this wasn't a shared hallucination, a mass delusion. It was crazy, impossible—but real. The radio had been . . . possessed. Some of the pieces of the Sony were still smoking. The air was thick with an acrid, charred-plastic odor.

Melanie moaned softly. Twitched.

"Easy, honey, easy."

The girl looked up at her mother, and Laura was jolted by the eye contact. Melanie was no longer gazing through her. She had come back from her dark world again, and Laura prayed that this time the girl was back for good, although that was unlikely.

"I . . . want," Melanie said.

"What is it, honey? What do you want?"

The girl's eyes searched Laura's. "I . . . need."

"Anything, Melanie. Anything you want. Just tell me. Tell Mommy what you need."

"It'll get them all," Melanie said, her voice heavy with dread.

Earl had looked up from the smoldering scraps of the radio and was watching intently.

"What?" Laura asked. "What will get them, honey?"

"And then it'll . . . get . . . me," the girl said.

"No," Laura said quickly. "Nothing's going to get you. I'll take care of you. I'll—"

"It'll . . . come up from . . . inside."

"Inside where?"

". . . from inside . . ."

"What is it, honey? What're you afraid of. What is it?"

". . . it'll . . . come . . . and eat me . . ."

"No."

". . . eat me . . . all up," the girl said, and she shuddered.

"No, Melanie. Don't worry about . . ." She let her voice trail away because she saw that the girl's eyes had shifted subtly. They were not entirely out of focus, but neither were they fixed on Laura anymore.

The child sighed and her breathing changed. She had gone back into that private place where she had been hiding ever since they'd found her wandering naked in the street.

Earl said, "Doc, can you make anything of this?"

"No."

"Because I can't figure it at all."

"Me neither."

Earlier, cooking dinner, she had begun to feel better about Melanie and the future. She'd begun to feel almost normal. But their situation had changed for the worse, and now her nerves were frayed again.

In this city, there were people who wanted to kidnap Melanie in order to continue experimenting with her. Laura didn't know what they hoped to achieve or why they had picked on Melanie, but she was certain they were out there. Even the FBI seemed sure of that. Other people wanted the girl dead. The discovery of Ned Rink's body seemed to prove that Melanie's life was indisputably in danger. But now it appeared that those faceless people were not the only ones who wanted to get their hands on Melanie. Now there was another enemy as well. That was the essence of the warning that had come to them through the radio.

But who or what had been controlling the radio? And how? Who or what had sent the warning? And why?

More important, who was this new enemy?

"It," the radio had said, and the implication had been that this enemy was more frightening and more dangerous than all the others combined. *It* was loose, the radio had said. It was coming. They had to run, the radio said. They had to hide. From it.

"Mommy? Mom?"

"Right here, honey."

"Mommmeeeee!"

"Right here. It's okay. I'm right here."

"I'm . . . I'm . . . I'm . . . scared."

Melanie was not speaking to Laura or Earl. She seemed not to have heard Laura's reassurance. She was talking only to herself, in a tone of voice that was the essence of loneliness, the voice of the lost and abandoned. "So scared. Scared."

part three
THE HUNTED

WEDNESDAY, 8:00 P.M.–THURSDAY, 6:00 A.M.

chapter twenty-two

Still sitting at Joseph Scaldone's desk in the office-storeroom behind the shop on Ventura Boulevard, Dan Haldane looked through the diskette storage wheel that stood beside the IBM computer. He read the labels on the floppy disks and saw that most held nothing of interest for him; however, one of them was marked CUSTOMER MAILING LIST, and that one seemed worth examining.

He switched on the computer, studied the menu of options, loaded the proper software, and brought up the mailing list. It appeared in white letters on a blue screen, divided into twenty-six documents, one for each letter of the alphabet.

He summoned the M document and scrolled slowly through it, searching for Dylan McCaffrey. He found the name and address of the house in Studio City.

He called up the H document and located Willy Hoffritz.

In the C file, he found Ernest Andrew Cooper, the millionaire businessman whose mangled body had been in that Studio City house last night, with McCaffrey and Hoffritz.

Dan called up the R file. Ned Rink was there.

He had discovered a cord that tied all four victims together: an interest in the occult and, more specific, patronage of the late Joseph Scaldone's bizarre little shop.

He checked under U. There was an address in Ojai and a telephone number for Albert Uhlander, the author of those quirky volumes about the occult, which someone had attempted to remove from Ned Rink's house and which now were safely stored in the trunk of the department sedan that Dan was using.

Who else?

He pondered that question, then called up the S file and searched for Regine Savannah. She was the young woman who had been under Hoffritz's total control and whose beating had resulted in the psychologist's removal from the UCLA faculty four years ago. She wasn't one of Scaldone's customers.

The G file. Just in case. But he could find no listing for Irmatrude Gelkenshettle.

He hadn't actually expected to find her there. He was slightly ashamed of himself for even checking on it. But it was the nature of a homicide detective to trust no one.

Calling up the O file, he searched for Mary Katherine O'Hara of Burbank, the secretary of Freedom Now, the organization which Cooper and Hoffritz served as president and treasurer, respectively.

Apparently, Mary O'Hara didn't share her fellow officers' enthusiasm for occult literature and paraphernalia.

Dan couldn't think of any more names to look for, but there would most likely be others of interest when he read through the entire mailing list. He ordered a printout.

The laser printer produced the first page in seconds. Dan snatched the sheet of paper from the tray and read it while the machine continued to print. There were twenty names and addresses, two columns of ten each. He didn't recognize anybody in that first section of the list.

He picked up the second page, and toward the bottom of the second column, he saw a name that was not merely familiar but startling. Palmer Boothe.

Owner of the *Los Angeles Journal*, heir to a huge fortune, but also one of the shrewdest businessmen in the country, Palmer Boothe had vastly increased the wealth that he had inherited. He kept his hands in not only the newspaper and magazine business but also in real estate, banking, motion-picture production, transportation, a variety of high-technology industries, broadcasting, agriculture, thoroughbred horse breeding, and probably anything else that made money. He was widely and well regarded, a political power broker, a philanthropist who annually earned the gratitude of a score of charities, a man known for his hardheaded pragmatism.

Yeah? How did hardheaded pragmatism coexist with a belief in the occult? Why would a canny businessman, with an appreciation for the no-nonsense rules and methods and laws of capitalism, patronize a strange place like the Sign of the Pentagram?

Curious.

Of course there was virtually no chance whatsoever that Palmer Boothe was involved with men like McCaffrey, Hoffritz, and Rink. The appearance of his name on Scaldone's mailing list did not link him to the McCaffrey case. Not everyone who bought from the Sign of the Pentagram was involved in that conspiracy.

Nevertheless, Dan opened Scaldone's personal address book—the item that had precipitated the confrontation with Mondale—and paged to the B listings, to see if Palmer Boothe was more than merely one of Scaldone's customers. The businessman's name wasn't there. Which probably meant that his sole contact with Joseph Scaldone was as an occasional purchaser of occult books and other items.

Dan reached to an inside coat pocket and withdrew Dylan McCaffrey's address book. Boothe's name wasn't in that one, either.

Dead end.

He had known that it would be.

As an afterthought, he checked McCaffrey's book for Albert Uhlander. The author was there: the same address and phone number in Ojai.

He looked in Scaldone's book again. Uhlander was also listed there. The writer was evidently more than just another customer of the Sign of the Pentagram. He was an integral part of whatever project McCaffrey and Hoffritz had been engaged upon.

They sure had a jolly little group. Dan wondered what they did when they got together. Compare favorite brands of bat shit? Whip up tasty dishes featuring snake eyes? Discuss megalomaniacal schemes to brain-wash everyone and rule the world?

Torture little girls?

The printer spewed out the fifteenth and final page long before Dan finished scanning the first fourteen. He collected them, stapled them together, folded the sheets, and put them in his pocket. Nearly three hundred names appeared on the mailing list, and he wanted to go over them later, when he was alone at home, with a beer, and could concentrate better.

He located an empty stationery box and filled it with Dylan McCaffrey's address book, Scaldone's smaller address book, and several other items. He carried the box out of the office, through the store, where the coroner's men were bagging Joseph Scaldone's hideously battered corpse, and he went outside.

The crowd of curiosity seekers had grown smaller, maybe because the night was colder. A few reporters still lingered in the vicinity of the occult shop, standing with shoulders drawn up, hands in their pockets, shivering. A heat-leaching wind alternately hissed and howled along Ventura Boulevard, sucking the warmth out of the city and everyone in it. The air was heavy, moist. The rains would return before morning.

Nolan Swayze, the youngest of the uniformed officers on duty in front of the Sign of the Pentagram, accepted the box when Dan handed it to him.

"Nolan, I want you to take this back to East Valley and give it to clerical. There're two address books among this stuff. I want the contents of both books transcribed, and all the detectives on the special task force should have a copy of the transcriptions in their information packets by tomorrow morning."

"Can do," Swayze said.

"There's also a diskette. I want the contents printed out with copies to everyone. There's an appointments calendar in there too."

"Copies to everyone?"

"You catch on fast."

Swayze nodded. "I intend to be chief someday."

"Good for you."

"Make my mother proud."

"If that's your goal, it's probably wiser to stay a patrolman. There's also a sheaf of invoices here—"

"You want the information transcribed into a less cumbersome format."

"Right," Dan said.

"With copies to everyone."

"Maybe you could even be mayor."

"I've already got my campaign slogan. 'Let's Rebuild L.A.'"

"Why not? It's worked for every other candidate for thirty years."

"This ledger—?"

"It's a checkbook," Dan said.

"You want the information transcribed from the stubs, with copies to everyone. Maybe I could even be governor."

"No, you wouldn't like the job."

"Why not?"

"You'd have to live in Sacramento."

"Hey, that's right. I prefer civilization."

•

Dinner was late because they had to clean up the kitchen. The water for the spaghetti had to be poured out; bits of the demolished radio were floating in it. Laura scrubbed the pot, refilled it, and put it back on the stove to boil.

By the time they sat down to eat, she wasn't hungry anymore. She kept thinking of the radio, which had been infused with a strange and demonic life of its own, and that memory spoiled her appetite. The air was rich with the mouthwatering aromas of garlic and tomato sauce and Parmesan cheese, but there was also an underlying hint of scorched plastic and hot metal that seemed (this was crazy, but true, God help her) like the olfactory trace of an evil spiritual presence.

Earl Benton ate more than she did, but not much. He didn't talk much either. He stared at his plate even when he took a long pause between bites, and the only time he looked up was when he glanced, occasionally, toward that end of the kitchen counter where the Sony had been. His usual efficient, no-nonsense manner wasn't in evidence now; his eyes had a faraway look.

Melanie's eyes were still focused on a far place too, but the girl ate more than either Laura or Earl Benton. Sometimes she chewed slowly and absentmindedly, and sometimes she gobbled up four or five bites in rapid succession, with wolflike hunger. Now and then she altogether forgot that she was eating, and she had to be reminded.

Feeding her daughter, repeatedly wiping spaghetti sauce off the child's chin, Laura could not avoid thinking about her own blighted childhood. Her mother, Beatrice, had been a religious zealot who had permitted no singing or dancing or reading of books other than the Bible and certain religious texts. A recluse with a persecution complex, Beatrice had labored hard to ensure that Laura would remain shy, withdrawn, and frightened of the world; if Laura had turned out like Melanie was now, Beatrice no doubt would have been delighted. She would have interpreted schizophrenic catatonia as a rejection of the evil world of the flesh, would have seen it as a deep communion with God. Beatrice would not only have been unable but unwilling to help Laura back into the real world.

But I can help you, honey, Laura thought as she wiped a smear of sauce off her daughter's chin. I am able and willing to help you find your way back, Melanie, if only you'll reach out to me, if only you'll let me help.

Melanie's head dropped. Her eyes closed.

Laura twisted more spaghetti onto the fork and put it to the girl's lips, but the child seemed to have slipped from apathy into some deeper level, perhaps even sleep.

"Come on, Melanie, have another bite. You've got to gain some weight, honey."

Something clicked loudly.

Earl Benton looked up from his plate. "What was that?"

Before Laura could respond, the back door flew open with shocking force. The security chain ripped out of the doorjamb, and wood cracked with a hard splintering sound.

The first click had been the dead-bolt lock snapping open. All by itself.

Earl had jumped to his feet, knocking over his chair. From the patio behind the house, out of the darkness and wind, something came through the door.

•

At 9:15, after talking to the owner of the shop next door to the Sign of the Pentagram and learning nothing of interest, Dan stopped at a McDonald's for dinner. He bought two cheeseburgers, a large order of fries, and a diet cola, and he ate in the car while he used the unmarked sedan's datalink to try to locate Regine Savannah.

The video display terminal was in the dashboard, mounted at a slant, facing up, so he didn't have to bend over to read it. The programmer's keyboard nearly filled the console between the seats. All LAPD patrol cars and half the unmarked sedans had been fitted with new computer terminals over the past two years. The mobile VDT was linked by microwave transmissions to the underground, high-security, bombproof police communications command center, which in turn had access, via modem, to a variety of government and private-industry data banks.

Taking a bite of a cheeseburger, Dan started the sedan's engine, switched on the VDT, punched in his personal code, and accessed the telephone-company records. He requested a number for Regine Savannah at any address in the Greater Los Angeles area.

In a few seconds, glowing green letters appeared on the screen:

NO LISTING:
SAVANNAH, REGINE

&

NO LISTING:
SAVANNAH, R.

He typed in a request for any unlisted numbers being billed to an R. or Regine Savannah, but that was a dead end too.

He ate a few french fries.

The screen glowed softly, patiently.

He accessed the Department of Motor Vehicles' license files and requested a search for Regine Savannah. That, too, was negative.

As he mulled over another approach, he finished his first cheeseburger and watched the traffic passing on the windswept street. Then he tapped into the DMV files again and requested a search for a driver's license issued to anyone whose first name was Regine and whose middle name was Savannah. Perhaps she had been married and had not abandoned her maiden name altogether.

Pay dirt. The screen flashed up the answer:

REGINE SAVANNAH HOFFRITZ

Dan stared in disbelief. Hoffritz?

Marge Gelkenshettle hadn't said anything about this. Had the girl actually married the man who had beaten her senseless and put her in the hospital?

No. As far as he knew, Wilhelm Hoffritz had been unmarried. Dan hadn't been to Hoffritz's house yet, but he had read over the available background information, which contained no reference to a wife or family. Others had tracked down the next of kin: a sister who was flying in from somewhere—Detroit or Chicago, someplace like that—to handle the funeral arrangements.

Marge Gelkenshettle would have told him if Regine and Hoffritz had married. Unless she didn't know about it.

According to the DMV files, Regine Savannah Hoffritz was female, with black hair and brown eyes. She was five-six, one hundred and twenty-five pounds. She had been born on July 3, 1971. That was about the right age for the woman about whom Marge had spoken. The address on her driver's license was in Hollywood, in the hills, and Dan jotted it down in his notebook.

Wilhelm Hoffritz had lived in Westwood. If he had been married to Regine Savannah, why would they have kept two houses?

Divorce. That was a possibility.

However, even if it had ended in divorce, the very fact of the marriage was nonetheless bizarre. What kind of life could it have been for her, married to a vicious sadist who had brainwashed her, who could completely control her, and who had once beaten her so severely that she had wound up in the hospital? If Hoffritz had savagely abused Regine when she was a student of his—at a time when he had his entire career to lose by indulging in such perverse urges—then, how much worse might he have treated her when she was his wife, when they were alone in the privacy and sanctity of their own home?

Thinking about that gave Dan the creeps.

•

Earl Benton had his gun in his hand, but what came into the kitchen from the darkness outside wasn't something that he could blow away with a few well-placed rounds from his .38. With a resounding crash, the door was thrown against the wall, and a cold whirlwind surged into the kitchen, a wind like a living beast, hissing and growling, sniffing and capering. And if the substance of the beast was wind, then its coat was made of flowers, for the air was suddenly filled with flowers, yellow and red and white roses, stalky impatiens of every hue, scores of blossoms from the garden behind the house, some with stems attached and some without, some that had been snapped off and some that had been torn out by the roots. The wind-beast shook itself; its coat of flowers flapped and, as if shedding loose hairs, threw off torn leaves, bright petals, crushed stems, clumps of moist earth that had been adhering to the roots. The calendar leaped off the wall and darted halfway around the room on wings of paper before settling to the floor. With a soft rustle not unlike the flutter of feathers, the curtains flew up from the windows and fought to free themselves from the anchoring rods, eager to join this demonic dance of the inanimate. Dirt spattered over Earl, and a rose struck his face; he was aware of a thorn lightly nicking his throat as the flower rebounded from him, and he raised one arm to protect himself. He saw Laura McCaffrey shielding her daughter, and he felt helpless and stupid in the face of this amorphous threat.

The door slammed shut as abruptly as it had been forced open. But the churning column of flowers continued to spin, as if this wind was not part of that greater wind which scoured the night outside but was, instead, a self-sustaining offspring. That was impossible, of course. Crazy. But real. The whirling turbulence whined, hissed, spat out more leaves and blossoms and broken stems, shook off more dirt and buds and bright petals. In its many-windowed, ragtag coat of rolling vegetation, the wind-creature stopped just inside the door (though its breath could be felt in every corner) and remained there, as if watching them, as if deciding what it would do next—and then it simply expired. The wind didn't die slowly; it stopped all at once. The remaining flowers, which it hadn't yet cast off, dropped to the kitchen tiles in a heap, with a soft thump and rustle and whoosh. Then silence, stillness.

•

In the unmarked police sedan in the McDonald's parking lot, Dan terminated the link with the DMV computer and accessed the telephone-company data banks once more. He got a number and address for Regine Hoffritz. It was the same address the DMV had provided.

He glanced at his watch: 9:32. He had been working with the VDT for about ten minutes. In the bad old days, before the advent of the mobile computer, he would have wasted at least two hours gathering this information. He switched off the screen, and a deeper darkness crept into the car.

As he finished his second cheeseburger and sipped his cola, he thought about the rapidly changing world in which he lived. A new world, a science-fictional society, was growing up around him with disconcerting speed and vigor. It was both exhilarating and frightening to be alive in these times. Mankind had acquired the ability to reach the stars, to take a giant leap off this world and spread out through the universe, but the species had also acquired the ability to destroy itself before the inevitable emigration could begin. New technology—like the computer—freed men and women from all kinds of drudgery, saved them vast amounts of time. And yet . . . And yet the time saved did not seem to mean additional leisure or greater opportunities for meditation and reflection. Instead, with each new wave of technology, the pace of life increased; there was more to do, more choices to make, more things to experience, and people eagerly seized upon those experiences and filled the hours that had only moments ago become empty. Each year life seemed to be flitting past with far greater speed than the year before, as if God had cranked up the control knob on the flow of time. But that wasn't right, either, because to many people, even the concept of God seemed dated in an age in which the universe was being forced to let go of its mysteries on a daily basis. Science, technology, and change were the only gods now, the new Trinity; and while they were not consciously cruel and judgmental, as some of the old gods had been, they were too coldly indifferent to offer any comfort to the sick, the lonely, and the lost.

How could a shop like the Sign of the Pentagram flourish in a world of computers, miracle drugs, and spaceships? Who could turn to the occult, seeking answers, when physicists and biochemists and geneticists were providing more answers, day by day, than all the Ouija boards and seances and spiritualists since the dawn of history? Why would men of science, like Dylan McCaffrey and Wilhelm Hoffritz, associate with a purveyor of bat shit and bunkum?

Well, clearly, they hadn't believed it was all bunkum. Some aspect of the occult, some paranormal phenomena, must have been of interest to McCaffrey and Hoffritz and must have seemed, to them, to have a bearing or an application in their own research. Somehow, they had wanted to join science and magic. But how? And why?

As he finished his diet cola, Dan remembered a fragment of rhyme:

> We'll plunge into darkness,
> into the hands of harm,
> when Science and the Devil
> go walking arm in arm.

He couldn't recall where he had heard it, but he thought it was part of a song, an old rock-'n'-roll number perhaps, from the days when he had regularly listened to rock. He tried hard to remember, almost had it, thought maybe it was from a protest song about nuclear war and destruction, but he couldn't quite seize the memory.

Science and the Devil, walking arm in arm.

It was a naive image, even simpleminded. The song had probably been nothing but propaganda for the New Luddites who yearned to dismantle civilization and go back to living in tents or caves. Dan had no sympathy for that point of view. He knew that tents were drafty and damp. But for some reason the image of "Science and the Devil, walking arm in arm" had a powerful effect on him, and a chill spread through his bones.

Suddenly he was no longer in the mood to visit Regine Savannah Hoffritz. He'd put in a long day. Time to go home. His forehead hurt where he'd been hit, and a score of bruises throbbed all over his body. His joints felt as if they were on fire. His eyes were burning, watering, itching. He needed a beer or two—and ten hours of sleep.

But he still had work to do.

•

Laura looked around in shock and disbelief.

Dirt, flowers, leaves, and other debris were scattered across the kitchen table and through the uneaten portions of their dinners. Battered roses littered the floor and the counters. Gnarled, broken bunches of red and purple impatiens bristled out of the sink. One white rose hung through the handle of the refrigerator door, and bits of greenery and hundreds of detached petals were stuck to the curtains, the walls, and the doors of the cabinets. On the floor, a mound of limp, ragged greenery and windburned blossoms marked the spot where the whirlwind had died.

"Let's get out of here," Earl said, the gun still in his hand.

"But this mess," Laura began.

"Later," he said, going to Melanie, pulling the somnolent child up from her chair.

Dazed, Laura said, "But I've got to clean up—"

"Come on, come on," Earl said impatiently. His ruddy, country-boy complexion had vanished. He was now pallid and waxy. "Into the living room."

She hesitated, surveying the tangled debris.

"Come on," Earl said, "before something worse comes through that door!"

chapter twenty-three

Regine Savannah Hoffritz lived on one of the less expensive streets in the Hollywood Hills. Her house was a prime example of the eclectic-anachronistic-madcap architecture which was actually rare in California but which chauvinistic New Yorkers pointed to as an example of typical West Coast tastelessness. Judging by its use of brick and exposed exterior wall beams, Dan supposed that the house was intended to be English Tudor, though there were elaborately carved Victorian eaves, American colonial shutters—and big brass carriage lamps, of no discernible period or style, flanking the front door and the garage. The two pilasters framing the entrance to the walk were stucco with Mexican-tile trim, bearing heavy wrought-iron lamps utterly different from—yet no nearer the Tudor ideal than—the brass fixtures employed elsewhere.

A black Porsche was parked in the driveway. In the ghostly white radiance of the various and clashing lamps, the curvature and sheen of the car's long hood was reminiscent of a beetle's carapace.

Dan rang the doorbell, withdrew his police ID, waited with his shoulders hunched in the chilly wind, and then rang the bell again.

When the door finally opened, it was on a security chain.

Half of a lovely face peered out at him: lustrous black hair, porcelain skin, one large and clear brown eye, half a precisely sculpted nose in which the one visible nostril was as delicately formed as if it had been made from blown glass, and one-half of a ripe and alluring mouth.

She said, "Yes?"

Her voice was soft, breathy. Although it might have been her God-given voice, completely unaffected, it nevertheless sounded phony, calculated.

Dan said, "Regine Hoffritz?"

"Yes."

"Lieutenant Haldane. Police. I'd like to talk with you. About your husband."

She squinted at his identification. "What husband?"

He heard another quality in her voice: a pliancy, a meekness, a tremulous and yielding weakness. She seemed to be waiting only for a command that would reduce her to unquestioning obedience.

He didn't think her tone had anything to do with his being a cop. He suspected that she was always like this, with everyone. Or, rather, she had always been like this since Willy Hoffritz had changed her.

"Your husband," he said. "Wilhelm Hoffritz."

"Oh. Just a minute."

She closed the door, and it stayed closed for ten seconds, twenty, half a minute, longer. Dan was just about to ring the bell again when he heard the security chain being disengaged.

The door opened. She stepped back, and Dan entered past three pieces of luggage that stood to one side. In the living room, he sat in an armchair, and she chose the rust-brown sofa. Her posture and manner were demure, yet her primary effect was powerfully seductive.

Although she was a striking woman, something about her was not quite right. Her considerable femininity seemed studied, exaggerated. Her hair was so perfectly coiffed and her makeup was so exactingly and faultlessly applied that she looked as if she were about to step before the cameras to film a Revlon commercial. She wore a floor-length, cream-colored silk robe cinched tightly at the waist to emphasize her full breasts, flat belly, and flaring hips. The robe was excessively frilly as well, with silk ruffles up the lapels, at the collar and cuffs and hem. At her tender throat she wore a gold mesh dog collar; it was one of those close-fitting necklaces that had been popular years ago. These days, among the general population, where such jewelry had no significance beyond mere decoration, dog collars could be seen only occasionally, though among sadomasochistic couples, such items remained in demand, because they were seen as a symbol of sexual subservience. And though Dan had met Regine only a minute ago, he knew that she wore her collar with that submissive and masochistic intent, for a crushed and obedient spirit was evident in the way she averted her face, in the graceful and yet humbled way she moved (as if anticipating and perversely welcoming a blow, a slap, a cruel pinch), and in her avoidance of eye contact.

She waited for him to begin.

For a moment he said nothing, listened to the house. Her delay in removing the security chain from the door led him to suspect that she was not alone. She had hurriedly consulted with someone and had obtained permission before letting Dan in. But the rest of the house was quiet and apparently deserted.

Half a dozen photographs were arranged on the coffee table, and all were of Willy Hoffritz. Or at least the three facing Dan were of Hoffritz, and he imagined that the others were too. It was the same unremarkable face, the same wide-set eyes, the same slightly plump cheeks and piggish nose that Dan had seen in the driver's license photo in the wallet of one of the dead men in Studio City, the previous night.

He finally said, "I'm sure you know that your husband is dead."

"Willy, you mean?"

"Yes, Willy."

"I know."

"I'd like to ask you some questions."

"I'm sure I can't help you," she said softly, meekly, looking at her hands.

"When was the last time you saw Willy?"

"More than a year ago."

"Divorced?"

"Well . . ."

"Separated?"

"Yes, but not . . . in the way you mean."

He wished that she would look at him. "Then in what way do *you* mean it?"

She nervously shifted positions on the sofa. "We were never . . . legally married."

"No? But you have his name now."

Still considering her hands, she nodded. "Yes, he let me change mine."

"You went to court, had your name changed to Hoffritz? When? Why?"

"Two years ago. Because . . . because . . . you won't understand."

"Try me."

Regine didn't answer at once, and as Dan waited for her to form her explanation, he looked around the room. On the mantel above the white brick fireplace was another gallery of photographs of Willy Hoffritz: eight more.

Although the house was warm, Dan felt as though he were in a Rocky Mountain January night as he stared at those silver-framed, carefully arranged images of the dead psychologist.

Regine said, "I wanted to show Willy that I was his, completely and forever his."

"He didn't object to your taking his name? He didn't think you might be setting him up for a palimony case?"

"No, no. I'd never have done something like that to Willy. He knew I'd never do something like that. Oh, no. Impossible."

"If he wanted you to have his name, why didn't he marry you?"

"He didn't want to be married," she said with unmistakable disappointment and regret.

Although Regine's face was bowed, Dan saw sadness, like a sudden gravitational force, pull at her features.

Amazed, he said, "He didn't want to marry you, but he wanted you to carry his name. To indicate that you . . . belonged to him."

"Yes."

"Taking his name was like . . . being branded?"

"Oh, yes," she said in a hoarse whisper, and upon her face blossomed a smile of genuine pleasure at the memory of this strange act of submission. "Yes. Like being branded."

"He sounds like a sweetheart," Dan said. But she was unaware of his ironic tone, so he decided to needle her, hoping to break through her whipped-dog demeanor. "Jesus, he must've been a real egomaniac!"

Her head jerked up, and she met his eyes at last. "Oh, no," she said, frowning. She did not speak with anger or impatience but with warmth, eager to correct what she saw as his misapprehension of the dead man's character. "Oh, no. Not Willy. There was no one like Willy. He was wonderful. There wasn't anything I wouldn't have done for Willy. Not anything. He was so special. You didn't know him, or you wouldn't say a word against him. Not against Willy. You couldn't. Not if you'd known him."

"There are those who did know him who don't speak so highly of him. I'm sure you're aware of that."

She lowered her gaze to her hands again. "They're all just envious, jealous, lying bastards," she said, but in the same soft, sweet, breathlessly feminine manner, as if she had been forbidden to mar her perfect femininity with a shrill tone of voice or any other display of anger.

"He was thrown out of UCLA."

She said nothing.

"Because of what he did to you."

Regine still said nothing, continued to avert her eyes, but she shifted uneasily again. Her robe fell open to reveal one perfectly formed calf. A bruise the size of a half dollar marred the creamy flesh. Two smaller bruises were visible at the ankle.

"I want you to talk about Willy."

"I won't."

"I'm afraid you must."

She shook her head.

"What was he doing with Dylan McCaffrey in Studio City?"

"I'll never say a word against Willy. I don't care what you do to me. Throw me in jail if you want. I don't care. I don't care." This was said quietly but with fierce emotion. "Too many bad things have been said about poor Willy by people not good enough to lick his shoes."

Dan said, "Regine, look at me."

She raised one hand to her mouth, put a knuckle to her teeth, and gently chewed on it.

"Regine? Look at me, Regine."

Nervously sucking-chewing at that knuckle, she raised her head, but she didn't meet his eyes. She stared over his shoulder, past him.

"Regine, he beat you up."

She said nothing.

"He put you in the hospital."

"I loved him," she said, speaking around the knuckle upon which her attention was becoming increasingly fixated.

"He used sophisticated brainwashing techniques on you, Regine. He somehow got in your mind, and he changed you, twisted you, and that is not the work of a sweet and wonderful man."

Tears sprang from her and streamed down her cheeks, and her face contorted in grief. "I loved him so much."

The sleeve of Regine's robe slid up her arm when she brought her hand to her mouth. Dan saw a small bruise on the meaty part of her forearm—and what appeared to be rope abrasions on her wrist.

She had told him that she hadn't seen Willy Hoffritz for a year, but someone had been playing bondage games with her, and recently.

Dan studied the ornately framed photographs on the coffee table, the thin smile on the dead psychologist's face. The air suddenly seemed thick, oily, unclean. A desire for fresh air almost propelled him from the chair, almost sent him stumbling toward the door.

He stayed where he was. "But how could you love a man who hurt you so?"

"He freed me."

"No, he enslaved you."

"He freed me to be . . ."

"To be what?"

"What I was meant to be."

"And what were you meant to be?"

"What I am."

"And what is that?"

"Whatever is wanted of me."

Her tears had stopped.

A smile flickered at the corners of her mouth as she considered what she had said. "Whatever is wanted of me." And she shivered, as though the very thought of slavery and degradation sent a current of physical pleasure through her.

With growing frustration and anger, he said, "Are you telling me that you were born to be only what Willy Hoffritz wanted you to be, born to do anything he wanted you to do?"

"Whatever is wanted," Regine repeated, looking directly into his eyes now.

He wished that she had continued staring into space beyond him, for he saw—or imagined that he saw—grave torment, self-loathing, and desperation of an intensity that made his heart clutch up. He glimpsed a soul in rags: a tattered, wrinkled, frayed, and soiled spirit. Within this woman's ripe, full, exquisitely sensuous body, and within the outwardly visible persona of the submissive child-woman, there was another Regine, a better Regine, trapped, buried alive, existing beyond whatever psychological blocks Hoffritz had implanted but unable to escape or even to imagine any hope of escape. In that brief moment of contact between them, Dan saw that the real woman, the woman who had existed before Hoffritz had come along, was like a withered straw doll, dried out by all these years of ceaseless abuse, now a juiceless, miserable creature who'd been transformed into kindling by a nightmare of humiliation and torture; she longed for the match that would ignite and, mercifully, extinguish her.

Horrified, he could not look away.

She lowered her eyes first.

He was relieved. And sick.

His lips were dry. His tongue stuck to the roof of his mouth. "Do you know what research Willy was doing after he was booted out of UCLA?"

"No."

"What project were he and Dylan McCaffrey working on?"

"I don't know."

"Did you ever see the gray room in Studio City?"

"No."

"Do you know a man named Ernest Andrew Cooper?"

"No."

"Joseph Scaldone?"

"I wish you would go away."

"Ned Rink?"

"No. None of them."

"What did those men do to Melanie McCaffrey? What did they want from her?"

"I don't know."

"Who was funding their project?"

"I don't know."

Dan was sure she was lying. Along with her self-assurance and self-respect and independence, she had also lost the ability to prevaricate with confidence or conviction.

Now that he'd seen Regine and knew the amazing, monstrous thing that had been done to her, Dan had no respect for Hoffritz as a man, but more than ever he feared Hoffritz's manipulative abilities, his vicious cruelty, and his dark genius, and more than ever he realized the need to arrive at a timely solution in this case. If Hoffritz had transformed Regine this completely, what might he have achieved in his research with Dylan McCaffrey, for which he'd had more time and resources? Dan had a new sense that time was swiftly running out, a growing urgency. Hoffritz had set some terrible engine in motion, and it would crush many more people, soon, unless it was understood, located, and stopped. Regine was lying to him, and he couldn't allow that. He had to find some answers quickly, before he was too late to help Melanie.

chapter twenty-four

They retreated from the flower- and dirt-strewn kitchen, but Laura felt no safer. One weirdness had followed another since they had come home that afternoon. First, Melanie had awakened from her nap, screaming in terror, clawing and punching herself as if she were a penitent religious fanatic scourging the devil from her flesh. Then the radio had come to life, followed by the whirlwind that had burst through the back door. If someone had told her that the house was haunted, she would not have scoffed.

Apparently, the move from kitchen to living room didn't make Earl feel any safer. He shushed Laura when she tried to talk. He led her and Melanie into the study, found a pad of paper and a pen in the desk drawer, and quickly scribbled a message.

Baffled by his mysterious behavior, Laura stood beside him and read what he wrote. *We're leaving the house.*

Laura wasn't reluctant to comply. She vividly remembered the warning that had been delivered to them through the radio: *It* was coming. The flower-filled whirlwind had seemed to be another warning with the same message. It was coming. It wanted Melanie. And It knew where they were.

Earl wrote more: *Pack a suitcase for yourself and one for Melanie.*

Evidently, he was prepared to believe that someone had planted listening devices in the house.

Apparently, he also believed he might not be able to spirit Laura and Melanie away if the listeners knew that they planned to leave. That made sense. Whoever had financed Dylan and Hoffritz would want to know where Melanie was at all times, so they would eventually have a chance to either kill her or snatch her away. And the FBI would want to know where she was at all times, so they would be able to nab the people who tried to nab Melanie. Unless it was the FBI that wanted her in the first place.

Laura had that trapped-in-a-nightmare feeling again.

Maybe everyone in the world wasn't out to get them, but it sure seemed that way. Worse, it wasn't only someone out to get them—it was some*thing.*

Hide. That was all they could do right now. They had to go where no one could follow or find them.

Laura grabbed the pencil and wrote: *Where will we go?*

"Later," he said softly. "Now, we've got to hurry."

It was coming.

In the bedroom, he helped Laura pack two suitcases, one for Melanie and one for herself.

It was coming. And the fact that she didn't know what It was—that she even felt slightly foolish for believing It existed in the first place—did nothing whatsoever to alleviate her fear of It.

When the bags were packed, when they had their coats on, Laura repeatedly called Pepper. The cat wouldn't respond to her, and a quick tour of the house didn't turn it up anywhere. Pepper was hiding, being difficult, as any self-respecting cat would have been in those circumstances.

"Leave it," Earl whispered. "Someone can stop by to feed it tomorrow."

They went through the laundry room into the garage. They didn't switch off any lights behind them, because that might have signaled their intentions. Earl put the suitcases in the trunk of Laura's blue Honda.

She didn't need to ask why they were taking her car instead of his. His was parked outside, at the curb, and if those FBI agents across the street saw Laura and Melanie heading for it, they'd want to know where they were going and why; they might even prevent them from leaving.

Of course, their hurried flight might be a mistake because the FBI might want nothing more than to help. Or it might not. In either case, their best hope was to trust only in Earl Benton.

He put Melanie in the backseat and fastened the belt across her lap.

From the front seat, Laura glanced back and was startled by her daughter's appearance. In the closed garage, illuminated only by the car's ceiling light, the girl's gaunt face was fleshed out by shadows; the harsh lines and sharp bones were softened by the moon-pale glow. For the first time, Laura realized how very pretty her little girl would be when she had gained some weight. She would be utterly and miraculously transformed by a few pounds and by peace of mind, both of which would come with time. Abruptly, Laura was able to see the potential within the battered clay, the familiar within the alien, the beauty within the grayness. Time, like a painter's brush, would layer other experiences and emotions over Melanie's now-bright agony, and when the paint of days and weeks and years had become sufficiently thick to all but conceal the horror of her ordeal with her father, she would no longer be a skeletal, angular, strange creature with death-pale skin and wounded eyes; she would, in fact, be quite lovely. That realization made Laura's breath catch, and it renewed her hope.

More important, the kind light and caressing shadows allowed her to perceive much of herself in her daughter, and that perception had an even more profound effect on her. Intellectually, she had known that Melanie resembled her—evidence in her genes was clear in the child's haunted face, in spite of the abuse that had pulled it into a tortured mask—but until now she had not quite related to that likeness on a deep emotional level. Seeing herself in her daughter, she had a more intense awareness that her child's suffering was her own suffering, that her child's future was her own future, and that she could have no happiness until Melanie was happy too. Whereas the realization of the girl's underlying beauty had renewed Laura's hope, this second insight renewed her determination to find the truth and to beat their enemies even if the whole damned world *was* aligned against them.

Earl got behind the wheel. He looked over at Laura and said, "It's going to get a little wild for the next few minutes."

"It's already gotten wild," she said, buckling her seat belt.

"I've had a driving course that teaches avoidance of terrorists and kidnappers, so I'm not being as reckless as it's going to seem."

"Recklessness won't bother me in the least," she said. "Not after seeing that wind-thing smash its way into my kitchen. Besides, I've always thought it would be a lot of fun to drive like James Bond."

He smiled at her. "You've got grit."

As he started the engine, she picked up the automatic garage-door opener that lay on the console tray between the seats.

He said, "Now."

Laura pressed the button on the remote-control device, and the garage door started to swing up. Before the door had lifted all the way. Earl threw the car into reverse and backed under it with only an inch to spare, moving fast.

Laura expected to crash through the rising door, but they slipped out of the garage and reversed away from the house at high speed. They slowed where the driveway met the street, but not much, and Earl pulled the steering wheel hard right, so they were facing down the long hill.

The FBI, in its fake telephone-company van, had not yet reacted. Earl hit the brakes, shifted the Honda out of reverse into drive and jammed his foot down on the accelerator. Tires squealed, and the car seemed to stick to the pavement, but then they rocked forward, down the dark and sloping street.

Two blocks downhill, Earl glanced at the rearview mirror and said, "They're coming."

Laura looked through the rear window, and saw the van just pulling away from the curb.

Earl tapped the brakes and swung the steering wheel hard to the right, and the Honda half turned, half slid around the corner, into the cross street. At the next intersection, he turned left, then right again at the end of that block, speeding and weaving through the quiet residential neighborhood, finally out of Sherman Oaks altogether, to the top of the valley wall, over the ridge line, into Benedict Canyon, and down the forested slopes, through the darkness, toward the distant light of Beverly Hills and Los Angeles beyond.

"We've lost them," he said happily.

Laura was not completely relieved. She wasn't convinced that they could lose their inhuman enemy—the unseen *It*—as easily as they had shaken the FBI van.

chapter twenty-five

Dan watched Regine closely, trying to figure how he could force her to tell him what she knew. She was so pliable that he could surely bend her to his purposes if he could only determine how and where to apply pressure.

Regine was no longer biting on her knuckle. She had slipped a thumb into her mouth and gently sucked on it. Her pose was so provocative— innocence waiting to be despoiled—that he was certain it was something that Hoffritz had taught her to do. Something he had *programmed* her to do? But it was clear that she also was soothed by the thumb-sucking; her inner torment was so severe that it had driven her to seek solace in the simplest, most infantile rituals of reassurance.

From the moment that she had put her thumb in her mouth, she had stopped sitting erect and ladylike. Now she slumped into the corner of the sofa. The neckline of her robe had parted, revealing deep, smooth, shadowed cleavage.

Dan had a pretty good idea how to make her talk, but he didn't like doing what he would have to do.

She took her thumb out of her mouth long enough to say, "I can't help you. I really can't. Will you go now? Please?"

He didn't answer. He got up from the armchair, walked around the coffee table, and stood over her, frowning down at her.

She kept her head bowed.

Sternly, almost harshly, he said, "Look at me."

She looked at him. In a tremulous voice that indicated she expected to be ignored, she said, "Will you go now? Please? Will you go now?"

"You're going to answer my questions, Regine," he said, scowling at her. "You're not going to lie to me. If you won't answer, or if you lie to me . . ."

"Will you hit me?" she asked.

He was confronted not by a woman any longer but by a sick, lost, miserable creature. Not a frightened creature, however. The prospect of being struck did not fill her with terror. Quite the opposite. She was sick, lost, miserable—and hungry. Hungry for the thrill of being hit, starving for the pleasure of pain.

Repressing his revulsion, making his voice as cold as he could, he said, "I won't hit you. I won't touch you. But you'll tell me what I want to know because that's the reason you exist right now."

Her eyes shone with a curious light, like those of an animal seen at night.

"You always do what's wanted of you, right? You are what you're expected to be. I expect you to be cooperative, Regine. I want you to answer my questions, and you will, because that's the only damned thing you're good for—answering questions."

She stared up at him expectantly.

"Have you ever met Ernest Andrew Cooper?"

"No."

"You're lying."

"Am I?"

Suppressing all the sympathy and compassion he felt for her, he made his voice even colder, and he raised one fist over her, although he had no intention of using it. "Do you know Cooper?"

She didn't answer, but her eyes focused on his big fist with an unholy adoration that he couldn't bear to contemplate.

With sudden inspiration, he feigned an anger that he didn't feel and said, "Answer me, you bitch!"

She flinched at the derogatory address, but not because it hurt or surprised her. She flinched, instead, as if a shock of delight had passed through her. Even that meager verbal abuse had been a key that unlocked her.

Gazing at his fist, she said, "Please."

"Maybe."

"You'd like to."

"Maybe . . . if you tell me what I want to know. Cooper."

"They don't tell me their last names. I knew an Ernie somebody, but I don't know if it was Cooper."

He described the dead millionaire.

"Yeah," she said, her gaze shifting between his fist and his eyes. "That was him."

"You met him through Willy?"

"Yes."

"And Joseph Scaldone?"

"Willy . . . introduced me to this guy named Joe, but I never knew his last name, either."

Dan described Joseph Scaldone.

She nodded. "That was him."

"And Ned Rink?"

"I don't think I ever met him."

"A short, stocky, rather ugly man."

As he fleshed out that description, she began to shake her head. "No. I never met that one."

"You've seen the gray room?"

"Yes. I dream of it sometimes. Of sitting in that chair, and they do it to me, the shocks, the electricity."

"When did you see it? The room, the chair?"

"Oh, a few years ago, when they were first painting the room, putting in the equipment, getting it ready. . . ."

"What were they doing with Melanie McCaffrey?"

"I don't know."

"Don't lie to me, damn it. You are what you're expected to be, and you do what's wanted of you, always what's wanted of you, so cut the shit and answer me."

"No, really, I don't know," she said meekly. "Willy never told me. It was secret. An important secret. It'd change the world, he said. That's all I know. He didn't include me in those things very much. His life with me was separate from his work with those other men."

Dan continued to stand over her, and she continued to cower in a corner of the sofa, and although the threat he posed to her was entirely theatrical, he nevertheless felt uncomfortably like a bully. "What did the occult have to do with their experiments?"

"I haven't any idea."

"Did Willy believe in the supernatural?"

"No."

"Why do you say that?"

"Well . . . because Dylan McCaffrey believed indiscriminately in it—all of it, ghosts and seances and even goblins for all I know—and Willy used to make fun of him, said he was gullible."

"Then why was he working with McCaffrey?"

"Willy thought Dylan was a genius."

"In spite of his superstitions?"

"Yeah."

"Who was funding them, Regine?"

"I don't know."

She moved in such a way that her robe parted further, revealing more cleavage, most of one full breast.

"Come on," he said impatiently. "Who's been paying their bills? Who, Regine?"

"I swear, I don't know."

He sat on the couch beside her. He took her by the chin, held her face, not gently, not with erotic intention, but as an extension of the threat first embodied by his raised fist.

Meaningless as the threat was, she nevertheless responded to it. This was what she wanted: to be intimidated, to be commanded, and to obey.

"Who?" he repeated.

She said, "I don't know. I really, really don't. I'd tell you if I did. I swear. Anything you want, I'd tell you."

This time he believed her. But he didn't let go of her face. "I know Melanie McCaffrey endured a lot of mental and physical abuse in that gray room. But I want to know . . . Christ, I don't want to know, but I've got to know . . . was there sexual abuse too?"

Regine's mouth was somewhat compressed by his grip on her chin and jaws, so her voice was slightly distorted. "How would I know?"

"You would have known," he insisted. "One way or the other, you would have sensed a thing like that, even if Hoffritz didn't talk to you much about what went on in Studio City. He might not have talked about what he was trying to achieve with the girl, but he would have bragged about his control of her. I'm sure of that. I never met him, but I know him well enough to be sure of that."

"I don't believe there was anything sexual about it," Regine said.

He squeezed her face, and she winced, but he saw (with dismay) that she liked it nonetheless, so he relaxed his hand, though he didn't let go of her. "Are you sure?"

"Almost certain. He might have liked . . . to have her. But I think you're right: He would have told me that, if he'd done it, if he'd been with her like that . . ."

"Did he even hint at it?"

"No."

Dan was profoundly relieved. He even smiled. At least the child hadn't been subjected to that indignity. Then he remembered what indignities she *had* endured, and his smile quickly died.

He let go of Regine's face but stayed beside her on the couch. Gradually fading red spots marked where his fingers had pressed into her tender skin. "Regine, you said you hadn't seen Willy in more than a year. Why?"

She lowered her eyes, bent her neck. Her shoulders softened even more, and she slumped farther into the corner of the sofa.

"Why?" he repeated.

"Willy . . . got tired of me."

That she should care so much about Willy made Dan ill.

"He didn't want me anymore," she said in a tone of voice more suited to announcing imminent death from cancer. Willy not wanting her anymore was clearly the worst, most devastating development that she could imagine. "I did everything, anything, but nothing was enough. . . ."

"He just broke it off, cold?"

"I never saw him after he . . . sent me away. But we talked on the phone now and then. We had to."

"Had to talk on the phone? About what?"

Almost whispering: "About the others he sent around to see me."

"What others?"

"His friends. The other . . . men."

"He sent men to you?"

"Yes."

"For sex?"

"For sex. For anything they wanted. I do anything they want. For Willy."

Dan's mental image of the late Wilhelm Hoffritz was growing more monstrous by the minute. The man had been a viper.

He not only brainwashed and established control of Regine for his own sexual gratification, but even after he no longer wanted her, he continued to control her and abuse her secondhand. Apparently, the mere fact that she continued to be abused, even beyond his sight, gratified him sufficiently to maintain an iron grip on her tortured mind. He had been a singularly sick man. Worse than sick: demented.

Regine raised her head and said, not without enthusiasm, "Do you want me to tell you some of the things they made me do?"

Dan stared at her, speechless with revulsion.

"I don't mind telling you," she assured him. "You might enjoy hearing. I didn't mind doing those things, and I don't mind telling you exactly what I did."

"No," he said hoarsely.

"You might like to hear."

"No."

She giggled softly. "It might give you some ideas."

"Shut up!" he said, and he nearly slapped her.

She bowed her head as if she were a dog that had been cowed by a scolding master.

He said, "The men Hoffritz sent to you—who were they?"

"I only know their first names. One of them was Andy, and you've told me his last name was Cooper. Another one was Joe."

"Scaldone? Who else?"

"Howard, Shelby . . . Eddie."

"Eddie who?"

"I told you, I don't know their last names."

"How often did they come?"

"Most of them . . . once or twice a week."

"They still come here?"

"Oh, sure. I'm what they need. There was only one guy who came once and never came back."

"What was his name?"

"Albert."

"Albert Uhlander?"

"I don't know."

"What did he look like?"

"Tall, thin, with a . . . bony face. I don't know how else to describe him. I guess you'd say he sort of looked like a hawk . . . hawkish . . . sharp features."

Dan had not looked at the author's photograph on the books now in the trunk of his car, but he intended to do so when he left Regine.

He said, "Albert, Howard, Shelby, Eddie . . . anybody else?"

"Well, like I said, Andy and Joe. But they're dead now, huh?"

"Very."

"And there's one other man. He comes by all the time, but I don't even know his first name."

"What's he look like?"

"About six foot, distinguished. Beautiful white hair. Beautiful clothes. Not handsome, you know, but elegant. He carries himself so well, and he speaks very well. He's . . . cultured. I like him. He hurts me so . . . beautifully."

Dan took a deep breath. "If you don't even know his first name, what do you call him?"

She grinned. "Oh, there's only one thing he wants me to call him." She looked mischievous, winked at Dan. "Daddy."

"What?"

"I call him Daddy. Always. I pretend he's my daddy, see, and he pretends I'm really his daughter, and I sit on his lap and we talk about school, and I—"

"That's enough," he said, feeling as if he had stepped into a corner of Hell, where knowing the local customs was an obligation to live by them. He preferred not knowing.

He wanted to sweep the photographs off the table, smash the glass that shielded them, pull the other pictures off the mantel and throw them in the fireplace and light them with a match. But he knew that he would be of no help to Regine merely by destroying those reminders of Hoffritz. The hateful man was dead, yes, but he would live for years in this woman's mind, like a malevolent troll in a secret cave.

Dan touched her face again, but briefly and tenderly this time. "Regine, what do you do with your time, your days, your life?"

She shrugged.

"Do you go to movies, dancing, out to dinner with friends—or do you just sit here, waiting for someone to need you?"

"Mostly I stay here," she said. "I like it here. This is where Willy wanted me."

"And what do you do for a living?"

"I do what they want."

"You've got a degree in psychology, for God's sake."

She said nothing.

"Why did you finish your degree at UCLA if you didn't intend to use it?"

"Willy wanted me to finish. It was funny, you know. They threw him out, those bastards at the university, but they couldn't throw me out so easily. I was there to remind them about Willy. That pleased him. He thought that was a terrific joke."

"You could do important work, interesting work."

"I'm doing what I was made for."

"No. You aren't. You're doing what Hoffritz said you were made for. That's very different."

"Willy knew," she said. "Willy knew everything."

"Willy was a rotten pig," he said.

"No." Tears formed in her eyes again.

"So they come here and use you, hurt you." He grabbed her arm, pulled up the sleeve of her robe, revealing the bruise that he had spotted earlier and the rope burns at her wrist. "They hurt you, don't they?"

"Yeah, in one way or another, some of them more than others. Some of them are better at it. Some of them make it feel so sweet."

"*Why* do you put up with it?"

"I like it."

The air seemed even more oppressive than it had a few minutes ago. Thick, moist, heavy with a grime that couldn't be seen, a filth that settled not on the skin but on the soul. Dan didn't want to breathe it in. It was dangerously corrupting air.

"Who pays your rent?" he asked.

"There is no rent."

"Who owns the house?"

"A company."

"What company?"

"What can I do for you?"

"What company?"

"Let me do something for you."

"What company?" he persisted.

"John Wilkes Enterprises."

"Who's John Wilkes?"

"I don't know."

"You've never had a man here named John?"

"No."

"How do you know about this John Wilkes Enterprises?"

"I get a check from them every month. A very nice check."

Shakily, Dan got to his feet.

Regine was visibly disappointed.

He looked around, spotted the suitcases by the door, which he had noticed when he'd first come in. "Going away?"

"For a few days."

"Where?"

"Las Vegas."

"Are you running, Regine?"

"What would I be running from?"

"People are getting killed because of what happened in that gray room."

"But I don't know what happened in the gray room, and I don't care," she said. "So I'm safe."

Staring down at her, Dan realized that Regine Savannah Hoffritz had a gray room all of her own. She carried it with her wherever she went, for her gray room was where the real Regine was locked away, trapped, imprisoned.

He said, "Regine, you need help."

"I need to be what you want."

"No. You need—"

"I'm fine."

"You need counseling."

"I'm free. Willy taught me how to be free."

"Free from what?"

"Responsibility. Fear. Hope. Free from everything."

"Willy didn't free you. He enslaved you."

"You don't understand."

"He was a sadist."

"There's nothing wrong with that."

"He got inside your mind, twisted you. We're not talking about some half-baked psychology professor, Regine. This lunatic was a heavyweight. This was a guy who worked for the Pentagon, researching behavior modification, developing new methods of brainwashing. Ego-repressing drugs, Regine. Subliminal persuasion. Willy was to Big Brother what Merlin was to King Arthur. Except Willy did bad magic, Regine. He transformed you into . . . into this . . . into a masochist, for his amusement."

"And that's how he freed me," she said serenely. "You see, when you no longer fear pain, when you learn to love pain, then you can't be afraid of anything anymore. That's why I'm free."

Dan wanted to shake her, but he knew that shaking her would do no good. Quite the opposite. She would only beg for more.

He wanted to get her in front of a sympathetic judge and have her committed without her consent, so she could receive psychiatric treatment. But he wasn't related to her; he was virtually a stranger to her; no judge would play along with him; it just wasn't done that way. There seemed to be nothing he could do for her.

She said, "You know something interesting? I think maybe Willy's not really dead."

"Oh, he's dead, all right."

"Maybe not."

"I saw the body. We got a positive ID match from dental records and fingerprints."

"Maybe," she said. "But . . . well, I get the feeling he's still alive. Sometimes I sense him out there . . . I feel him. It's strange. I can't explain it. But that's why I'm not as broken up as I might have been. Because I'm not convinced he's dead. Somehow, he's still . . . out there."

Her self-image and her primary reasons for continuing to live were so dependent upon Willy Hoffritz, upon the prospect of receiving his praise and his approval or at least upon hearing his voice on the telephone every once in a while, that she was never going to be able to accept his death. Dan suspected that he could take her to the morgue, confront her with the bloody corpse, force her to place her hands upon the cold dead flesh, make her stare into the grotesquely battered countenance, shove the coroner's report in front of her—and nevertheless fail to convince her that Hoffritz had been killed. Hoffritz had gotten inside her, had shattered her psyche, then had rejoined the pieces in a pattern that was more pleasing to himself, with himself as the bonding agent holding her together. If Regine accepted the reality of his death, there would be no glue binding her anymore, and she might collapse into insanity. Her only hope—or so it must seem to her—was to believe that Willy was still alive.

"Yes, he's out there," she said again. "I feel it. Somehow, somewhere, he's out there."

Feeling utterly ineffectual, loathing his powerlessness, Dan headed toward the door.

Behind him, Regine rose quickly from the sofa and said, "Please. Wait."

He glanced back at her.

She said, "You could . . . have me."

"No, Regine."

"Do anything to me."

"No."

"I'll be your animal."

He continued to the door.

She said, "Your little animal."

He resisted the urge to run.

She caught up with him as he opened the door. Her perfume was subtle but effective. She put one hand on his shoulder and said, "I like you."

"Where are your folks, Regine?"

"You make me hot."

"Your mother and father? Where do they live?"

She put her slender fingers to his lips. They were warm.

She traced the outline of his mouth.

He pushed her hand away.

She said, "I really, really like you."

"Maybe your folks could help you through this."

"I like you."

"Regine—"

"Hurt me. Hurt me very badly."

He pushed her away from him as a compassionate hypochondriac might push away a grasping leper: firmly, with distaste, with fear of contagion, but with a regard for the delicacy of her condition.

She said, "When Willy put me in the hospital, he came to visit me every day. He arranged a private room for me and always closed the door when he came, so we'd be alone. When we were alone, he kissed my bruises. Every day he came and kissed my bruises. You can't know how good his lips felt on my bruises, Lieutenant. One kiss, and each spot of soreness—each little tender contusion—was transformed. Instead of pain, each bruise was filled with pleasure. It was as if . . . as if a clitoris sprang up in the place of every bruise, and when he kissed me I climaxed, again and again."

Dan got the hell out of there and slammed the door behind him.

chapter twenty-six

With a cold and gusty wind blowing scraps of litter along the night streets, and with the portent of rain heavy in the air, Earl Benton took Laura and Melanie to an apartment on the first floor of a rambling three-story complex in Westwood, south of Wilshire Boulevard. It had a living room, a dining alcove, a kitchen, one bedroom, and one bath. The place didn't seem quite as small as it actually was, because big windows looked out on a lushly landscaped courtyard which, at that time of night, was illuminated by blue- and green-filtered spotlights concealed throughout the shrubbery.

The apartment was owned by California Paladin and was used as a "safe house." The agency was occasionally hired to retrieve teenagers and college-age kids from fanatical religious cults with which they had become entangled; immediately upon being freed, they were brought to that apartment, where they underwent several days of deprogramming before returning to their parents. The safe house also had been used as a secure way station for wives who were threatened by estranged husbands, and on several occasions high corporate executives in a variety of industries had met there for days at a time to plan secret and hostile takeover bids of other companies because they could be free of worry about electronic eavesdropping and corporate espionage. California Paladin had also once stashed a Baptist minister in those rooms after a youth gang in south-central L.A. had put out a contract on his life to repay him for testimony against one of their brothers. A rock-music star had passed through while dodging a particularly onerous subpoena in an expensive civil suit. And a big-name actress had needed just this degree of total privacy in just such an unlikely location as this, in order to recuperate from secret cancer surgery that, if revealed, would have cost her roles in upcoming pictures; producers were reluctant to hire stars who would be ineligible for completion bonds and who might get sick or even die halfway through filming.

Melanie and Laura would make use of those quiet, modest rooms, at least for the night. Laura hoped that the hideaway would be as safe from the strange force pursuing them as it was from youth gangs and process servers.

Earl turned on the heat and went into the kitchen to brew a pot of coffee.

Laura tried to interest Melanie in some hot chocolate, but the girl wanted none. Melanie moved like a sleepwalker to the largest chair in the living room, climbed onto it, curled her legs beneath her, and sat staring down at her hands, which lethargically pulled and rubbed and scratched and massaged each other. Her fingers interlaced and knotted and then untied themselves and then knotted together again. She stared at her hands so raptly that it almost began to seem as if she didn't realize that they were a part of her but thought, instead, that they were two small, busy animals at play in her lap.

The coffee countered the chill they had gotten while coming from the windswept parking lot to the apartment, but it could not relieve that other chill—the one caused not by physical stimuli but by their unexpected and unwanted encounter with the unknown.

While Earl called his office to report their move from the house in Sherman Oaks, Laura stood at the living-room window, holding the coffee mug in both hands, breathing in the fragrant vapors. As she stared out at the lakes of shadow, at the sprays and pools of green and blue light, the first fat droplets of rain began to snap against the palm fronds.

Somewhere in the night, something was stalking Melanie, something beyond human understanding, an invulnerable creature that left its victims looking as if they had gone through half the cycle in a trash compactor before someone had pushed the emergency-stop button. Laura's university degrees, her doctorate in psychology, might make it possible for her to eventually bring Melanie out of quasi-autistic withdrawal, but nothing taught and nothing learned in any university could help her deal with *It*. Was it demon, spirit, psychic force? Those things did not exist. Right? Did not exist. Yet . . . what had Dylan and Hoffritz unleashed? And why?

Dylan had believed in the supernatural. Periodically, he had been obsessed with one aspect of the occult or another, and during those periods he had been more intense and nervous and argumentative than usual. In fact, when thus obsessed, he reminded Laura of her mother because his adamant belief in—and constant preaching about—the reality of the occult was akin to the religious fanaticism and superstitious mania that had made Beatrice such a terror; it was this, as much as anything, that had driven Laura to divorce, for she could not abide anything that reminded her of her fear-ridden childhood.

Now, she tried to remember specific enthusiasms that had gripped Dylan, theories that had obsessed him. She strove to recall something that might explain what was happening now, but she could not remember anything important, because she had always refused to listen to him when he had spoken of those things that had seemed, to her, like the sheerest flights of fancy—or madness.

In reaction to her mother's irrationality and gullibility, Laura had built a life strictly on logic and reason, trusting in only those things that she could see, hear, touch, smell, and feel. She did not believe that a cracked mirror meant seven years of bad luck, and she did not throw spilled salt over her shoulder. Given the choice, she would always walk *under* a ladder rather than around it, merely to prove that there was nothing of her mother in her. She didn't believe in devils, demons, possession, and exorcism. In her heart, she felt there was a God, but she didn't attend church or identify with any particular religion. She didn't read ghost stories, had no interest in movies about vampires and werewolves. She didn't believe in psychics, premonitions, clairvoyant visions.

She was profoundly unprepared for the events of the past twenty-four hours.

While logic and reason made the most solid foundation on which to construct a life, she realized that the mortar ought to be mixed with a sense of wonder, with a respect for the unknown, or at least leavened with open-mindedness. Otherwise, it would be brittle mortar that would dry, crack, and flake away. Her mother's extreme reliance on religion and superstition was undoubtedly sick. But perhaps it wasn't wise to have rushed to the other extreme of the philosophical spectrum. The universe seemed considerably more complicated than it had been before.

Something was out there.

Something she couldn't understand.

And it wanted Melanie.

But even as she stood by the window and studied the rainy night with a new respect for things mysterious and uncanny, her mind sought more rational explanations, tangible villains of flesh and blood. She heard Earl talking on the telephone with someone at his office, and suddenly it occurred to her that no one except California Paladin knew where she and her daughter were. For a terrible moment, she felt that she had done something very wrong, very stupid, in allowing herself to be spirited away from the watchful eyes of the FBI, from contact with friends and neighbors and the police. Melanie had not been targeted solely by the unseen It of which they had been warned, but by real people too, people like that hired killer who had been found in the hospital parking lot. And what if those people had contacts inside California Paladin? What if Earl himself was the executioner?

Stop!

She took a deep breath. Another.

She was standing on a slope of slippery emotions, sliding toward hysteria. For Melanie's sake, if not her own, she had to maintain control of herself.

chapter twenty-seven

Dan stepped out of Regine's house and slammed the door behind him, but he didn't head down the walk. He waited, listening at the door, and his suspicion was confirmed when he heard a man's voice: She hadn't been alone.

The man was furious. He shouted, and she called him Eddie and responded in a meek and wheedling voice. The flat, hard, unmistakable sound of a slap was followed by her cry—a bleat composed partly of pain, partly of fear, but also partly of pleasure and excitement.

Around Dan, the wind huffed noisily and the branches of the trees were scraping against one another, and it wasn't possible to hear exactly what was being said in the house. He picked up enough words to know that Eddie was angry because Regine had revealed too much. In a miserable, servile voice, Regine tried to explain that she'd had no choice but to tell Dan what she knew; Dan hadn't asked for answers, he had *demanded* answers—and, more important, he had demanded in a way that pushed all her buttons. She was an obedient creature who found meaning, purpose, and joy only in doing what she was told to do. Eddie and his friends liked her that way, she said, wanted her that way, she said, and it wasn't possible for her to be that way with them and not that way with other people. "Don't you understand, Eddie? Don't you understand?" He might have understood, but her explanation did nothing to ameliorate his fury. He slapped her again, again, and her tortured but dismayingly eager cry did not bear contemplation.

Dan moved away from the door, along the front of the house, to the first window. He wanted to get a look at Eddie.

Through a gap in the drapes, he saw a portion of the living room and a man of about forty-five. The guy had red hair, a mustache, and doughy features. He was dressed in black slacks, white shirt, gray sweater-vest, and bow tie. His face was that of an aging, spoiled child. He had an effete quality, and he moved with a bantam-rooster strut that wasn't natural to him, as if he thought that authority must always be expressed by a puffing of the chest, a rolling of the shoulders, and a cocky attitude. In spite of his posturing, he looked weak and ineffectual, like a wimpy high school English teacher who had trouble controlling his students. He was not at all the kind of man who would slap a woman around; very likely, he would not have been slapping Regine if she'd been any other woman than she was, for another woman might have slapped him back.

More than anything else, Eddie was distressed that Regine had told Dan about John Wilkes Enterprises, the company that was her keeper, that owned the house in which she lived, and that sent her a check each month. Regine was on her knees before him, head bowed, like a vassal humbling herself before her feudal lord, and he loomed over her, shifting from foot to foot, gesticulating with nervous energy, repeatedly castigating her for having such a loose tongue.

John Wilkes Enterprises.

Dan knew he had been given another key to another lock in this many-doored mystery.

He turned away from the house and returned to the street where he had parked the car. He opened the trunk and plucked one of the seven Albert Uhlander books from the carton that he had carried out of Ned Rink's house earlier in the evening. Regine had said that a man named Albert had visited her once and, unlike the others who used her, had never visited her again; she had said that he'd had a bony face with sharp features, hawklike. Now, in the ghostly radiance of a mercury-vapor streetlight and in the even more eldritch glow of the bulb in the car's trunk, Dan studied the photograph of the author on the book jacket. Uhlander's face was long, narrow, almost cadaverous, with prominent brow, cheekbones, and jawline; his eyes were cold and predatory, at least in the context of his hooked and beakish nose, and he did indeed have the aspect of a hawk or some other ferocious bird of prey.

So it had been Uhlander who had visited Regine, but only on one occasion, not motivated by overpowering and perverse sexual needs, as were the others, but perhaps by curiosity, as if he needed to see for himself that she was real and that Hoffritz had thoroughly enslaved her. Maybe Uhlander had wished to satisfy himself as to Hoffritz's genius in these matters before joining him and Dylan McCaffrey on the strange project that they had undertaken with Melanie.

Whatever the case, Dan wanted to talk to him. He added Uhlander to the mental list of those whom he intended to question, a list that already included Mary O'Hara, Ernest Andrew Cooper's wife, Joseph Scaldone's wife (if he had one), the executives and/or owners of John Wilkes Enterprises, the silver-haired and distinguished pervert who visited Regine regularly and whom she knew only as "Daddy," and the other men who used her—Eddie, Shelby, and Howard.

He put the book back in the carton, closed the trunk, and got into the car just as a few fat drops of rain began to splatter the pavement. Scaldone's mailing list was still in his pocket, and he was certain that he would soon find last names for Eddie, Shelby, and Howard among those three hundred customers of the Sign of the Pentagram. The light there was poor, however, and he was tired, and his eyes felt sandy, and he still wanted to talk to Laura McCaffrey before it got too late, so he left the list in his pocket, started the engine, and drove out of the Hollywood Hills.

At 10:44, when he reached Laura's house in Sherman Oaks, a cold rain was falling. Although lights were on in several rooms, no one answered the door. He rang the bell, then knocked, then pounded on the door, to no avail.

Where was Earl Benton? He was supposed to remain there until midnight, when another agent from California Paladin was scheduled to relieve him.

Dan thought of the crushed and disfigured corpses in Studio City the previous night, and he thought of the dead hit man, Ned Rink, and with growing anxiety he moved away from the door, squished across the wet lawn, pushed between two flower-laden hibiscus bushes, and peered in the nearest window. He saw nothing out of the ordinary, no bodies or blood or wreckage. He went to the next window, and still he saw nothing, so he hurried to the gate at the side of the house and went through it and along the walk to the rear, his heart racing and an ulcerous pain flaring in his gut.

The kitchen door was unlocked. As he pushed it open and stepped inside, he noted that the doorframe was splintered and that a ruined security chain hung from its mounting. Then he saw the mess in the room beyond: torn and wilted flowers, shredded and wadded leaves, other greenery, clods of moist earth.

No blood.

On the table were three unfinished spaghetti dinners speckled with dirt and debris.

One overturned chair.

A tangled mass of impatiens bristled from the sink.

But no blood. Thank God. No blood. So far.

He drew his revolver.

Full of dread, with incipient grief welling in anticipation of the battered corpses that must lie somewhere in the house, he edged out of the kitchen and moved cautiously from one room to the next. He found nothing but a wary cat that dashed away from him.

Checking the garage, he saw that Laura McCaffrey's blue Honda was gone. He didn't know what to make of that.

When he uncovered no bodies anywhere, his relief was as great as if he had been trudging along an ocean floor with billions of tons of water pressing on him and was now abruptly transported to dry land where only air weighed on his shoulders. The extent and depth of his relief, and the great exhilaration that accompanied it, forced him to admit to himself that his feelings for this woman and her troubled child were different from his feelings for all the other victims whom he had known in fourteen years of policework. Nor could his unusual involvement and empathy be attributed to the vague parallels between this case and that of Fran and Cindy Lakey, years ago; he was not drawn to Laura McCaffrey solely because, by saving her and Melanie, he could atone for his failure to save Cindy Lakey's life. That was part of it, certainly, but he was also attracted to this woman. The influence that she had on him was not quite like anything he'd ever known before; he was drawn to her not only because of her beauty, which was undeniably affecting, and not only because of her intelligence, which was important to him since he had never shared most men's fascination with dumb blondes and airhead brunettes, but also because of her incredible strength and determination in the face of horror and adversity.

But even if she and Melanie get out of this predicament alive, Dan thought, there's probably little hope of a relationship between her and me. She's a doctor of psychology, for God's sake. I'm a cop. She's better educated than I am. She makes more money than I do. Forget it, Haldane. You're out of your class.

Nevertheless, when he found no bodies anywhere in the house, he was immensely relieved, and his heart swelled with a particular joy that he would not have felt if the escapees from death had been any other escapees than this woman and her daughter.

When he returned to the kitchen to have a closer look at the wreckage there, Dan found that he was no longer alone in the house. Michael Seames, the FBI agent he'd met a few hours ago at the Sign of the Pentagram, was standing by the table, hands in the pockets of his raincoat, studying the floral debris that filled the room. Beneath his graying hair, above his apparently aged shoulders, a troubled and puzzled expression lay upon Seames's anachronistically young face.

"Where have they gone?" Dan asked.

"I was hoping *you* could tell *me*," Seames said.

"At my suggestion, she hired around-the-clock bodyguards—"

"California Paladin."

"Yeah, that's right. But as far as I know, they weren't going to recommend that she go into hiding or anything like that. They were going to stay here with her."

"One of them was here. An Earl Benton—"

"Yes, I know him."

"Until about an hour ago. Then, without warning, he split with Laura McCaffrey and the girl, went out of here like a bat out of hell. We have a surveillance van across the street."

"Oh?"

"They tried to follow Benton, but he was moving too fast." Seames frowned. "In fact, it seemed like he was trying to give us the slip as much as anything else. You have any idea why he'd want to do that?"

"Just a wild guess. I'm probably totally off the wall to even suggest it. But maybe he doesn't trust you."

"We're here to protect the child."

"You sure our government wouldn't like to have her for a while, to try to figure out what McCaffrey and Hoffritz were doing with her in that gray room?"

"We might," Seames admitted. "That decision hasn't been made yet. But this is America, you know—"

"So I've heard."

"—and we wouldn't kidnap her."

"What would you call it—'borrowing' her?"

"We'd want to have her mother's permission for whatever tests we'd run."

Dan sighed, not sure what to believe.

Seames said, "You didn't maybe tell Benton that he should get them out from under us, did you?"

"Why would I do that? I'm a public servant, same as you."

"Then you always work these hours, all day and half the night, on every case you handle?"

"Not every case."

"Most cases?"

Dan could honestly say, "Yeah, in fact, on most cases I put in long hours. You get going on an investigation, and one thing leads to another, and it isn't always possible to stop cold at five o'clock each day. Most detectives work long hours, irregular shifts. You must know that."

"You work harder than most, I hear."

Dan shrugged.

Seames said, "They say you're a bulldog, that you love your work and you really sink your teeth into it, really hang on."

"Maybe. I guess I work pretty hard. But in a homicide, the trail can get cold fast. Usually, if you don't get a lead on your killer in three or four days, you'll never hang it on anyone."

"But you're putting more into this case than even the average homicide detective usually does, more than even you usually do. Aren't you, Lieutenant?"

"Maybe."

"You know you are."

"Arf, arf."

"What?"

"The bulldog in me."

"Why such a bulldog on *this* case?"

"I guess I was just in the mood for some action."

"That's no answer."

"I just ate too much Purina Dog Chow, have too much energy, got to work it off."

Seames shook his head. "It's because you've got a special stake in this one."

"Do I?"

"Don't you?"

"Not that I'm aware of," Dan said, although an image of Laura McCaffrey's lovely face rose unbidden in his memory.

Seames regarded him with suspicion and said, "Listen, Haldane, if someone was bankrolling McCaffrey and Hoffritz because their project had a military application, then those same—let's call them *financiers*—those same financiers might be willing to spread a lot of money around to get their hands on the girl again. But any money they spread would be dirty, damned dirty. Any guy who took it would probably come down with an infection from it. Know what I mean?"

At first it had appeared that Seames was somehow aware of Dan's romantic inclinations toward Laura. Now it was suddenly clear that a darker worry nagged the agent.

For God's sake, Dan thought, he's wondering if I've sold out to the Russians or someone!

"Jesus, Seames, are you ever on the wrong track!"

"They might be willing to pay a lot to get their hands on her, and while a police detective is reasonably well paid in this city, he's never going to get rich—unless he moonlights."

"I resent the implication."

"And I regret your reluctance to make a plain denial of that implication."

"No. I haven't sold out to anyone, anywhere, at anytime. No, *nyet,* negative, definitely not. Is that plain enough for you?"

Seames didn't answer. Instead, he said, "Anyway, when the surveillance team lost Benton, they drove right back here to wait, to see if the woman and girl would return, or whether maybe somebody else would show up. As an afterthought, they came to have a look around the house, found the door the way you found it—and this weird mess."

Dan said, "What about the mess? What do you make of it?"

"The flowers are from the garden in the back."

"But what're they doing here? Who brought them inside?"

"We can't figure it."

"And why's the security chain been torn out of the door?"

"Looks like somebody forced their way inside," Seames said.

"Really? Gee, you Bureau guys don't miss a trick."

"I'm at a loss to understand your attitude."

"So is everyone else."

"Your lack of cooperation."

"I'm just a very bad boy." Dan went to the telephone, and Seames wanted to know what he was doing, and Dan said, "Calling Paladin. If Earl felt Laura and Melanie were in danger here, he might've moved them in a hurry, the way you say he did, but when he got wherever he was going, he'd call his office and tell them where he was."

The night operator at California Paladin, Lonnie Beamer, knew Dan well enough to recognize his voice. "Yeah, Lieutenant, Earl took them to the safe house."

Lonnie seemed to think Dan knew the address of that place, which he didn't. Earl had spoken of it a few times, when he'd been telling tales about various cases on which he'd worked, but if he had ever said exactly where the safe house was, Dan had forgotten. He could not ask Lonnie Beamer for the address without alerting Seames, who was watching intently. He'd have to call the night operator again from another phone, once he had slipped away from the FBI agent.

On the phone, Lonnie said, "But they probably won't be there much longer."

"Why not?"

"Haven't you heard? Mrs. McCaffrey and the kid won't be needing our protection anymore—though she hasn't decided to let us go just yet. She may want us to hang around too, but for the most part, you people are taking over for us. You're giving them police protection."

"Are you serious?"

"Yeah," Lonnie said. "Around-the-clock police protection. Right now, Earl's over there in Westwood, at the safe house, waiting for a couple of your people to show up and take the McCaffreys off his hands. They'll probably be there any minute."

"Who?"

"Uh . . . let's see . . . Captain Mondale ordered the protection, and Earl's been told to relinquish our clients to Detectives Wexlersh and Manuello."

Something was wrong. Very wrong. The department was too short-handed to provide around-the-clock protection even in a case like this. And Ross wouldn't have called Paladin himself; that was always delegated to assistants. Besides, if protection were to be offered, it would be in the form of uniformed officers, not vitally needed plainclothes detectives who were in even shorter supply than patrolmen.

And why Wexlersh and Manuello, in particular?

"So you might as well stay there in Sherman Oaks," Lonnie said, "because I imagine your people will bring the McCaffreys straight back there."

Dan wanted to know more, but he couldn't talk freely with Seames breathing down his neck. He said, "Well, thanks anyway, Lonnie. But

I think it's inexcusable that you don't know where your operative is or what's happening to your clients."

"Huh? But I just said he was—"

"I've always thought Paladin was the best, but if you can't keep track of your agents and your clients, especially clients whose lives might be in jeopardy—"

Lonnie said, "What's wrong with you, Haldane?"

"Sure, sure," Dan said for Seames's benefit, "they're probably safe. I know Earl's a good man, and I'm sure he won't let anything happen to them, but you better start running a tighter ship there or, sooner or later, something will happen to a client, and then there goes the whole agency's license."

Lonnie started to say something more, but Dan hung up.

He was desperate to get away from there, to find another phone and get back to Lonnie to hear more details. However, he didn't want to appear eager to depart, because he didn't want Seames to come with him. And if Seames thought that Dan knew where Laura and Melanie were, there would be no hope of leaving alone and unobstructed.

The FBI agent was staring hard at him.

Dan said, "They don't know anything at Paladin."

"Is that what he told you?"

"Yeah."

"What else did he tell you?"

He wanted and needed to trust Seames and the Bureau. He was, after all, a cop by choice, and he believed in authority, in systems of law and enforcement. Ordinarily, he would have given Seames his trust automatically, unthinkingly.

But not this time. This was a twisty situation, with stakes so high that the usual rules did not apply.

"He didn't tell me shit," Dan said. "What do you mean?"

"Something's got you really scared all of a sudden."

"Not me."

"You just broke into a sweat."

Dan felt it on his face, cool and trickling. Thinking fast, he said, "It's this knock I took on the forehead. It feels okay, and I forget about it, and then all of a sudden the pain starts up again so bad it makes me weak."

"Hats?" Seames said.

"What?"

"At the Sign of the Pentagram, you told me you'd hurt yourself while trying on hats."

"Did I? Well, I was just being a smart-ass."

"So . . . what really happened?"

"Well, see, usually I don't think very much or very hard. Not used to it. Big dumb cop, you know. But today I had to think so hard that my head got hot, blistered the skin right off."

"I believe you're thinking hard all the time, Haldane. Every minute."

"You give me too much credit."

"And I want to warn you to think hard about this: You're just a city cop, while I'm a federal agent."

"I am acutely aware of your exalted status and the hovering ghost of J. Edgar Hoover."

"Though I can't meddle in your jurisdiction on just any excuse, I can find ways to make you wish you'd never crossed me."

"I never would, sir. I swear."

Seames just stared at him.

Dan said, "Well, I guess I'll be going."

"Where?"

"Home, I guess," Dan lied. "It's been a long day. You're right: I've been working too much. And this head hurts like hell. Ought to take a few aspirins and make up an ice pack."

"All of a sudden you're no longer worried at all about the McCaffreys?"

"Oh, well, sure, I'm concerned about them," Dan said, "but there's nothing more I can do right now. I mean, this mess here, it's sort of on the suspicious side, but it doesn't necessarily indicate foul play, does it? I figure they're safe with Earl Benton. He's a good guy. Besides, Mr. Seames, a homicide cop has to have a pretty thick skin. Can't start identifying with the victims, you know. If we did that, we'd all be basket cases. Right?"

Seames stared, unblinking.

Dan yawned. "Well, time to have a beer and hit the sack." He crossed to the door.

He felt hopelessly obvious, transparent. He had no talent for deception.

Seames spoke to him as he was about to step over the threshold. "If the McCaffreys are in danger, Lieutenant, and if you really want to help them, you'd be wise to cooperate with me."

"Well, like I said, I don't suppose they *are* in danger right this minute," Dan said, although he could still feel the sweat trickling down his face and though his heart was racing and though his stomach was again tied in a burning knot.

"Damn it, why are you being so stubborn? Why aren't you cooperating, Lieutenant?"

Dan met his eyes. "Remember when you pretty much accused me of selling out, turning the McCaffreys over to someone?"

"It's part of my job to be suspicious," Seames said.

"Mine too."

"You mean . . . you suspect me of being opposed to that little girl's best interests?"

"Mr. Seames, I'm sorry, but though you have the round, unlined face of a cherub, that doesn't mean you're an angel at heart."

He left the house, went out to his car, and drove away. They didn't try to follow him, probably because they realized it would be wasted effort.

•

The first telephone that Dan saw was one of those artifacts whose steady disappearance seemed to symbolize the decline of modern civilization: a fully enclosed glass booth. It stood at the corner of a property occupied by an Arco service station.

By the time that he saw the booth and parked beside it, he was shaking badly, not in a panic yet but certainly within sight of one, which wasn't like him. Ordinarily he was calm, collected. The worse that things got, the faster a situation deteriorated, the cooler he became. But not this time. Perhaps it was because he couldn't get Cindy Lakey out of his mind, couldn't forget that tragic failure, or perhaps it was because the murders of his own brother and sister had been much on his mind in the past twenty-four hours, or perhaps the attraction Laura McCaf-frey had for him was even far greater than he was yet willing to admit and perhaps the loss of her would be far more devastating than he could imagine. But whatever the cause of his crumbling self-control, he was becoming undeniably more frantic by the moment.

Wexlersh.

Manuello.

Why was he suddenly so frightened of them? He had never liked either of them, of course. They were originally vice officers, and word was that they had been among the most corrupt in that division, which was probably why Ross Mondale had arranged for them to transfer under his command in the East Valley; he wanted his right-hand men to be the type who would do what they were told, who wouldn't question any questionable orders, whose allegiance to him would be unshakable as long as he provided for them. Dan knew that they were Mondale's flunkies, opportunists with little or no respect for their work or for concepts like duty and public trust. But they were still cops, lousy cops, lazy cops, but not hit men like Ned Rink. Surely they posed no threat to Laura or Melanie.

And yet . . .

Something was wrong. Just a hunch. He couldn't explain the inten-sity of his sudden dread, couldn't give concrete reasons for it, but over the years he had learned to trust his hunches, and now he was scared.

In the booth, he hastily and anxiously fumbled in his pockets for coins, found them. He punched the number for California Paladin into the keypad.

His breath steamed the inner surface of the glass walls, while rain streamed down the exterior. The service station's silvery lights shim-mered in the rippling film of water and were diffused through the opal-escent condensation.

That curious lambent luminescence, combined with the unsettling harmonics of the storm, gave him the extraordinary sensation of being encapsulated and set adrift outside the flow of time and space. As he punched in the last digit of Paladin's number, he had the weird feeling that the booth door had closed permanently behind him, that he would not be able to force his way out of it, that he would never see or hear or touch another human being again, but would forever remain adrift in that rectangular prison in the Twilight Zone, unable to warn or to help Laura and Melanie, unable to alert Earl to the danger, unable to save even himself. Sometimes he had nightmares of being utterly helpless, powerless, paralyzed, while right before his eyes a vaguely defined but monstrous creature tortured and murdered people whom he loved; however, this was the first time that such a nightmare had attempted to seize him while he was awake.

He finished entering the number. After a few electronic beeps and clicks, a ringing came across the line.

At first even the ringing did not dispel the miasma of fear so thick it inhibited breathing. He half expected it to go on and on, without response, for everyone knew that there were no telephone lines between reality and the Twilight Zone. But after the third ring, Lonnie Beamer said, "California Paladin."

Dan almost gasped with relief. "Lonnie, it's Dan Haldane again."

"Have you regained your senses?"

"All that stuff I said . . . that was just for the benefit of a guy who was listening over my shoulder."

"After you hung up, I figured it out."

"Listen, as soon as I hang up this time, I want you to call Earl and tell him there's something fishy about all this police-protection crap."

"What're you talking about?"

"Tell him the guys who come to his door might not really be cops and he shouldn't open up to them."

"You aren't making sense. Of course they'll be cops."

"Lonnie, something bad is about to go down. I don't know exactly what or why—"

"But I know I talked to Ross Mondale. I mean, I recognized his voice, but I still called him back at his office number. Just to double-check who he was before I told him where Earl was keeping the McCaffreys."

"All right," Dan said impatiently, "even if it's actually Wexlersh and Manuello who show up, tell Earl it stinks. Tell him I said he's in deep shit if he lets them in."

"Listen, Dan, I can't tell him to shoot it out with a couple of cops."

"He doesn't have to shoot it out. Just tell him not to let them in. Tell him I'm on my way. He's got to hold out until I get there. Now, what the hell's the address of this safe house?"

"It's actually an apartment," Lonnie said. He gave Dan an address in Westwood, south of Wilshire. "Hey, you really think they're in danger?"

"Call Earl!" Dan said.

He slammed down the receiver, threw open the steam-opaqued door of the booth, and ran to the car.

chapter twenty-eight

"Under arrest?" Earl repeated, blinking at Wexlersh, frowning at Manuello.

Earl looked every bit as surprised and baffled as Laura felt. She was on the sofa, with Melanie, where the detectives had indicated that they wanted her to remain when they had first come into the room. She felt terribly vulnerable and wondered why she should feel vulnerable when they were only policemen who said they were there to help her. She had seen their identification, and Earl apparently had met them before (although he didn't seem to know them well), so there was every indication that they were what they claimed to be. Yet dark buds of doubt and fear began to flower, and she sensed that something was not right about this, not right at all.

She didn't like the looks of these two cops, either. Manuello had mean eyes, a superior smirk. He moved with a macho swagger, as if waiting for his authority to be questioned so he could kick and stomp someone. Wexlersh, with his waxy white skin and flat gray eyes, gave her chills.

She said, "What's going on? Mr. Benton is working for me. I hired his company." And then she had a crazy thought that she voiced at once: "My God, you didn't think he was holding us here against our will, did you?"

Ignoring her, speaking to Earl Benton, Detective Manuello said, "You carrying any iron?"

"Sure, but I have a permit," Earl said.

"Let me have it."

"The permit?"

"The piece."

"You want my weapon?"

"Now."

Drawing his own revolver, Wexlersh said, "Be real careful when you hand it over."

Clearly astonished by Wexlersh's tone and suspicion, Earl said, "You think I'm dangerous, for Christ's sake?"

"Just be careful," Wexlersh said coldly.

Handing his gun to Manuello, Earl said, "Why would I draw down on a cop?"

As Manuello stuck the pistol in the waistband of his trousers, the telephone rang.

Laura started to get up, and Manuello said, "Let it ring."

"But—"

"Let it ring!" Manuello repeated sharply.

The phone rang again.

A dark stain of worry appeared on Earl's face and grew darker even as Laura watched.

The phone rang, rang, and everyone seemed transfixed by the sound.

Earl said, "Hey, listen, there's been a serious mistake here."

The phone rang.

•

Dan had clipped the detachable emergency beacon to the edge of the sedan's roof. Although the car was unmarked, there was a siren too, and he used it and the flashing beacon to command the roadway ahead. Traffic pulled obediently out of his path. Considering the weather, he drove with too little regard for his own safety and for that of everyone else on the streets, plunging toward Westwood with uncharacteristic recklessness.

If someone had corrupted Ross Mondale—and that possibility was far from unthinkable—and had arranged for him to betray Melanie,

Mondale would have had no difficulty whatsoever persuading Wexlersh and Manuello to cooperate in the scheme. They could go to the safe house, gain admission with their police ID, and take the child. They would probably have to kill Laura and Earl to cover up the treachery, but the more Dan thought about it, the more certain he became that they wouldn't have any qualms about murder if they stood to gain enough from it. And they weren't taking much of a risk because they could always say that they'd found the bodies when they had arrived and that the child had already been missing when they got there.

He came to a place where the street passed beneath a freeway, and the depression in the pavement at the underpass was flooded, barring further progress. One car was stuck out in the middle of the whirling torrent, with water halfway up its doors, and several other vehicles were halted at the edge of the flood zone. A truck from the city's department of streets had just arrived. Workers in reflective orange safety vests were setting up a pump and erecting barriers and starting to get traffic turned away and redirected, but for a minute or more Dan was caught in the jam-up, in spite of the flashing beacon on the roof of his sedan.

As he sat there, furious, cursing, blocked in by a car in front and a truck behind, rain drummed a monotonous rhythm on the roof and hood. The beat of each drop was like the tick of a precious second cast off by a clock, time raining away, valuable minutes streaming over him and pouring down the gutters.

•

The phone rang ten times, and each ring increased the tension in the room.

Earl knew something was wrong, but he couldn't quite figure it out. He had met Wexlersh and Manuello before, and he'd heard stories about them, so he knew that they weren't two of the sharpest men on the city's payroll. They could be expected to make mistakes. And this was surely a mistake. Lonnie Beamer had said they were coming to put Laura and Melanie under police protection; he'd said nothing about a warrant for Earl's arrest, and there couldn't be a warrant because Earl hadn't done anything illegal. From what Earl had heard of Wexlersh and Manuello, it would be like them to screw up, to come charging in here misinformed, confused, operating under the gross misapprehension that they had not merely been sent to protect the McCaffreys but to arrest him as well.

But why wouldn't they answer the telephone? The call might be—probably was—for them. He couldn't figure it.

The phone finally stopped ringing. Briefly, the silence seemed as absolute as that in a vacuum. Then Earl again became aware of the pounding of rain on the roof and in the courtyard.

To his partner, Wexlersh said, "Cuff him."

Earl said, "What the hell is this? You still haven't told me what I'm being arrested for?"

As Manuello produced a pair of flexible and disposable plastic handcuffs from one of his jacket pockets, Wexlersh said, "We'll read the charges when we get you to the stationhouse."

They both seemed nervous, eager to get this over with. Why were they in such a hurry?

•

Dan swung hard off Wilshire Boulevard, onto Westwood Boulevard, heading south. He passed through a foot-deep puddle, and on both sides water plumed up as if vaguely phosphorescent wings had suddenly sprouted from the car.

As he squinted through the rain-smeared windshield the wet black pavement appeared to roll and squirm under the scintillant reflections of streetlights and neon signs. His eyes, already weary and burning, began to sting even worse. His battered head throbbed, but there was another pain as well, an inner pain that grew from unwanted thoughts of failure, from unwelcome and unavoidable premonitions of death and despair.

•

Holding the plastic handcuffs, Manuello came toward Earl and said, "Turn around and put your hands together behind your back."

Earl hesitated. He looked at Laura and Melanie. He looked at Wexlersh, holding the Smith & Wesson Police Special. These guys were cops, but Earl suddenly was not sure that he should have done what they told him to, wasn't sure that he should have given up his gun, and he damned sure didn't like being handcuffed.

"Are you going to resist arrest?" Manuello demanded.

Wexlersh said, "Yeah, Benton, for Christ's sake, you realize resisting arrest will be the end of your PI license?"

Reluctantly, Earl turned and put his hands behind his back. "Aren't you going to read me my rights?"

"Plenty of time for that in the car," Manuello said as he slipped the plastic handcuffs around Earl's wrists and drew them tight.

To Laura and Melanie, Wexlersh said, "Better get your coats."

Earl said, "What about my coat? You should have let me put it on before you cuffed me."

"You'll manage without a coat," Wexlersh said.

"It's raining out there."

"You won't melt," Manuello said.

The phone began to ring again.

As before, the detectives ignored it.

•

The siren failed.

Dan tapped the control switch with his foot, clicked it on and off and on again, but the siren refused to come back to life. He was left with only the flashing red emergency beacon and his horn to get him through the rain-slowed traffic.

He was going to be too late. Again. As with Cindy Lakey. Too late. Whipping and weaving from lane to lane, cutting dangerously in and out of traffic, blasting the horn, he was increasingly sure that they were dead, all dead, that he had lost a friend, and the innocent child he had hoped to protect, and the woman whose impact on him—admit it— had been somewhere in the hundred-megaton range. All dead.

•

Laura picked up Melanie's coat and dressed her first. It was a slower procedure than it might have been because the girl didn't help at all.

Manuello said, "What is she—a retard or something?"

Astonished and angry, Laura said, "I can't believe you actually said that."

"Well, she don't act normal," Manuello said.

"Oh, *don't* she?" Laura said scathingly. "Jesus. She's a very sick little girl. What's your excuse?"

While Laura got Melanie into the coat, Earl was directed to sit on the sofa. He perched on the edge. His arms were cuffed behind him.

When Laura finished buttoning her daughter's raincoat, she picked up her own coat.

Wexlersh said, "Never mind that. You sit there on the sofa beside Benton."

"But—"

"*Sit!*" Wexlersh said, pointing at the sofa with his gun.

His ice-gray eyes were unreadable.

Or maybe Laura simply didn't want to read what was evident in them.

She looked at Detective Manuello. He was smirking.

Turning to Earl for guidance, Laura saw that he looked more uneasy than ever.

"Sit," Wexlersh repeated, not stressing the word this time, almost speaking in a whisper, yet somehow conveying more authority—and a greater potential for violence—with that soft tone than he had when he'd spoken more harshly.

Laura's stomach clenched and twisted. A sickening wave of dread swept through her.

When Laura sat down, Wexlersh went to Melanie, took the girl by the hand, and led her away from the sofa, brought her to where he had been standing, and kept her between himself and Manuello.

"No," Laura said miserably, but the two detectives ignored her.

Looking at Wexlersh, Manuello said, "Now?"

"Now," Wexlersh said.

Manuello reached under his coat and brought out a pistol. It wasn't the weapon that he had taken off Earl, and Laura didn't think that it was the detective's own service weapon either, because she was pretty sure policemen usually used revolvers. That was what Wexlersh was holding: a revolver. The moment she saw the new pistol in Manuello's hand, she had a sharper sense that something was amiss.

Then Manuello took a burnished metal tube from his coat pocket and began to screw it onto the barrel of the pistol. It was a silencer.

Earl said, "What the hell are you doing?"

Neither Wexlersh nor Manuello answered him.

"Jesus Christ!" Earl said in shock and horror as a sudden and unacceptable realization dawned upon him.

"No shouting," Wexlersh said. "No screaming."

Earl thrust off the sofa, to his feet, uselessly struggling to free himself of the handcuffs.

Wexlersh rushed at him, clubbed him with the revolver, once on the shoulder, once alongside the face.

Earl fell backward onto the sofa.

Manuello had gotten the threads of the silencer misaligned with those that had been machined into the barrel of the pistol, and he had to unscrew it and try again.

Still looming over Earl, Wexlersh looked at his partner and said, "Will you hurry up?"

"I'm trying, I'm trying," Manuello said, wrestling with the stubborn attachment to the pistol.

"You crazy bastards are going to kill us," Earl said through split and bleeding lips.

When Laura heard their fate put into blunt words, she wasn't surprised. She realized that she had known, if only subconsciously, what was coming, had sensed it when the detectives had first entered the room, had felt it even more strongly when they had handcuffed Earl, and had been convinced of it when Wexlersh had taken Melanie away from her, but hadn't wanted to accept the truth.

Manuello had misthreaded the silencer again. "This thing's a piece of shit."

"It'll fit if you start it right," Wexlersh said.

Laura understood that they didn't want to use their own revolvers for fear the murders would be traced to them. And they didn't want to fire the pistol without a silencer, if they could avoid it, because the gunshots would bring neighbors to windows in other apartments, and then someone would see them leaving with Melanie.

Melanie. She was standing near Manuello, whimpering. Her eyes were closed, her head bowed, and she was making small, lost, pathetic sounds. Did she know what was about to happen in this room, that her mother was about to die, or was she whimpering about something else, something in her private inner fantasy world?

In a tone that was part disbelief but mostly rage, Earl said, "You're cops, for God's sake."

Wexlersh said, "You just sit there and be quiet."

Laura's gaze had settled on a heavy glass ashtray on the coffee table. If she grabbed it, threw it at Wexlersh, and managed to hit him in the head, it might knock him unconscious or cause him to drop his gun, and if he dropped his gun, she might be able to reach it before either he or Manuello could react. But she needed a diversion. She was desperately trying to think of something to distract Wexlersh when Earl evidently decided they had nothing to lose by resisting; he distracted both detectives at exactly the right moment.

As Manuello continued to struggle with the poorly fitted silencer, Earl looked at Wexlersh and said, "No matter what we do, no matter how loud we scream, you're not going to use your own gun or mine." Then, shouting for help at the top of his voice, Earl launched himself up toward Wexlersh, using his head as a ram.

Wexlersh stumbled back two steps as Earl butted him in the stomach. But the detective didn't fall. In fact, he struck down with the gun, clubbing the bodyguard to the floor, putting an abrupt end to the attack and to the shouting.

In the brief confusion, Laura snatched up the ashtray even as Wexlersh struck Earl. Manuello saw her and said, "Hey," just as she heaved the object at Wexlersh, which was sufficient warning for the detective, who ducked and let the ashtray sail past him. It thudded into the wall, thumped to the floor.

Wexlersh pointed his service revolver straight at Laura, and within the muzzle was the deepest blackness that she had ever seen. "Listen, you bitch, if you don't sit down right now and keep your trap shut, we'll make this a lot harder on you than it has to be."

Melanie was mewling softly now, in increasing distress. Her head was still bowed, her eyes closed, but her mouth was open and slack as the pitiful sounds issued from her.

Flopping onto his back, pulling himself up against the sofa, streaming blood from a scalp wound, Earl glared at Wexlersh. "Yeah? Is that so? Make it harder on us, huh? What the hell could be worse than what you're already planning to do?"

Wexlersh smiled. It was a singularly unsettling expression on his bloodless lips and moon-pale face. "We could tape your mouth shut and torture you for a while. Then torture this bitch here."

Shuddering, Laura looked away from his gray eyes.

The room seemed cold, colder than it had been.

"She's a nice piece of ass," Manuello observed.

"Yeah, we could screw her," Wexlersh said.

"Screw the kid too," Manuello said.

"Yeah," Wexlersh said, still smiling. "That's right. We could screw the kid."

"Even though she is a retard," Manuello said, then cursed the pistol and silencer that wouldn't fit together properly.

Wexlersh said, "So if you don't just sit there quiet like, we'll tape your mouths shut and screw the kid right in front of you—and then kill you, anyway."

Gagging, choking down the vomit that rose into her throat, Laura settled back on the sofa, subdued by this crudest of all threats.

Earl had been silenced too.

"Good," Wexlersh said, massaging his stomach with one hand, where Earl had butted him. "Much better."

Melanie's mewling had grown louder and was punctuated with a few words—"open . . . door . . . open . . . no"—and with deep, quavering gasps.

"Shut up, kid," Wexlersh said, lightly slapping her face.

Her whimpering subsided, but she wasn't silenced altogether.

Laura wanted to go to the girl, hug her, hold her close, but for her own sake, and Melanie's, she had to stay where she was.

The room was definitely cold and getting colder.

Laura remembered how the kitchen had grown frigid just before the radio had come to life. And again just before the wind-thing had thrown open the door and surged in from the darkness. . . .

Wexlersh said, "Don't they have heat in this damned place?"

"There!" Manuello said, finally screwing the silencer onto the barrel of the gun.

Colder . . .

Holstering his own revolver now that his partner was at last ready to do the deed, grabbing Melanie by one arm and pulling her out of the way, Wexlersh edged backward toward the front door of the apartment.

Colder . . .

Laura was electrified, charged with tension and anticipation. Something was about to happen. Something strange.

Manuello stepped closer to Earl, who regarded him with more contempt than terror.

The temperature of the room plunged precipitously now, and behind Wexlersh and Melanie, the apartment door flew open with a crash—

But nothing supernatural burst into the room. It was Dan Haldane. He came through the door fast, even as he opened it. He took in the situation with remarkable alacrity and jammed his revolver into Wexlersh's back as that detective was starting to swing toward the door.

Manuello spun around, but Haldane said, "Drop it! Drop it, you bastard, or I'll blow you away."

Manuello hesitated, probably not because he was worried about his partner getting killed, but because it was clear that Wexlersh's body would stop the first bullet meant for Dan, and because it was equally clear that Manuello wouldn't have a chance to fire twice before Dan took his head off. He glanced at Melanie too, as though calculating the chances of leaping toward her, grabbing her. But when Dan shouted at him again—"Drop it!"—Manuello finally conceded the game and let the silencer-equipped pistol fall to the floor.

"He's got Earl's gun," Laura warned Dan.

"And his own service revolver too," Earl added.

Keeping a grip on Wexlersh's coat, the revolver still jammed hard in the man's back, Dan said, "Okay, Manuello, get rid of the other two pieces, slow and easy. No funny stuff."

One at a time, Manuello rid himself of the weapons, then backed across the room and stood against the wall, as Dan directed.

Laura came forth to gather up the three firearms while Dan relieved Wexlersh of his service revolver.

"Why the hell is it so cold in here?" Dan asked.

But even as he voiced the question, the air grew warm again as swiftly as it had turned frigid.

Something almost happened, Laura thought. Something like what happened in the kitchen at our house earlier.

But she didn't think that they had been about to get just another warning. Not this time. No, this would have been worse. She had the unsettling feeling that *It* had been within seconds of making an appearance.

Dan was looking at her strangely, as if he knew that she had an answer for him.

But she couldn't speak. She didn't know how to put it into words that would make any sense at all to him. She knew only that, if *It* had come, the slaughter here would have been far worse than any that the two corrupt detectives had been planning. If *It* had come, would they all have wound up like the battered, torn, and mangled bodies in the house in Studio City?

chapter twenty-nine

In the emergency room at UCLA Medical Center, Earl was admitted for immediate treatment of his scalp wound and split lips.

Laura and Melanie waited in the lounge adjacent to the emergency admitting desk while Dan went to the nearest pay phone. He called the East Valley Division number and got Ross Mondale's extension.

"Working late, aren't you, Ross?"

"Haldane?"

"Didn't know you were so industrious."

"What do you want, Haldane?"

"World peace would be nice."

"I'm not in the mood for—"

"But I guess I'd settle for a solution to this case."

"Listen, Haldane, I'm busy here, and I—"

"You're going to be even busier, 'cause you're going to have to spend a lot of time thinking up alibis."

"What're you talking about?"

"Wexlersh and Manuello."

Mondale was silent.

Dan said, "Why'd you send them down to Westwood, Ross?"

"I guess you didn't know, but I've decided to provide police protection for the McCaffreys."

"Even with the current manpower shortage?"

"Well, considering the Scaldone killing tonight and the extreme violence of these crimes, it seemed prudent to—"

"Stuff a sock in it, you son of a bitch."

"What?"

"I know they were going to kill Earl and Laura—"

"What are you talking about?"

"—and snatch Melanie—"

"Have you been drinking, Haldane?"

"—and then go back later and report that Earl and Laura were already dead when they got there."

"Am I supposed to be making sense out of this?"

"Your confusion almost sounds genuine."

"These are serious accusations, Haldane."

"Oh, you're so smooth, Ross."

"These are fellow officers we're talking about here. They—"

"Who'd you sell out to, Ross?"

"Haldane, I advise you—"

"And what did you get for selling out? That's the big question. Listen, listen, hold on a sec, bear with me, let me theorize a bit, okay? You wouldn't have sold out just for money. You wouldn't put your entire career on the line just for money. Not unless it was a couple of million, and nobody would've paid that kind of dough for a job like this. Twenty-five thousand. Tops. Probably fifteen. That's more like it. Now, I can believe Wexlersh and Manuello would have done it for that kind of money, maybe even less, but neither of them would've whacked Earl and Laura without your approval, without a guarantee of your protection. So I'd say they got the money, and you got something else. Now what could that something else be, Ross? You'd sell out for power, for a really important promotion maybe, for a guarantee of the chief's post and maybe even a mayoral nomination. So whoever bought you is somebody who controls political machinery. Am I getting warm, Ross? Did you trade Laura and Melanie McCaffrey for those kinds of promises?"

Mondale was silent.

"Did you, Ross?"

"This sounds worse than drunk, Dan. This is spacey. Are you on drugs, or what?"

"Did you, Ross?"

"Where are you, Dan?"

Dan ignored the question. He said, "Manuello and Wexlersh are at that apartment in Westwood right now, gagged and hog-tied, one on the commode and the other in the bathtub. I'd have flushed them both down the drain if they'd have fit."

"You *are* high on something, by God!"

"Give it a rest, Ross. Paladin is sending a couple of men over there to babysit your boys, and I've already called a reporter at the *Times* and another one at the *Journal*. Called the division over there, too, told them who I was, told them there'd been an attempted murder, so they've got uniforms on the way. It's going to be a circus."

After another silence, Mondale said, "Is Mrs. McCaffrey going to give a statement accusing Wexlersh and Manuello of attempted murder?"

"Beginning to worry, Ross?"

"They're my officers," Mondale said. "My responsibility. If they've actually done what you say, then I want to be absolutely sure they're eventually indicted and convicted. I don't want any damned rotten apples in my barrel. I don't believe in covering up for my men out of some misguided sense of police brotherhood."

"What's the matter, Ross? Do you think I'm recording this call? You think someone's listening in? Well, there's no one listening, no tape, so you can drop the act."

"I don't understand your attitude, Dan."

"Nobody does."

"I don't know why you suspect me of being involved." He was a lousy actor; his insincerity was as obvious as a lisp or a stutter. "And you haven't answered my question. Is Mrs. McCaffrey going to give a statement accusing Wexlersh and Manuello of attempted murder, or isn't she?"

Dan said, "Not tonight. I've taken Laura and Melanie away from there, and I'm keeping them with me, well hidden, for the duration. I know you're disappointed to hear that. They'd have sure made easy targets for a sniper if they'd hung around, wouldn't they? But I'm not telling anyone where they are. I'm not letting them meet with any cops from any division, either to give a statement or to identify Wexlersh and Manuello in a lineup. I don't trust anyone anymore."

"You're not talking like a responsible cop, Dan."

"I'm such an imp."

"For God's sake, you can't take personal responsibility for the McCaffreys."

"Just watch me."

"If they need protection, you've got to arrange it through the department, which is what I thought I was doing when I sent Wexlersh and Manuello over there. You can't handle this by yourself. Good heavens, these people aren't your own family, you know. You can't just take charge of them as if it's your legal right or something."

"If they want me to, I can. They aren't my family—you're right—but just the same . . . I've got something at stake here."

"What're you talking about?"

"You said it yourself, at the Sign of the Pentagram tonight. This isn't an ordinary case for me. That's why I'm holding on so tight. I'm attracted to Laura. And I pity the girl. What I feel for them *is* stronger than anything I've ever felt for other victims, so you keep that in mind, Ross."

"Right there's reason enough to disassociate yourself from this case. You're no longer an objective officer of the law."

"Fuck you."

"This explains why you're so hostile, hysterical, filled with all these paranoid conspiracy theories."

"It's not paranoia. It's real, and you know it."

"I understand now. You're distraught."

"I'm just warning you, Ross—back off. That's why I even bothered calling you. Those two words: back off." Mondale said nothing, so Dan said, "This woman and this child are important to me."

Mondale breathed softly into the phone but made no promises.

Dan said, "I swear to God I'll destroy anyone who tries to hurt them. *Anyone.*"

Silence.

Dan said, "You may be able to keep Wexlersh and Manuello quiet. You might even find a way to have the charges dropped and the whole thing covered up. But if you keep coming after the McCaffreys, I'll find a way to break your ass. I swear it, Ross."

At last Mondale spoke, but not to the point, as if he had heard none of Dan's warning. "Well, if you won't let Mrs. McCaffrey make a statement, then Wexlersh and Manuello can't be arrested."

"Oh, yes. Earl Benton can make a statement. He was pistol-whipped. By Wexlersh. Earl's at a hospital, getting patched up."

"Which hospital?"

"Get serious, Ross."

Finally, out of frustration, Mondale showed a little of what he was really feeling. The dam didn't break, but a hairline crack appeared in it: "You bastard. I'm sick of you, sick of you and your threats, sick to death of having you hanging over me like a goddamned sword."

"That's good. Get it out, Ross. Get it off your chest."

Mondale was silent again.

Dan said, "Anyway, if Earl's released from the hospital, he's going back to that apartment to talk with the uniforms who answered my call, give them a statement, see to it that Wexlersh and Manuello are booked on charges of assault and battery plus assault with intent to kill."

Mondale had control of himself now. He wouldn't lose it again.

Dan said, "And if the doctors want to hold him overnight for observation, then police from this division will be coming here for his statement. Either way, Wexlersh and Manuello aren't going to skip out on this one . . . unless you work your buns off to slip them free of the hook. Which I figure you'll have to do in order to keep them quiet."

No response. Just heavy breathing.

"When and if you finally smooth it over, Ross, you might be able to convince Chief Kelsey that you and Wexlersh and Manuello weren't involved in a plot to snatch the girl and kill her mother, but the press will still figure something was going on, and they'll never quite trust you again. Reporters will always be sniffing around you for the rest of your career, waiting for you to put a foot wrong."

Silence.

"You hear what I'm saying, Ross?"

Silence.

"At best, you'll hold on to your captain's bars, but you won't be on the mayor's short list for chief. Not anymore. Now, see, this is a warning, Ross. This is why I called you. Listen close. Listen good. If you keep coming after the McCaffreys, you'll be *completely* ruined. I'll see to it. I'll personally guarantee it. You're half ruined now, but if you keep coming after them, you won't even remain a captain. I'll bring you down all the way. No matter who put you up to this, no matter how powerful and influential he is, he won't be able to save your ass if you try to touch the McCaffreys again. He won't be able to save you from *me*. You get the picture?"

Silence. But it was a silence with an emotional quality now, and the emotion it radiated was hatred.

Dan said, "I still have to worry about the FBI, and I have to worry about whoever was financing Dylan McCaffrey and Willy Hoffritz, because somebody out there wants that little girl real bad, but I'll be damned if I'm going to keep worrying about you, Ross. Tonight, you're going to relinquish your place on the special task force and hand the whole case over to someone else until you've cleared up this cloud of suspicion hanging over Wexlersh and Manuello. Understand? I'm not suggesting this, Ross. I'm telling you."

"You shithead."

"Sticks and stones. Listen good: If you don't say what I want to hear, Ross, I'm going to hang up, and when I hang up, it's too late for you to change your mind."

Silence.

"Well . . . good-bye, Ross."

"Wait."

"Sorry, got to go."

"All right, all right. I agree."

"What?"

"What you said."

"Make it plainer."

"I'll take myself off the case."

"Very wise."

"I'll even take a week of sick leave."

"Ahhh, not feeling well?"

Mondale said, "I'll get out of this, walk away from it, but I want something from you."

"What?"

"I don't want Benton or you or the McCaffreys giving any statements about Wexlersh and Manuello."

"Fat chance."

"I mean it."

"Nonsense. The only way we have a hold on you is if we get those two creeps booked for attempted murder."

"Okay. Let Benton give his statement. But in a couple days, when you feel the McCaffreys are safe, then Benton retracts his accusations."

"He'd look like a fool."

"No, no. He can say someone else beat him up and that he took a bad knock on the head, he was confused and he mistakenly accused Wexlersh and Manuello. In a couple days, he can say his head cleared and then he remembered what really happened. He can say it was some other bum who beat on him and that Wexlersh and Manuello actually saved his ass."

"You're in no position to demand anything from me, Ross."

"Goddammit, if you don't give me an out, a glimpse of light, then I don't have any reason for playing along with you."

"Maybe. But if we're bargaining, then I want something else too. I want the name of the man who got to you, Ross."

"No."

"Who wants the girl, Ross? Tell me, and we've got a deal."

"No."

"Who convinced you to use Wexlersh and Manuello this way?"

"Impossible. I tell you, and I'm really finished. I'm dog meat. I'd rather go down now, fighting, than rat on anybody and maybe wind up like those bodies in Studio City—or worse. I give you the McCaffreys, and after a few days, you give me Wexlersh and Manuello. That's the deal."

"You've got to at least tell me if he's the one who financed the work in that gray room."

"I think so."

"Is he government?"

"Maybe."

"You have to do better."

"I just don't know. He's the kind of guy who could be a conduit for the government, or maybe he financed it himself."

"Rich?"

"I'm not giving you his name, and I'm not giving you so many details you could *guess* his name. Hell, I'd be signing my own death warrant."

Dan thought a moment. Then: "He say anything about what they were trying to prove in that gray room?"

"No."

"This guy, this one who got to you, this one who financed that crazy research . . . is he doing the killing, Ross?"

Silence.

"Is he, Ross? Come on. Don't be afraid to talk. You've already said too much. I'm not insisting on his name, but I've got to have an answer to this one. Is he responsible for Scaldone and those bodies in Studio City?"

"No, no. Just the opposite. He's scared that he's going to be the next target."

"Well, who's he afraid of?"

"I don't think it's a who."

"What?"

"This is crazy . . . but the way these people talk, they're so scared you'd think it was Dracula who was after them. I mean, from things I've heard, I somehow get the idea it's not a person they're afraid of. It's a thing. Some *thing* is killing everyone connected with the gray room. I know that sounds like horseshit, but it's the feeling I get. Now, damn it, do we have a deal or not? I back out of this, give you the McCaffreys, and you give me Wexlersh and Manuello. Is that agreeable?

Dan pretended to think about it. Then: "Okay."

"We got a deal?"

"Yeah."

Mondale laughed nervously. His laughter had a filthy edge to it, as well. "You realize what this means, Haldane?"

"What's it mean?"

"You make a deal like this, you drop charges against men you believe to have intended murder . . . well, then you're just as dirty as anybody."

"Not as dirty as you. I could float in a sewer for a month and eat whatever drifted by, and I still wouldn't be half as dirty as you, Ross."

He hung up. He had eliminated one threat. No one would be using police badges to get close to Melanie. They still had an army of enemies, but now there was one less variety of them.

And the beauty of it was that he had not given up anything in return for Ross Mondale's retreat, had not even slightly dirtied his hands, because he didn't intend to uphold his end of the bargain. He would never ask Earl to withdraw his accusations against Wexlersh and Manuello. In fact, when the case was finally broken and it was safe for Laura and Melanie to appear in public, Dan would encourage them to testify, as well, against the two detectives, and he would add his own testimony to the record. Manuello and Wexlersh were finished—and by extension, so was Ross Mondale.

chapter thirty

At twenty-five past midnight, the hospital released Earl Benton.

Laura was shocked by the bodyguard's battered appearance even after the blood had been cleaned off his face. On the side of his head, doctors had shaved a spot half as large as the palm of a hand and had closed the wound with seven sutures. Now it was covered with a bandage. His lips were purple and swollen. His mouth was distorted. One eye was black. He looked as if he'd had a close encounter with a truck.

His appearance affected Melanie. The girl's eyes cleared. She seemed to swim up from her trance to peer more closely at him, as if she were a fish rising to the surface of a lake to examine a curious creature standing on the shore.

"Ahhh," she said sadly.

She seemed to want to say something more to Earl, so he leaned toward her.

She touched his battered face with one hand, and her gaze moved slowly from his bruised chin to his split lips, to his black eye, to the bandage on his head. As she studied him, she chewed worriedly on her lower lip. Her eyes filled with tears. She tried to speak, but no sound came from her.

"What is it, Melanie?" Earl asked.

Laura stooped beside her daughter and put one arm around her.

"What're you trying to tell him, honey? Think one word at a time. Take it nice and slow. You can get it out. You can do it, baby."

Dan, the doctor who had treated Earl, and a young Latino nurse were watching attentively, expectantly.

The child's tear-blurred gaze continued to move over Earl's face, from one battle scar to another, and at last she said, "For m-m-me."

"Yes," Laura said. "That's right, baby. Earl was fighting for you. He risked his life for you."

"For me," Melanie repeated with awe, as if being loved and protected was an entirely new and amazing concept to her.

Excited by this crack in Melanie's autistic armor, hoping to widen it or even shatter the armor completely, Laura said, "We're all fighting for you, baby. We want to help. We *will* help you, if you'll let us."

"For me," Melanie said again, but she would say no more. Although Laura and Earl continued to coax her, Melanie did not speak again. Her tears dried, and she lowered her hand from Earl's injured face, and that faraway look returned to her eyes. She bowed her head, weary.

Laura was disappointed but not despairing. At least the child seemed to want to come back from her dark and private place, and if she had a strong desire to recover, she would probably do so, sooner or later.

The emergency-room physician suggested that Earl stay overnight for observation, but in spite of the drubbing that he had taken, Earl resisted. He wanted to return to the safe house and make a statement to the police, thereby pounding a few nails into a tandem coffin for Wexlersh and Manuello.

They had all come to the hospital in Dan's car, but now Dan didn't want to go back to the safe house. He didn't want Laura and Melanie to be near any other cops, so they called a taxi for Earl.

"Don't wait with me," Earl said. "You guys get out of here."

"We might as well wait," Dan said, "because we've got a few things to talk over anyway."

Without discussing it, they grouped around Melanie, shielding her. They stood just inside the front entrance of the medical center, where they could see the rain-lashed night and the place where the taxi would pull up. Half the fluorescent lights in the lobby were switched off, for it was well after visiting hours, and the other half cast fuzzy bars of cold, unpleasant light across the large room. The air smelled vaguely of rose-scented disinfectant. Except for the four of them, the place was deserted.

"You want Paladin to send someone out here to take over for me?" Earl asked.

"No," Dan said.

"Didn't think you would."

"Paladin's damned good," Dan said, "and I've never had reason to doubt their integrity, and I still don't have reason—"

"But, in this particular case, you don't trust anyone at Paladin any more than you trust anyone on the police force," Earl said.

"Except you," Laura said. "We know we can trust you, Earl. Without you, Melanie and I would be dead."

"Don't credit me with anything heroic," Earl said. "I was plain stupid. I opened the door to Manuello."

"But you had no way of knowing—"

"But I opened the door," Earl said, and the expression of self-disgust on his face was unmistakable in spite of the way his injuries distorted his features.

Laura could see why Dan and Earl were friends. They shared a devotion to their work, a strong sense of duty, and a tendency to be excessively self-critical. Those were qualities seldom found in a world that seemed daily to put more stock in cynicism, selfishness, and self-indulgence.

To Earl, Dan said, "I'll find a motel, get a room, and hole up there with Laura and Melanie the rest of the night. I thought of taking them back to my place, but someone might be expecting me to do just that."

"And tomorrow?" Earl asked.

"There're several people I want to see—"

"Can I help?"

"If you feel up to it when you get out of bed in the morning."

"I'll feel up to it," Earl assured him.

Dan said, "There's a woman named Mary Katherine O'Hara, in Burbank. She's secretary of an organization called Freedom Now." He gave Earl the address and outlined the information he wanted from

O'Hara. "I also need to find out about a company called John Wilkes Enterprises. Who are its officers, majority stockholders?"

"Is it a California corporation?" Earl asked.

"Most likely," Dan said. "I need to know when the incorporation papers were filed, by whom, what business they're supposed to be in."

"How's this John Wilkes outfit come into it?" Earl asked, which was something Laura wondered about too.

"It'll take a while to explain," Dan said. "I'll tell you about it tomorrow. Let's get together for a late lunch, say one o'clock, and try to make something out of the information we've gathered."

"Yeah, I should have dug up what you want by then," Earl said. He suggested a coffee shop in Van Nuys because, he said, it was a place in which he had never seen anyone from Paladin.

"It's not a cop hangout, either," Dan said. "Sounds good."

"Here's your cab," Laura said as headlights swept across the glass doors and briefly sparkled in the raindrops that quivered on those panes.

Earl looked down at Melanie and said, "Well, princess, can you give me a smile before I go?"

The girl peered up at him, but Laura saw that her eyes were still strange, distant.

"I'm warning you," Earl said, "I'm going to hang around and bother you until you finally give me a smile."

Melanie just stared.

To Laura, Earl said, "Keep your chin up. Okay? It's going to work out."

Laura nodded. "And thanks for—"

"For nothing," Earl said. "I opened the door for them. I've got to make up for that. Wait until I make up for that before you start thanking me for anything." He stepped to the lobby doors, started to push one open, then glanced back at Dan and said, "By the way, what the hell happened to you?"

"What?" Dan asked.

"Your forehead."

"Oh." Dan glanced at Laura, and she could tell by his expression that he'd come by his injury while working on the case, and she could also tell that he didn't want to say as much and make her feel at all responsible. He said, "There was this little old lady . . . she hit me with her cane."

"Oh?" Earl said.

"I helped her across the street."

"Then why would she hit you?"

"She didn't *want* to cross the street," Dan said.

Earl grinned—it was a macabre expression on his battered face— pushed the door open, ran through the rain, and disappeared into the waiting taxi.

Laura zipped up Melanie's jacket. She and Dan kept the girl between them as they hurried out to his unmarked department sedan.

The air was chilly.

The rain was cold.

The darkness seemed to breathe with malevolent life.

Out there, somewhere, *It* waited.

•

The motel room had two queen-size beds with purple-and-green spreads that clashed with the garish orange-and-blue drapes that, in turn, clashed with the loud yellow-and-brown wallpaper. There was a certain kind of eye-searing decor to be found in about one-fourth of the hotels and motels in every state of the union, from Alaska to Florida, an unmistakable bizarre decor of such a particular nature that it seemed, to Dan, that the same grossly incompetent interior decorator must be traveling frantically from one end of the country to the other, papering walls and upholstering furniture and draping windows with factory-rejected patterns and materials.

The beds had mattresses that were too soft, and the furniture was scarred, but at least the place was clean. On the credit side of the ledger, the management provided a percolator and complimentary foil packets of Hills Brothers and Mocha Mix. Dan made coffee while Laura put Melanie to bed.

Although the girl had seemed to drift through the day with all the awareness of a sleepwalker, expending little energy, it was late, and she fell asleep even as her mother was tucking the covers around her.

A small table and two chairs stood by the room's only window, and Dan brought the coffee to it. He and Laura sat mostly in shadow, with one small lamp burning just inside the door. The drapes were partly open to reveal a section of the rain-swept parking lot, where ghostly bluish light from mercury-vapor lamps made strange patterns on the glass and chrome of the cars and shimmered eerily on the wet macadam.

While Dan listened with growing amazement and disquiet, Laura told him the rest of the story that she had begun in the car: the levitating radio that seemed to broadcast a warning, the whirlwind filled with flowers that had burst through the kitchen door. She clearly found it difficult to credit these apparently supernatural events, though she had witnessed them with her own eyes.

"What do you make of it?" he asked when she had finished.

"I was hoping you could explain it to me."

He told her about Joseph Scaldone being killed in a room where all the windows and doors had been locked from inside. "Considering that impossibility on top of what you've told me happened at your place, I guess we've got to accept that there's something here—some power, some force that's beyond human experience. But what the hell is it?"

"Well, I've been thinking about it all evening, and it seems to me that whatever . . . whatever *possessed* that radio and carried those flowers into the kitchen is not the same thing that's killing people. In retrospect, scary as it was, the presence in my kitchen wasn't fundamentally threatening. And like I said, it seemed to be warning us that what killed Dylan and Hoffritz and the others is eventually going to come for Melanie too."

"So we've got both good spirits and bad spirits," Dan said.

"I guess you could think of them that way."

"Good ghosts and bad ghosts."

"I don't believe in ghosts," she said.

"Neither do I. But, somehow, in their experiments in that room, your husband and Hoffritz seem to have tapped into and then unleashed occult entities, some of which are murderous and some of which are at least benign enough to issue warnings about the bad ones. And until I can think of something better . . . well, 'ghosts' seems to be the best word for them."

They fell silent. They sipped the last of their coffee.

The rain came down hard, harder. It roared.

At the far end of the room, Melanie murmured in her sleep and shifted under the covers, then grew still and quiet again.

At last Laura said, "Ghosts. It's just . . . crazy."

"Madness."

"Insanity."

He switched on the dim light over the table. From a jacket pocket, he withdrew the printout of the Sign of the Pentagram's mailing list. He unfolded it and put it in front of her. "Aside from your husband, Hoffritz, Ernest Cooper, and Ned Rink, is there anyone on this list with whom you're familiar?"

She spent ten minutes scanning names and found four additional people who she knew.

"This one," she said. "Edwin Koliknikov. He's a professor of psychology at USC. He's a frequent recipient of Pentagon grants for research, and he helped Dylan make some connections at the Department of Defense. Koliknikov's a behaviorist with a special interest in child psychology."

Dan figured that Koliknikov was also the "Eddie" who had been at Regine's house in the Hollywood Hills and who had, by now, taken her to Las Vegas.

She said, "Howard Renseveer. He represents some foundation with lots of money to spend. I'm not sure which one, but I know he backed some of Hoffritz's research and talked with Dylan several times about a grant for his work. I didn't know him well, but he seemed to be a thoroughly unpleasant man, distant and arrogant."

Dan was certain that this was the "Howard" whom Regine had mentioned.

"This one too," Laura said, indicating another name on the list. "Sheldon Tolbeck. His friends call him Shelby. He's a heavyweight, a psychologist *and* a neurologist, who's done definitive research on various forms of dissociative behavior."

"What's that?" Dan asked.

"Dissociative behavior? Psychological withdrawal, catatonia, autism— conditions of that sort."

"Like Melanie."

"Yes."

"I've reason to believe these three men were all involved with your husband and with Hoffritz in the research being done in that damned gray room."

She frowned. "I could believe it of Koliknikov and Renseveer, but not Sheldon Tolbeck. His reputation is spotless." She was still looking at the list. "Here's another. Albert Uhlander. He's an author, writes strange—"

"I know. That box I brought in from the car is full of his books."

"He and Dylan carried on an extensive correspondence."

"About what?"

"Various aspects of the occult. I'm not sure exactly."

She found no other familiar name on the long list, but she had identified every member of the conspiracy except that tall, white-haired, distinguished-looking man whom Regine knew only as "Daddy." Dan had a hunch that "Daddy" was more than just a sadistic pervert, that he was more than just another member of Dylan McCaffrey's ad hoc research team, that he was the key to the entire case, the central figure behind the conspiracy.

Dan said, "I think these men—Koliknikov, Renseveer, Tolbeck, and Uhlander—are all going to die. Soon. Something is methodically killing everyone involved with the project in that gray room, the something we're calling a 'ghost' for want of a better word. It's something that they themselves unleashed but couldn't control. If I'm correct, these four men don't have much time left."

"Then we should warn them—"

"Warn them? They're responsible for Melanie's condition."

"Still, as much as I'd like them all punished . . ."

"Anyway, I think they already know something's coming for them," Dan said. "Eddie Koliknikov left town tonight. And the others are probably getting out too, if they're not already gone."

She was silent a moment. Then: "And whatever wants them . . . once it's gotten them . . . it's also coming after Melanie."

"If we can believe the message that came through your radio."

"We can believe it," she said grimly.

Melanie began to murmur again, and the murmurs quickly escalated into groans of fear. As the girl thrashed under the blankets, Laura got up and took a step toward the bed—but halted suddenly and looked around anxiously.

"What's wrong?" Dan asked.

"The air," she said.

He felt it even as she spoke.

The air was getting colder.

chapter thirty-one

The late shuttle flight from LAX landed in Las Vegas before midnight, and Regine and Eddie went straight to the Desert Inn, where they had a room reserved. They were registered and unpacked by one o'clock in the morning.

She had been to Vegas with Eddie twice before. They always registered under her name, so she never learned his name from the desk clerks or the bellmen.

One thing that she *had* learned was that something about Vegas was a turn-on for Eddie. Maybe it was the lights and the excitement, maybe the sight and smell and sound of money. Whatever the cause, his sexual appetite was substantially greater in Vegas than it was back in L.A. Each evening, when they went to dinner and a show, she would wear a low-cut dress that he picked out for her, and he would put her on display, but the rest of the time he made her stay in the room, so she would always be available to him when he came back from a session at the craps or black-jack tables. Two or even three times a day, he would return to the room, keyed-up, his eyes a little wild, tense but not nervous, and he would use her to work off his excess energy. Sometimes he would stop just inside the room, standing with his back against the door, unzip, make her come to him, make her get on her knees, and when he was finished, he would push her away and leave without saying a word. Sometimes he would want to do it in the shower, or on the floor, or in bed but in weird positions that ordinarily would not have interested him. In Vegas, he found greater satisfaction in sex, approached it almost fiercely, and exhibited an even more delicious cruelty than he did back in Los Angeles.

Therefore, when they got settled into their room at the Desert Inn, she expected him to jump her, but he wasn't interested tonight. He had been on edge since he'd come to her house several hours ago, and then he had relaxed a bit when their flight had taken off from LAX, but his relaxation had been short-lived. Now he seemed almost . . . frantic.

She knew that he was running from someone, from whomever or whatever had killed the others. But the depth and tenacity of his fear surprised her. In her experience, he was always cool, detached, superior. She hadn't thought that he was susceptible to the stronger emotions like joy and terror. If Eddie was afraid, then the threat must be truly horrendous. It didn't matter. She wasn't afraid. Even if someone learned that Eddie had gone to hide in Vegas and came all the way there to get Eddie, and even if she was in danger while with him, she would not be afraid. She had been freed from all fear. Willy had freed her.

But Eddie had not been freed, and he was so afraid that he didn't want to screw or sleep. He wanted to go downstairs to the casino and gamble for a while, but—and this was the unusual part—he wanted her to go with him. He didn't want to be alone among strangers, not even in a crowded public place like a casino.

Indirectly, he was asking her for moral and emotional support, which was something neither he nor any of his friends had ever wanted from her before, and it was something that she was not equipped to give them— not since Willy had changed her. Indeed, she could relate to Eddie only when he used her, when he was dominant and abusive. She was actually disgusted and repelled by his expression of weakness and need.

Nevertheless, at 1:15 in the morning, she accompanied him downstairs to the casino. He wanted her companionship, and she always provided what was wanted of her.

The casino was relatively busy now but would be jammed in half an hour, when the showroom had emptied from the midnight performance. At the moment there were hundreds of people at the blinking-flashing-

sparkling slot machines, at the semielliptical blackjack tables, and standing around the craps tables: people in suits and evening gowns; people
in slacks and jeans; conscientiously rustic cowboy types standing next to
people who looked as if they had just survived an explosion in a polyes-
ter factory; grandmothers and young hookers; Japanese high rollers in
from Tokyo on a junket flight and a flock of secretaries from San Diego;
the rich and the not-so-rich; losers and winners; more losers; a three-
hundred-pound lady in a bright yellow caftan and a matching turban,
who was betting a thousand dollars a hand at blackjack, but who knew
so little about the game that she was routinely splitting pairs of tens; an
inebriated oilman from Houston who was betting fifty dollars a hand,
every hand, for the dealer, and only twenty-five dollars a hand for himself; uniformed security guards so big that they looked as if they ate
furniture for breakfast, but who were soft-spoken and unfailingly polite;
blackjack and craps dealers in black slacks and white shirts and black
string ties; a tuxedo-clad crew at the baccarat table; pit bosses and their
assistants, all in well-tailored dark suits, all with the same sharp, quick,
suspicious eyes. It was a people-watcher's paradise.

Staying at Eddie's side as he prowled restlessly around the enormous
room, drifting from game to game but playing at none of them, Regine
reacted to the Vegas turmoil in a way that was, for her, uncommon. A
quickening of the pulse, a sudden rush of adrenaline, a strange electric
crackle of excitement that made her skin tingle—all led her to believe
that something big was going to happen. She didn't know what it would
be, but she knew it was coming. She sensed it. Maybe she would win a
lot of money. Maybe this was what people meant when they said they
"felt lucky." She had never felt lucky before. She had never *been* lucky
before. Maybe she wouldn't be lucky tonight, either, but she sensed that
something was going to happen. Something big. And soon.

•

The air in the motel room grew colder.

Though apparently still asleep, Melanie writhed and kicked her legs
beneath the covers. She gasped and whimpered softly and said, "The . . .
door . . . *the door* . . ."

Dan went to the door, checked the lock, because the girl seemed to sense that something was coming.

"... keep it *shut*!"

The door was locked.

The air temperature dropped even lower.

Softly but urgently: *"Don't ... don't ... don't let it out!"*

In, Laura thought. She should be afraid of it getting *in*.

Melanie thrashed, gasped, shuddered violently, but didn't wake.

Oppressed by a feeling of utter helplessness, Laura surveyed the small room, wondering which inanimate objects, like the radio in her kitchen, might abruptly come to life.

Dan Haldane had drawn his revolver.

Laura turned, expecting the window to explode, expecting the door to burst into splinters, expecting the chairs or the television to be infused with sudden malevolent life.

Dan stayed near the door, as if anticipating trouble from that quarter.

But then, as abruptly as the disturbance had begun, it ended. The air grew warm again. Melanie stopped whimpering and gasping, ceased speaking. She was also utterly motionless on the bed, and her breathing was unusually slow and deep.

"What happened?" Dan asked.

Laura said, "I don't know."

The room was now as warm as it had been before the disturbance.

"Is it over?" Dan asked.

"I don't know."

Melanie was death-pale.

•

Because she was wearing a dress that bared her shoulders, Regine felt the change in the air before Eddie did. They were standing at a craps table, watching the action, and Eddie was deciding whether or not to put a bet down and go with the shooter. People were crowding in on every side, and the casino was warm, so warm that Regine wished that she had something with which to fan herself. Then, abruptly, there was a change of atmosphere. Regine shivered and saw gooseflesh on

her arms. For an instant she thought that the management had over-
reacted to the heat and had turned the air-conditioning too high, but
then she realized that the temperature had plummeted too quickly and
too steeply to be explained merely by the air-conditioning.

A couple other women noticed the change, and then Eddie became
aware of it, and the effect on him was astonishing. He turned from the
craps table, hugging himself, shaking, a look of horror on his face. His
skin was bloodless alabaster, and his eyes were bleak. He looked wildly
left and right, then pushed through the crowd that had formed around
the table, shoving and elbowing toward the broad aisle between rows
of gaming tables, moving away from Regine, a desperate jerkiness to
his movements.

"Eddie?" she called after him.

He didn't glance back.

"Eddie!"

It was bitterly cold now, at least immediately around the craps tables,
and people were commenting on this sudden and inexplicable frigidity.

Regine pushed through the crowd, following Eddie. He shouldered
into the main aisle and reached a clear space. He was turning in a circle,
his arms raised, as if expecting to be attacked and preparing to ward off
the assailant. But no assailant was in sight, and Regine wondered if he
had cracked up or something. She continued to make her way toward
him, and now she saw that a security guard had noticed Eddie's strange
behavior and was heading in his direction too.

She called to Eddie again, but even if he heard her, he had no opportunity to answer, for at that moment he was struck so hard that he
stumbled sideways. He collided with people streaming past the blackjack tables, and he went to his knees.

But who had struck him?

For that brief moment, he had been in an island of open space
between surging rivers of people. No one had been closer to him than
six or eight feet. But he had been hit. His hair was in disarray, and his
face was covered with blood.

Jesus, so much blood.

He began to scream.

A torrent of sound had been pouring through the busy casino—the happy shouts and squeals of winning craps shooters, the age-old litany of blackjack dealers and players, the snap of cards, the click of dice, the *ticka-ticka-ticka* of the wheel of fortune, the clack and rattle of the ball in the roulette wheel, laughter, groans of dismay at the wrong turn of a card, stridently ringing bells and wailing sirens from those slot machines that were making payoffs, pounding music from the quartet playing in the lounge—but it all ground to a silence when Eddie began to scream. His cries were as bone-shaking, as marrow-piercing as the shrieks of any creature in a nightmare. Alone, this shocking series of screeches and ululations would have been enough to turn heads, but now unseen amplifiers—or some strange sound-enhancing quality inherent in the cold and smoky air—seemed to take up his scream, echo and reecho it, double and triple the volume. It was as if some invisible and monstrous presence were mocking him by rebroadcasting his screams at an even more hysterical pitch. All conversation ceased, and then all gambling, and then even the band stopped playing, and the only sound—other than Eddie's tortured cries of pain and terror—was the ringing of a slot machine in some far corner of that vast chamber.

People fell back from Eddie, giving him even more space.

Regine stopped too, when she got a closer look at him. His right ear was limp and mangled, half ripped off, streaming blood. That entire side of his face was abraded and bleeding, and some of the hair had been torn out of his head. He appeared to have been clubbed by someone damned strong and in a rage, but he wasn't yet unconscious. He spat blood and broken teeth, started to get up from his knees, and was struck again so hard that his screaming was cut off. He was lifted from the floor and thrown into a crowd of onlookers who stood by one of the craps tables. People scattered, and the brief preternatural silence was broken by their shouts and screams, and now even the security guard, who had been approaching Eddie, stopped in perplexity and fear.

Eddie collapsed in a bloody heap but, in an instant, sprang to his feet again, though not of his own accord. He was jerked erect, as though he were a marionette controlled by a mysterious puppeteer. He took several ungainly, bouncing steps away from the craps table, twisted, turned, stumbled, staggered sideways, leaped, whirled, as if terrible bolts of lightning were striking the unseen puppeteer overhead and then were passing through the strings into this bloody marionette, causing it to cavort spastically.

Regine stepped out of the way as Eddie lurched past her. He was berserk, arms swinging and flapping as if the control strings were tangled. His right eye was smashed shut, but his left was blinking and rolling and searching frantically for his ghostly assailant. He crashed into the untenanted stools of a blackjack table, knocking one over, and the dealer, who had been watching in astonishment, scurried away.

As the pit boss shouted into a phone, demanding additional guards from the security office, Eddie clutched at the blackjack table the way a drowning man might cling to a raft in a storm-tossed sea, trying to resist the unknown entity or force that was pulling at him. But it was far stronger than he, and it lifted him off the floor. He hung above the blackjack table, kicking and squirming in midair, sorcerously suspended there, a sight that elicited from the crowd a babble and then a roar of bewilderment, shock, and terror. Suddenly Eddie was thrown down hard onto the top of the blackjack table, scattering cards and casino chips and half-finished drinks that had been abandoned by the players who had fled from him a moment ago. And he was picked up and thrown down onto the table again, so hard this time that the table collapsed under him; his back surely must have been broken.

But his ordeal was not over. He was pulled to his feet once more and was propelled headlong through the aisle between craps tables and blackjack games, toward the forest of brightly glowing slot machines. His clothes were ragged, blood-soaked, and blood flew from him as he plunged involuntarily across the casino. He was no longer conscious and might even have been dead, hardly more than a limp sack of broken bones and ruptured flesh, supernaturally animated.

The crowd's morbid curiosity ceased to be more powerful than its terror. People ran, pushing, shoving, some heading toward the front doors, some toward the showroom or the coffee shop or the stairs to the mezzanine level: in any direction that put distance between them and the shattered, shambling nightmare man who, among these dedicated escapists in this adult Disneyland, was a most unwelcome reminder of death and of the mystery and the perversity of the universe.

In a daze, in the grip of a dark thrill that she could not have defined but that was no less powerful for its lack of definition, Regine followed Eddie on his macabre pilgrimage toward the banks of slot machines. She remained fifteen feet behind him and was aware of the casino's security guards following in her wake.

One of them said, "Lady, stop. Stop where you are!"

She glanced at them. Three big uniformed men. They had their guns drawn. They were all pale and bewildered.

"Get out of the way," one of them said, and another one was pointing a revolver at her.

She realized that they might think she was somehow responsible for the impossible things that had just happened to Eddie. But what exactly did they think? That she was gifted with psychic powers and now in the grip of homicidal mania?

She stopped as they directed, but she turned to Eddie again. He was now only ten feet from the slot machines.

Immediately in front of Eddie, twenty chrome-plated, one-armed bandits—one entire bank of them—were magically activated. Twenty sets of cylinders spun at once. In the display windows, blurred processions of cherries and bells and limes and other symbols moved so fast that they flowed together in formless bands of color. The cylinders whirled for a few seconds, and then all twenty sets stopped simultaneously, and in every window of every machine, lemons were visible.

Eddie bolted forward, tucking his head down—or, rather, the unseen thing tucked his head down for him—and ran straight into a glowing slot machine, ramming it with his skull hard enough to crack thick bone. He collapsed. But he was instantly picked up, hustled backward, then rushed forward a second time, brutally slammed into the machine again. Collapsed. Was picked up. Pulled back. Was thrown forward. This time he hit the machine with such force that he cracked its Plexiglas window and dislodged it from its mountings.

The dead man dropped to the floor.

He lay there, demolished, still.

The air remained freezing cold for a moment.

Regine hugged herself.

She had the feeling that something was watching her.

Then the air grew warm, and Regine sensed that the thing, whatever it had been, had now departed.

She looked at Eddie. He was an unrecognizable mess. In her heart, Regine found a small measure of pity for him, but mostly she was thinking about what his death must have been like, how it must have felt to live through those final brutal minutes of unimaginably intense pain, all-encompassing pain, excruciating and sweetly fulfilling pain.

•

Melanie had been quiet and at rest for a few minutes, long enough for Laura to have decided that the worst had passed and for Dan to put away his revolver. As they were returning to the small table by the window, the girl began to writhe and moan again. The room grew cold. Heart racing, Laura went to the bed again.

Melanie's features were grotesquely distorted—not by pain, but (it seemed) by horror. At the moment, she didn't resemble a child at all. She looked . . . not old, exactly . . . but wizened, possessed of some hideous and hurtful knowledge far beyond her years, a knowledge that caused anxiety and anguish, a knowledge of dark things best left unknown.

It was coming or was already present. By primitive, instinctive means that she could not understand, Laura sensed a malevolent force bearing down on them. The fine hairs on her arms prickled, and along the nape of her neck too. *It.*

Laura looked desperately around the room. No demonic creature. No hell-born shape.

Show yourself, damn you, she thought angrily. Whoever you are, whatever you are, wherever you come from, give us something to focus on, something to strike at or shoot.

But it remained beyond the reach of her senses, and the only thing about the creature that could be apprehended was the chill in which it always cloaked itself.

The air temperature sank impossibly fast, lower than ever, until their breath gushed out in visible roiling plumes. Condensation appeared on the windows and on the mirror, crystallized into frost, then hardened into ice. But after only thirty or forty seconds, the air began to warm again. The child stopped groaning, and once more the unseen enemy departed without harming her.

Melanie's eyes popped open, but she still seemed to be staring at something in a dream. "It'll get them."

Dan Haldane bent over her, put one hand on her small shoulder. "What is it, Melanie?"

"*It*. It'll get them," the girl repeated, not to him as much as to herself.

"What is the damned thing?" Dan asked.

"It'll get them," the girl said, and shuddered.

"Easy, honey," Laura said.

"And then," Melanie said, "it'll get me too."

"No," Laura said. "We'll take care of you, Mellie. I swear we will."

The girl said, "It'll come up . . . from . . . inside . . . and eat me . . . eat me all up. . . ."

"No," Laura said. "No."

"Inside?" Dan said. "From inside what?"

"Eat me all up," the girl said forlornly.

Dan said, "Where does it come from?"

The child issued a long, slowly fading whimper that seemed more a sigh of resignation than an expression of fear.

"Was something here just a moment ago, Melanie?" Dan asked. "The thing you're so afraid of . . . was it here in this room?"

"It wants me," the girl said.

"If it wants you," he said, "then why didn't it take you while it was here?"

The girl wasn't hearing him. Softly, thickly, she said, "The door . . ."

"What door?"

"The door to December."

"What's that mean, Melanie?"

"The door . . ."

The girl closed her eyes. Her breathing changed. She slipped into sleep.

Looking across the bed at Dan, Laura said, "It wants the others first, the people involved with the experiments in that gray room."

"Eddie Koliknikov, Howard Renseveer, Sheldon Tolbeck, Albert Uhlander, and maybe more we don't know about yet."

"Yes. As soon as they're all dead, then it . . . *It* will come for Melanie. That's what she said earlier tonight, at the house, after the radio was . . . possessed."

"But how does she know this?"

Laura shrugged.

They stared at the slumbering girl.

At last Dan said, "We've got to break through this . . . this trance she's in, so she can tell us what we need to know."

"I tried earlier today. Hypnotic-regression therapy. But it wasn't terribly successful."

"Can you try again?"

Laura nodded. "In the morning, when she's rested a little."

"We shouldn't waste time—"

"She *needs* her rest."

"All right," he said reluctantly.

She knew what he was thinking: If we wait until morning, let's hope we're not too late.

chapter thirty-two

Laura slept with Melanie in the second bed, and Dan lay in the first bed because it was nearer the door, which was the most likely source of trouble. He was wearing his shirt, trousers, shoes, and socks; he was ready to move fast. They had left a single lamp lit because, after the events of the past day, they distrusted the dark. Dan listened to their deep and even breathing.

He could not sleep. He was thinking about Joseph Scaldone's battered body, about all the dead people in that Studio City house, and about Regine Savannah Hoffritz, who was physically and mentally alive but whose soul had been murdered. And as always, when he thought too long about murder in its myriad forms and wondered about humanity's capacity for it, his thoughts led inexorably to his dead brother and sister.

He had never known them. Not alive. They had been dead by the time that he had learned their names and had gone in search of them. As far as his own name was concerned, he had been born with neither "Dan" nor "Haldane." Pete and Elsie Haldane had adopted him when he'd been less than a month old. His real parents had been Loretta and Frank Detwiler, two Okies who had come to California in search of their fortune but who had never found it. Instead, when Loretta had been carrying her third child, Frank had been killed in a traffic accident; and Loretta, whose pregnancy had been plagued by serious complications, died two days after giving birth to Dan. She had named him James. James Detwiler. But because there had been no relatives, no one to take custody of the three Detwiler children, they had been separated and put up for adoption.

Peter and Elsie Haldane had never concealed the fact that they weren't Dan's actual parents. He loved them and was proud to carry their name, for they were good people to whom he owed everything. At the same time, however, he had always wondered about his natural parents and had longed to know about them.

Because of the rules that governed adoption agencies in those days, Elsie and Pete had been told nothing about their baby's real parents, other than the fact that both the natural mother and father were dead. That single fact made Dan more eager to learn what kind of people they had been, for they had not abandoned him by choice but had been taken from him by a whim of fate.

By the time he got to college, Dan had started wrestling with the child-placement bureaucracy in order to obtain copies of their records. The search took time, but after considerable effort and some expense, he learned his real name and the names of his blood parents, and he was startled to discover that he had a brother and a sister. The brother, Delmar, had been four when Loretta Detwiler died, and the sister, Carrie, had been six.

Through the adoption agency's records, which had been partially damaged in a fire and which were not as complete as Dan would have hoped, he began an even more ardent search for his lost siblings. Pete and Elsie Haldane always gave him a deep and abiding sense of family; he thought of their brothers and sisters as his true aunts and uncles, thought of their parents as his grandparents, and felt that he belonged with them. Nevertheless . . . well, he was plagued by a peculiar emptiness, a vague and uneasy sense of being adrift, that he knew would be with him until he had found and embraced his kin. A thousand times since then, he wished that he'd never gone looking for them.

Tracking back through the years, he eventually found Delmar, his brother. In a grave. The names on the tombstone weren't Delmar or

Detwiler. Rudy Kessman, it said. That was the name Delmar's adoptive parents had given him.

Four years old when their mother died, Delmar had been eminently adoptable and had been placed quickly with a young couple—Perry and Janette Kessman—in Fullerton, California. But the adoption agency had not performed a sufficiently thorough investigation and had not discovered Mr. Kessman's enthusiasm for new, dangerous, and sometimes even unlawful experiences. Perry Kessman drove stock cars, which was legal, of course. He was a motorcycle enthusiast, which was potentially dangerous but certainly not prohibited by law. On paper he was a Catholic, but he frequently experimented with new cults, even attended a pantheists' church for several months, and was for a long while involved with a group that worshiped UFOS; but no one could fault a man who sought God, even if he sought Him in all the wrong places. Kessman also used marijuana, which had been more of an offense at that time than it was now, though it was still illegal. After a while he started using hashish, uppers, downers, and various other substances. One night, hallucinating in a drug-induced state of paranoia or perhaps making a blood offering to some new god, Perry Kessman had killed his wife, his adopted son, and then himself.

Rudy-Delmar Kessman-Detwiler was seven when he was murdered. He had been a Kessman less time than he had been a Detwiler.

Now, lying on the motel bed in the dim light that dispelled little of the darkness but draped every familiar object in mysterious shadows, Dan did not even have to close his eyes to see the cemetery in which he had, at last, found his older brother. The headstones had been all alike, set flat in the ground, so as not to spoil the lovely contours of the rolling land. Each stone was a rectangle of granite, and centered in each rectangle was a polished copper plate bearing the name of the deceased, date of birth, date of death, and in some instances a line of Scripture or a sentiment. In Delmar's case, there had been no Scripture, no words of tribute, only his name and dates, cold and impersonal. Dan could recall that mild October day in the cemetery: the softness of the breeze, the birch and laurel shadows banding the lush green grass. But most of all he recalled what he had felt when he had dropped to his knees and had placed one hand on the copper plaque that marked his unmet brother's resting place: a piercing, wrenching loss that drove the breath out of him.

Though many years had passed, though he had long ago resigned himself to having a brother forever unknowable, Dan felt his mouth go dry again. His throat tightened. A tightness filled his chest too. He might have wept quietly then, for he had wept other nights when that memory had come to him unbidden; he was so weary that tears would have risen easily. But Melanie murmured and made a small sound of fear in her sleep, and her distress brought him instantly off his own bed.

The girl writhed beneath the sheets, but not like before, not with her previous vitality. She groaned softly in terror, not loud enough to wake her mother. Melanie struggled as if fending off an attacker, but she seemed to lack the strength to resist effectively.

Dan wondered what nightmare monster stalked her.

Then the room suddenly grew cold, and he realized that the monster might be stalking her not in a nightmare but in reality.

He stepped quickly to his own bed and picked up the gun that lay on the nightstand.

The air was arctic. And getting colder.

•

The two men sat at a table by a large mullioned window, playing cards, drinking Scotch and milk, and pretending to be just a couple of guys baching it and having a good time.

Wind soughed in the eaves of the cabin.

The night was bitterly cold and blustery outside, as befitted February in the mountains, but there would be no new snow anytime soon. Beyond the window, a large moon drifted in a star-spattered sky, casting pearly luminescence on the snow-caked pines and firs and on the white-clad mountain meadow.

They were a long way from the busy streets and bright lights of the Big Orange.

Sheldon Tolbeck had fled from Los Angeles with Howard Renseveer in the desperate hope that distance would provide safety. They had told no one where they were going—in the equally desperate hope that the murderous psychogeist would be unable to follow them to a place that it did not know.

Yesterday afternoon, they had driven north and then northeast, into the high Sierras, to a ski chalet near Mammoth, where they had settled in a few hours ago. The place was owned by Howard's brother, but Howard himself had never used it before, had no association with it, and could not be expected to go there.

It'll find us anyway, Tolbeck thought miserably. It'll sniff us out somehow.

He didn't voice the thought because he didn't want to anger Howard Renseveer. Howard, still somewhat boyish at forty, was an outgoing type who, until recently, had been certain that he was going to live forever. Howard jogged; Howard was careful not to eat much fat or refined sugar; Howard meditated half an hour every day; Howard always expected the best from life, and life usually obliged. And Howard was optimistic about their chances. Howard was—or said he was—absolutely convinced that the creature they feared could not journey this far and could not follow them if they took care to cover their trail. Yet Tolbeck couldn't fail to notice that Howard glanced nervously at the window each time that the gusty wind raised a louder protest in the eaves, that he jumped when the burning logs popped in the fireplace. Anyway, the very fact that they were awake at that dead dark hour of the morning was enough to put the lie to Howard's supposed optimism.

Tolbeck was pouring more Scotch and milk for himself, and Howard Renseveer was shuffling the cards when the room turned cold. They glanced at the fireplace, but the flames were leaping high; the fans in the Heatolator were purring, driving currents of hot air outward from the hearth. No window or door had come open. And in a moment it became frighteningly clear that the chill they felt was not merely a vagrant draft, for the air grew rapidly colder, colder.

It had come. A miraculous, malevolent advent. One moment it was not there, and the next moment it was in their midst, a demonic and deadly coalescence of psychic energy.

Tolbeck got to his feet.

Howard Renseveer leaped up so abruptly that he knocked over his Scotch and milk, then his chair, and dropped the deck of cards. The interior of the cabin had become a freezer, although the fire continued to blaze undiminished.

A large round rag rug lay on the floor between the two hunter-green sofas, and now it rose into the air until it was six feet off the floor. It hung there, not floppy and rumpled the way it should have been but stiff, rigid. Then it spun around, faster and faster, as though it were a giant phonograph record whirling on an unseen turntable.

With fevered thoughts of escape that seemed foolish and hopeless even as they took possession of him, Tolbeck backed toward the rear door of the cabin.

Renseveer stood by the table, transfixed by the sight of the spinning rug, apparently unable to move.

Abruptly, the rug dropped in a lifeless heap. One of the sofas was pitched across the room with such force that it knocked over a small table and lamp, snapped off two of its own legs, and smashed a magazine rack, sending glossy publications tumbling and flapping along the floor, like a flock of birds incapable of taking flight.

Tolbeck had retreated from the living room of the cabin into the kitchen annex, which was really part of one large chamber that constituted the entire ground floor of the structure. He had almost reached the rear door. He was beginning to think he might make it. Not daring to turn his back to the invisible but undeniable entity in the living-room area, he extended one arm behind him, scrabbling at the empty air with his hand, seeking the doorknob.

Around Renseveer, the dropped cards whirled up from the floor, full of a magical and menacing life not unlike that which had made mere brooms such a tribulation for the Sorcerer's Apprentice. They swarmed around Renseveer as if they were leaves caught in a wind devil, clicked and scraped against one another in a dizzying dance. Something about the sound made Tolbeck think of small knives being sharpened. Even as that unsettling image occurred to him, he saw that Howard Renseveer, who was frantically flailing at the storm of plastic-coated rectangles, was bleeding from both hands and was nicked all over the head and face. Surely, cards were neither rigid enough nor sharp enough to inflict even minor wounds . . . yet they slashed, slashed, and Renseveer shrieked in pain.

Groping behind him with one hand, Tolbeck found the doorknob. It wouldn't turn. Locked. He could have swung around, found the thumb latch, and been out of the cabin in a wink, but he was half mesmerized by the spectacle in the living room. Fear both energized and paralyzed him, filled him with an urgent desire to flee but simultaneously numbed his mind and his legs.

The cards collapsed into lifelessness as the rug had done before them. Howard Renseveer's wounded hands appeared to be encased in tight crimson gloves.

Even as the cards were falling, the fire screen was pitched off the stone hearth. A blazing log erupted from the fireplace, shot across the room, and struck Renseveer, who was too dazed to attempt to dodge that projectile. The log was half eaten away by flames, a missile composed of wood and crumbly coals and ashes and licking fire. When it struck Renseveer in the gut, the charred and brittle part of the log dissolved into black smoking rubble that rained down on his shoes. The unburned core of the wood, however, was hard and jagged, a crude and particularly sadistic spear that punctured his stomach and stabbed brutally, not merely severing blood vessels and rupturing organs as it went, but also carrying fire deep into him.

That grotesque and heart-freezing sight was sufficient to cure the paralysis of fear that had left Tolbeck standing at the kitchen door for long, precious seconds. He found the lock, twisted the knob, threw open the door, burst out into the night and wind and darkness, and ran for his life.

•

The air temperature had risen as quickly as it had fallen. The motel room was warm again.

Dan Haldane wondered what the hell had happened—or had *almost* happened. What did the change of temperature signify? Had some occult presence been there for a few seconds? If so, why had it come, if not to attack Melanie? And what had made it leave?

Melanie seemed to sense the dissipation of the threat, for she grew still and quiet under the covers.

Standing by the bed, Dan stared at the gaunt child and, for the first time, realized that she would grow up to be as beautiful as her mother. That thought made him turn to Laura, who was lying beside her daughter, fast asleep, undisturbed by the girl's brief spate of soft murmuring and unaware of the bitter cold that had gripped the room for half a minute or more. In repose, her lovely face reminded him of the faces of Madonnas that he'd seen in paintings in museums. Fanned out across the pillow in the pale amber light of the single lamp, Laura's thick, silky auburn hair looked as if it had been spun from the red-gold light of an autumn sunset, and Dan had an urge to put his hands into it and let it spill through his fingers.

He returned to his own bed.

He lay on his back, staring at the ceiling.

He thought of Cindy Lakey. Dead at the hands of her mother's crazy-jealous boyfriend.

He thought of his brother, Delmar. Dead at the hands of his drug-blasted, hallucinating, adoptive father.

He thought of his sister too, of course. It was an inevitable progression of memory, the same on any night when he had trouble sleeping: Delmar, Carrie, Cindy Lakey.

Eventually, through the records of the child-placement agency that had dispersed the Detwiler family on the death of their mother, Dan had found the sister from whom he had been separated when he had been a month-old infant and she had been six. Like Delmar, she was in a graveyard by the time Dan finally tracked her down.

Six years old when their mother died, Carrie had not reacted or adapted well to the dissolution of her family. She was emotionally and psychologically damaged by the experience, and her behavioral problems made her a difficult candidate for adoption. She drifted from an orphanage to a series of foster homes, back to the orphanage, then to another series of foster homes, apparently with a growing sense that she belonged nowhere and was wanted nowhere. Her attitude grew worse, until she began running away from her foster homes, and each time that she ran away, the authorities found it increasingly difficult to locate her and bring her back. By the time that she was seventeen, she knew how to dodge those searching for her, and she stayed free, on her own, thereafter. All available photographs revealed that Carrie was a lovely girl, but she didn't do well in school, and she had no job experience, and like a lot of other lovely girls from broken homes, she chose prostitution as the best way to support herself—or, rather, prostitution chose her, for she had little choice.

She was twenty-eight years old and a high-priced call girl by the time her short, unhappy life came to an end. One of her johns wanted something kinkier than she was willing to provide, and the argument swiftly led to violence. She was killed five weeks before Dan located her, and she was one month in the ground by the time that he paid a visit. He had missed meeting his brother by twelve years, and that had been sad but not as painful as missing a meeting with his sister by only thirty days.

He told himself that she would have been a stranger to him. They would have had little or nothing in common. She might not have been glad to see him, what with him being a cop and her a call girl. And he very well might have been sorry to meet the woman his sister had become. Almost certainly, given the circumstances, a reunion and any subsequent relationship would have been filled with much anguish and little joy. But he had been only twenty-two, a rookie on the force, when he had found his sister's grave, and at twenty-two he hadn't been as tough emotionally as he was now; he had wept for her. Hell, even these days, after more than fifteen years of policework, fifteen years of seeing people who'd been shot and knifed and beaten and strangled, after being considerably roughened by the work he did, he still sometimes wept for her and for his lost brother when, in the darkest hour of a sleepless night, he dwelt too intently upon the past that might have been.

He held himself, in part, responsible for Carrie's death. He felt that he should have worked harder to track her down, should have located her in time to save her. Yet he also knew that he deserved none of the blame. Even if he had found her sooner, no words or actions would have influenced her to give up life as a call girl; nothing he could have done would have kept her from that rendezvous with the homicidal john. The guilt that nagged at him wasn't earned. It was, instead, just one more example of his Atlas complex: he had a tendency to take the whole world on his shoulders. He understood himself; he could even laugh at himself, and sometimes he said that (considering his capacity and enthusiasm for guilt) he should have been Jewish. But being able to laugh at himself did not in any way lessen his sense of responsibility.

Therefore, when sleep remained teasingly beyond his reach, his thoughts often went to Delmar, Carrie, and Cindy Lakey. In the dark he would ponder humanity's capacity for murder, and he would consider his own frequent inability to save the living, and sooner or later he would even explore the idea that his mother had died at his own hands because complications from childbirth had taken her life. Crazy. But the subject made him a little crazy. The fact of death. The fact of murder. The fact that a violent savage hid deep within every man and woman. He wasn't able to come to terms with those inescapable facts, and he supposed he never would. He persisted in believing that life was precious and that humanity was noble—or at least was meant for nobility. Delmar to Carrie to Cindy Lakey: that was the usual late-night progression of memories. When he got that far, he often found himself teetering on the edge of an abyss of irrationality and guilt and despair, and he would sometimes—not often but sometimes—get up, switch on a lamp, and drink until he knocked himself unconscious.

Delmar, Carrie, Cindy Lakey.

If he failed to save the McCaffreys, their names would be added to that list, and henceforth the progression of unwanted memories would be longer: Delmar, Carrie, Cindy Lakey . . . Melanie, and Laura.

He wouldn't be able to live with himself then. He knew he was only one cop, only a man like any other, not Atlas, not a knight in shining armor, but deep inside, there was a part of him that *wanted* to be that knight; and it was that part—the dreamer, the noble fool—that made living worthwhile. If that part of him were ever snuffed out, he couldn't imagine going on. That was why he had to protect Laura and Melanie as if they were his own family. He had come to care for them, and if he let them die now, he too would be dead—at least emotionally and psychologically.

Delmar, Carrie, Cindy Lakey . . . The progression ran its course, and at last he drifted off to sleep with the soft breathing of Laura and Melanie in the background, like the susurration of a faraway sea.

•

Sheldon Tolbeck ran into the night, across the white meadow, through snow that was almost knee-deep in places. The mountainside was doubly frosted by both severe cold and frigid lunar light. As he raced from the cabin, he exhaled plumes of vapor and kicked up clouds of snow that drifted away like ghosts behind him; the appearance of ectoplasm was imparted to them by the phantasmagorical radiance of the moon.

From the cabin came Renseveer's screams, which carried well on the bitter air and echoed back from some far-off vale. The clarity of the air and the peculiarities of the terrain were such that even the echo reechoed, again and again, until there was a hideous chorus of screams. From that unnerving cacophony, one might have thought the door of Hell itself lay in this high fastness and was open wide. The screams put the fear of the devil in Tolbeck, and he ran as if the hounds of Hell were nipping at his heels.

He was wearing boots but no coat, and at first the piercingly cold wind was painful. But then, as he persisted in his mad plunge toward the far end of the meadow, the wind became like a thousand needles delivering a dose of powerful anesthetic. Within fifty or sixty yards of the cabin, his face and hands went half numb. The sharp air penetrated his flannel shirt and his jeans, and within a hundred yards his entire body seemed to be under the influence of Novocain. He knew this merciful lack of feeling would not last more than a few minutes; it was nothing more than shock. Soon, the pain would return, and the cold would be like a crab moving through his bones and tearing out bits of his marrow with its icy claws.

Not sure where he was going, driving not by reason but by stark terror, he floundered through a drift that was piled up along one edge of the meadow, and then he was into the woods. Massive firs and spruces and pines towered over him. The phosphoric moonlight reached the forest floor only through a few scattered holes between the giant and closely packed trees. Where the rays of the moon got through, they were like wan searchlight beams, and everything in those shafts of faint luminescence seemed unreal, otherworldly. Elsewhere, the forest was wrapped in darkness that varied from pitch-black to blue, to purple, to charcoal-gray.

Tolbeck staggered forward, his hands held out in front of him. He walked into trees. He tripped over rocks and exposed roots. He plunged unexpectedly down the side of a gully, fell on his face, got up, went on. His eyes were adjusting to the darkness but not quickly, and for the most part he could see little of the land ahead of him, yet he rushed forward at a fast walk, often at a run, for Renseveer's screams had come to an end a few minutes ago—which meant that Tolbeck himself was now the prey. He stumbled and dropped painfully to his knees. He got up. He went on. He blundered through ice-sheathed brush that crackled, poked at him, scratched, and scraped. He went on. He ran into a low-hanging pine branch that lacerated his scalp, and the blood that flowed down his face seemed boiling hot by contrast with his half-frozen skin. He went on.

He found himself in a wide, shallow wash bottomed with rocks, pieces of deadwood, and occasional heaps of withered brush and silt deposited by the runoff from the last rain before autumn had phased into winter. There was some ice, a little snow where the densely packed boughs of the trees parted to let it in, but for the most part the going was easier than it had been outside the wash. He followed it upward for a few hundred yards until it narrowed and then choked off near the top of the ridge.

He scrambled up a short steep slope, into an area where the trees thinned out, clutching at brush and granite outcroppings that were partly crusted with snow and partly swept clean by the wind. His hands were so cold and stiff that he could not feel the cuts and bruises that he surely had sustained in the climb.

Finally, on the high crest of the ridge, his total exhaustion overcame his panic. Tolbeck crumpled in a heap, unable to go another step.

The trees were sparse, the wind found him again, and moonlight and snow were all around. After a moment in which he unsuccessfully tried to catch his breath, Tolbeck crawled into the shelter and the shadows afforded by a nearby tooth of granite. He slumped there, peering down the wall of the ravine, squinting with bleak expectation into the lightless lower slopes of the wash through which he had ascended.

The only sound was the wind hissing through the needled branches of the evergreens and whispering across the rocky crag of the ledge. Of course, that didn't mean the psychogeist was not stalking him. It might be down there, coming toward him out of the trees, but it would make no sound as it approached.

Nothing moved except occasional snow devils whirling across the crest of the ridge and evergreen boughs stirred by the wind. But even as he squinted into the darkness below, Tolbeck realized that watching for his enemy was pointless, stupid, for if the psychogeist was moving in on him, he would not see it. It had no substance, but infinite power. It had no form, only strength. It had no body, just consciousness and will . . . and a maniacal thirst for vengeance and blood.

He would not detect it until it was upon him.

If it found him, he could do nothing to defeat it.

However, he was not a quitter, never had been and never would be, so he was unable to accept the hopelessness of his situation. Hugging himself and shivering, pressing up against the sheltering granite formation, Tolbeck peered intently into the forest below, strained to hear any sound that was not produced by the wind—and told himself, over and over, that the thing would not come, would not find him, would not tear him limb from limb.

Immobility meant less body heat, and within minutes the cold had sunk numberless talons into his flesh. He shuddered uncontrollably, and his teeth chattered, and he found that he couldn't completely uncurl the bent fingers of his gloveless hands. His skin was not only cold but dry, and his lips were cracking, bleeding. His misery was so complete that he couldn't restrain his tears, which collected in his mustache and beard stubble, where they quickly froze.

With all his heart, Tolbeck wished that he had never met Dylan McCaffrey and Willy Hoffritz, wished that he had never seen that gray room or the girl who had been taught to find the door to December.

Who would have imagined the experiments could get this far out of hand or that such a thing as this would be unleashed?

Something moved below.

Tolbeck gasped, and the sudden intake of subfreezing air hurt his throat and made his lungs ache.

Something cracked, thudded, snapped.

A deer, he thought. There are deer in these mountains.

But it wasn't a deer.

He remained on his knees, cowering against the rocks, hoping that he might still be able to hide, although he knew that he was deluding himself.

Something rattled below. The queer noise grew louder, closer. A small, hard object snapped against Tolbeck's chest, startling him, then clattered to the frozen ground.

He saw it roll away from him and come to rest in the moonlight. A pebble.

From below, the malign, psychotic spirit-thing had thrown a pebble at him.

Silence.

It was playing with him.

More rattling. He was struck again, twice, not hard, but harder than he had been struck the first time.

He saw another stone drop to the ground in front of him: a white pebble about the size of a marble. The clattering was made by pebbles rolling and bouncing and skipping up the side of the ravine, snapping against larger stones and rebounding as they came.

The psychogeist pitched with unerring accuracy.

Tolbeck wanted to run. He had no strength.

He looked wildly left and right. Even if he had possessed the strength to run, he had nowhere to go.

He looked at the night sky. The stars were sharp and cold. He had never seen a sky so forbidding.

He realized that he was praying. The Lord's Prayer. He hadn't prayed in twenty years.

Suddenly a lot more rattling arose, a torrent of uprushing pebbles, dozens, scores, hundreds of little stones, a rattle-tick-snick-snap-click-clack-crack that built until it was like the sound of a hailstorm on a concrete parking lot. Abruptly a squall of stones burst over the crest of the ridge, spewing out of the darkness, waves of half-glimpsed missiles in the pale moonlight, spinning at Tolbeck, ricocheting off his skull, rapping his face and arms and hands and body. None of the projectiles was traveling at the speed of a bullet or even half fast enough to be lethal, but all of them were painful.

And now it was not as if the pebbles were being thrown at him but as if the laws of gravity had been suspended on the slope, at least in respect to small stones, for they came up in a veritable river, Jesus, hundreds of them, and he was caught in the center of those punishing currents. He drew his knees up. He tucked his head down and covered it with his arms. He tried to squeeze even farther into the granite niche where he had hoped to hide, but the pebbles found him.

Occasionally, he was pummeled by pieces of stone too large to be called pebbles. Small rocks. And some that were not so small. He cried out each time that one of those found him, for it was worse than taking a blow from a fist.

He was bleeding and bruised. He thought one of the rocks had broken his left wrist.

The hard music on the slope, a deadly song of pure percussion, changed: The hailstorm patter of upwardly cascading pebbles was now punctuated by heavier thuds and cracks. Those noises were made by the small rocks bounding along the ridge wall to take their whacks at him. He was being stoned to death by something he could not see, and he was no longer praying but was screaming instead. However, even above his screams, he could hear the distant and terrible sound of *boulders* rolling inexorably toward the top of the ridge.

The entire slope below seemed to be tearing loose and churning upward, cataclysmically divorcing itself from the crust of the earth, as though divine judgment had required the planet to disperse its substance, and as though the fulfillment of that harsh judgment was beginning here. The ground shook with a series of violent concussions transmitted through the rough granite beneath him, as each bounce of each oncoming boulder generated the energy equivalent to a grenade explosion.

He was screaming at the top of his lungs now, but he couldn't hear himself above the thunderous roar of the antigravity avalanche. The boulders exploded over the crest and rained down around him with earsplitting force. Splinters of stone broke from them and gouged him, drew more blood, but he was not crushed as he expected. Two, three, half a dozen, ten boulders slammed down around him and piled up above him, though he was not struck by anything other than the shards cast off by each jarring impact.

Then the rocks were still.

Tolbeck waited, breathless with terror.

Gradually, he became aware of the cold again. And the wind.

Feeling around, he discovered that the boulders had piled on all sides and had stacked up overhead, forming a rude tomb. They were too heavy to be shoved out of the way. There were chinks in the tomb, hundreds of them, and a few admitted the moon's radiant gaze. The wind whistled and moaned and hissed at other openings, but no hole large enough to permit Tolbeck to escape.

In essence, though air could still reach him, he had been buried alive.

For a moment his terror swelled, but then he thought of what had happened to McCaffrey and Hoffritz and some of the others, and this death seemed almost merciful. The cold was painful again, as if some rodent with teeth of ice were chewing on his guts and nibbling on his bones. But that would pass, and quickly. In a few more minutes he would grow numb again, and this time the numbness would last. The blood had already begun to drain inward, away from his freezing skin, in a desperate effort to protect vital organs. The blood supply to his brain would be reduced as well, to a minimal maintenance level, and he would become drowsy. He would go to sleep and never wake up. Not so bad. Not as bad as what had been done to Ernie Cooper and the others.

He relaxed, resigned to death, afraid of it but willing to face it now that he knew it would not be too painful.

But for the wind, the winter night was silent.

With great weariness, Tolbeck curled up in his tomb and closed his eyes.

Something grabbed his nose, pinched and twisted it so hard that tears burst from his eyes.

He blinked, flailed out, struck empty air.

Something clawed at his ear. Something unseen.

"No," he pleaded.

Something poked him hard in the right eye, and the pain was so excruciating that he knew he had been blinded.

The psychogeist had slipped through the chinks and had joined him in his makeshift tomb of winter-chilled stone.

His death would not be easy, after all.

•

During the night, Laura woke and did not know where she was. A lamp with a cocked shade cast faint amber light, created odd and menacing shadows. She saw a bed beside her own. In it, Dan Haldane was sleeping, fully clothed.

The motel. They were hiding out, holed up in a motel room.

Still fuzzy-minded and having trouble keeping her eyes open, she turned over and looked at Melanie, and then she realized what had awakened her. The air temperature was plummeting, and Melanie was squirming weakly under the covers, softly sobbing, murmuring in fear.

Within the room there was now a . . . presence, something either more or less than human but unquestionably alien, invisible yet undeniable. In her drowsiness, Laura was more acutely aware of the entity than she had been when it had twice intruded into her kitchen or when it had earlier visited this very room. Freshly roused from sleep, she was still largely guided by her subconscious, which was far more open to these fantastic perceptions than was the conscious mind, which, by comparison, was conservative and a vigilant doubting Thomas. Now, although she still had no idea what the thing was, she could sense it drifting across the room and hovering above Melanie.

Suddenly Laura was certain that her daughter was about to be beaten to death before her eyes. With a panic that was half like the dreamy terror in a nightmare, she started to get up, shivering, each exhalation instantly transformed to frost. Even as she pushed the covers aside, however, the air grew warm again, and her daughter quieted. Laura hesitated, watching the child, glancing around the room, but the danger—if there had been any—seemed to have passed.

She could no longer sense the malignant entity.

Where had it gone?

Why had it come and then left within seconds?

She slipped back under the covers again and lay facing Melanie. The girl was terribly drawn, thin, and frail.

I'm going to lose her, Laura thought. It's going to come for her sooner or later, and It's going to kill her like It killed the others, and I won't be able to do a damned thing to stop It because I won't even be able to understand where It comes from or why It wants her or what It is.

For a while she huddled miserably under the covers, draped not only in blankets and sheets but in despair. Nevertheless, it was not in her nature to surrender easily to anyone or anything, and gradually she convinced herself that reason ruled the world and that all things, no matter how mysterious, could eventually be examined and understood if one only applied wit and logic to the problem.

In the morning she would use hypnotic-regression therapy with Melanie once more, and this time she would press the child harder than she had the first time. There was some danger that Melanie would crack completely if forced to recall traumatic memories before she was ready to handle them, but it was also true that risks had to be taken if the child's life was to be saved.

What was the door to December? What lay on the other side of it? And what was the monstrous thing that had come through it?

She asked herself those questions again and again, until they flowed through her mind like the endlessly repeated verses of a lullaby, rocking her down into darkness.

When dawn came, Laura was deep asleep and dreaming. In the dream she was standing in front of an enormous iron door, and above the door hung a clock that ticked toward midnight. Only seconds remained before all three hands of the clock would point straight up (tick), at which time the door would open (tick), and something eager for blood would burst out upon her (tick), but she couldn't find anything with which she could bar the door, and she couldn't move away from it, could only wait (tick), and then she heard sharp claws scraping at the far side of the door, and a wet slobbering sound. *Tick*. Time was running out.

part four
IT

THURSDAY

8:30 A.M.–5:00 P.M.

chapter thirty-three

Laura was at the small table by the window, where she had sat with Dan last night. Melanie sat across from her, the table between them. The girl was in a hypnotic state; she had been regressed back in time. In every sense but the physical, she was in that Studio City house once more.

Outside, no rain was falling, but the winter day was sunless and somber. The night fog had not lifted. Beyond the motel parking lot, the traffic on the street was barely visible through curtains of gray mist.

Laura glanced at Dan Haldane, who was perched on the edge of one of the beds.

He nodded.

She turned again to Melanie and said, "Where are you, honey?"

The girl shuddered. "The dungeon," she said softly.

"Is that what you call the gray room?"

"The dungeon."

"Look around the room."

Eyes closed, in a trance, Melanie turned her head slowly to the left, then to the right, as if studying the other place in which she believed that she was now standing.

"What do you see?" Laura asked.

"The chair."

"The one with the electric wires and the shock plates?"

"Yes."

"Do they ever make you sit in that chair?"

The girl shuddered.

"Be calm. Relax. No one can hurt you now, Melanie."

The girl quieted.

Thus far, the session had been considerably more successful than the one that Laura had conducted the previous day. This time, Melanie answered directly, forthrightly. For the first time since their reunion in the hospital the night before last, Laura knew for sure that her daughter was listening to her, responding to her, and she was excited by this development.

"Do they ever make you sit in that chair?" Laura repeated.

Eyes closed, the girl fisted her small hands, bit her lip.

"Melanie?"

"I hate them."

"Do they make you sit in the chair?"

"I hate them!"

"Do they make you sit in the chair?"

Tears squeezed out of the girl's eyes, although she tried to hold them back. "Y-yes. Make me . . . sit . . . hurts . . . hurts so bad."

"And they hook you up to the biofeedback machine beside it?"

"Yes."

"Why?"

"To teach me," the girl said in a whisper.

"To teach you what?"

She twitched and cried out. "It hurts! It *stings*!"

"You aren't in the chair now, Melanie. You're only standing beside it. You aren't being shocked now. It doesn't sting. You're all right now. Do you hear me?"

The agony faded from the child's face.

Laura felt sick, but she had to proceed with the session regardless of how painful it was for Melanie, for on the other side of this pain, beyond these nightmare memories, there were answers, explanations, truth.

"When they make you sit in the chair, when they . . . hurt you, what are they trying to teach you, Melanie? What are you supposed to learn?"

"Control."

"Control of what?"

"My thoughts," the girl said.

"What do they want you to think?"

"Emptiness."

"What do you mean?"

"Nothingness."

"They want you to keep your mind blank. Is that it?"

"And they don't want me to feel."

"Feel what?"

"Anything."

Laura looked at Dan. He was frowning and seemed as perplexed as she was.

To Melanie, she said, "What else do you see in the gray room."

"The tank."

"Do they make you go into the tank?"

"Naked."

Tremendous emotion was conveyed in the single word "naked," more than merely shame and fear, an intense sense of utter helplessness and vulnerability that made Laura's heart ache. She wanted to end the session right then and there, go around the table and hug her daughter, hold the girl tight and close. But if they were to have any hope of saving Melanie, they had to know what she had endured and why; and for the time being, this was the best way they had of discovering what they needed to know.

"Honey, I want you to climb that set of gray steps and go into the tank."

The girl whimpered and shook her head violently, but she didn't open her eyes or break loose of the trance in which her mother had put her.

"Climb the steps, Melanie."

"No."

"You must do as I say."

"No."

"Climb the steps."

"Please . . ."

The child was frighteningly pale. Tiny beads of sweat had appeared along her hairline. The dark rings around her eyes seemed to grow darker and larger as Laura watched, and it was agonizingly difficult to force the girl to relive her torture.

Difficult but necessary.

"Climb the steps, Melanie."

An anguished expression distorted the girl's face.

Laura heard Dan Haldane shift uneasily on the edge of the bed where he sat, but she didn't look at him. She couldn't take her eyes off her daughter.

"Open the hatch to the tank, Melanie."

"I'm . . . afraid."

"Don't be afraid. You won't be alone this time. I'll be with you. I won't let anything bad happen."

"I'm afraid," Melanie repeated.

Those two words seemed, to Laura, to be an accusation: You couldn't protect me before, Mother, so why should I believe that you can protect me now?

"Open the hatch, Melanie."

"It's in there," the girl said shakily.

"What's in there?"

"The way out."

"The way out of what?"

"The way out of everything."

"I don't understand."

"The . . . way out . . . of me."

"What does that mean?"

"The way out of me," the girl repeated, deeply distressed.

Laura decided that she didn't yet know enough to make sense of this twist that the interrogation had taken. If she pursued it, the child's answers would only seem increasingly surreal.

First of all, she had to get Melanie into the tank and find out what happened in there. "The hatch is in front of you, honey."

The girl said nothing.

"Do you see it?"

Reluctantly: "Yes."

"Open the hatch, Melanie. Stop hesitating. Open it now."

With a wordless protest that somehow managed to express dread and misery and loathing in a few wretched and meaningless syllables, the child raised her hands and gripped a door that was, in her trance, very real to her, though it could not be seen by Laura or Dan. She pulled on it, and when she had it open, she hugged herself and trembled as though she were in a cold draft. "I . . . it . . . I've opened it."

"Is this the door, Melanie?"

"It's . . . the hatch. The tank."

"But is it also the door to December?"

"No."

"What is the door to December?"

"The way out."

"The way out of where?"

"Out . . . out of . . . the tank."

Baffled, Laura took a deep breath. "Forget about that for now. For now, I just want you to go inside the tank."

Melanie began to cry.

"Go inside, honey."

"I . . . I'm s-scared."

"Don't be afraid."

"I might . . ."

"What?"

"If I go inside . . . I might . . ."

"You might what?"

"Do something," the girl said bleakly.

"What might you do?"

"Something . . ."

"Tell me."

"Terrible," Melanie said in a voice so soft that it was almost inaudible.

Not sure that she understood, Laura said, "You think something terrible is going to happen to you?"

Softer: "No."

"Well, then—"

"Yes."

"Which is it?"

Softer still: "No . . . yes . . ."

"Honey?"

Silence.

The lines in the child's face were no longer entirely lines of fear. Another emotion shared her features, and it might have been despair.

Laura said, "All right. Don't be afraid. Be calm. Relax. I'm right here with you. You've got to go into the tank. You've got to go in, but you'll be all right."

The tension drained out of Melanie, and she sagged in her chair. Her face remained grim. Worse than grim. Her eyes were impossibly sunken; they appeared to be in the process of caving into her skull, and it was not difficult to imagine that within minutes she would be left with two empty sockets. Her face was so white that it might have been a mask carved out of soap, and her lips were nearly as bloodless as her skin. She possessed an extremely fragile quality—as if she were not composed of flesh and blood and bone, but as if she were a construct of the thinnest tissue and the lightest powder—as if she would dissolve and blow away if someone spoke too loudly or waved a hand in her direction.

Dan Haldane said, "Maybe we've gone far enough for one day."

"No," Laura said. "We have to do this. It's the quickest way to find out what the hell's been going on. I can guide her through the memories, no matter how bad they are. I've done this sort of thing before. I'm good at it."

But as Laura looked across the table at her wan and withered daughter, a sinking feeling filled her, and she had to choke back a wave of nausea. It seemed as if Melanie were already dead. Slumped in her chair, eyes closed, the child appeared lifeless; her face was the face of a cold corpse, the features frozen in the final, painful grimace of death.

Could these memories be terrible enough to kill her if she were forced to bring them into the light before she was ready?

No. Surely not. Laura had never heard of hypnotic-regression therapy being dangerous to any patient's physical health.

Yet . . . being taken back into that gray room, being forced to speak of
the chair where she had received electric-shock aversion therapy, being
forced to climb into the sensory-deprivation tank . . . well, it seemed to
be draining the life out of the girl. If memories could be vampiric, these
were exactly that, sucking the blood and vitality from her.

"Melanie?"

"Mmmmmm?"

"Where are you now?"

"Floating."

"In the tank?"

"Floating."

"What do you feel?"

"Water. But . . ."

"But what?"

"But that's fading too . . ."

"What else do you feel?"

"Nothing."

"What do you see?"

"Darkness."

"What do you hear?"

"My . . . heart . . . beating, beating . . . But . . . that's fading too. . . ."

"What do they want you to do?"

The girl was silent.

"Melanie?"

Nothing.

With sudden urgency, Laura said, "Melanie, don't drift away from
me. Stay with me."

The girl stirred and breathed, though shallowly, and it was as though
she had come back from the faraway and lightless shore of the river that
flowed darkly between this world and the next.

"Mmmmmm."

"Are you with me?"

"Yes," the girl said, but so quietly that the spoken word was barely more than a shadow of the thought.

"You're in the tank," Laura said. "It's like it always is in the tank . . . except that I'm there with you this time: a safety line, a hand to grasp. You understand? Now . . . floating. Feeling nothing, seeing nothing, hearing nothing . . . but *why* are you there?"

"To learn to . . ."

"What?"

". . . to let go."

"Let go of what?"

"Everything."

"I don't understand, honey."

"Let go. Of everything. Of me."

"They want you to learn to let go of yourself? What does that mean, exactly?"

"Slip out."

"Out where?"

"Away . . . away . . . away . . ."

Laura sighed with frustration and tried a different tack. "What are you thinking?"

An even colder and more haunting note entered the child's voice. "The door . . ."

"The door to December?"

"Yes."

"What *is* the door to December?"

"Don't let it open! Keep it *shut*!" the girl cried.

"It's shut, honey."

"No, no, no! It's going to come open. I hate it! Oh, please, please, help me, Jesus, Mommy, help me, Daddy, help me, don't do it, please, help me, I hate it when it comes open, I *hate* it!"

Melanie was screaming now, and the muscles in her neck were taut. The blood vessels in her temples swelled and throbbed. In spite of this new agitation, she regained no color; if anything, she grew even paler.

The child was terrified of whatever thing lay beyond the door, and that terror was transmitted to Laura. She felt the skin prickle at the back of her neck and all the way down her spine.

•

With considerable admiration, Dan watched Laura calm and quiet the frightened girl.

The session had wound his own nerves so tight that he felt as if he might pop apart like a self-destructing clockwork mechanism.

To Melanie, Laura said, "Okay. Now . . . tell me about the door to December."

The girl was reluctant to reply.

"What is it, Melanie? Explain it to me. Come on, honey."

In a hushed voice, the child said, "It's like . . . the window to yesterday."

"I don't understand. Explain."

"It's like . . . the stairs . . . that go only sideways . . . neither up nor down. . . ."

Laura looked at Dan.

He shrugged.

"Tell me more," Laura said to the girl.

Her voice rising and falling in an eerie rhythm, never too loud, often too soft, the girl said, "It's like . . . the cat . . . the hungry cat that ate itself all up. It's starving. There's no food for it. So . . . it starts chewing on the tip of its own tail. It begins eating its tail . . . chewing higher . . . higher and faster . . . until the tail is all gone. Then . . . then it eats its own hindquarters, and then its middle. It keeps on eating and eating, gobbling itself up . . . until it's eaten every last bit of itself . . . until it's even eaten its own teeth . . . and then it just . . . vanishes. Did you see it vanish? How could it vanish? How could the teeth eat themselves? Wouldn't at least one tooth be left? But it isn't. Not one tooth."

Sounding as puzzled as Dan felt, Laura said, "That's what they want you to think about when you're in the tank?"

"Some days, yes. Other days they tell me to think about the window to yesterday, nothing else but the window to yesterday, for hours and hours and hours . . . just concentrating on that window . . . seeing it. . . . *believing* in it. . . . But the one that always works best is the door."

"To December."

"Yes."

"Tell me about that, honey."

"It's summer . . . July . . . "

"Go on."

"Hot and sticky. I'm so warm. . . . Aren't you warm?"

"Very warm," Laura agreed.

"I'd give anything for . . . a little cool air. So I open the front door of the house . . . and beyond the door it's a cold winter day. Snow is falling. Icicles hanging off the porch roof. I step back to look at the windows on both sides of the door . . . and through the windows I can see it's really July . . . and I know it's July . . . warm . . . everywhere, it's July . . . except through this door . . . on the other side of this one door . . . this door to December. And then . . ."

"Then what?" Laura urged.

"I go through. . . ."

"You step through the door?" Laura asked.

Melanie's eyes flew open, and she bolted off her chair, and to Dan's astonishment she began to strike herself as hard as she could. Her small fists delivered a flurry of blows to her frail chest. She thumped her sides, whacked herself on the hips, shouting, "No, no, no, no!"

"Stop her!" Laura said.

Dan was already off the bed, hurrying to the girl. He grabbed her hands, but she wrenched loose with an ease that startled him. She couldn't be that strong.

"Hate!" Melanie screamed, and she struck herself hard in the face.

Dan made another grab for her.

She dodged him.

"Hate!"

She took fistfuls of her own hair and tried to tear it out of her scalp.

"Melanie, honey, stop!"

Dan grabbed the girl by the wrists and held her tightly. She felt as if she had been reduced to mere bones, and he was afraid of hurting her. But if he released her, she would hurt herself.

"Hate!" she screeched, spraying spittle.

Laura approached cautiously.

Melanie released her own hair, at which she had been tearing, and tried to claw at Dan and pull free of him.

He held on and finally managed to pin her arms at her sides, but she wrenched left and right, kicked his shins, and said, "Hate, hate, *hate*!"

Laura put one hand on each side of the girl's face, held her head tightly, trying to force her to pay attention. "Honey, what is it? What do you hate so much?"

"Hate!"

"What do you hate so much?"

"Going through the door."

"You hate going through the door?"

"And *them*."

"Who are they?"

"I hate them, I hate them!"

"Who?"

"They make me . . . think about the door, and they make me *believe* in the door, and then they make me . . . go *through* it, and I hate them!"

"Do you hate your daddy?"

"Yes!"

"Because he makes you go through the door to December?"

"I hate it!" the girl wailed in fury and misery.

Dan said, "Melanie, what happens when you go through the door to December?"

In her trance, the girl could hear no voices but her own and her mother's, so Laura repeated the question. "What happens when you go through the door to December?"

The girl gagged. She'd had no breakfast yet, so there was nothing in her that she could bring up, but she succumbed to dry heaves so violent that they frightened Dan. Holding her, he felt each spasm rack her entire body, and it seemed that she would tear herself apart before she was done.

Laura continued to hold the girl's face, but now she didn't keep a tight grip on it. She held Melanie but stroked her too, smoothed the lines out of her tortured countenance, cooed to her.

At last Melanie stopped struggling, went limp, and Dan released her into her mother's arms.

The girl allowed herself to be embraced by her mother and, in a forlorn voice that chilled Dan's heart, she said, "I hate them . . . all of them . . . Daddy . . . the others. . . ."

"I know," Laura said soothingly.

"They hurt me . . . hurt me so much . . . I hate them!"

"I know."

"But . . . but most of all . . ."

Laura sat on the floor and pulled her daughter into her lap. "Most of all? What do you hate most of all, Melanie?"

"Me," the girl said.

"No, no."

"Yes," the girl said. "Me. I hate me . . . I hate *me*."

"Why, honey?"

"Because . . . because of what I do," the girl sobbed.

"What do you do?"

"I go . . . through the door."

"And what happens?"

"I . . . go . . . through . . . the door. . . ."

"And what do you do on the other side, what do you see, what do you find over there?" Laura asked.

The girl was silent.

"Baby?"

No response.

"Talk to me, Melanie."

Nothing.

Dan stooped to examine the child's face. Since she had been found wandering in the street, naked, two nights ago, her eyes had been unfocused and distant, but now they were far emptier and far more strange than ever before. They didn't even seem like eyes anymore. Peering into them, Dan thought they were like two oval windows offering a view of an immense void that was as empty as the cold reaches of space at the center of the universe.

Sitting on the floor of the motel room, clutching her daughter, Laura wept but made no sound. Her mouth softened and trembled. She rocked her girl, and tears spilled from her eyes, coursed down her cheeks. The perfect quietness of her grief indicated its intensity.

Shaken by the look on her face, Dan wanted to take her in his arms and rock her the way she cradled her daughter. All he could do was put one hand upon her shoulder.

When Laura's tears began to dry, Dan said, "Melanie says she hates herself because of what she's done. What do you think she means by that? What has she done?"

"Nothing," Laura said.

"She evidently thinks she has."

"It's a common syndrome in cases like this, in almost *all* child-abuse cases," Laura said.

Although Laura's voice was for the most part low and even, Dan could hear tension and fear just below the surface. Clearly, she was making a major effort to control the emotional turmoil that Melanie's deteriorating condition stirred in her.

She said, "There's so much *shame* involved. You can't imagine. Their sense of shame is overwhelming, not just in cases of sexual abuse, but in other kinds of abuse as well. Frequently, an abused child isn't only ashamed of having been abused, but she actually feels *guilty* about it, as if she were somehow responsible. See, these kids are confused, shattered by their experiences. They don't know what to feel, except that they know what happened to them was wrong, and by some tortuous logic they come to blame themselves rather than the adults who abused them. Well, after all, they're accustomed to the idea that adults are wiser and more knowledgeable than kids, that adults are always right. God, you'd be surprised how often they fail to realize they're victims, that they've nothing to be ashamed about. They lose all sense of self-worth. They hate themselves because they hold themselves responsible for things they didn't do and couldn't prevent. And if they hate themselves enough, they withdraw . . . further and further . . . and the therapist finds it increasingly difficult to bring them back."

Melanie seemed totally insensate now. She lolled limply, silently, almost lifelessly in her mother's arms.

Dan said, "So you think when she says she hates herself because she's done terrible things, she's really just blaming herself for what was done *to* her."

"No doubt about it," Laura said emphatically. "I can see now that her guilt and self-hatred are going to be even worse than in most cases. After all, she was mistreated—*tortured*—for nearly six years. And it was extremely intense and bizarre psychological abuse, even considerably more destructive than what the average child-victim endures."

Dan understood everything Laura had said, and he was sure there was much truth in it. But a minute ago, while listening to Melanie, a monstrous possibility had occurred to him, and now he could not dismiss it. A shocking and disturbing suspicion had planted itself with hooks and barbs. The suspicion didn't entirely make sense. The thing he suspected seemed impossible, ludicrous. And yet . . .

He thought he knew what *It* was.

And it wasn't anything he had previously imagined. It was something far worse than all the nightmarish creatures he had thus far considered.

He stared at the girl with a mixture of sympathy, compassion, awe, and cold hard fear.

•

After Laura had gone through all the necessary steps to talk Melanie up from her deep hypnotic state, the girl's condition did not change. Both in a trance and out, her withdrawal from the world was virtually complete. They would not be able to elicit any more information from her.

Laura appeared to be almost physically ill with worry. Dan didn't blame her.

They moved Melanie to one of the unmade beds, where she lay in a catatonic state, moving only to bring her left thumb to her mouth so she could suck on it.

Laura called the hospital where she was on staff and from which she had taken a leave of absence, to make certain that no emergencies had arisen that would require her attention, and she checked in with her secretary at her own office to ascertain if all of her private patients had been placed with other psychiatrists for the duration of her leave. Then, not yet having had her shower, she said, "I'll be ready in half an hour or forty-five minutes," and went into the bathroom and closed the door.

Occasionally casting a glance at Melanie, Dan sat at the small table and paged through books written by Albert Uhlander, which he'd obtained at Rink's house the previous day. All seven volumes dealt with the occult: *The Modern Ghost*; *Poltergeists*; *Twelve Startling Cases*; *Voodoo Today*; *The Lives of the Psychics*; *The Nostradamus Pipeline*; *OOBE: The Case for Astral Projection*; and *Strange Powers Within Us*. One had been published by Putnam, one by Harper & Row, and to his surprise the other five had been published by John Wilkes Press, which was no doubt an operation controlled by John Wilkes Enterprises, the same company that owned the house in which Regine Savannah Hoffritz now lived.

His first reaction to the colorfully jacketed books was that they were trash, filled with junk thoughts aimed at the same people who faithfully read every issue of *Fate* and believed every story therein, the same people who joined UFO clubs and believed that God was either an astronaut or a two-foot-tall blue man with eyes the size of saucers. But he reminded himself that something inhuman was stalking the people involved with the experiments in the gray room, something that was probably more understandable to *Fate*'s regular readers, even with all the junk thought cluttering their minds, than to people who, like he himself, had always viewed believers in the occult with smug superiority or outright disdain. And now, since observing the hypnotic-regression therapy session with Melanie, he had an unsettling theory of his own that was every bit as fantastical as anything in the pages of *Fate*. Live and learn.

He found the publisher's address on the copyright page. The office was on Doheny Drive in Beverly Hills. He made a note of it, so he could compare it with the address of John Wilkes Enterprises's corporate headquarters, which was one of the things Earl Benton would be looking into this morning.

Next, he went through all seven volumes, reading the dedications and acknowledgments, in hope of coming across a familiar name that would further tie Uhlander to the McCaffrey-Hoffritz conspiracy or perhaps identify other as-yet-unknown conspirators, but he found nothing that seemed to be of value.

He looked at all the books again and chose one for closer examination. It was the volume that, at a glance, seemed the most likely to offer confirmation of the horrible possibility that had occurred to him while he'd been observing the hypnotic-therapy session with Melanie. He had read thirty pages by the time Laura showered, gave Melanie a bath, and declared herself ready to begin the day; in those pages he had indeed found things that lent substance to his worst fears.

The mists were clearing, the mystery dissolving. He felt that he stood on the edge of an understanding that would make sense of the events of the past two days: the gray room, the hideously battered bodies, the fact that the men in that Studio City house had been able to do nothing to defend themselves, Melanie's miraculous escape from that carnage, Joseph Scaldone's death in a locked room, and all the poltergeistlike phenomena.

It was madness.

Yet . . . it made sense.

And it scared the hell out of him.

He wanted to share his ideas with Laura, obtain her point of view as a psychiatrist. But what he would be proposing to her was so shocking, so horrible, and so hopeless that he wanted to think it through better than he had thus far. He wanted to be very sure of his chain of reasoning before he broached the subject. If what he suspected was true, Laura would need all the physical, mental, and emotional strength she could muster in order to deal with it.

They left the motel and went to the car. Laura sat in back with Melanie, because she didn't want to stop holding, stroking, and comforting the child, and the computer terminal left room for only two people up front.

Dan had intended to make a brief stop at his place to change clothes. His jacket, shirt, and trousers were limp and rumpled, for he had more or less slept in them. However, now that he believed that he was on the brink of a breakthrough in the case, he no longer cared if he looked seedy. He was eager to find and talk with Howard Renseveer, Sheldon Tolbeck, and others who had been a part of the conspiracy. He wanted to confront them with the ideas that had come to him during the past hour and see how they reacted.

Before driving out of the motel lot, he turned in his seat and studied Melanie.

She was slumped against her mother.

Her eyes were open but vacant.

Am I right, kid? he wondered. Is *It* what I think It is?

He half expected her to hear the unspoken questions and shift her eyes toward him, but she did not.

I hope I'm wrong, he thought. Because if that's what's been killing all these people, and if it's going to come after you when all the rest are dead, then there's nowhere you can hide, is there, honey? Not from a thing like that. Nowhere in the world you can hope to hide.

He shivered.

He started the car and drove away from the motel.

The previous night's fog continued to linger in the city. Rain began to fall once more. As each cold drop snapped hard against the windshield, the frigid impact seemed to be transmitted through the glass, through Dan's clothes, through his flesh and bones, and into his very soul.

chapter thirty-four

Dan and Laura accomplished nothing of importance that morning, though they didn't fail for lack of trying. The renewed rainfall hampered them because it slowed traffic to a crawl throughout the city. The weather was bad, but the real problem was that the rats who could provide some answers were all deserting the ship: Neither Renseveer nor Tolbeck could be found at work or home. Dan wasted a lot of time tracking them down before he finally had sufficient reason to believe that both men had fled the city for destinations unknown.

At one o'clock, they met Earl Benton at the coffee shop in Van Nuys, as they had arranged the night before. Fortunately, the head wound that he'd suffered at the hands of Wexlersh had not appreciably slowed him down, and his morning had been more productive than Dan's and Laura's. The four of them sat in a booth at the back of the restaurant, as far as possible from the jukebox that was playing country music. They were beside a large plate-glass window, down which a gray film of rain rippled, blurring the world beyond. The place smelled pleasantly of french fries, sizzling hamburgers, bean soup, bacon, and coffee. The waitress was cheerful and efficient, and when she had taken their order and gone, Earl told Dan and Laura everything that he had uncovered.

First thing that morning, he had called Mary Katherine O'Hara, the secretary of Freedom Now, and had arranged to see her at ten o'clock.

She lived in a neat little bungalow in Burbank, a place half shrouded in bougainvillea, so typical of the architecture of the 1930s and in such good repair that Earl had half expected to see a Packard parked in the driveway.

"Mrs. O'Hara is in her sixties," Earl said, "and she's almost as well kept as her house. She's a very handsome woman now, and she must have been a knockout when she was young. She's a retired real-estate sales-woman. Though she isn't rich, I'd say she's definitely comfortable. The house is very nicely furnished, with several superb Art Deco antiques."

"Was she reluctant to talk about Freedom Now?" Dan asked.

"On the contrary. She was eager to talk about it. You see, your police file on the organization is out of date. She's no longer an officer. She resigned in disgust several months ago."

"Oh?"

"She's a dedicated libertarian, involved with a dozen different organizations, and when Ernest Cooper invited her to play a major role in a libertarian political-action committee that he had formed, she was happy to volunteer her time. The problem was that Cooper clearly wanted her name in order to lend some legitimacy to his PAC, and he expected her to be manipulable. But manipulating Mary O'Hara would be about as easy as playing football with a live porcupine without getting hurt."

Dan was surprised and pleased to hear Laura's laughter. She had laughed so little in the past couple of days that he'd forgotten how deeply affected he could be by her delight.

"She sounds tough," Laura said.

"And smart," Earl said. "She reminds me of you."

"Me? Tough?"

"Tougher than you think you are," Dan assured her, with the same admiration that Earl evidently felt.

Outside, thunder rolled like great broken wheels of stone across the day. Driven by a gusty wind, rain pummeled the window harder than ever.

Earl said, "Mrs. O'Hara was there almost a year but, like several legit libertarians before her, she finally walked away from it, because she found out the organization wasn't doing what it was supposedly formed to do. It was taking in a lot of money, but it wasn't supporting a wide array of libertarian candidates or programs. In fact, most of the funds were going to a supposedly libertarian research project headed by Dylan McCaffrey."

"The gray room," Dan said.

Earl nodded.

Laura said, "But what was libertarian about that project?"

"Probably nothing," Earl said. "The libertarian label was just a convenient cover. That's what Mary O'Hara finally decided."

"A cover for what?"

"She didn't know."

The waitress returned with three cups of coffee and a Pepsi. "Your lunch will be ready in a couple minutes," she said. She considered Earl's battered face and the bandage on his head, glanced at the bruise and abrasion on Dan's forehead, and said, "You guys in a wreck or something?"

"Fell up some stairs," Dan said.

"Fell *up*?" she asked.

"Four flights," Earl said.

"Ah, you're kidding me."

They grinned at her.

Smiling, she hurried away to take an order at another table.

As Laura unwrapped the straw, put it in the Pepsi, and tried to get Melanie to drink, Dan said to Earl, "Mrs. O'Hara sounds like the type who would've done more than just walk away from a situation like that. I would expect her to write the Federal Elections Commission and get that PAC closed down."

"She did write them," Earl said. "Twice."

"And?"

"No reply."

Dan shifted uneasily in the booth. "You're saying the people behind Freedom Now have a grip on the Federal Elections Commission?"

"Let's just say they apparently have influence."

"Which means this is a secret government project," Dan said. "And we were smart to get out from under the FBI."

"Not necessarily."

"But only the government would be able to pinch off an inquiry by the elections commission, and even they would find it difficult."

"Patience," Earl said, lifting his cup.

"You know something," Dan said.

"I always know something," Earl said, smiling, pausing to sip his coffee.

Dan saw that Melanie had drunk some of her Pepsi, though not without difficulty. Laura had already used up one napkin, blotting spilled soda from the girl's chin.

Earl said, "First, let me back up and explain where Freedom Now gets its money. Mrs. O'Hara was only the secretary, but when she began to sense that something was rotten, she went behind Cooper's and Hoffritz's backs and checked the treasurer's records. Ninety-nine percent of the PAC's funds were received as grants from three other PACS: Honesty in Politics, Citizens for Enlightened Government, and the Twenty-second Century Group. Furthermore, when she looked into those groups, she discovered that Cooper and Hoffritz had roles in all of them and that all three of those PACs were primarily funded not, as you would expect, by contributions from ordinary citizens but by two other nonprofit organizations, two charitable foundations."

"Charitable foundations? Are they permitted to mix in politics?"

Earl nodded. "Yes, as long as they tread very carefully and if they're properly chartered to support 'public-service and better-government programs,' which these two foundations were."

"So where do these foundations get their money?"

"Funny you should ask. Mrs. O'Hara didn't explore any further, but I called the Paladin office from her place and had some of our people start making inquiries. Both of these foundations are funded by another, larger charitable organization."

Laura said, "My God, it's a Chinese-box puzzle!"

"Let me get this straight," Dan said. "This larger charity funded the two smaller ones, and the two smaller ones funded three political-action committees—Honesty in Politics, uh, Citizens for Enlightened Government, and the Twenty-second Century Group—and then *those* committees contributed toward the funding of Freedom Now, which did virtually nothing with its money but fund Dylan McCaffrey's work in Studio City."

"You got it," Earl said. "It was an elaborate laundering system to keep the original backers well separated from Dylan McCaffrey in case anything should go wrong and the authorities should find out that he was performing a series of cruel and abusive experiments on his own child."

The cheerful young waitress arrived with their lunches, and they exchanged innocuous comments about the weather while she put the food in front of them.

When she was gone, no one touched lunch. To Earl, Dan said, "What's the name of the charitable organization at the center of this Chinese-box puzzle?"

"Hold on to your hat."

"I don't have a hat."

"The Boothe Foundation."

"I'll be damned."

Laura said, "The same one that supports orphanages and child-welfare groups and senior-citizen aid programs?"

"The same one," Earl said.

Dan had been fumbling in a coat pocket. Now he produced the computer printout of the mailing list of customers from the Sign of the Pentagram. He leafed to the third page and showed it to them: Palmer Boothe, heir to the Boothe fortune, current head of the Boothe family, owner and publisher of the *Los Angeles Journal*, one of the city's most prominent citizens, the guiding force of the Boothe Foundation.

He said, "I saw this last night, in Joseph Scaldone's office, behind that weird occult shop he was running. It amazed me that a hardheaded businessman like Boothe would be interested in the supernatural. Of course even the hardest heads have soft spots. We all have some weakness, some foolishness in us. But considering Boothe's reputation, his enlightened image . . . hell, it never occurred to me that he'd be involved in something like this."

"The devil has advocates in the least likely places," Earl said.

As Elton John came on the jukebox, Dan looked out at the driving gray rain. "Two days ago I didn't even believe in the devil."

"But now?"

"But now," Dan said.

Laura began to cut Melanie's cheeseburger into bite-size pieces that she might be persuaded to take off a fork. The girl was staring at the wriggling patterns of rain on the window—or at something light-years beyond.

In a far part of the restaurant, a busboy or a waitress dropped a few dishes, and the crash was followed by a burst of laughter.

"Anyway," Earl said, "you remember those two letters Mary O'Hara wrote to the Federal Elections Commission? Well, there's not much mystery about why there was no follow-up. Palmer Boothe is a big contributor to both political parties, always a little more to the party currently in power, but always large contributions to both. And here several years ago, when political-action committees first came into vogue, when Boothe apparently saw how useful they could be for things like indirect funding of Dylan McCaffrey's research, he set out to get one or two of his own men on the commission that oversees them."

Laura finished cutting up the cheeseburger and said, "Listen, I don't know much about the Federal Elections Commission, but it seems to me that its members wouldn't be political appointees."

"They aren't," Earl said. "Not directly. But the people who manage the bureaucracy that manages the elections commission *are* political appointees. So if you want to plant someone there, if you want it badly enough, and if you're rich and determined enough, you can accomplish it in a roundabout fashion. Of course, you can't get away with completely corrupting the commission, with outrageous misuse of it, because both political parties watch it intently for abuses. But if your intentions are modest—say, like keeping the commission from looking too closely at a couple of political-action committees that you've established for less than legitimate purposes—then no one's going to notice or particularly care. And if you're as resourceful as Palmer Boothe, you don't use obvious henchmen; you arrange for civic-minded, reputable men from one of the nation's largest charitable foundations to provide their services to the Federal Elections Commission, and everyone is delighted to see such educated, well-meaning types selflessly offering their time and energies to their government."

With a sigh, Dan said, "So it's Palmer Boothe, not the government, financing McCaffrey's research. Which means we didn't have to worry that the FBI might want to make Melanie disappear again."

"I'm not so sure about that," Earl said. "It's true that the government wasn't providing the money to support McCaffrey and Hoffritz or to pay for the research that was conducted in that gray room. But now that they've seen the place and had a chance to poke through the papers McCaffrey had there, they might figure there's national-defense applications to what he was doing, and they might like to have a chance to examine and work closely with Melanie . . . unobstructed."

"Over my dead body," Laura said.

"So we're still on our own," Dan said.

Earl nodded. "Besides, Boothe apparently managed to get to Ross Mondale, to use the police department against us—"

"Not the department itself," Dan said. "Just a few rotten apples in it."

"Still, who's to say he doesn't have friends in the FBI too? And while we'd be able to get Melanie back from the government if they took her away from us, we'd probably never find her again if Boothe regained control of her."

For a couple of minutes they were silent. They ate lunch, and Laura tried to feed Melanie, though with little success. A Whitney Houston number faded away on the jukebox, and in a couple of seconds Bruce Springsteen began to sing a haunting song about how everything dies but some things come back and, baby, that's a fact.

In their present situation, there was something decidedly macabre and disquieting about Springsteen's lyrics.

Dan looked at the rain and considered how this new information about Boothe helped them.

They now knew that the enemy was powerful, but that he wasn't as all-powerful as they had feared. That was a damned good thing to know. It improved morale. It was better to deal with an ultrawealthy megalomaniac—with one enemy, regardless of how crazy and influential he might be—than to be confronted by a monolithic bureaucracy determined to carry out a course of action in spite of the fact that it was an *insane* course of action. The enemy was still a giant, but he was a giant that might be brought down if they found the right slingshot, the perfectly shaped stone.

And now Dan knew the identity of "Daddy," the white-haired and oh-so-distinguished pervert who regularly visited Regine Savannah Hoffritz in that Hollywood Hills house that couldn't decide if it wanted to be Tudor or Spanish.

"What about John Wilkes Enterprises?" he asked Earl. Even as he voiced the question, he saw what he should have seen earlier, and in part he answered his own inquiry: "There's no John Wilkes. It's entirely a corporate name, right? John Wilkes Boothe. The man who assassinated Lincoln, although I think that was spelled B-O-O-T-H, without the E. So this is another company owned by Palmer Boothe, and he called it John Wilkes Enterprises as—what?—a joke?"

Earl nodded. "Seems like an inside joke to me, but I guess you'd have to ask Boothe himself if you want an explanation. Anyway, Paladin looked into the corporation this morning. It's no deep dark secret or anything. Boothe is listed as sole stockholder. He uses John Wilkes Enterprises to manage a collection of small endeavors that don't fit under his other corporate or foundation umbrellas, one or two of which don't even turn a profit."

"John Wilkes Press," Dan said.

Earl raised his eyebrows. "Yeah, that's one of them. They publish only occult-related books, and they break even some years, lose a few bucks other years. John Wilkes also owns a small legit theater in the Westwood area, a chain of three shops that sells homemade chocolates, a Burger King franchise, and several other things."

"Including the house where Boothe keeps his mistress," Laura said.

"I'm not sure he thinks of her as his mistress," Dan said with considerable distaste. "More like his pet . . . a pretty little animal with some really good tricks in its repertoire."

They finished lunch.

The rain beat on the windows.

Melanie remained silent, empty-eyed, lost.

At last Laura said, "Now what?"

"Now I go see Palmer Boothe," Dan said. "If he hasn't run like all the other rats."

chapter thirty-five

Before they paid their check and left the coffee shop, they decided that Earl would take Laura and Melanie to a movie. The girl needed a place to hide for a few hours, until Dan had a chance to speak with Palmer Boothe either in person or on the telephone, and seeking shelter in yet another motel room was too depressing to consider. Neither the FBI nor the police—not even the minions that Boothe could marshal—would think of looking for them at an anonymous shopping-center multiplex, and there was virtually no chance that they would be accidentally spotted by someone in the darkness of a theater. In addition, Laura suggested that the right film might hold therapeutic value for Melanie: The forty-foot images, unnaturally bright color, and overwhelming sound of a motion picture sometimes gained the attention of an autistic child when nothing else could.

Newspaper vending machines stood in front of the restaurant, and Dan dashed into the rain to buy a *Journal* for its film listings. The irony of using Palmer Boothe's own publication for the purpose of finding a place to hide from him was not lost on any of them. They settled on a Steven Spielberg adventure fantasy and a theater in Westwood. It was a multiplex that was showing a second film suitable for Melanie, so after the Spielberg picture they could take in another feature and pass the rest of the afternoon and the early evening there if necessary.

Their intention was to remain at the theater until Dan had either found Boothe or had given up searching for him, at which time he would return for them and relieve Earl.

When they went outside to Earl's car, Dan got in with them for a moment. While the rain fell from a roiling gray sky, he said to Laura, "There's something you've got to do for me. When you're in the theater, I want you to keep an even closer watch on Melanie than you've done so far. Whatever happens, don't let her go to sleep. If she closes her eyes for any length of time longer than a blink, shake her, pinch her, do whatever you have to do to make sure she's awake."

Laura frowned. "Why?"

Not answering the question, he said, "And even if she remains awake but just seems to be slipping into an even deeper catatonic state, do what you can to pull her back. Talk to her, touch her, *demand* more of her attention. I know what I'm asking isn't easy. The poor kid's already extremely detached, so it's not going to be easy to tell that she's drifting off a little further, especially not in a dark theater, but do the best you can."

Earl said, "You know something, don't you?"

"Maybe," Dan admitted.

"You know what was going on in that gray room."

"I don't *know*. But I have some . . . vague suspicions."

"What?" Laura leaned forward from the backseat with pathetic eagerness, so desperate to understand what was happening, so frantic for any knowledge that would shed light on Melanie's ordeal, that she gave no thought to the possibility that knowing might be even worse than not knowing, that knowledge might be a far greater horror than mystery. "What do you suspect? Why is it so important for her to stay awake, alert?"

"It would take too long to explain right now," he lied. He wasn't certain that he knew what was happening, and he didn't want to worry her unnecessarily. And there was no doubt, if he were to tell her what he suspected, she would be considerably more distraught than she was now. "I've got to get moving, find out if Boothe is still in the city. You just keep Melanie as awake and as alert as you can."

"When she's asleep or deeply catatonic," Laura said, "she's more vulnerable, isn't she? Somehow, she's more vulnerable. Maybe . . . maybe *It* even senses when she's asleep and comes for her then. I mean, last night, in the motel, when she slept, the room got cold and something came, didn't it? And yesterday evening, at the house, when the radio became . . . possessed . . . and when that whirlwind full of flowers burst through the door, she had her eyes closed and she was . . . not asleep but more catatonic than she is most of the time. You remember, Earl? She had her eyes closed, and she seemed unaware of the uproar around her. And somehow *It* knew when she was the least alert, and It came then because she was vulnerable. Is that it? Is that why I have to keep her awake?"

"Yes," Dan lied. "That's part of it. And now I've really got to go, Laura." He wanted to put his hand to her face. He wanted to kiss the corners of her mouth and say good-bye with more feeling than he had any right to express. Instead, he looked at Earl. "You take good care of them."

"Like they were my own," Earl said.

Dan got out of the car, slammed the door, and sprinted across the storm-lashed parking lot to the unmarked sedan that he had left on the other side of the restaurant. By the time Dan started the engine and switched on the windshield wipers, Earl had already pulled out of the lot and was moving off through the hesitant traffic on the rainy street.

Dan wondered if he would ever see them again.

Delmar, Carrie, Cindy Lakey . . .

The hated, long-remembered, dream-haunting string of failures cycled through his mind for at least the ten thousandth time.

Delmar, Carrie, Cindy Lakey . . . Laura, Melanie.

No.

He wouldn't fail this time.

In fact, he might be the only cop in the city—the only person within a thousand miles—who was sufficiently fascinated with murder and murderers, sufficiently well versed in their aberrant behavior and psychology, to be able to find his way into the heart of this bizarre case; he was, perhaps, the only one who had any chance of successfully resolving it.

He knew more about murder than most men ever would, because he had thought more about it than anyone else he knew and because it had played such an important role in both his personal and his professional life. His contemplation of the subject had long ago brought him to the dismal realization that the capacity for murder existed in everyone, and he was not surprised when he found it in even the least likely suspects. Therefore, he was not now surprised by the suspicions that had grown even more concrete during the past several hours, although Laura and Earl would have been not only surprised but probably devastated by them.

Delmar, Carrie, Cindy Lakey.

The chain of failure ended there.

He drove away from the restaurant, and although he worked hard at keeping his confidence high, he felt almost as bleak as the gray, rain-filled day through which he moved.

•

The Spielberg film had come out a few weeks before Christmas, but almost three months later, it was still popular enough to fill half the large theater for a weekday matinee. Now, five minutes before the feature was scheduled to start, the audience was murmuring and laughing and shifting in their seats in happy anticipation.

Laura, Melanie, and Earl took three seats on the right side of the auditorium, halfway down the aisle. Sitting between Laura and Earl, Melanie stared at the giant blank screen, expressionless, unmoving, unspeaking, hands limp in her lap, but at least she seemed awake.

Although it would be more difficult to monitor the girl in the dark, Laura wished that the lights would go down and that the movie would start, for she felt vulnerable in the light, naked and observed among all those strangers. She knew it was silly to worry that the wrong people would see them there and make trouble for them. The FBI, crooked police officers, Palmer Boothe and his associates might all be eager to find her, but that meant they would be out searching, not taking in a movie. They were safe. If any place in the world was a haven from harm, it was that ordinary theater on a rainy afternoon.

But then, of course, she had decided some time ago that nowhere in the world was safe anymore.

•

Having decided that a forceful, blunt, and surprise approach would be most effective with Palmer Boothe, Dan drove directly from the coffee shop to the *Journal* building on Wilshire Boulevard, just a couple of blocks east of the point at which Beverly Hills gave way to the enfolding, octopodal city of Los Angeles. He didn't know if Boothe was even in the city any longer, let alone in his office, but it was the best place to start.

He parked in the underground garage beneath the building and rode the elevator to the eighteenth floor, where all the executives of the *Journal* communications empire—which included nineteen other papers, two magazines, three radio stations, and two television stations—had their offices. The elevator opened on a plushly furnished lounge with ankle-deep carpet and two original Rothko oils on the walls.

Unavoidably impressed and overwhelmed by the knowledge that there was probably four or five million dollars' worth of artwork represented in those two simply framed pieces, Dan wasn't able to slip into his Intimidating Homicide Detective role as smoothly and completely as he had planned. Nevertheless, he used his ID and authority to get by the armed security guard and past the coldly polite and supremely efficient receptionist.

A polite young man who might have been an executive secretary or an executive trainee or a bodyguard—or all three—arrived at the receptionist's summons. He led Dan back down a long hall so silent that it could have been in deep space between distant stars instead of in the middle of a large city. The hallway terminated in another reception area, an exquisitely appointed decompression chamber outside the sanctum sanctorum of the starship commander himself, Palmer Boothe.

The young man introduced Dan to Mrs. Hudspeth, who was Boothe's secretary, then departed. Mrs. Hudspeth was a handsome, elegant, gray-haired woman in a plum-colored knit suit and a pastel blouse with a plum-colored bow at the throat. Though she was tall and thin and refined and obviously proud of her refinement, she was also brisk and efficient; that no-nonsense aspect of her personality reminded Dan of Irmatrude Gelkenshettle.

"Oh, Lieutenant," she said, "I'm so sorry, but Mr. Boothe isn't in the building right now. You've missed him by only a few minutes. He had a meeting to attend. It's been a terribly busy day for him, but then most days are, you know."

Dan was unsettled to hear that Boothe was carrying on with work as usual. If his theory was correct, if he had correctly identified *It*, then Palmer Boothe should be in desperate fear for his life, on the run, perhaps barricaded in the basement of some heavily fortified castle, preferably in Tibet or the Swiss Alps, or in some other far and difficult-to-reach corner of the world. If Boothe was attending meetings and making business decisions as usual, that must mean that he was not afraid, and if he was not afraid, that meant Dan's theory about the gray room was incorrect.

He told Mrs. Hudspeth: "I absolutely must talk with Mr. Boothe. It's an urgent matter. You might say it's even a matter of life or death."

"Well, of course, he's most anxious to speak with you as well," she said. "I'm sure that must have been clear from his message."

Dan blinked. "What message?"

"But isn't that why you're here? Didn't you receive the message he left for you at your precinct headquarters?"

"The East Valley Division?"

"Yes, he called first thing this morning, anxious to arrange a meeting with you. But you weren't in yet. We tried your home and got no answer there."

"I haven't been back to East Valley today," he said. "I didn't get any message. I came here because I must talk to Mr. Boothe as soon as possible."

"Oh, I know he shares your desire for a conference," she said. "Indeed, I've got a copy of his schedule for the day—every place he'll be and the time he'll be there—and he asked me to share it with you if you showed up. He requested that you attempt to connect with him at some point that would be convenient for you."

All right. This was more like it. Boothe was desperate, after all, so desperate that he hoped Dan would either be corruptible or would agree to act as intermediary between Boothe and the particular devil that was stalking the people from the gray room. He wasn't on the run or hiding in some foreign port because he knew perfectly well that it would do no good to run or hide. He was conducting business as usual because the alternative—staring at the walls and waiting for *It* to come—was simply unthinkable.

Mrs. Hudspeth went to her enormous Henredon desk, opened a leather folder, and pulled out the top sheet of paper—her boss's schedule for the day. She studied it and said, "I'm afraid you won't be able to catch him where he is now, and then he'll be in transit for a while—the limousine, of course—so I think the earliest you can hope to connect with him is at four o'clock."

"That's more than an hour and a quarter. Are you sure I can't get hold of him sooner?"

"See for yourself," she said, handing him the schedule.

She was right. If he tried driving around the city after Boothe, he'd just keep missing him; the publisher was a busy man. But according to the schedule, at 4:00 he expected to be home.

"Where does he live?"

Mrs. Hudspeth told Dan the address, and he wrote it down. It was in Bel Air.

When he finished writing, closed his small notebook, and looked up, she was watching him intently. There was an avaricious curiosity in her eyes. Clearly, she was aware that something extraordinary was happening, but Boothe had for once not taken her into his confidence, and she required all of her refinement and self-control to keep from pumping Dan for information. She was obviously eaten alive by worry too, an emotion which she had thus far been able to conceal from him, but which now surfaced like a drowned and bloated corpse soaring up through dark waters. She would be this worried only if she knew that Boothe himself was worried, and he would have permitted her to see his own concern only if it was too overwhelming to conceal. For a hard-nosed and crafty businessman like him, it would have been impossible to conceal only if it was the next thing to panic.

The young executive—or the human equivalent of an attack dog, whichever he was—returned and escorted Dan back to the reception area. The armed guard was still standing alertly by the elevators.

The beautiful but cool receptionist typed at high speed on her computer keyboard. In the muffling acoustics of the room, the nearly silent keys made soft clicking sounds that reminded Dan of ice cubes rattling against one another.

•

The movie had started ten minutes ago, much to Laura's relief, and they were now as anonymous as all the other shadowy theatergoers slumped in the high-backed seats.

Melanie stared toward the front of the theater with the same expression that had been on her face when the screen had been blank. The backsplash of light illuminated her face. Distorted reflections of the images in the film moved across her features, bringing moments of artificial color to her, but for the most part the strange light made her look even paler than she was.

At least she's awake, Laura thought.

And then she wondered what Dan Haldane knew. More than he had told her. That was for sure.

On the other side of Melanie, Earl Benton reached a hand inside his suit jacket, quietly reassuring himself that his revolver was in his shoulder holster and that he could draw it unobstructed. Laura had seen him check the weapon twice even before the film had started; she was sure he would check it again in a few minutes. It was a nervous habit, and for a man who was not the type for nervous habits, it was a disconcerting indication of how profoundly worried he was.

Of course, if It came to them here in the theater, and if It was finally ready to take Melanie, the revolver would provide no defense, regardless of how quickly Earl could draw and fire it.

•

With an hour and a quarter to kill before he could meet Palmer Boothe in Bel Air, Dan Haldane decided to drop around to the precinct house in Westwood where, the previous night, charges had been filed against Wexlersh and Manuello. The two detectives were being held solely on Earl Benton's sworn statement, and Dan wanted to add his testimony as another weight against their cell door. He had left Ross Mondale under the impression that he would not accuse Wexlersh and Manuello of assault with intent to kill, and he had told Mondale that Earl would withdraw his accusations in a couple of days, when the McCaffreys were safe, but he had been lying. If he achieved nothing else in this case, if he failed to save Melanie and Laura, he would at least see Wexlersh and Manuello behind bars and Ross Mondale ruined.

At the precinct house, the officer in charge of the case, one Herman Dorft, was glad to see Dan. The only thing that Dorft wanted more than Dan's statement was one from Laura McCaffrey. He was not happy to learn that Dr. McCaffrey was unavailable for the foreseeable future. He took Dan to a small interrogation room with a battered desk, VDT, table, and five chairs, and he offered to provide either a stenographer or a tape recorder.

"I'm so familiar with this routine," Dan said, "I'd rather just compose the statement myself. I can use the computer if that's all right with you."

Herman Dorft obligingly left Dan alone with the computer, with the harsh fluorescent light and the sound of rain on the roof, and with the stale, bitter smell of cigarette smoke that had precipitated a thin yellowish film on the walls since the last time the room had been painted.

Twenty minutes later, he had just finished typing the statement and was about to go looking for a police notary, in whose presence he would sign what he had written, when the door opened and Michael Seames, the FBI agent, took one step inside. He said, "Hello there." He still seemed, to Dan, to be suffering chronological confusion: His face was that of a thirty-year-old, but his slumped shoulders and stiff movements made him seem like a seasoned Social Security recipient. "I've been looking for you, Haldane."

"Good day for ducks, huh?" Dan said, getting to his feet.

"Where are Mrs. McCaffrey and Melanie?" Seames asked.

"Hard to believe that everyone was worried about the drought just a few years ago. Now the winters get rainier every year."

"Two detectives charged with attempted murder, police violations of civil rights, several potential breaches of national security—the Bureau now has plenty of reasons to step into this case, Haldane."

"Myself, I'm building an ark," Dan said, picking up his typed statement and moving toward the door.

Seames didn't get out of his way. "And we *have* moved in. We're no longer just observers here. We've exercised the right of federal jurisdiction in these homicides."

"Good for you," Dan said.

"You are, of course, obliged to cooperate with us."

"Sounds like fun," Dan said, wishing Seames would get the hell out of his way.

"Where are Mrs. McCaffrey and Melanie?"

"Probably at the movies," Dan said.

"Damn it, Haldane—"

"On a dreary day like this, they aren't going to be at the beach or at Disneyland or having a picnic in Griffith Park, so why not the movies?"

"I'm beginning to think you're an asshole, Haldane."

"Well, at least it's comforting to hear that you're beginning to think."

"Captain Mondale warned me about you."

"Oh, don't take that seriously, Agent Seames. Ross is such a kidder."

"You're obstructing—"

"No, it's you who's obstructing," Dan said. "You're in my way." And as he spoke, he shouldered past Seames, through the door.

The FBI agent followed him down the hall to the busy uniformed-operations room, where Dan located a notary. "Haldane, you can't protect them all by yourself. If you insist on handling it this way, they're going to get snatched or killed, and you're going to be to blame."

Signing his statement in front of the notary, Dan said, "Maybe. *Maybe* they'll get killed. But if I turn them over to you, they'll *positively* be killed."

Seames gaped at him. "Are you implying that I . . . that the FBI . . . that the *government* would murder that little girl? Because maybe she's a Russian or Chinese research project? Or maybe because she's one of *our* projects and she knows too much and now we want to shut her up before this mess becomes too public? Is *that* what you think?"

"Crossed my mind."

Spluttering and fuming, filled with either genuine outrage or a good imitation of it, Seames followed Dan from the notary to another desk where Herman Dorft was drinking black coffee and looking through a file of mug shots.

"Are you crazy, Haldane, or what?" Seames demanded.

"Or what."

"We're the government, for Christ's sake. The *United States* government."

"I'm happy for you."

"This isn't China, where the government knocks on a couple of hundred doors every night and a couple of hundred people disappear."

"How many disappear here? Ten a night? Makes me feel so much better."

"This isn't Iran or Nicaragua or Libya. We aren't killers. We're here to protect the public."

"Does this stirring speech come with background music? It ought to, but I don't hear any."

"We don't murder people," Seames said flatly.

Handing his notarized statement to Dorft, Dan said to Seames, "All right, so the government itself, the institution of government in this country, doesn't make a *policy* of killing people—except maybe with taxes and paperwork. But the government is composed of people, individuals, and your agency is composed of individuals, and don't tell me that some of those individuals aren't capable of murdering the McCaffreys in return for money or for political concerns, misguided idealism, or any of a thousand other reasons. Don't try to tell me that everyone in your agency is so saintly and so God-fearing that a homicidal thought has never entered any of their minds, because I remember Waco, Texas, and the Weaver family in Idaho and more than a few other Bureau abuses of power, Agent Seames."

Dorft stared up at them, startled, as Seames shook his head violently and said, "FBI agents are—"

"Dedicated, professional, and generally damned good at what they do," Dan finished for him. "But even the best of us have the capacity for murder, Mr. Seames. Even those of us who appear to be the most dependable—or the most innocent, the gentlest. Believe me, I know. I know all about murder, about the murderers among us, the murderers *within* us. More than I want to know. Mothers murder their own children. Husbands get drunk and murder their wives, and sometimes they don't have to be drunk, just suffering from indigestion, and sometimes it doesn't even take indigestion. Ordinary secretaries murder their two-timing boyfriends. Last summer, right here in L.A., on the hottest day in July, an ordinary salesman murdered his next-door neighbor over an argument about a borrowed lawn mower. We're a twisted species, Seames. We mean well, and we want to do good for each other, and we *try*, God knows we try, but there's this darkness in us, this taint, and we've got to struggle against it every minute, struggle against letting the taint spread and overwhelm us, and we do struggle, but sometimes we lose. We murder for jealousy, greed, envy, pride . . . revenge. Political idealists go on murderous rampages and make life hell on earth for the very people whose lives they profess to want to make better. Even the best government, if it's big enough, is *riddled* with idealists who'd open up extermination camps and feel *righteous* about it, if they were just given a chance. Religious zealots kill each other in the name of God. Housewives, ministers, businessmen, plumbers, pacifists, poets, doctors, lawyers, grandmothers, and teenagers—all have the capacity to murder, given the right moment and mood and motivation. And the ones you've got to mistrust the most are the ones who tell you they're men and women of peace, the ones who tell you they're absolutely nonviolent and safe, because they're either lying and waiting for an advantage over you—or they're dangerously naive and know nothing important about themselves. Now, you see, two people I care about— the two people I care about most in the world, it seems—are in danger of their lives, and I won't entrust their care to anyone but me. Sorry. No way. Forget it. And anybody who tries to get in my way, tries to stop me from protecting the McCaffreys, is at least going to get his ass kicked up between his shoulder blades. Oh, at least. And anyone who tries to harm them, tries to lay a finger on them . . . well, hell, I'll waste the son of a bitch, sure as hell. I have no doubts about that, Seames, because I have absolutely no illusions about my *own* capacity for murder."

Shaking, he walked away, heading toward the door that opened onto the parking lot beside the precinct house. As he went, he became aware that the room had fallen silent and that everyone was looking at him. He realized that he had been speaking not only angrily and passionately but at the top of his voice as well. He felt fevered. Sweat sheathed his face. People moved out of his way.

He had reached the door and put his hand on it by the time Michael Seames had recovered from that emotional outburst and had come after him. "Wait, Haldane, for Christ's sake, it just can't work that way. We can't let you play the Lone Ranger. *Think*, man! There are eight people dead in two days, which makes this case just too damned big to—"

Dan stopped before opening the door, turned sharply to Seames, and interrupted him. "*Eight?* Is that what you said? Eight dead?"

Dylan McCaffrey, Willy Hoffritz, Cooper, Rink, and Scaldone. That made five. Not eight. Just five.

"What's happened since last night?" Dan demanded. "Who else has been hit since Joseph Scaldone?"

"You don't know?"

"Who else?" Dan demanded.

"Edwin Koliknikov."

"But he got out. He ran, went to Las Vegas."

Seames was furious. "You knew about Koliknikov? You knew he was an associate of Hoffritz's, in on this gray room business?"

"Yes."

"We didn't know until he was dead, for God's sake! You're withholding information from a police investigation, Haldane, and it doesn't matter a rat's ass that you're a cop!"

"What happened to Koliknikov?"

Seames told him about the gaudy public execution in the Vegas casino. "It was like a poltergeist," the agent repeated. "Something unseen. An unknown, unimaginable power that reached into that casino and beat Koliknikov to death in front of hundreds of witnesses! Now there's no longer any doubt that Hoffritz and Dylan McCaffrey were working on something with serious defense applications, and we're goddamned determined to know what it was."

"You've got his papers, the logbooks and files from the house in Studio City—"

"We *had* them," Seames said. "But whatever reached into that casino and wasted Koliknikov also reached into the evidence files in this case and set fire to all of McCaffrey's papers—"

Astonished, Dan said, "What? When was this?"

"Last night. Spontaneous fucking combustion," Seames said.

Obviously Seames was teetering on the edge of blind rage, for a federal agent simply did not shout the F-word at the top of his voice in a public place. Such behavior wasn't good for the image, and to the feds, their image was as important as their work.

"You said eight," Dan reminded him. "Eight dead. Who else besides Koliknikov?"

"Howard Renseveer was found dead in his ski chalet this morning, up in Mammoth. I guess you know about Renseveer too."

"No," Dan lied, afraid that the truth would so enrage Seames that he would put Dan under arrest. "Harold Renseveer?"

"*Howard,*" Seames corrected in a sarcastic tone that indicated he was still half convinced that Dan knew the name well. "Another associate of Willy Hoffritz and Dylan McCaffrey. Evidently he was hiding up there. People in another chalet, farther down the mountain, heard screaming during the night, called the sheriff. They found a mess when they got there. And there was another man with Renseveer. Sheldon Tolbeck."

"Tolbeck? Who's he?" Dan asked, playing dumb in the name of self-preservation.

"Another research psychologist who was involved with Hoffritz and McCaffrey. Indications are that Tolbeck was in the cabin when this thing . . . this *power*, whatever it is, showed up and started to bash Renseveer's brains in. Tolbeck ran into the woods. He hasn't been found yet. He probably never will be, and if he is . . . well, the odds are pretty damned high that the best we can hope for is that he froze to death."

This was bad. Terrible. The worst.

Dan had known that time was running out, but he hadn't known that it was pouring away like floodwater through the broken breast of a dam. He had thought that at least five of the conspirators from the gray room remained to be disposed of before *It* would turn Its attention to Melanie. He had figured those executions would require another day or two and, long before the last of the conspirators had been destroyed, he would have confirmed his suspicions about the case and would have found a way to bring the slaughter to an end in time to save Melanie. He'd thought he might even be in time to save one or more of those manipulative and amoral men, although they didn't deserve to be saved. But suddenly his chances of saving anyone were diminished: Three more were gone. As far as he knew, two conspirators remained: Albert Uhlander, the author; and Palmer Boothe. As soon as they were terminated, *It* would turn to Melanie with a special rage. It would tear her apart. It would hammer her head to bits, hammer the last glimmer of life out of her brain before finally releasing her. Only Boothe and Uhlander stood between the girl and death. And even now, either the publisher or the author—or both—might be in the merciless grip of their invisible but powerful adversary.

Dan turned away from Seames, jerked open the door, and plunged out into the parking lot, where a cold wind and a stinging rain and an early fog were industriously putting the lie to the standard postcard image of Southern California. He sloshed through several puddles, getting water in his shoes.

He heard Seames shouting at him, but he didn't pause or reply. When he got in the car, dripping and shivering, he looked back and saw Seames standing in the open door of the precinct house. From this distance the agent's face seemed to have aged in the past few minutes; now it was more in harmony with his gray hair.

Driving out of the lot, into the street, Dan was surprised that Seames let him go. After all, a great deal was at stake, perhaps even grave national-defense issues; eight people were dead, and the FBI had officially stepped into the case. Seames would have been justified in detaining him; in fact, it was a dereliction of duty not to have done so.

Dan was relieved to be free, of course, because it was more important than ever that he talk to Boothe soon, damned soon. If Melanie's life had been hanging by a string, it was now hanging by a thread, and time like a razor was relentlessly sawing through that fragile filament.

Delmar, Carrie, Cindy Lakey . . .

No.

Not this time.

He would save this woman, this child. He would not fail again.

He drove through Westwood, reached Wilshire, swung left, heading toward Westwood Boulevard, which would take him to Sunset and to the entrance to Bel Air. He would be arriving at the Boothe house ahead of schedule, but maybe Boothe would be early too.

Dan went three blocks before it dawned on him that Michael Seames had probably had his car bugged while he was in the precinct house preparing his statement against Wexlersh and Manuello. That was why he hadn't been detained for questioning or arrested for obstructing a federal officer. Seames had realized that the quickest method of finding Laura and Melanie McCaffrey was to allow Dan to lead the way.

As a traffic light turned red ahead of him, Dan braked and glanced repeatedly in the rearview mirror. Traffic was heavy. Spotting a tail would be difficult and time-consuming when there was precious little time to consume. Besides, those tracking him were not necessarily within sight of his car; if they had bugged his car, if they were running an electronic tail, they could be several blocks away, watching his progress on a lighted scope overlaid with a computer-generated map of the streets.

He had to lose them.

He wasn't going to the McCaffreys yet, but he didn't want to be followed to Boothe's place, either. A tagalong band of FBI agents would not particularly encourage Boothe to open up. Furthermore, if Boothe did spill everything he knew, Dan didn't want anyone to hear what the publisher had to say, for if Melanie did—by some miracle—survive, that information would be used against her. Then she would have no chance whatsoever of finding her way back from autism, no hope of leading a normal life.

Already, there was little hope for her, though there was at least a spark. Right now, it was Dan's job to preserve that spark of hope and try to nurture it into a flame.

The traffic light changed to green.

He hesitated, not sure which way to go, what action to take in order to rid himself of his tail.

Delmar, Carrie, Cindy Lakey . . .

He looked at his watch.

His heart was pounding.

The soft ticking of his watch, the thump-tick of his heartbeat, and the ticking of the rain on the car all blended together in one metronomic sound, and it seemed as though the entire world were a time bomb about to explode.

chapter thirty-six

Melanie's eyes followed the action on the screen. She didn't make a sound, and she didn't shift an inch in her seat, but her eyes moved, and that seemed to be a good sign. It was one of the few times in the past two days that Laura had seen the girl actually looking at something in *this* world. For almost an hour, the movement of her eyes had indicated that she was involved with the movie, which was certainly the first that she had focused on external events for any substantial length of time. Whether Melanie was following the plot or was merely fascinated by the bright images didn't matter. The important thing was that the music and the color and Spielberg's cinematic artistry—his imaginative scenes and archetypal characters and bold use of the camera—had done what nothing else could do, had begun to draw the child out of her self-imposed psychological exile.

Laura knew there would be no miraculous recovery, no spontaneous rejection of autism simply because of the movie. But it was a start, however small.

In the meantime, Melanie's interest in the film made it easier for Laura to monitor her and keep her awake. The girl exhibited no signs of being sleepy or of slipping back into a more profound catatonic state.

•

Dan drove back and forth through Westwood, winding from street to street. Each time that he came to a stop sign or a red traffic light, he shifted the car into park, got out, and hastily searched one small portion of the sedan's body for the compact transmitter that he knew must be attached to some part of the vehicle. He could have pulled to the curb and examined the entire car methodically from end to end, but then the Bureau agents tailing him would catch up and see what he was doing. If they realized that he suspected being monitored they would not give him an opportunity to find and discard the bug and slip away from them; they would most likely arrest him and take him back to Michael Seames. So at the first stop sign, he frantically checked up under the left front fender and in the wheel well around the tire, groping for a magnetically attached electronics package about the size of a pack of cigarettes. At the next stop he checked the left rear wheel well; during the two stops after that, he ran to the right side of the car and explored under those fenders. He knew other motorists were gawking, but because of his zigzagging route of randomly chosen streets, none of them were behind him for more than two stops, so none had enough time to begin to think that his behavior was suspicious rather than merely odd or eccentric.

Eventually, at a stop sign at an intersection in a residential neighborhood, two blocks east of Hilgarde and south of Sunset Boulevard, when he was the only motorist in sight, with rain pasting his hair even tighter to his scalp and drizzling under the collar of his coat, he found what he was looking for under the rear bumper. He tore it loose, pitched it into a line of plum-thorn shrubs in the front yard of a big pale yellow Spanish house, got behind the wheel of the sedan again, slammed his door, and got the hell out of there. He repeatedly checked the rearview mirror during the next few blocks, afraid that the men tailing him had gotten close enough to see him discard the bug and were following visually. But he was not pursued.

His pants legs and shoes were soaked, and a lot of water had gotten under the collar of his coat while he'd twisted and strained to feel beneath various portions of the car. Waves of shivers swept through him. His teeth chattered.

He turned the car's heater control to its highest position. But this was a cheapjack city vehicle, and even when the equipment worked, it didn't work well. The vents spewed a vaguely warm, moist, slightly fetid breeze in his face, as if the car had halitosis, and he didn't stop shivering until he had driven all the way into the heights of Bel Air, had wound through the tangled network of very private streets, and had found the Boothe estate on the most secluded street of all.

Beyond the massive pines and intermingled oaks that were almost equally enormous as the ancient evergreens, rose a brick wall the color of old blood, between seven and eight feet tall, capped with black slate and black iron spikes. The wall was so long that it seemed to delineate the property line of an institution—a college, hospital, museum—rather than that of a private residence. But in time Dan came to a place where the brick ramparts curved in on both sides of a driveway, flanking it for twenty feet and terminating at a formidable iron gate.

The cross-supported bars of the gate were two inches thick. The entire structure, which was flanked and capped by intricately wrought scrolls and fleurs-de-lis of iron, was impressive and elegant and beautifully crafted—and seemed capable of withstanding any number of bomb blasts.

For a moment Dan thought he was going to have to get out in the rain and search for a call button to announce himself, but then he noticed a guardhouse subtly incorporated into one of the curved brick ramparts. A guard, wearing galoshes and a gray rain slicker with the hood pulled up, stepped out from behind a brick baffle that concealed the door to his small domain; for the first time Dan noticed the round window through which the guard had seen the sedan approaching.

The man came directly to the car, inquired if he could help, checked Dan's ID, and informed him that he was expected. He said, "I'll open the gate, Lieutenant. Just follow the main drive and park along the circle in front of the house."

Dan cranked up his window while the guard returned to the booth, and the colossal gates swung inward with ponderous grace. He drove through them with the curious science-fictional feeling that this was not a residence in the same world that he inhabited, but a place in another, better dimension; the gates guarded a magic portal through which one might jump into stranger and more wonderful realms.

The Boothe estate appeared to encompass eight or ten acres and must have been one of the larger properties in Bel Air. The driveway led up a gentle rise and then curved to the left, through exquisitely maintained, parklike grounds. The house, standing just beyond that point at which the driveway curved back on itself to form a circle, was where God would have lived—if He'd had sufficient money. It resembled one of those baronial homes in films with British settings, like *Rebecca* and *Brideshead Revisited*, a great pile of bricks with granite coins and granite window lintels, three stories high, with a black-slate mansard roof and many gables, with half-seen wings and unseen wings angling off from the front-facing portion of the structure. A dozen steps under a portico led up to a set of antique, mahogany entry doors that had probably cost the life of at least one big tree or two younger ones.

He parked beside a limestone fountain that was centered in the looped circular turnaround. It wasn't spouting at the moment, but it looked like a backdrop to a love scene featuring Cary Grant and Audrey Hepburn in one of those old movies about European romance and intrigue.

Dan climbed the steps, and one of the front doors opened before he could begin searching for the bell. Evidently the guard in the gatehouse had called ahead to announce him.

The entry hall was so grand and large that Dan figured he could have lived comfortably in just that space, even if someday he married and produced two children.

Forgoing the formal wear of movie butlers in favor of a gray suit and white shirt and black tie, a soft-spoken servant with a British accent took Dan's streaming coat and had the courtesy not to look askance at his damp, rumpled, day-old clothes.

"Mr. Boothe is waiting for you in the library," the butler said.

Dan checked his watch. It was 3:55. Delayed by the necessity of locating and removing the transmitter that had been attached to his car, he'd not arrived too early, after all. He was again seized by an urgent sense of time running out.

The butler led him through a series of huge serene rooms, each more elaborately and graciously furnished than the one before it, across antique Persian rugs and Chinese carpets. The deeply coffered ceilings with inlaid-woods might have been imported from classic estates in Europe. They passed through superbly hand-carved doorways and walked past Impressionist paintings by all the masters of that school (and no reason to believe that even one piece was a print or imitation).

The wealth of antiques and the great beauty of the house were awesome and visually appealing, but surprisingly, the succession of paradisiacal rooms gave rise to an increasing uneasiness in Dan. He had a sense of powerful and ominous forces lying dormant but easily disturbed just beyond the walls and under the floors, a pseudopsychic perception of colossal dark machinery purring with malevolent purpose somewhere just out of sight. In spite of the exquisite taste and apparently infinite resources with which the house had been built and appointed, in spite of its soaring spaces—or perhaps in part *because* of its superhuman scale—it had a quality of medieval oppressiveness.

Furthermore, Dan could not help but grimly wonder how Palmer Boothe could possess the refinement and taste to appreciate a house like this—and still be capable of condemning a little girl to the horrors of the gray room. That contradiction would seem to require a personality so duplicitous as to be virtually indistinguishable from schizophrenic multiplicity. Dr. Jekyll and Mr. Hyde. The great publisher and liberal and philanthropist who, by night, stalks the mean streets with a bludgeon disguised as an innocent walking stick.

The butler opened one of the heavy, paneled doors to the library and stepped through, announcing Dan as he went, and Dan followed with more than a little trepidation, passing between bookcases into which the entry was recessed. The butler immediately withdrew, closing the door behind him.

A twenty-foot-high, richly paneled mahogany ceiling curved down to ten-foot-high mahogany shelves filled with books, some accessible only with the aid of a library ladder. At the far end of the room, enormous French windows occupied the only wall not given completely to books; they presented a view of lush gardens, though heavy green drapes were drawn across more than half the glass. Persian rugs decorated the highly polished wood floor, and groupings of heavily padded arm-chairs offered elegant comfort. On a desk almost as big as a bed, a Tif-fany stained-glass lamp cast such rich colors and exquisite patterns of light that it seemed to be made not of mere glass but of precious gems. Around the side of that desk and through the red-yellow-green-blue beams of filtered lamplight, Palmer Boothe came to greet his guest.

Boothe was six feet tall, broad in the shoulders and chest, narrow in the waist, in his mid- or late-fifties, with the physique and aura of a much younger man. His face was too narrow and his features too elon-gated to be called handsome. However, a certain ascetic quality in his thin lips and straight thin nose, and a trace of nobility in his chin and jawline, made it impossible to deny him the approbative "distinguished."

Holding out his hand as he approached, Boothe said, "Lieutenant Haldane, I'm so pleased you could come."

Before Dan realized what he was doing, he found himself shaking Boothe's hand, though the very idea of touching this evil lizard of a man should have repelled him. Furthermore, he saw himself manipu-lated into reacting to Boothe partly like a vassal unaccountably admit-ted to the court of the king, partly like a valued acquaintance answering the summons of a nobleman whose approval he wished to elicit by the performance of any favor asked and whose friendship he hoped to gain. How this subtle manipulation was accomplished remained a mystery to him. Which was why Palmer Boothe was worth several hundred million and Dan, by contrast, did far more shopping at Kmart than at Neiman-Marcus. Anyway, he sure as hell hadn't initiated their encounter in the manner of a hard-nosed cop who had come to break someone's ass, which was the impression he had intended to make straightaway.

Dan noticed movement in a shadowed corner of the wood-dark room and turned to see a tall, thin, hawk-faced man rise from an armchair, a glass of ice and whiskey in one hand. Although he was twenty feet away, the hawkish man's unusually bright and intense eyes conveyed everything essential about his personality: high intelligence, strong curi-osity, aggressiveness—and a touch of madness.

As Boothe began to make introductions, Dan interrupted and said, "Albert Uhlander, the author."

Uhlander apparently knew that he did not possess Palmer Boothe's uncanny manipulative powers. He didn't smile. He made no attempt to shake hands. That they were of opposing camps and hostile ideologies seemed as apparent to Uhlander as it was to Dan.

"Can I get you a drink?" Boothe asked with a misplaced gentility and excessive civility that was beginning to be maddening. "Scotch. Bourbon? Perhaps a glass of dry sherry?"

"We don't have time to sit here and drink, for God's sake," Dan said. "You're both living on borrowed time, and you know it. The only reason I want to try to save your lives is so I can have the great pleasure of putting both of you bastards in prison for a long, long time."

There. That was better.

"Very well," Boothe said coldly, and he returned to his desk. He settled into the brass-studded, dark green leather club chair behind the desk and was almost entirely in shadow, except for his face, which was part blue and part green and part yellow in the spears of multicolored light from the Tiffany lamp.

Uhlander went to one window that was not concealed by green drapes, and he stood with his back to the French panes. Outside, because the storm-gray afternoon was waning toward an early-winter twilight, not much daylight found its way past the lush vegetation of the formal gardens and to the library window. Nevertheless, sufficient brightness lay behind Uhlander to reduce him to only a silhouette, leaving his face in deep shadows that concealed his expression.

Dan approached the desk, stepped into the circle of jeweled light, and looked down at Boothe, who had lifted a glass of whiskey. "Why would a man of your position and reputation get involved with someone like Willy Hoffritz?"

"He was brilliant. A genius in his field. I have always sought out and associated with the brightest people," Boothe said. "They're the most interesting people, for one thing. And for another, their ideas and enthusiasms are often of great practical use in one of my businesses or another."

"And besides, Hoffritz could supply you with an utterly passive, totally submissive young woman who would endure any humiliation you wanted to heap on her. Isn't that right, *Daddy*?"

At last a crack appeared in Boothe's self-possession. For a moment his eyes narrowed hatefully, and his jaw muscles bulged as he clenched his teeth in anger. But his control slipped only one notch, and the crack closed up again in seconds. His face recomposed itself, and he sipped his whiskey.

"All men have . . . weaknesses, Lieutenant. In that regard, I'm a man like any other."

Something in his eyes, in his expression, and in his tone of voice belied any admission of weakness. Rather, it seemed as if he were merely being magnanimous by claiming to share the weaknesses of ordinary men. It was all too clear that he didn't believe there was anything wrong or even slightly morally suspect in his behavior with Regine, and his admission was not an act of contrition or humility but one of smug condescension.

Shifting to another tack, Dan said, "Hoffritz might have been a genius, but he was bent, twisted. He applied his knowledge and his talents not to legitimate behavior-modification research but to developing new techniques of brainwashing. I'm told by people who knew him that he was a totalitarian, a fascist, an elitist of the worst sort. How does that square with your own widely heralded liberalism?"

Boothe regarded Dan with pity, disdain, and amusement. As if speaking to a child, he said, "Lieutenant, everyone who believes that the problems of society can be solved through the political process is an elitist. Which means most people. It doesn't matter if you're a right-winger, a conservative, a moderate, a liberal, or an extreme left-winger. If you define yourself by *any* political label, then you're an elitist because you believe that problems could be solved if only the right group of people held power. So Willy Hoffritz's elitism was of no concern to me. I happen to believe the masses *need* to be guided, controlled—"

"Brainwashed."

"Yes, brainwashed, but for their own good. As the world's population grows ever larger and as technology leads to a wider dissemination of information and ideas, the old institutions like family and Church break down. There are new, more dangerous ways for the discontented to express their misery and alienation. So we must find methods of eliminating discontent, of controlling thought and action, if we're to have a stable society, a stable world."

"I see why you used libertarian political-action committees as a front for financing McCaffrey and Hoffritz."

Boothe raised his eyebrows. "You know about that, do you?"

"I know considerably more than that."

Boothe sighed. "Libertarians are such hopeless dreamers. They want to reduce government to a minimum, virtually eliminate politics. I thought it would be amusing to work toward exactly the opposite ends while employing the cover of a libertarian crusade."

Albert Uhlander still stood with his back to the French window, attentive but unreadable, a silent silhouette that moved only to raise the black outline of a whiskey glass to unseen lips.

"So you supported Hoffritz and McCaffrey and Koliknikov and Tolbeck and God knows how many other twisted 'geniuses,'" Dan said. "And now, while searching so diligently for a way to control the masses, you've *lost* control. One of these experiments has run wild, and it's rapidly destroying everyone involved in it. Soon it's going to destroy you as well."

"I'm sure you find this ironic turn of events to be enormously satisfying," Boothe said. "But I don't believe you know as much as you think you do, and when you hear the entire story, when you know what's happening, I think you'll be as eager as we are to stop the killing, to put an end to the terror that came out of that gray room. You're sworn to protect and preserve lives, and I am familiar enough with your record to know that you take your oath seriously, even solemnly. Though the lives you'll have to protect are mine and Albert's, and though you despise us, you'll do what's necessary to help us, once you know the whole story."

Dan shook his head. "You have nothing but disdain for the honor and integrity of common people like me, yet you're relying on that honor to save your ass."

"That . . . and certain inducements," Uhlander said from his place at the window.

"What inducements?" Dan asked.

Boothe studied him intently. Bright miniature patterns of Tiffany stained glass reflected in his icy eyes. Finally he said, "Yes, I suppose it won't hurt to explain the inducements first. Albert, would you bring it here, please?"

Uhlander returned to the chair where he had been sitting, put his whiskey glass on a nearby table, and picked up a suitcase which had been standing beside the chair but which Dan hadn't noticed until now. He brought the piece of luggage to Boothe's desk, put it down, and opened it. The suitcase was filled with fifty- and hundred-dollar bills in neatly banded stacks.

"Half a million dollars, cash," Boothe said softly. "But that's only part of what I'm offering you. There's also a position available with the *Journal*. Head of security. It pays more than twice your current salary."

Ignoring the cash, Dan said, "You pretend to be so cool, but this makes it clear just how desperate you are. This is out of panic. You say you know me, so you know an offer like this would almost surely have the opposite effect intended."

"Yes," Boothe said, "*if* we wanted you to do something that was wrong in order to earn the money. But I hope to show you that what we want you to do is the *right* thing, the best thing, the only thing that a man of conscience could possibly do under the circumstances. I believe that, once you know what's happening, you'll do the right thing. Which is all that we want. Really. You'll see that the money isn't being offered to alleviate your guilt, but . . . well, as a bonus for good deeds well done." He smiled.

"You want the girl," Dan said.

"No," Uhlander said, his eyes glittering, his face more hawklike than ever in the queer mix of shadows and colored light. "We want her dead."

"And quickly," Boothe said.

"Did you offer Ross Mondale this much money? Wexlersh and Man-uello?" Dan asked.

"Good heavens, no!" Boothe said. "But now you're the only one who knows where to find Melanie McCaffrey."

Uhlander said, "You're the only game in town."

From their side of the desk, they watched Dan with carnivorous anticipation.

He said, "Apparently, you're even more depraved than I thought. You think killing an innocent child could in any way be construed as the *right* thing, a *good* deed?"

"The operative word is 'innocent,' " Boothe said. "When you understand what happened in that gray room, when you realize what's been killing all these people—"

"I think maybe I already know what's been killing them," Dan said. "It's Melanie, isn't it?"

They stared at him, surprised by his perception.

"I read some of your book, the one about astral projection," he told Uhlander. "With that and other things, I've begun to piece it together."

He had hoped that he was wrong, had dreaded finding out that his worst suspicions were correct. But there was no escaping the truth. A cold despair, as real and almost as tangible as the drizzling rain outside, poured over him.

"She's killed all of them," Uhlander said. "Six men so far. And she'll kill the rest of us if she has the chance."

"Not six," Dan said. "Eight."

•

The Spielberg film had ended. Earl had bought tickets for the next showing of another PG film in the same multiplex. He and Laura had settled into seats in the new theater, with Melanie ensconced between them once more.

Laura had watched her daughter closely through the first movie, but the child had shown no sign of going to sleep or crawling deeper into her sheltering catatonia. Her eyes had continued to follow the action on the screen through the end of the story, and once a smile had flickered so very briefly at the corners of her mouth. She had not spoken or even made a wordless sound in response to the celluloid fantasy, and she had moved only once or twice, no more than slightly shifting in the theater seat, but even the minimal attention that she had paid to the movie constituted an improvement in her condition. Laura was more hopeful than she had been at any time in the past two days, although she was far from sanguine about the girl's prospects for total recovery.

Besides, *It* was still out there.

She checked her watch. Two minutes until showtime.

Earl scanned the crowd, which was half the size of that for the previous movie. He appeared to be merely people watching, neither suspicious nor tense. He was less concerned than he had been before the other show had begun; this time, he reached inside his coat to check for his gun only once before the house lights dimmed and the big screen lit up.

Melanie was slumped in her seat more than she had been before, and she looked wearier. But her eyes were open wide, and she seemed to be focused on the screen as previews of coming attractions began.

Laura sighed.

They had gotten through most of the afternoon without incident. Maybe everything would be all right now.

•

"Eight?" Uhlander was aghast. "You say she's killed *eight*?"

"Six," Boothe insisted. "Only six so far."

"You know about Koliknikov in Vegas?" Dan said.

"Yes," Boothe said. "He was the sixth."

"You know about Renseveer and Tolbeck up in Mammoth?"

"When?" Uhlander asked. "My God, when did she get them?"

"Last night," Dan said.

The two men looked at each other, and Dan could feel a surge in the current of fear that passed between them.

Uhlander said, "She's been disposing of people in a certain order, according to how much time they spent in that gray room and according to how much discomfort they caused her. Palmer and I were there far less often than any of the others."

Dan was tempted to crack sarcastic about Uhlander's choice of the word "discomfort" instead of the more accurate "pain."

He saw why they had been so low-key when he had first arrived, so confident that they had time to enjoy a drink and to proceed cautiously; they had expected to be the last of the ten conspirators to be killed, and as long as they had thought Howard Renseveer and Sheldon Tolbeck were still alive, they had been frightened but not yet panicked.

Beyond the huge French windows, even the dim gray sunlight was fading.

Within the library, shadows were growing and shifting as though they were living creatures.

The glow from the Tiffany lamp seemed to grow brighter as the daylight dimmed. The multicolored, luminescent spots, when combined with the encroaching shadows, made the large room seem smaller, and somehow brought to the decreasing space the feeling of a Gypsy wagon or tent or other fantastic carnivalesque setting.

"But if Howard and Shelby are dead," Boothe said, "then we're next and . . . she . . . she could come at any time."

"Any time," Dan confirmed. "So we don't have the leisure for drinks or bribery. I want to know *exactly* what went on in that gray room— and why."

Boothe said, "But there's no time to tell it all. You've got to stop her! You evidently know we were encouraging OOBE—out-of-body experiences—in the girl, and that she—"

"I know some of it, and I suspect more, but most of it I don't yet understand," Dan said. "And I want to know it all, every detail, before I decide what to do."

A tremor shook Boothe's voice: "I need another drink." He got up and went unsteadily to the bar, which was tucked in one corner of the room.

Uhlander collapsed into the chair that Boothe had vacated. He looked up at Dan. "I'll tell you about it."

Dan pulled up another chair.

At the bar, Boothe was so nervous that he dropped a couple ice cubes. When he poured more bourbon for himself, the neck of the Wild Turkey bottle chattered against the rim of his glass before he could steady his shaky hand.

•

Laura kept leaning over to look in Melanie's face.

The girl had slumped even farther in her chair.

This film, only ten minutes old, obviously wasn't going to be as engaging as the Spielberg movie. Thus far, Melanie's eyes were open and seemed to follow the action, but Laura wondered how long the girl would remain involved.

•

Palmer Boothe paced and drank bourbon with an uncharacteristic lack of self-control.

Albert Uhlander sat with his head low on his sharp shoulders, bird-like in every aspect of his face and body, explaining the project in the gray room.

Though he had been a doctor of psychology, Dylan McCaffrey had nurtured a lifelong fascination with various aspects of the occult. He'd read Uhlander's first few books and conducted a correspondence with him, which eventually had centered on the subject of OOBE, out-of-body experiences, or what was also known as astral projection. The phenomenon of astral projection was based on the theory that two entities existed in each human being: a physical body of flesh, and an astral or etheric body—sometimes called a psychogeist. In other words, each person has a dual nature, including a double that can function separately of the physical body, making it possible to be in two places at one time. Usually the double, the astral body (or as Uhlander called it, "the body of feeling and sensation"), resided in the physical body and animated it. But under extremely special circumstances (and routinely upon death) the astral body left the physical body.

"Some mediums," Uhlander said, "claim to be able to instigate out-of-body experiences at will, though they are very likely lying. There are, however, many fascinating stories told by reputable people who report having dreamed about rising out of their bodies while sleeping; they tell stories about traveling in an invisible state, often to places where loved ones are dying or are in risk of death. Ten years ago, for example, a woman in Oregon had such an experience while sleeping: She rose out of her body, sailed over the rooftops of houses, went out into the countryside, and came to a place where her brother's car was overturned on a lonely stretch of a little-traveled back road. He was pinned in the wreckage and bleeding to death. She couldn't help him while she was in her astral state, for the astral body frequently has no strength, only sensation, no power of any kind other than the ability to observe. But she returned to her sleeping body, woke, called the police, reported the location of her brother's accident, and saved his life."

"Usually," Boothe said, "the astral body isn't visible. It's entirely spiritual."

"Although visibility and even physical solidity aren't entirely unheard of," Uhlander said. "In 1810, while Lord Byron, the poet, was in Patras, Turkey, unconscious with a high fever, several of his friends saw him in London. They said he passed them on the street without speaking and was seen to write down his name on a register of people inquiring about the king's health. Byron thought this was odd but he never realized he'd experienced an OOBE of rare intensity—and then had forgotten it after recovering from his fever. Anyway, every serious occultist has consciously attempted to initiate an OOBE at some time or other . . . usually without success."

Boothe had already returned to the bar to pour more bourbon into his glass.

Dan said, "Don't get drunk. There's sure as hell no safety in being unconscious. It'll just complicate things."

"I've never been drunk in my life," Boothe said icily. "I don't run from problems, Lieutenant. I solve them." He paced again, but he didn't suck at the bourbon as greedily as he had done previously.

Uhlander said, "Dylan not only believed in astral projection, but he thought he knew why it was so hard to achieve an OOBE."

Dylan, Uhlander explained, had been certain that people were born with the ability to step in and out of their bodies whenever they wished—all people, everyone. But he was equally sure that the confining, limiting nature of all human society and teaching—with its long list of dos and don'ts, its overly restrictive definitions of what was possible and impossible—effectively brainwashed children so early that the development of their astral-projection potential was, like many other psychic powers, never realized. Dylan believed that a child could discover and develop that potential if raised in cultural isolation, if permitted to learn only those things that sharpened awareness of the psychic universe—and if subjected to long and frequent sessions in a sensory-deprivation chamber from a young age, in order to direct the mind inward upon its own hidden talents.

"Isolation," Boothe interrupted, "was a way of purifying the child's concentration, a way of sealing out all the distractions of day-to-day life in order to focus her mind more intensely upon psychic matters."

Uhlander said, "When Mrs. McCaffrey decided to divorce Dylan, he saw an opportunity to raise Melanie according to his own theories, so he abducted her with that intention."

"And you supported him," Dan said to Boothe. "Accessory to a kidnapping, a conspirator in child abuse."

The white-haired publisher approached Dan's chair, loomed over him, stared down with undisguised disdain. He had a haughty disregard for the pain that he'd caused. "It was necessary. An opportunity that could not be missed. Think of it! If astral projection could be proved possible, if the child could be taught to leave her body at will, then perhaps a system could be developed for teaching adults as well . . . *selected* adults. Imagine what it would mean if a select group, an intellectual elite, possessed the ability to enter undetected into any room in the world, no matter how heavily guarded, could listen in on any conversation no matter how secret. No government, no business competitor, no one in the *world*, could hide their plans or intentions from us. Without anyone knowing what we were doing or how, we could at last orchestrate the evolution of one worldwide government without effective opposition or, indeed, without any opposition at all. How could opposition exist if we could sit in on their strategy sessions, know their names, intentions, and secret organizations?"

Boothe was breathing hard, partly because of the effect of the whiskey, but largely due to the dark dreams of power that filled him with a megalomaniacal excitement. The Tiffany lamp cast amber circles of light on his cheeks, smaller spots of blue on his chin, stained his lips yellow, and painted his nose and forehead green, so he again reminded Dan of someone from a carnival, a malevolent roadshow like that in Bradbury's *Something Wicked This Way Comes*. He was a bizarre and demented clown in whose eyes one could see the crimson flickering fires of Hell, a soul in damnation.

"The world would be ours," Boothe said.

Both the publisher and Uhlander smiled, and they seemed to have forgotten how badly their scheme had worked out and how deep was the trouble in which they now found themselves.

"You're both insane," Dan said thinly.

"Farsighted," Uhlander said.

"Insane."

"Visionaries," Boothe said. He turned away from Dan and began to pace once more.

Uhlander's smile gradually bled away as he remembered why they were there, and he continued the explanation that Dan had demanded. Dylan McCaffrey had lived in that Studio City house twenty-four hours a day, seven days a week, year after year, staying close to Melanie, making himself nearly as much a prisoner as she was, seeing only a handful of sympathizers from his small circle of friends who bridged the scientific and occult communities and shared his interests—and who were all on the Palmer Boothe dole, one way or another. Dylan became increasingly obsessed with his project, and the regimen he designed for Melanie became ever more harsh, more demanding, less forgiving of her human failings, weaknesses, and limitations. The gray room, which was painted and soundproofed and furnished in such a way as to reduce all distraction to a minimum, became Melanie's entire universe and also the center of her father's world. Those privileged few who knew of the experiment all thought that they were involved in a noble attempt to transform the human race, and they held the secret of Melanie's torture as though they were protecting something magnificent and holy.

"Then," Uhlander said, "two nights ago, Melanie finally broke through. During her longest session ever in the sensory-deprivation tank, in her cocoon, she achieved what Dylan had always believed she could achieve."

From the purple-gray twilight by the windows, Boothe said, "The girl seized her full psychic potential. She separated her astral body from her physical body and rose out of that tank."

"But what happened after that was something none of us had anticipated," Uhlander said. "In a rage, she killed her father, Willy Hoffritz, and Ernie Cooper, who happened to be there at the time."

"But how?" Dan asked, although he had already decided that it must be true. "You said the astral body usually has the power to observe but can perform no physical act. And even if that wasn't the case this time . . . well, she's only a frail little girl. Those people were beaten to death. Savagely beaten."

Palmer Boothe had moved to the deepening shadows along one wall of books and had vanished within them. His disembodied voice rose from the gloom: "Her talent for astral projection wasn't the only psychic ability the little bitch learned how to use that night. She's apparently discovered how to teleport her astral body great distances—"

"To Las Vegas, to the mountains above Mammoth," Albert Uhlander elaborated.

"—and how to move objects without touching them. Telekinesis," Boothe said. He paused. In the darkness where he stood, his whiskey glass clicked against his teeth. The swallowing sound he made was preternaturally loud. "Her strength is psychic, the strength of the mind, which is virtually beyond limit. She's stronger than ten men, a hundred, a *thousand*. She easily disposed of her father, Hoffritz, and Cooper . . . and now she's been coming after the rest of us, one by one, and she seems to be able to sense where we are, regardless of how hard we try to hide."

•

Melanie sighed.

Laura leaned over and looked at her in the dim backwash of light from the movie screen.

The girl's eyes were getting heavy.

Worried, Laura put a hand on her daughter's shoulder and shook gently, then harder.

Melanie blinked.

"Watch the movie, honey. Watch the movie."

The child's eyes swam back into focus and reconnected with the action on the screen.

•

Boothe had moved out of the shadows.

Uhlander was leaning forward in his chair.

They both seemed to be waiting for Dan to say something, to assure them that he would kill the girl and stop the slaughter.

Instead, he said nothing because he wanted them to sweat for a while. Besides, his emotions were in such turmoil that he didn't trust himself to speak yet.

Murder, Dan knew, was a human potential as universal as love. It existed in the kind and the meek, in the gentle and the innocent, though perhaps it lay more deeply buried in them than in others. He was no more surprised to discover it in Melanie McCaffrey than he had been surprised by the murderous impulses of the scores of killers that he'd put in prison over the years—though this discovery left him distraught, sick, and profoundly depressed.

Indeed, Melanie's homicidal urges were more understandable than most. Imprisoned, physically and psychologically tortured, denied love and comfort and understanding, treated more like a laboratory monkey than like a human being, forced to endure long years of mental and emotional and physical pain, she had developed a superhuman rage and hatred, diamond-hard and gas-flame-bright, that could have been relieved only by violent, brutal, bloody revenge. Perhaps her rage and hatred—and the need to relieve those inner pressures—were as much responsible for her psychic breakthrough as any of the exercises and conditions that her father had imposed upon her.

Now she stalked her tormentors, a frail nine-year-old girl, yet as deadly and dangerous and efficient a killer as Jack the Ripper or as any member of the Manson Family. But she wasn't entirely depraved. That was a thought to cling to. Evidently a part of her was shocked and repelled by what she had done. After all, horrified by her own thirst for blood, she'd sought refuge in a catatonic state, crawling down into that dark place where she could hide the terrible truth of the murders from the world . . . and even from herself. As long as she had a conscience, she hadn't descended all the way into savagery, and maybe her sanity was retrievable.

She was the power that had taken possession of the radio in the kitchen. She could not throw off the heavy weight of guilt and self-disgust that kept her pressed down in her quasi-autistic subworld, could not bear to speak of what she had done or might do, but she could send warnings and pleas for help through the radio. That's what those messages had meant: "Help me, stop me. Help me. Stop me."

And the whirlwind filled with flowers had been . . . what? Not at all threatening, of course. It had seemed threatening to Laura and Earl, but only because they hadn't understood. No, the flower-laden whirlwind had been a pathetic, desperate expression of Melanie's love for her mother.

Her love for her mother.

In that love, the girl might find salvation.

Boothe was impatient with Dan's silence. "When she broke through, when she finally cast off all restraints of the flesh, and found her great powers and saw how to use them, she should have been grateful to us. The rotten little bitch should have been grateful to her father and to all of us who helped her to become more than just a child, more than just human."

"Instead," Uhlander whined with childish self-pity, "the vicious little brat turned on us."

Dan said, "So you told Ned Rink to kill her."

Boothe was as quick as ever with the self-justifications. "We had no choice. She was infinitely valuable, and we wanted to study and understand her. But we knew she was after us, and recapturing her and studying her was a risk we simply couldn't take."

"We didn't want to kill her," Uhlander said. "We created her, after all. We made her what she became. But we had to remove her. It was self-preservation. Self-defense. She'd become a monster."

Dan stared at Uhlander and Boothe, as though peering through the bars of a cage, into a cell in a zoo. It must have been an alien zoo as well, on some distant planet, for it didn't seem that *this* world could have produced creatures as bizarre, bloodless, and cruel as these. He said, "Melanie wasn't the monster. *You* were. You *are*." He got up, too tense and angry to remain seated, and stood with his hands fisted at his sides. "What the hell did you expect to happen if she ever actually achieved this breakthrough you wanted? Did you think she'd say, 'Oh, thank you so much, now what can I do for you, what wishes can I grant, what deeds perform?' Did you think she would be like a genie let loose of a lamp, subservient and eager to please those who'd rubbed the brass and let her out?" He realized he was shouting. He tried to lower his voice, but he couldn't. "For God's sake, you people imprisoned her for six years! Tortured her! Do you think prisoners are usually *grateful* to their jailers and torturers?"

"It wasn't torture!" Boothe protested. "It was . . . education. Guidance. Scientifically encouraged evolution!"

"We were showing her The Way," Uhlander said.

•

Melanie murmured.

Laura barely heard the girl above the music and screeching of car tires in the movie. She leaned closer to her daughter. "What is it, honey?"

"The door . . ." Melanie whispered.

In the pulsating light from the film, Laura saw that the girl's eyes were going shut again.

"The door . . ."

•

Beyond the French windows, night had come to Bel Air.

Boothe had gone to the bar for more bourbon.

Uhlander had gotten up too. He was standing behind the desk, staring down into the panoply of colors that composed the Tiffany lampshade.

Dan said, "What is this 'door to December,' this door that opens onto a different season of the year than any other door or window in the house? I read a little about it in your book. You said it was a paradoxical image used as a key to the psyche, but I didn't have a chance to finish the chapter, and I wasn't entirely sure I grasped the concept, anyway."

Uhlander spoke without looking up from the lamp. "As part of the attempt to get Melanie to view *anything* as possible, to open her to fantastic concepts like astral projection, she was given specially designed concepts on which to concentrate during long sessions in the sensory-deprivation chamber. Each concept was an impossible situation . . . a carefully designed paradox. Like that door to December about which you read. It was my theory . . . it still *is* my theory that these mind-stretching exercises are useful for people who want to develop their psychic potential. It's a way of training yourself to explore the unthinkable, a way to readjust your worldview to include what you formerly thought impossible."

From the bar, Boothe said, "Albert is brilliant, a genius. He's spent years developing a synthesis of science and the occult. He's found places where both those disciplines intersect. He has so much to teach us, so much to contribute. He mustn't die. That's why you mustn't let that little bitch kill us, Lieutenant. We both have so much to give the world."

Uhlander continued to stare into the jewel-rich colors of the lamp. "By *visualizing* impossibilities, by working hard to make each of these strange concepts seem possible and real and familiar, you can eventually liberate your psychic powers from the mental box in which you've sealed them with your socially acquired, culturally imposed disbelief. Preferably, the visualization would take place during deep meditation or after being hypnotized in order to fully concentrate the mind. This theory has never been proved, because scientists are barred from subjecting human subjects to the lengthy and somewhat painful steps necessary to reshape the psyche."

"Too bad you weren't around in Germany when the Nazis were in power," Dan said bitterly. "I'm sure they would have provided hundreds of human subjects for such an interesting experiment, and they wouldn't have given a damn what you had to do to reshape their psyches."

As if he hadn't heard the insult, Uhlander said, "But then, with Melanie, subjected as she was to years of drug-induced states of prolonged and intense concentration, then those longer sessions floating in the sensory-deprivation chamber . . . well, it was an ideal approach, and the breakthrough was at last achieved."

There had been other mind-stretching concepts besides the door to December, the occultist explained. Sometimes Melanie had been instructed to concentrate on a staircase that went only sideways. Uhlander said, "Imagine you are on an enormous, eternal Victorian staircase with an elaborately carved handrail. Suddenly you become aware that you're neither climbing higher nor descending. Instead, you're on a stairway that leads only sideways, which has no beginning or end." Other concepts included the cat that ate itself, beginning with its tail, the story that Melanie recounted while hypnotically regressed in the motel room that morning, and there was one about a window to yesterday. "You are standing at a window in your bedroom, looking out on the lawn. You don't see the lawn as it is today, but as it was yesterday, when you were out there, sunbathing. You see yourself out there, lying on a beach towel. This isn't the same scene you can see through the other windows in the room. This isn't an ordinary window. It's a window looking out on yesterday. And if you went through that window, would you be back there in yesterday, standing beside yourself as you were sunbathing?"

Boothe left the bar, glided through shadows, and stopped in the penumbra at the edge of the lamp's rainbow glow. "Once the subject is able to *believe* in the paradox, then he must not only believe in it but actually *enter* it. For instance, if the stairway to nowhere had worked best for Melanie, there would have come a point at which she would've been told to step *off* the end of those stairs, even though there was no end. And the instant she'd done that, she would have left her body as well and begun her first out-of-body experience. Or if the window to yesterday had worked for her, she would have stepped into yesterday, and the dislocation involved in becoming *part* of the impossible would have triggered an astral projection. That was the theory, anyway."

"Madness," Dan said again.

"Not madness at all." Uhlander finally looked up from the lamp. "It worked, you see. It was the door to December that the girl was most able to visualize, and as soon as she stepped through it, she was in touch with her psychic abilities. She learned how to control them."

Contrary to what Dan and Laura had thought, the girl was not afraid of what would come through the door from some supernatural dimension. Instead, she had been afraid, once she opened the door, that she would go through it and kill again. She had been torn between two opposing and powerful desires: the urge to kill every last one of her tormentors, and the desperate need to *stop* killing.

Jesus.

Boothe stepped to the desk and put his hand on some of the tightly banded hundred-dollar bills that filled the open suitcase. He looked hard at Dan. "Well?"

Instead of answering him, Dan said to Uhlander, "When she enters this psychic state, uses these powers, is there a change in the air around her that people would notice?"

A new intensity entered Uhlander's bird-bright eyes. "What sort of change?"

"A sudden, inexplicable chill."

"Could be," Uhlander said. "Perhaps an indication of a rapid accumulation of occult energies. Such a phenomenon is associated with the poltergeist, for instance. You've been present when this has happened?"

"Yes. I think it happens each time she leaves her body—or returns to it," Dan said.

•

Suddenly the air in the theater turned cold.

Laura had just looked away from Melanie, no more than two or three seconds ago, and the girl's eyes had been open wide. Now they were closed, and already *It* was coming. It must have been waiting, watching, ready to take advantage of the girl's first moment of vulnerability.

Laura grabbed Melanie and shook her, but her eyes did not open. "Melanie? Melanie, wake up!"

The air grew colder.

"Melanie!"

Colder.

In the grip of panic, Laura pinched her daughter's face. "Wake up, wake up!"

Two rows back in the theater, someone said, "Hey . . . quiet over there."

Colder.

•

Boothe's hand was on the money, caressing it. "You know where she is. You've got to kill her. It's the right thing to do."

Dan shook his head. "She's only a child."

"She's killed eight men already," Boothe said.

"Men?" Dan laughed humorlessly. "Could men have done to her what you people did? Tortured her with electric shock? Where did you put the electrodes? On her neck? On her arms? On her little backside? On her genitals? Yes, I'll bet you did. On the genitals. Maximum effect. That's what torturers always go for. Maximum effect. Men? Eight *men,* you say? There's a certain level of amorality, a bottom line of ruthlessness below which you can't call yourself a man anymore."

"Eight men." Boothe refused to acknowledge what Dan had said. "The girl's a monster, a psychopathic monster."

"She's deeply disturbed. She can't be held accountable for her actions." Dan had never imagined that he could enjoy seeing another human being squirm as much as he was enjoying the growing horror and desperation on these bastards' faces as they realized that their last hope of survival had been a false hope.

"You're an officer of the law," Boothe said angrily. "You have a duty to prevent violence wherever you can."

"Shooting a nine-year-old girl is the commission of violence, not the prevention."

"But if you don't kill her, she'll kill us," Boothe said. "Two deaths instead of one. Kill her, and the net effect is that you save one life."

"A net balance of one life to my credit, huh? Gee, what an interesting way to think of it. You know, Mr. Boothe, when you get down there in Hell, I'll bet the devil makes you an accountant of souls."

A sudden all-consuming fury pulled the white-haired publisher's face into a grotesque mask of hatred and impotent rage. He threw his whiskey glass at Dan's head.

Dan ducked, and the fine crystal struck the floor far behind him, shattering on impact.

"You stupid fucking son of a bitch," Boothe said.

"My, my. Mustn't ever let your friends at the Rotary Club hear you talking like that. Why, they'd be shocked."

Boothe turned away from him, stood facing the darkness where the books waited silently on their shelves. He was shaking with rage, but he did not speak.

Dan had learned everything he needed to know. He was ready to leave.

•

Laura couldn't wake Melanie. She was causing an ever greater disturbance in the theater, angering other patrons, but she couldn't make the child respond with even a murmur or a flutter of her eyes.

Earl had stood up and put his hand on the gun inside his coat.

Laura looked around wildly, waiting for the first sign of the apparition, the explosion of occult force.

But the chill abruptly went away, and the air grew warm again without any supernatural violence.

Whatever had been there a moment ago had now gone.

•

Uhlander's gaze had drifted back to the mosaic of stained glass through which the room's only light rose in colorful beams. Though he stared at the scene depicted on the shade, he did not seem to see it; the unfocused nature of his stare was reminiscent of Melanie's haunting detachment. The author was probably seeing his future in that light, although his future was only darkness. In a thin and tremulous voice, he said, "Lieutenant, listen, please . . . you don't have to agree with what we did . . . don't have to like us . . . to take pity on us."

"Pity? You think it would be an appropriate expression of pity for me to blow the brains out of a nine-year-old girl?"

Trembling, Palmer Boothe swung back to him. "It won't just be *our* lives you'll be saving. For God's sake, don't you see? She's running amok. She has a taste for blood, and it's not very damned likely that she'll stop with us. She's crazy. You said so yourself. You said we drove her crazy and she's not responsible for what she's done. All right!

She's not responsible, but she's out of control, and she's probably getting more powerful all the time, learning more about her psychic abilities every hour, and maybe if somebody doesn't stop her soon, maybe nobody will *ever* be able to stop her. It's not just Albert and me. How many others may die?"

"No others," Dan said.

"What?"

"She'll kill the two of you, the last of the conspirators from the gray room, and then . . . then she'll kill herself."

When he put it in words, it hit him hard. A sudden, heavy ache bloomed in his chest at the prospect of Melanie taking her own life in despair over what she had done.

"Kill herself?" Boothe said.

"Where'd you get an idea like that?" Uhlander asked.

Succinctly, he told them about Laura's hypnotic-therapy sessions and about the strange things that Melanie had said regarding her own vulnerability. "When she said *It* would come after her once It had killed everyone else, we had no idea what the creature might be. Spirit, demon—it seemed impossible that such a thing could exist, but we saw evidence that something strange was loose in the world. Now we know it wasn't a spirit or a demon, and we know that . . . well, once she's eliminated the two of you, she plans to take her own life, turn her psychic powers upon herself. So you see, the only lives hanging in the balance are yours and hers, and I'm afraid hers is the only one I have any chance of saving."

Boothe, whose morality was about as admirable as that of Adolf Hitler or Joseph Stalin, who had hired torturers and murderers with a clear conscience, who would clearly have committed any number of murders with his own bare hands if that were the only way he could save his own damned skin, this thoroughly corrupted and corrupting snake was aghast that Dan, an officer of the law, was not only going to let them die but seemed to welcome the idea that they would soon be removed from this world. "But . . . but . . . if she kills us, and you could have stopped her and didn't . . . then you're just as guilty of our murder as she is."

Dan stared at him, then nodded. "Yes. But that doesn't shock me.

I've always known I'm like everyone else in that regard. I've always known, given the right circumstances, I have the capacity for cold-blooded murder."

He turned his back on them.

He walked away from them, toward the library door.

When Dan was halfway to the door, Uhlander said, "How long do you think we have?"

Dan paused, looked back at them. "After reading part of your book this morning, I thought I understood at least some of what was going on. So when I left them, I warned Laura to keep Melanie awake and to keep her from slipping into a deeper catatonic state. I didn't want her to come for you until we had a chance to talk. But tonight I don't intend to keep Melanie from going to bed. And when she goes to bed and finally sleeps . . ."

They were all silent.

The only sound was the faraway gurgle and sizzle of rain.

"So we have a few hours," Boothe said at last, and he sounded like a different man from the one who had welcomed Dan into the library a short while ago, a much weaker and less impressive man. "Just a few hours . . ."

But they didn't even have that much time. As Palmer Boothe's voice faded into a silence composed of terror and self-pity, the air temperature in the library dropped twenty degrees from one second to the next.

Laura hadn't been able to keep Melanie alert.

"No!" Uhlander gasped.

Books exploded off one of the highest library shelves and rained over Boothe and Uhlander.

The two men cried out and threw their arms over their heads.

A heavy chair rose off the floor, eight feet into the air, hung there, spinning around and around, then was thrown all the way across the library, where it struck the French windows. The brittle sounds of breaking glass and splintering mullions was followed by the crash of the chair rebounding from the window frame and falling to the floor.

Melanie was there. The etheric half of her. The astral body or psychogeist.

Dan thought of trying to speak to her and reason with her now, before she killed again, but he knew there was no hope of getting through to her, no more hope than her mother had had in hypnotic-therapy sessions. He could not save Boothe and Uhlander, and he really had no desire to save them. The only life he might be able to save now was Melanie's, for he had thought of something—a plan, a trick—that might stop her from turning her psychic power upon herself in a suicidal response to her self-loathing and horror. It was a shaky plan. Not much chance that he could make it work. But in order even to try, he had to be with the girl's body, with her physical self, when her astral body returned. Which meant he had to get back to Westwood, to the theater, before she was finished in Bel Air, and he didn't have time to waste in a fruitless attempt to dissuade her from destroying Boothe and Uhlander.

Unseen hands swept another shelf clean of books, and the volumes crashed to the floor, all across the room.

Boothe was screaming.

The bar exploded as if a bomb had gone off in it, and the air reeked of whiskey.

Uhlander was begging for mercy.

Dan saw the Tiffany lamp rising into the air, floating up like a balloon on its cord. Before the lamp had risen to the length of that tether, Dan recovered his wits, regained his sense of urgency. He ran the last few steps to the end of the room. As he pulled open the door, the light went out behind him, and the library was plunged into darkness.

He pulled the door shut as he stepped out of the room. He raced back through the house, retracing the route along which the butler had brought him earlier.

In a room with peach-colored walls and an elaborately molded white ceiling, he encountered that servant rushing in the opposite direction in response to the hideous screaming in the library.

Dan said, "Call the police!" He was sure that Melanie wouldn't harm anyone other than those who had been in the gray room or those closely associated with the conspiracy against her. Nevertheless, as the butler stopped in confusion, Dan said, "Don't go in the library. Call the police. For God's sake, *don't* go in there yourself!"

•

The dark theater no longer seemed like a sanctuary to Laura. She was claustrophobic. The rows of seats were confining. The darkness threatened her. Why in the name of God had they taken refuge in a place of darkness. *It* probably thrived on darkness.

What would happen if the air grew cold again and the thing returned.

And It would return.

She was sure of that.

Soon.

•

The enormous iron gates began to swing slowly open when Dan had descended half the long driveway.

Ordinarily, the butler probably called ahead to the gatehouse, and the guard opened the gates even as the guest was pulling his car out of the parking circle in front of the house. But at the moment, the butler was calling 911, scared witless by the bloodcurdling screams and battle sounds coming from the library, so the guard had activated the gate controls only when he'd seen headlights knifing down toward him through the early darkness and rain.

Dan had also slapped the detachable emergency beacon to the roof. He rocketed down the long hill, pressing the accelerator almost to the floor, counting on the gateman to get the barrier out of his way in time to prevent a nasty collision. That ironwork had appeared to be capable of stopping a tank. If he hit it, he would most likely be decapitated or skewered by a jagged bar that would pierce the windshield.

He could have descended the hill at a more reasonable pace, but seconds counted. Even if the girl's astral body did not finish with Boothe and Uhlander for a few minutes, it would no doubt return to that Westwood theater well ahead of Dan; the spirit surely didn't travel as slowly as an automobile, but moved from place to place in the wink of an eye. Besides, the butler might soon collect his wits and get the idea that Dan had done something to cause all the screaming in the library. If such a suspicion arose, the gatehouse guard might be alerted to close the gates again the instant that they finished opening, blocking Dan's escape; then whole minutes would be lost.

Thirty feet from the gates, as they continued to swing open, he finally eased up on the accelerator and touched the brakes. The car started to slide, but he held it to the road and kept its nose pointed where it should be. A sharp snap, a thin squeal: the rear bumper scraped one of the still-moving portals. Then he was on that short length of driveway beyond the walls of the estate. No traffic on the street ahead. He didn't slow down when he turned left. The sedan fishtailed to the far curb, but he maintained control, losing only a little momentum.

Emergency beacon flashing, he pushed the car to its limits, plunging down from the heights of Bel Air, from one twisting street to another, taking unconscionable chances with his own life and the lives of anyone who might have been in his way around any of several blind and half-blind curves.

His thoughts arced back in time: Delmar, Carrie, Cindy Lakey . . .

Not again.

Melanie was a killer, yes, but she did not deserve to die for what she had done. She'd not been in her right mind when she killed them. Besides, if murder in self-defense had ever been a justifiable plea, it was now. If she hadn't killed them, every last one, then they would have come for her, not necessarily to exact revenge, but to conduct further experiments with her. If she hadn't killed all ten men, the torture would have continued.

He had to get that idea through to her. He thought he knew a way of doing it.

God, please, let it work.

Westwood was not far away. With the beacon, with no thought for his own mortality, he should reach the theater in a lot less than five minutes.

Delmar, Carrie, Cindy Lakey . . . Melanie . . .

No!

•

The theater was a refrigerator.

Melanie whimpered.

Laura leaped up from her seat, not sure what to do, knowing only that she couldn't sit still as *It* approached.

The air temperature plummeted. In fact, it seemed colder than it had been in the kitchen the previous night or in the motel room, when It had paid them other visits.

From the row behind, someone asked Laura to please sit down, and heads turned her way from across the aisle too. But after a moment, everyone's attention shifted to the incredibly abrupt chill that had gripped the theater.

Earl was on his feet too, and this time he'd drawn the revolver from his shoulder holster.

Melanie let out a thin, pathetic cry, but her eyes didn't open.

Laura grabbed her, shook her. "Baby, wake up! Wake up!"

Soft exclamatory comments swept in a wave across the auditorium as other patrons reacted not to Laura and Melanie but to the fact that they were freezing. Then the crowd was shocked into a brief silence as the giant movie screen tore open from top to bottom with a ripping noise that sounded as though God had rent the heavens. A jagged line of blackness appeared through the center of the projected images, and the figures on the screen rippled and acquired distorted faces and bodies as the silvery surface on which they existed began to wrinkle and bulge and sag.

Melanie writhed in her seat and struck at the empty air. Her blows landed on Laura, who tried to force the girl to wake up.

No sooner had the screen torn, silencing the audience, than the heavy curtains flanking it were pulled out of the tracks in the ceiling. They flapped in the air like great wings, as if the devil himself had risen into the theater and was unfolding his batlike appendages; then they collapsed with a *whoosh!* into huge piles of lifeless material.

That was too much for the audience. Confused and frightened, people rose from their seats.

After taking a score of hard blows on her arms and face, Laura got hold of Melanie's wrists and kept her still. She looked over her shoulder, toward the front of the theater.

The projectionist had not touched his equipment yet, so a queer luminosity still bounced off the ruined screen, and a vague amber radiance was provided by the torch-shaped emergency lamps along the walls. The light was just sufficient for everyone to see what happened next. Empty seats in the front row tore loose of the floor to which they were bolted, and shot violently up and backward, into the air. They struck the large screen, punched through the fabric, destroying what remained of it.

People began to scream, and a few ran toward the exits at the back of the theater.

Someone yelled, "Earthquake!"

An earthquake didn't explain it, of course, and it wasn't likely that anyone believed that explanation. But that word, much dreaded in California since the Northridge temblor, stoked the panic. More seats—those in the second row—erupted from the floor: bolts snapped, metal shredded, concrete burst.

It was, Laura thought, as if some gigantic invisible beast had entered at the front of the theater and was making its way toward them, destroying everything in its path.

"Let's get out of here," Earl shouted, though he knew as well as she did that they could not run from this thing, whatever it was.

Melanie had ceased struggling. She was limp, like a pile of knotted rags, so limp that she might have been dead.

The projectionist switched off his machinery and turned up the house lights. Everyone but Laura, Melanie, and Earl had surged to the back of the theater, and half the audience had already spilled out into the lobby.

Heart jackhammering, Laura scooped Melanie into her arms and stumbled along the row, into the aisle, with Earl following close behind her.

Now seats were exploding into the air from the fourth row and crashing backward into the demolished screen with thunderous impact. But the worst sound was coming from the emergency-exit doors that flanked the screen. They swung open and slammed shut, again and again, banging back and forth with such tremendous force that their pneumatic cylinders, which should have ensured a soft closing every time, could not cope.

Laura saw not doors but flapping mouths, hungry mouths, and she knew that if she was foolish enough to try to escape through those exits, she would find herself stepping not into the theater parking lot but into the gullet of some unimaginably foul beast. Crazy thought. Insane. She was teetering on the brink of mindless panic.

If she had not experienced the poltergeist phenomena on a smaller scale in her own kitchen, she would have been unhinged by the sight before her. What was it? What was *It*? And why the hell did It want Melanie?

Dan knew. At least he knew part of it.

But it didn't matter what he knew, because he couldn't help them now. Laura doubted that she would ever see him again.

Considering that she was hysterical and already emotionally over-charged, the thought of never seeing Haldane again hit her harder than seemed possible.

She had no sooner reached the aisle than her knees began to buckle under the combined weight of her terror and Melanie. Earl jammed his revolver back into its holster and took the girl out of Laura's arms.

Only a few people remained at the lobby doors, pressing against those in front of them. Some were looking back, wide-eyed, at the inexplicable chaos.

Laura and Earl took only a few steps along that same carpeted route of escape before seats stopped exploding into the air behind them—and erupted, instead, from the rows ahead. After a brief, clumsy, aerial ballet, the mangled seats crashed down into the aisle, blocking it.

Melanie would not be permitted to leave.

Holding the girl in his arms, Earl looked this way and that, unsure of his next move.

Then something shoved him. He staggered backward. Something tore Melanie out of his grip. The girl tumbled along the aisle until she slammed against a row of seats.

Screaming, Laura scurried to her daughter, rolled the girl over, put a hand to her neck. There was a pulse.

"Laura!"

She looked up when she heard her name, and with an enormous rush of relief she saw Dan Haldane. He had entered through the exiting people at the back of the theater. He rushed down the aisle toward them.

He vaulted the ruined seats that the unseen enemy had piled in the aisle, and as he drew nearer, he shouted, "That's it! Hold her in your arms, shelter her." He reached Laura and knelt beside her. "Put yourself between her and *It,* because I don't think It'll hurt you."

"Why not?"

"I'll explain later," he said. He turned to Earl, who had gotten to his hands and knees. "You okay?"

"Yeah. Just bruised."

Dan got to his feet.

Laura lay in the aisle, among scattered pieces of popcorn and crumpled paper cups and other debris, embracing Melanie, trying to fold herself around the child. She realized that the theater was silent, that the invisible beast was no longer on the rampage. But the air was cold, blood-freezing.

It was still there.

•

Dan turned slowly in a circle, waiting for something to happen.

As the silence continued, he said, "You can't kill yourself unless you kill your mother too. She won't let you do it unless you kill her first."

Looking up at him, Laura said, "Who are you talking to?" And then she cried out and pressed closer to Melanie. "Something's pulling at me! Dan, something's trying to tear me away from her!"

"Fight it."

She held tightly to Melanie, and for a moment she looked like an epileptic, jerking and twitching in a fit upon the floor. But the attack ended, and she stopped struggling.

"Gone?" Dan asked.

Gaunt, baffled, she said, "Yes."

Dan spoke to the air, for he could sense that the astral body was hovering out there in the theater somewhere. "She won't let you pry her away just so you can hammer yourself to pieces. She loves you. If she has to, she'll die to protect you."

Across the theater, three seats were torn loose of their moorings and were swept up into the air. They whirled and slammed against one another for a half minute before they dropped back to the floor.

"No matter what you think," Dan said to the psychogeist, "you don't deserve to die. What you did was horrible, but it wasn't much more than you had to do."

Silence.

Stillness.

He said, "Your mother loves you. She wants you to live. That's why she's holding on to you with all her strength."

A wretched sound from Laura indicated that she understood the whole terrible truth, at last.

At the front of the theater, the crumpled curtains stirred and rose slightly, in a halfhearted attempt to spread themselves into menacing wing-shapes as before, but after a few seconds they sagged into a formless heap.

Earl had gotten to his feet. He stepped beside Dan. Surveying the theater, he said, "It was the girl herself?"

Dan nodded.

Weeping in shock and grief and fear, Laura cradled her daughter.

The air was still frigid.

Something touched Dan with invisible hands of ice and shoved him backward, but not hard.

"You can't kill yourself. We won't let you kill yourself," he told the unseen astral body. "We love you, Melanie. You've never had a chance, and we want to give you a chance."

Silence.

Earl started to say something, and then several rows down from them the psychogeist rushed along a line of seats, snapping the backs of them as it went, and the fallen curtains did rise this time, and the exit doors began to bang open and shut again, and scores of acoustic ceiling tiles rained down, and a cold keening arose that must have been an astral voice, for it came out of midair and filled the theater at such volume that both Earl and Dan clamped their hands over their ears.

Dan saw Laura wincing, but she didn't let go of Melanie to cover her own ears. She maintained her loving grip, squeezing the girl tight, holding on.

The noise rose to an unbearable level, and Dan thought he had misjudged the girl, thought she was going to bring the roof down on all of them and kill everyone in order to kill herself. But abruptly the cacophony stopped, and the animated wreckage crashed back onto the floor, and the doors stopped slamming open and shut.

One last ceiling tile sailed down, struck the aisle beyond them, and tumbled over twice before coming to rest.

Stillness again.

Silence again.

For more than a minute they waited fearfully—and then the air grew warm.

At the back of the theater, a man who might have been the manager said, "What the hell happened in here?"

An usher, standing at the manager's side, having apparently seen the start of the destruction, tried to explain but couldn't.

Dan noticed movement up at the projectionist's booth and saw a man peering out of one of the portals there. He looked amazed.

Laura finally pulled back from Melanie while Dan and Earl crouched at her side.

The child's eyes were open, but she wasn't looking at anyone. Her gaze remained unfocused. But it wasn't the same haunted look that had possessed her before. She was not yet focused on anything in this world, but she had ceased to gaze inward upon the haven in which she'd recently taken refuge. She was now on the borderline between that fantasy and this reality, between that introverted darkness and the world of light in which she would eventually have to make her life.

"If the suicidal urge is gone—and I think it is—then the worst is past," Dan said. "I think she'll come back all the way, in time. But it'll take an infinite amount of patience and a lot of love."

"I've got enough of both," Laura said.

"We'll help," Earl said.

"Yes," Dan said. "We'll help."

Years of therapy lay ahead for Melanie, and there was a chance she might remain autistic. But Dan had a feeling that she had closed the door to December for good, that she would never let it come open again. And if it was closed, if she could make herself forget how to open it, perhaps she could eventually forget the pain and violence and death that had occurred on the other side of that door.

Forgetting was the start of healing.

He realized that this was a lesson he himself needed to learn. A lesson in forgetting. He needed to forget the pain of his own failures. Delmar, Carrie, Cindy Lakey. A desperate, childish hope flooded him: If only he could at last put those grim memories behind him and close his own door, then perhaps the girl would be able to close hers too; perhaps her recovery would be encouraged by his own determination to turn away from death.

He decided to bargain with God: Look here, Lord, I promise I'll put the past behind me, stop dwelling too much on thoughts of blood and death and murder, take more time to live and to appreciate the blessings of life You've given me, be more *grateful* for what You've given me, and in return, God, all I want from You is, please, for Melanie to come all the way back. Please. Deal?

Holding and rocking her daughter, Laura looked at him. "You seem so . . . intense. What's wrong? What're you thinking?"

Even smeared with dirt and spotted with blood and disheveled, she was beautiful.

Dan said, "Forgetting is the start of healing."

"That's what you were thinking?"

"Yes."

"That's all?"

"It's enough," he said. "It's enough."

AFTERWORD

I originally published *The Door to December* under a pen name.

Novelists write under pen names for many reasons.

Perhaps you write bestselling novels about bricklayers and associated masonry trades, and after producing fifteen or twenty such tales, you wish to write a book about some of the intrepid, multitalented, four-hundred-pound men who are both Sumo wrestlers and FBI agents. With the quite reasonable expectation that the established audience for your bricklaying adventures might be displeased by such a sudden shift in your subject matter, you might concoct a pen name for this new work.

Or perhaps under your real and true name, you have contracted with Publisher A for several books, to be delivered at the rate of one per year, but because of weak moral character or because you're keeping company with the wrong crowd, you have gotten into a twenty-four-can-a-day Diet Pepsi habit, and the resultant surfeit of nervous energy requires that you either enter a Twelve Step program or write a second book each year. To you, in your caffeine buzz, a Twelve Step program seems like a dreary, plodding business, but no one is offering either a Three Step program or a Twelve Running Steps program; besides, this treatment requires an outlay of funds, whereas writing a second book produces additional income. Because Publisher A's contract gives it the *exclusive* use of your name, you must publish your second book under a pen name. Consequently, you make a deal with Publisher Q or Publisher Z (either has a more exotic and more thrilling name than does bland old Publisher A), and the world now knows you by your real and true identity, John Smith, and also by your pen name, Obadiah Furk.

In less enlightened days, a female novelist, writing in a genre with a largely male readership, often chose to disguise her gender under a pen name. Likewise, men writing romance novels often hid behind women's names. The danger here, obviously, is that ego and alter ego might become confused, whereupon you could discover one day that you have acquired an entirely different wardrobe from the one you owned just a year previously and that some of the most treasured parts of your anatomy have been left on a surgeon's table.

Writers of literary fiction have occasionally used pen names for work that people might actually enjoy reading. They believe that the existence of a satisfied audience is absolute proof that a work of fiction is utterly worthless, and while they wish to have the income produced by popular fiction, they are loath to be identified as the author of it. Until the late 1940s, the distinction between literary and popular fiction was so blurry as to be nearly nonexistent. Many authors wrote both literary and popular novels under their real names and suffered no diminution of their authorial reputations. One fine example was John P. Marquand, who won the Pulitzer Prize and critical acclaim for his literary fiction while at the same time producing a series of detective novels featuring a character named Mr. Moto. This couldn't happen in our time. For one thing, having died many years ago, Mr. Marquand can't be expected to meet contractual deadlines, to review copyedited manuscripts, or to make himself available for long publicity tours. Furthermore, since the end of World War II, the U.S. academic community has assumed an increasingly elitist viewpoint bordering on contempt for the masses, which is expressed in numerous ways, including the assiduous segregation of fiction into approved and condemned genres. This has the expected effect of making the most passionate genre writers into the best chroniclers of the common man and woman, a job once held by literary writers—and the *unanticipated* effect of turning most literary writers into creative cowards afraid to operate outside of the narrow boundaries drawn by the elites.

Some writers use pen names because they are on the "to-abduct" list of evil extraterrestrials and they feel the need to hide out to avoid unwanted proctological exams aboard the mother ship.

Some writers resort to pen names after waking in a strange city to discover that they suffer from permanent amnesia, that they are carrying no identification, that their fingerprints have been burned off with multiple applications of acid, and that they have recently undergone plastic surgery that will make it impossible for family and friends to recognize them from a photograph in the Do-You-Know-Who-I-Am? feature carried in every major newspaper. They sense in their bones that they were writers in their former lives, but being unable to recall a byline, they must reinvent themselves. Some will choose simple names related to the genres in which they wish to write: Joe Mystery, Bob Sci-fi, Brenda Romance. Others will be creative: Mickey Mysterioso, Robert Rocketblast, Britney Heather Slinkythighs. Still others will choose hopelessly improper names like Luke Phlegm and Kathleen Gastroenteritis, and their careers will flounder.

Compared to some reasons for using a pen name, my reasons for publishing The Door to December as by "Richard Paige" were prosaic if not downright boring, which is why I cleverly left the discussion of them for the latter part of this afterword. In 1984, when I wrote this novel, I was publishing successfully under my real and true name (Dean Koontz) and also under the pseudonym "Leigh Nichols." A nice gentleman who published the Koontz titles at Berkley Books had moved to New American Library, a competitor, and though he knew that I was unlikely to shift work under my own name to the new house at which he now labored, he also knew I was not entirely happy at Pocket Books, which at that time was publishing my Leigh Nichols titles. I had one unwritten Nichols book to deliver under contract. The nice gentleman suggested that I sign a contract with him for a book that fit the Nichols profile but under yet another pen name—Richard Paige; when I had delivered the final Nichols that I owed to Pocket Books, I could move Nichols to New American Library, where that established pen name could be applied in place of the Paige byline on the book that was under contract to him. This sounds nefarious, even demonic, but it was all on the up-and-up.

Then, as I was delivering the Nichols title to Pocket Books and had barely begun the Paige novel, the nice gentleman changed jobs again—moving to Pocket Books. He became Leigh Nichols's publisher and promised to solve the problems I had been having at Pocket Books. I embraced this serendipitous development—but wasn't able to persuade New American Library to accept repayment of my advance and cancel my contract. As a result, I wrote *The Door to December* and published it in 1985 as the first and last Richard Paige novel.

Nine years later, books under my own name were selling so well (in spite of the fact that I had declined Satan's final offer for my soul) that I no longer used any pen names. I had been reissuing the Leigh Nichols books under my name (*The Servants of Twilight*, *The Eyes of Darkness*, *The House of Thunder*, *The Key to Midnight*, *Shadowfires*), and they had all been paperback bestsellers upon reissue; therefore, New American Library suggested that the same be done with *The Door to December*. We worked out a new deal, they shipped two million copies into stores in 1994, and everyone but Satan was happy with the sales.

These days, when people ask me whatever happened to Richard Paige, I always tell them the (metaphorical) truth: I bludgeoned him with a blunt instrument purchased at a Kmart blunt-instrument sale, fed him into a wood chipper in my backyard, and stole his small but lucrative literary estate.

In an annotated bibliography in *The Dean Koontz Companion*, a book about my work, the generous bibliographer writes of *The Door to December*: "Its exploration of the corrupting influence of power and the totalitarian urge is as dark as anything the author has written, but this is nicely offset by the character of Dan Haldane, whose dialogue is frequently as witty as it is acerbic." Whether it's nicely offset or not is for the reader to judge, but the stated theme is indeed the one I intended to explore, though I'm also writing here about the power of family and love to overcome those ominous forces.

Those of you who have been my constant readers will know that

I *always* write about the power of family, love, faith, hope. As I have written elsewhere and more than once: none of us can ever save himself; we are the instruments of one another's salvation, and only by the hope that we give to others do we lift ourselves out of the darkness into light. I try to live by this philosophy, and except for that one episode with the wood chipper, I think maybe I've done so more successfully than not.